P9-CAD-777

THE REDHUNTER

OTHER NOVELS BY WILLIAM F. BUCKLEY JR.

A NOVEL BASED ON THE LIFE OF SENATOR JOE MCCARTHY

William F. Buckley Jr.

 Little, Brown and Company | Boston | New York | London

Copyright © 1999 by William F. Buckley Jr.

All rights reserved. No part of this book may be reproduced in any form or by any ele
mechanical means, including information storage and retrieval systems, without per
writing from the publisher, except by a reviewer who may quote brief passages in a re

First Edition

This book is a work of historical fiction. It contains some names of real people, and
torical events are described. It also describes events and characters that are the produ
author's imagination. Any resemblance of such nonhistorical persons or events to actu
purely coincidental.

Library of Congress Cataloging-in-Publication Data
Buckley, William F. (William Frank)
      The Redhunter : a novel based on the life of Senator Joe McCarthy / by Willia
   Buckley Jr. — 1st ed.
         p.   cm.
      ISBN 0-316-11589-4
      1. McCarthy, Joseph, 1908–1957—Fiction.   2. Anti-communist movements—
   United States—History—20th century—Fiction.   I. Title.
   PS3552.U344R44   1999
   813'.54—dc21   98-31

10 9 8 7 6 5 4 3 2 1

MV-NY

Book design by Julia Sedykh

Printed in the United States of America

TO L. BRENT BOZELL — *in grateful memory*

Acknowledgments

I knew Senator McCarthy and, with my brother-in-law the late L. Brent Bozell, wrote a book about him (*McCarthy and His Enemies*) in 1953. This book is a novel, but most of the events here recorded are true to life.

The McCarthy library is scant, but one book is central. It was written by Thomas C. Reeves, professor of history at the University of Wisconsin–Parkside, is titled *The Life and Times of Joe McCarthy: A Biography,* and was published in 1982 by Stein and Day. I am very grateful to Professor Reeves.

In chapter 7 I quote almost verbatim for several paragraphs a scene described by Nikolai Tolstoy in his book *The Great Betrayal, 1944–47.* It was published by Charles Scribner & Sons in 1977.

Christopher Weinkopf, formerly assistant editor at *National Review,* now at the Center for the Study of Popular Culture in Los Angeles, did research for this book over two winters and made fine suggestions. I am grateful for his work, as for his company. And grateful, too, to Julie Crane, for her useful last-minute reading.

Frances Bronson of *National Review* superintended the editorial effort with customary intelligence and dispatch, and Tony Savage patiently produced all seven drafts of this work, with punctilio and good humor.

I am grateful to several readers who were kind enough to read drafts and make suggestions. My sister Priscilla Buckley, brother Reid Buckley, Professor Chester Wolford of Penn State, Professor Thomas Wendel of San Jose State, Mr. Evan Galbraith of New York, Tracy Lee Simmons of *National Review,* my agent, Mrs. Lois Wallace, and my wife, Pat. Mr. William Phillips, my editor at Little, Brown, made valuable comments. I owe special thanks to M. Stanton Evans, the author and journalist who is preparing his own book on Senator McCarthy and is comprehensively informed on the issues of that period.

I come now, with some trepidation, to Samuel S. Vaughan. Harold Ross, the founding editor of *The New Yorker,* spoke impatiently of a contributor who in his manuscript had written of an "indescribable" event. Ross pounded into the margin of that essay, "*Nothing* is indescribable!" — a dictum that makes you feel good ("It can be done!"), but also a little scared ("But can *I* do it?"). Perhaps I can get by with saying that what Sam Vaughan did to encourage and refine this venture is unimaginable. This novel is not, at 400 pages, slight; yet his notes and references and asides and quotations and emendations were more extensive than my text. I wish this book were written about Mother Teresa, not Joe McCarthy, so that it might serve as a more fitting conduit for Sam's productive benignity. I leave it that the best that is here is his responsibility.

W. F. B.
Stamford, Connecticut
October 1, 1998

PROLOGUE

Enter Lord Herrendon

Harry Bontecou was tired, but also relaxed. He sat in one of the pleasant, comfortably tatterdemalion clubs patronized by English literati. He had been warned his host might be late for dinner so he had brought along the morning papers. The headline in the *Telegraph* spoke of the rumored capture the day before of Pol Pot in the Cambodian forests. There were two accounts, one in a news article, the second in the editorial section, telling the minihistory of Pol Pot, sometime plenipotentiary ruler of Cambodia.

They differed on the enumeration of Cambodians executed by Pol Pot during the years 1975 to 1979, when he ruled. The news account spoke of "over a million executed," the editorial of "two million." Harry sipped his sherry. He paused then and reflected on exactly what he was doing, reading about Pol Pot twenty-five years after the age of the killing fields, drinking sherry.

He supposed that there would not ensue, in the press accounts the next day, lively and informed discussions over which of the two figures was more nearly correct — one million killed by the self-designated Marxist-Leninist, or two. The population of Cambodia at the time of Pol Pot's rule was five million, the *Telegraph* reminded its readers. So, Harry Bontecou closed his eyes and quickly calculated. The variable estimates meant 20 percent of the population executed, or 10 percent of the population executed. The *Telegraph*'s account told that Pol Pot's genocide was the "gravest since those of the Second World War." Harry reflected. The executions in Nazi Germany might have reached 10 percent of the population; perhaps an equivalent percentage in the Soviet Union (twenty-five million shot or starved between 1917 and the death of Stalin in 1953 was a figure frequently encountered). Harry remembered his reaction on that winter day in 1946 when it became his job to expedite a genocidal operation. A mini genocidal operation. Now he could read the papers and sip sherry and speak softly and securely in this well-protected shelter for British men of letters. It was very different for him then, and very different those early years. Now he could focus on the statistics, on the round figures. Now he was Harry Bontecou, Ph.D. History.

The *Telegraph* noted also the transatlantic debate over whether Marcus Wolf was entitled to a visa to visit the United States. Herr Wolf, the paper reported, was indignant at having been held off. He had served as chief of intelligence for the Democratic Republic of Germany, which no longer existed. But when it did, East Germany's mission had been to do the will of Moscow. This included guarding the impermeability of the Berlin Wall. That was a special responsibility of Marcus Wolf, Harry knew — he scanned the story, would the reporter mention the wall? No. He went back to the paragraph reporting Wolf's displeasure. Harry knew, as did how many members of the Garrick Club? — 70 percent? 10 percent? — that as Secret Police (Stasi) chief, Wolf had engaged in the torture and killing of anyone who, between 1961 and 1989, when the wall came down, tried to escape from the Democratic Republic of Germany to West Germany. Marcus Wolf had taken considerable precautions to discourage trespassers to freedom. They included land mines and electrical fences and barbed wire and spotlights and machine guns and killer dogs. Now, in the morning paper, Wolf was reported as saying he did not *understand* being persecuted for carrying out a routine professional assignment. "I didn't kill anybody personally," he told the reporter.

Neither did Hitler, Harry reflected.

He was jolted by the hortatory tone of voice from a figure standing by the bar, who now, drink in hand, approached him, an elderly man stylishly dressed in dark gray. His abundant white hair framed an angular face with heavy tortoise-shell glasses that magnified the light blue eyes. Oh, my God, Harry Bontecou thought, Tracy. His freshman-year college roommate.

"Say." The insistent tone was off register in the quiet of the Garrick Club. One had the impression the leather volumes winced at Tracy's voice. "Didn't you used to be Harry Bontecou?"

Harry was irritated by the question. To begin with, the tired formulation, "Didn't you used to be . . ." Harry remembered that phrase used in the title of a book published in the 1960s, an autobiography of George Murphy. The author had been a genial Hollywood song-and-dance entertainer in the memory of an entire generation of moviegoers, and suddenly he was junior senator from the state of California. Clever title—back then. In the 1960s; not funny in 1991. There was that, there was the imperious tone of voice, and there were the—memories, many of them ugly, of the man who now addressed him. Harry remained in his chair but extended his hand. "Hello, Tracy. How you doing?"

"I'm fine, old boy. And you? I'll buy you a drink. What will you have?"

"Nothing, thanks. You living in England, Tracy?"

"Yes, old boy. But you—you still hunting political progressives for a living?"

Oh, please, Harry thought. Four decades had gone by. He would not take the bait. He had had more than enough, back then. Back in the years of the Korean war, of the rise of Mao Tse-tung, of the Soviet explosion of an atom bomb, of the Berlin blockade, the campaign of Henry Wallace for president. Above all . . . the years of Joe McCarthy. His mind turned determinedly to the likeliest way of avoiding the old subject.

"Yes, indeed, Tracy," he said submissively. And then quickly, "Trust everything is okay with you. Come to think of it, the last time I got any word about you was from the Washington, D.C., police."

"Oh?"

"Yes. After your surprise . . . visit to me . . . after they—escorted you home, they reported the next day that you were in law school and evidently had excess energies to spare." Harry did not tell him about the other call, from the security people. "—But all goes well for you, I gather."

"Well, I manage to make ends meet." Tracy Allshott extended his hand toward a waiter, who knew to bring him another drink. "You would discover this, dear Harry, if ever while in London — or, for that matter, anywhere else in the world — you needed a lawyer, and someone was benevolent enough, notwithstanding your Redhunting past, to give you the name of the . . . best in America — or in London — you would learn that I am indeed . . . paying my bills! Though if you came to me as a client, perhaps I would give you a compassionate discount, as a member of the Columbia class of 1950."

Talks rather more than he used to, Harry reflected. On the other hand, Allshott had clearly been drinking.

"That would be nice, Tracy." He permitted his eyes to wander over to the entrance of the lounge. Tracy did not miss the meaning intended.

"But you are waiting for somebody?"

To Harry's dismay, Tracy reached over to an adjoining table, drew a chair alongside, and sat down. "Evidently your host has not arrived yet. So I will take the opportunity. I am writing my memoirs, and I thought to try to dig up an address for you. I want in my memoirs to talk about Senator McCarthy."

"Which Senator McCarthy?" Harry asked, affecting innocence, though knowing it was fruitless. Clearly, with his background, Tracy was not talking about the other McCarthy. Eugene McCarthy, sometime senator from Minnesota, had derailed President Johnson in 1968 and soon after resigned political office to go back to his poetry. Harry might as well have asked, "Which Pope John Paul?"

"Don't waste my time, Harry. My assistant, after a few minutes in the library, confirms my impression: that after Presidents Truman and Eisenhower, your Senator McCarthy was the dominant figure in the United States from 1950 to 1955."

"I will not deny that."

Allshott stared at his drink as though the salons of history were assembled there to hear his charge. His voice was oracular. "Senator McCarthy was, by the consolidated holding of history, the most dangerous American of the half century, a savage, unscrupulous, fascistic demagogue —"

"Tracy. Would you please go away?"

"You don't want to talk about Joe McCarthy." Allshott's voice was insistent, the words rapidly pronounced. Now he paused. "I don't blame you."

He rose from his chair. "We'll leave it that there were those of us back in the fifties during the anti-Communist hysteria who were far-sighted and courageous enough to resist McCarthy and McCarthyism."

"Congratulations," Harry said, lowering his eyes to the newspaper.

"All right. I'll let you alone. But you're going to have a place in my memoirs, Harry. Harry Bontecou, the young McCarthyite. You've never written about those years. But I'm not surprised. What the hell would you say?"

Harry bit his lip. He said nothing, keeping his eyes on the paper. Tracy Allshott hesitated only a moment, and then turned and walked back to the bar.

Harry's eyes stayed on the newspaper, but they did not focus. It had been a long time since the subject of Joe McCarthy had been raised. But the memories would never entirely dissipate. When McCarthy died, Pol Pot was a young Marxist student in Paris; Khrushchev had succeeded Stalin as general secretary of the Communist Party of the Soviet Union, the most exalted office in the Soviet empire; Dwight David Eisenhower was one year into his second term as president. And Harry—

But again he was interrupted. This time by his host.

"We've never met." Lord Herrendon extended his hand.

2

London, the same day

The letter from Lord Herrendon had reached Harry Bontecou at the University of Connecticut a day or two after Harry's visit with Ed Furniss, UConn's provost. Furniss, age thirty-two, had snow white hair. When two years earlier the trustees nominated him as provost, he found the color of his hair useful in suggesting a seniority he hadn't biologically earned. It wasn't easy for a thirty-two-year-old to deal with scholars twenty, thirty, even forty years older. But Furniss had to do it, approving this project, disapproving the other, allocating funds here at the expense of requests there.

Harry Bontecou, sixty-four, had been thirty years with the department of history, teaching the politics and diplomacy of the nineteenth century. During his year in office Ed Furniss had never interfered with the history department, in which Bontecou was senior professor.

The summons had social dress — an invitation to Furniss's house for a drink before dinner. But it had, even so, an instrumental feel. The subject Harry knew had to come up at some point might now be coming up: the matter of Harry's retirement. The senior Storrs community, when the subject of retirement came up (not infrequently), called their talisman the "Old Age Act." It was the law-regulation that made it unlawful for any institution that received federal funds to discriminate against an employee on account of age. Professor Harry

Bontecou was mutely grateful for this protection, while aware that civilized behavior would require him, at some point, to hang up his hat and make way for younger scholars. But then too, in recent weeks he had found himself restless.

It had been just two months—the day after Valentine's Day. There had been no theater for a public dispute over whose fault the accident was, no lawsuits, no arraignments. But for an oppressive week or two, one thousand faculty and ten thousand students took it for granted that Professor Bontecou privately thought the responsibility for the accident lay with Mrs. Furniss—the late Mrs. Furniss—and that Professor Furniss privately thought the responsibility for the accident lay with Mrs. Bontecou—the late Mrs. Bontecou.

The official verdict: The accident was, in every respect, accidental. Approaching the bridge from the south, in a heavy snowstorm, Mrs. Furniss had swerved left to avoid the fourteen-year-old boy crossing the bridge, walking from right to left (he testified to seeing the oncoming car for only an instant). A police reconstruction had her slamming on her brakes, skidding diagonally left into Mrs. Bontecou's car, which had been approaching the bridge from the west road, going downhill. The impact edged both the Ford station wagon driven by Mrs. Furniss and the Bontecous' Volvo over the embankment, the two cars and their drivers dropping twenty feet into the icy water. The boy's telephone call from the half-hidden house on the point brought police and ambulance in fifteen minutes. Both drivers were drowned.

They had agreed, in a crisp telephone call the next morning, not to attend each other's funerals, and they both declined to give interviews to the *New London Press*. A month later the university chaplain invited them to a small dinner party to which just the right other people—two close friends of each of the widowers—had been invited. The dinner party worked. There had now been a meeting between the two widowers, who had professional reasons to be in touch.

Ed Furniss was a natural diplomat. He had no problem using his house for official purposes. As a widower, he recognized that he needed to give extraordinary attention to domestic arrangements. What on earth had his wife done, he made himself wonder out loud, pencil and pad in hand, to make one guest professor comfortable? On that list today were fresh limes, essential to a proper gin and tonic. That was the drink Harry Bontecou had requested at the chaplain's dinner.

"You know, of course, about Campari?" Furniss's voice sounded to Harry, seated in an armchair in the handsome book-lined living room with ornithological prints nicely spaced along three walls, as if he were speaking from deep inside the refrigerator.

"What do you mean, Ed? Do I know that Campari exists? Or are you asking me for recondite knowledge about Campari? My field is history." He attempted to make his voice sound solemnly reproachful—better to break the ice that way than to answer routinely.

"Don't slight Campari when you're making a proper gin and tonic. I use one teaspoonful per jigger of gin. Since I will be giving you two jiggers of gin, which I would not have been permitted to do by Edith—she insisted on three jiggers—I will be giving you two teaspoonfuls of Campari."

"That follows. How much tonic?"

"Ah. People are careless on the subject. The ratio must be exact. One and one-half ounces of tonic water for one ounce of gin. Otherwise the tonic taste simply takes over. I don't really like the taste of tonic, come to think of it."

"You know what, Ed," Harry moved into the orderly New England kitchen, where Furniss was mixing the drinks, "I don't know you very well, but I'd bet you have a cup there that holds five ounces, which is what the average cup holds. So to make it sound highly calibrated, you come up with the one-point-five measures of tonic for one gin, but what it all boils down to is a cup of tonic water and a regular two-jigger splash of gin."

"Plus the Campari bit."

"Plus the Campari bit."

Ed Furniss laughed and, seated back in the living room, raised his glass and started talking about the upcoming baseball season.

Harry let him go on a bit. But after the refill was served he took his pen from his pocket and tinkled his glass, as though summoning a dinner party to a toast. "Ed, you want to talk to me about when I plan to pull out of UConn?"

Furniss raised his own glass and sipped from it, a philosophical smile taking shape. "Well, yes."

"The Old Age Act no longer shelters me, Ed?"

"Yes, it does. But—well, who knows the situation better than you do? There's a lot of pressure, and not unreasonable pressure. All

WILLIAM F. BUCKLEY JR.

those young cubs gasping for the pure air of tenure. But," he said with resignation, "we can't move any without a corresponding vacancy, not with Hartford's budget, and that budget ain't going anywhere."

Harry had several years before resolved not to pay out his federal anchor line beyond the point he thought seemly. He had no financial obligations he couldn't handle. His third book, *Victorian Disharmony,* was on its way to the University of Chicago Press. He had fitfully planned to visit Europe (his wife hated to fly, so he had been there only twice). But everything was now different, and he knew that he really yearned to be away. He'd make it easy for Furniss.

"Tell you what, Ed. I'm not due for a sabbatical until 1992. Give it to me instead at the end of this semester. I'll go off for the summer and fall, come back after that and teach one more year, then quit. Okay?"

"Done," said the provost.

Harry was oddly grateful for this nudge by Official Connecticut. Before he had finished his second drink, Harry was talking to Ed about other matters, academic, national, collegiate, though never personal.

Lord Alex Herrendon was tall, spare, well-groomed, his abundant hair silver. A trace of a smile on his face. "I was told you were waiting for me here," he said. "I'm sorry if I kept you."

Harry stood. Herrendon motioned Harry back down with the deferential touch of a hand on his shoulder. "Please sit." He slid his limber frame onto the chair Tracy Allshott had left behind. "And I will join you in a sherry. I gave the order to the steward coming in. You selected the favorite of my father, I discovered."

Lord Herrendon was animated on a subject he and Harry had resolved by correspondence to pursue.

Herrendon eyed Harry. "It is very important to me that you were so intimately involved with Operation Keelhaul."

Harry Bontecou had served in the U.S. Army division that was involved in the repatriation of Russian refugees right after the world war. Three million Russians, against their will, had been sent back to the Soviet Union.

Herrendon addressed Harry. "Which division were you with?"

"The 103rd," Harry replied.

"Have you written on your experiences in 1946?"

"No," Harry said. "I never have."

Herrendon sipped his drink. For a few moments there was silence. Neither spoke. Then Herrendon said, "I had a jolly difficult time finding out where in the University of Connecticut to find you. Department of history, yes. But I did not know to put down 'Storrs.'" He sipped and suddenly he smiled. "I should have asked Marcus Wolf to advise me. You noticed the story in the newspapers? He is angry at having run into some bureaucratic difficulty in getting a visa to visit America—" Harry nodded. Yes, he had seen the story.

Another pause. And then, "I know about your late wife. I am sorry. But it is always easier, wouldn't you agree"—he looked up—"not to get into personal matters?"

"Yes," Harry said, with some emphasis.

"So let me quickly get to the matter I wrote to you about. My book. But now let me ease into the subject. Let me talk to you first, oh—permit an eighty-six-year-old historian to digress a little—talk a little about my Operation Keelhaul research, which will be a part of my bigger book. It will perhaps interest you to know that I received a call from the new Russian ambassador in February, telling me I would be receiving an invitation to visit the archives housed, as it happens, in Tolstoy's estate—Leo Tolstoy's estate—with permission to examine for my own purposes the archives the Soviet authorities wouldn't let Nikolai Tolstoy, when doing his book on the question twenty years ago, look at."

Harry nodded but said nothing.

"The offer came too late for Nikolai's book. But they will be important for my own." Harry looked at the eighty-six-year-old gentleman, admiring his confidence and apparent good health. "Which is . . . one reason I wrote to ask you to meet with me. A book about the Communist scene in the West—after the war. So I wrote back cautiously on the Tolstoy business. I am certain to want Russian cooperation on the book I am planning."

"You took the trip to Saint Petersburg?"

"Yes. The man who dealt with me was a General Lasserov. A scholarly gentleman. We spent some time together, and we surveyed the estate—it is twelve hundred acres. The dwelling places—the main

WILLIAM F. BUCKLEY JR.

house and the farmers' quarters—will sleep four hundred souls. Non-dead souls. Aleksandr Lasserov, I would learn after several evenings together, was as a young man in Gulag for four years, sent there by Brezhnev, for what infraction I forget. He is eager to sort out the history of Soviet suffering and to analyze compliant responsibility for it by the West."

"He is talking mostly about Operation Keelhaul?"

"Yes. Though not exclusively. He cares about American foreign policy and its neglect of Soviet suffering in the years that followed Keelhaul."

"You told him about your prospective book?"

"Yes." Herrendon took a worn leather packet from his jacket and—"Do you mind?"—lit a small cigar. He stretched out his legs.

"So what exactly is his interest in your project?"

"Lasserov is an ethicist. He wants to try to understand why presumably moral people simply stand by when huge crimes are not merely committed but institutionalized."

"He wants you to figure that out?"

Herrendon smiled. "You have the point exactly, yes, Professor Bontecou."

"—Harry." Odd, Harry thought, to be asking Herrendon to call him by his first name.

Herrendon nodded and went on. "There are not many senior officials alive who took part in the operations. But, at a junior level, you of course did. Most important, for me, is what came later. The great, turbulent, postwar Communist/anti-Communist/Red scare/McCarthy period. You were in it, deeply in it. And you are a trained historian. And I am here to ask you to spend time with me—as much time as is required—to help me to understand, retrospectively."

Harry drained his glass. His wife, Elena, had often teased him about his impetuosity, sometimes reproachfully. He recalled her summons to spend more time *deliberating* commitments he often made offhandedly. Accordingly, with a nod to her memory, he touched his napkin to his lips and said with mock deliberation, "Let me think about it." He was not ready to call him Alex.

He would say yes. Tomorrow. Actually—he was busy assembling supporting arguments for his decision—actually, he had nothing else to do. He had no plans on how to spend the sabbatical suddenly sprung on him. And just one hour ago, reading the news of Pol Pot, the old questions had stirred: Why? How come? He turned to Herrendon.

"I know. You want me to talk about Senator McCarthy."

Lord Herrendon took a puff on his cigar. "Yes."

"You probably know that I have never written about Senator McCarthy. You probably do not know that I have never spoken about him."

"I did know that. One of your students was a colleague in Cambridge. Jim Presley. He said he once tried to interview you for the college paper."

Harry paused. He had made his resolution in 1957, more than thirty years ago, and hadn't diverted from it. But he felt now not merely the weakening of an old resolve but an utterly unanticipated anxiety to reverse himself. The historian who shelters historical material profanes his calling—the point had been made to Harry before, both by fellow historians and by survivors of the great McCarthy wars, 1950 to 1954.

He spoke finally. "I'd need a lot of stuff."

"I'll bring over everything you want."

"Nobody can put his hands on everything I'd want. Though I know a bit about his boyhood, and the war years. I collected all that, way back then."

"From the widow?"

"Well, Jeanie McCarthy and I were close. But she died in 1979. I'm talking about way back. Let's put it this way—you can count on me to help."

"Even to telling all . . . telling everything you know about Joe McCarthy?"

Harry closed his eyes. "Even to telling about Joe McCarthy."

"That is what I hope you can tell me about. When is your next appointment?"

"What's the date today?"

"June thirtieth."

"Well, I should get back to Storrs in a year or so."

"In that case, we'd better get started."

WILLIAM F. BUCKLEY JR.

BOOK ONE

3

Joe McCarthy, age fourteen

Joe McCarthy left on the school bus on the opening day of classes. He didn't respond to the talk of his schoolmates, which surprised them: Joe was the very best fifteen-year-old to swap stories with, discuss the virtues and weaknesses of the faculty, all six of them. "What's the matter?" Billy asked him. "Just thinking," Joe said. "Well, I wouldn't want to interrupt *that,* you agree, Moe?" Joe ducked his head and shot his right elbow back as if preparing to deliver a blow. But he laughed, and when he turned his head again to the bus window, his companions left him alone.

When he descended the bus, the decision was made. He thought to take Billy to one side—it was 8:20, and class didn't begin for ten minutes. Take him aside and tell him what Joe had decided. Joe would tell him he wasn't learning anything, he was "bored out of my mind"—Joe had heard that formulation on the radio and thought it expressive. He would tell Billy that the shortage of hands on the farm—his father's, and also their neighbors'—meant there was need for extra help. And anyway, what harm had leaving school done to his two older brothers?

But he quickly reflected that it would be disloyal to his parents to tell anyone before they learned about it. What he knew he couldn't do, having made up his mind, was to enter that classroom and wait until bus time at three P.M. to go home. So instead of making his case to Billy, he leaned over and said, "I've got to go home, very important. Tell Miss Lockhart I won't be there." Billy tried to interrogate him, but, lunch box in hand, Joe simply wheeled about and started his five-mile walk back to the farm.

He had rehearsed how to say it to Tim and Bid. He didn't look forward to it, and delayed opening the door to the farmhouse until the lunch hour, noon. He spent two hours in his old tree house, well removed from his father's sight—he'd be tending the farm over the brow of the hill. But he had to do it and thought, after much self-interrogation, to do it matter-of-factly.

Tim and Bid were seated at the kitchen table with the big bowl of soup, the loaf of bread, and the platter of butter. "What you doing here at noon, Joe?" his mother asked.

Joe knew to direct the conversation to his father. "I'm sure you know, Dad, it's one of those things, just like it was for Steve and Bill." Joe knew his mother would make a fuss, never mind that his older brothers had done the same thing. But he knew also that his father would deal fatalistically with Joe's decision. His brothers too had been fifteen and had said they would join their father as farmhands, as now Joe was expected to do.

There was more of a problem with his mother. Bid closed her mouth tightly. But she knew instantly, knew from the way Joe had given them the news and from her close study of him as a boy, that there would be no changing his mind. Bid got up, left the table, and retreated to the bedroom, but returned moments later to the silent kitchen, neither husband nor son saying anything. Bid fancied her son Joe as someone who *ought* to continue in school. Joe listened, and let his eyes dart over for comfort to his father. Tim McCarthy had finished his soup and was now seated by the stove, idly petting the hound dog.

Joe was reassured: He could be confident that there would be no interference from that quarter. Joe rose and embraced his mother, propelling her into a cheek-to-cheek dance, Joe humming the tune.

Bid stopped resisting. She couldn't deny the handsome, dark, muscular boy whose school picture she always kept within reach. When Bid visited her cousin at Fond du Lac she would put up on the mirror in the room she shared with her hostess a picture of her husband, Tim. Tim never changed, neither in appearance nor in dress: always the blue overalls and the straw hat with the old pheasant feather, faded after five years, sticking up from the hatband that took icy snow in the winter and, in the summer, day after day of Tim's sweat-soaked hair. And alongside it, the picture of Joe, standing stiffly for the school portrait but unable to suppress entirely the smile that seemed always to animate his face, as also his spirit.

What was special about Joe, Bid thought, was that in his view of life *everything* was marvelous and *everybody* was wonderful. Joe packed so much pleasure into his waking hours that he resented even the hours given to sleeping. He was now, at fifteen, up earlier and earlier, going to bed later and later. Sometimes in the late hours he would read magazines, occasionally a book. He would listen to the radio and comment on whatever he heard, laughing uproariously when Jack Benny told a funny story. He took careful notes whenever the announcer gave the name of a product that could be had, free of charge, by just mailing in a request for it. He had his own special wooden box that he kept in the barn. He had built the box himself, though it was his brother Steve, three years his senior, who taught him how to use the lathe that made it possible.

Joe kept his box padlocked, and at age fourteen had announced to the family with some ceremony that it would be his own preserve, its contents not to be seen by any other McCarthy. He had in the box his array of samples. Listerine, Colgate, Pepsodent, Wrigley's, Mum— all in tiny, one-ounce bottles or in tubes smaller than Joe's thumb. There were specially wrapped single sticks of gum, lozenges, small packages of Smith Brothers cough drops. The box contained one document, a holographic will leaving his collection to his sister, Anna Mae, who was nine. Joe had got two of his teachers to witness his will. He did not want any family to witness it, as they would then be privy to the secret object of Joe's philanthropy.

His collection became something of a problem for him when, in the summer of 1923, the advertisers one after another changed their policy. Now the samples were no longer free: they required a nickel. Plus postage. That meant eight cents. This was a problem for Joe. His father paid him almost twice that sum for an hour's work, but Joe had a difficult time saving money. For one thing, he had taken to going to Billy's house, two miles down the country road, unpaved, hemmed in by the luxuriant Wisconsin green, speckled with tall oak trees. He would do this two, sometimes three times a week. There he would play poker tirelessly and joyously with Billy and his older brother Jerry. Sometimes Moe would join them, but Moe wasn't very welcome — he tended to lose his temper when he lost.

They played five-card stud, betting nickels and dimes, and every now and then a quarter. The house limit was a quarter. But often a night's gambling would lose (or gain) the player a dollar; on two memorable occasions, four dollars. Joe played with desperate zeal. Billy and Jerry and Moe learned that they would need to call Joe's bluff every now and then or else lose to him, hand after hand. Joe would always stay, and always raise.

The day of the upset was Thanksgiving Eve. Joe had accumulated very nearly ten dollars by intensive wood chopping in the hard Wisconsin cold for his father's winter supply. He arrived at Billy's with Thanksgiving presents — he was always bringing presents, especially after he had walked home the winner. For Jerry he brought the newest model of a Whizz — the rubber ball attached to the center of a paddle by a long elastic string. Joe was eager to demonstrate his skill with it and managed eleven hits before the ball eluded the paddle. For Billy he brought a box of ten jacks and, again, set out to show him how to bounce the ball on the floor and quickly snatch up a jack. Billy showed prowess, capturing six of the ten jacks before missing the ball. The two boys were engrossed with their toys. Joe enjoyed the pleasure they were taking, but now Moe came in, and he wanted to play cards. That meant getting out of the warm house and walking through the cold to the barn. There was the usual recitation of the house rules: five-cent limit, three-raise maximum.

It was after ten, and they had been playing for two hours. Now it was cold. They sat under the kerosene lamp on individual hay bales grouped around twin hay bales that were covered by a blanket. Jerry and Billy's father, Mr. Garvey, had set down his rule in mid-September, before the chill set in. His rule was that just ten pieces of coal could be used by the boys to keep warm. Mr. Garvey thought that rule a good idea from two points of view. There was the husbandry — coal was not to be treated as though it grew from the ground. And then too, putting a limit on the coal the boys could burn was a way of limiting the time they would stay up nights.

"What would happen," Joe asked, burying his hands in the pockets of his jacket to shield against the night's cold, "if we just, well, stuck a few more pieces in the stove? I mean," he asked Jerry, "your dad wouldn't notice. He doesn't *count* how many pieces are in that vat, does he?"

Joe thought his idea very funny, and without waiting for an answer, got up from his seat, walked over to the coal bin, and, in the voice of an auctioneer, counted out, "*Five thousand four hundred and eighty-seven coal pieces here, five thousand four hundred and eighty-eight, five thousand four hundred and eighty — who took number five thousand four hundred and eighty-nine!* Jerry! Billy! I'm going to whip your ass!"

Billy, freckled and chubby, wearing a winter jacket and a scarf, thought this funny too, as did Jerry, red haired and rangy, with traces of a beard. He rubbed his fingers together to keep warm. Moe, his wool cap pulled down to his ears, said nothing, his eyes fixed on the corner of the blanket and Joe's collection of silver after hours of successful poker — He must have *five dollars* in quarters and nickels, Moe reckoned.

Joe stood there by the coal bin with the grave countenance of an auctioneer deliberating over a critical bid. Joe was waiting for Jerry, the senior Garvey, to say, What the hell! Go ahead! Take a few forbidden pieces of coal!

But Jerry gave no such signal. Instead he said, "Cut it out, Joe. My dad trusts Billy and me. Let's call it a night. It's late. And," he shivered ostentatiously, "it's cold."

Joe paused. "Tell you what, Jerry. Suppose I *buy* some coal from your dad? How much is one piece worth? A penny? Two pennies? Hell, let's say *three* pennies! Five pieces, fifteen cents." He reached down to the corner where his stakes were sequestered, plucked out a dime and a nickel, and placed the coins in Jerry's corner. He then turned, opened the bin, and scooped up coals in the cups of both hands.

He was reaching down to put them in the stove when Jerry landed his fist on his chest, knocking him down. Joe got up, the smile gone. He lowered his head and, fists flying, tore into Jerry, two years older, fifteen pounds heavier. Jerry, who boxed at school, returned the blows lustily and with precision, and in moments Joe McCarthy was on the floor, his mouth bleeding. The blanket had been ripped away, the coins strewn about the hay-packed floor among the bales that served as chairs. Moe began collecting the silver pieces, frenzied, determined. Jerry leaned down, picked up the blanket, spread it out, and reconstituted the table. He turned to Moe.

"Put it all back on the table. We'll figure out who had what."

Joe, silent, looked on. In a few moments Jerry, his hand full of silver coins, approached him.

"I figure this is yours."

Joe did not extend his hand. Jerry reached to one side and dumped the money in Joe's pocket.

"Okay, that's it. Good night, Moe. Good night, Joe. And thanks for the Whizz ball. Come on, Billy." Jerry reached over and turned the kerosene light knob down. The light flickered out gradually on the four boys dressed for winter, one of them with a bloodstain over his chin, but the faltering light caught also the bright smile on Joe's face.

The next day was a holiday, and Tim McCarthy forbade work on holidays and holy days. Joe was gone when his parents and brothers woke at seven, but he was back in time for the Thanksgiving turkey, happy and talkative.

Where had he been? his mother asked.

Down to the school, he said.

But the school was closed.

Yes, but he wanted to track down Mr. Agnelli. The football coach.

"He teaches boxing too, you know. I wanted to get him to teach me."

"How're you going to do that," Steve wanted to know. "Now that you've pulled out of school?"

"Oh," said Joe happily, "no problem. We made a deal."

4

Joe McCarthy, age nineteen

Joe worked very long days, adding twenty hours for his uncle to his father's fifty-hour ration, but now, at seventeen, he was staying awake in bed at night. He had to do more, it was that simple, he concluded after several weeks, and one night he got the idea, and after making some notes on the inside cover of a magazine, he slept long and well. The next day he informed his father that he, Joe, was going into business "on my own," needing only permission to use a corner of his father's sixty-four-acre farm. He didn't say what it was he intended to do. But he did open his wallet to his father, and with some ceremony counted out the sixty-five dollars he had saved. Altering his habits, he had studiously sequestered the money he earned from his uncle as a farmhand. He kept it separate from the money he earned from his father. This he spent on cards and on the steady drizzle of little gifts he was always giving to family and friends.

"That's what they call capital," he said. "Just wait, Dad."

Joe McCarthy, a year and a half later, was by community standards a prosperous chicken farmer. He owned two thousand laying hens and ten thousand broilers. He would rise before dawn and tend his chickens, coming home at dark heavy with chicken offal, showering before dinner, and talking about his future as a chicken farmer—"The sky's the limit!" he told his mother buoyantly.

In late summer he bought the second-hand Chevrolet. He refitted it for his own uses and spent long days on the road selling cases of eggs, carefully memorizing the names of all his customers, some of whom, attracted to the energetic young man, were cheered by his ambition. Many would hold back on buying eggs from the local store, waiting to see Joe McCarthy come by in his converted old Chevy. They gave as their reason for doing so, when talking to members of the family, that it was a good thing in America to encourage youthful enterprise. Actually, they were buying their eggs from Joe McCarthy because they liked him, liked his cheerfulness and affability and the hint of a flirt when the buyer was the lady of the house.

In December he drove in his Chevy to pick up Jerry. They embarked on a considerable adventure, a drive to Chicago, where Jerry hoped to go to college. They would share a room at the hotel, saving on expenses. The 175 miles was an exciting trip. They were now in the Windy City, which would be the home of the World's Fair of 1939, an exuberant act of defiance of the terrible Depression. The great drive by the shore of Lake Michigan still gave off its old splendor. Both young men wanted to take Chicago on, Jerry to examine the University of Chicago, and Joe to cultivate prospective clients and attend festivities at the biannual twenty-four-hour convention of chicken farmers.

The day was full with speeches and meetings and seminars and an exchange of trade information. At the closing reception he spotted the name of Richie O'Neill, a seigneurial figure at age twenty-five with his hundred-thousand-broiler enterprise, a major player in southern Wisconsin.

Joe introduced himself, pointing to his mislettered name tag. "They got it wrong, Mr. O'Neill—"

"Richie."

"Richie. They got it wrong; it's *McCarthy*, one *t*."

Richie asked the routine questions about the business enterprise of the chicken farmer he was talking to. They ate dinner with two of Richie's friends, and after the evening lecture (on the need for federal price supports), Richie asked if Joe played poker. Joe whooped his delight at the thought of a game, and five of them went to Richie's hotel room, bringing in extra chairs to play their cards on the bed.

Richie ordained that there would be no house limit. Joe was startled when Richie, opening with two kings, put down a five-dollar bill.

WILLIAM F. BUCKLEY JR.

Joe, a single ace showing in his four up cards, saw him and raised five dollars. Gene, Benton, and Chuck dropped out. Richie raised Joe back. Joe paused for a moment, and then raised Richie ten dollars. Richie looked up at Joe, apparently unconcerned. The others froze on the scene, an opening-hand drama. Richie folded. Joe took the money, buried his cards—no one would know whether he had another ace as his down card.

It was Gene's deal. A half hour later Richie thought he had drawn the profile of young McCarthy, poker player. An hour later Joe lost seventy-five dollars on a single hand.

Gene said he was quitting, but Benton and Chuck and Richie said they were good for more. Benton volunteered to go find some beer. Richie looked up at Joe.

"You want to quit?"

"Hell, no! But I got to go get some stuff from my room. Be right back."

He prayed Jerry would be back from his tour of the university campus. He was there, sitting in the armchair, reading the next day's *Chicago Tribune.*

"Jerry, can you let me have a loan?"

"How much?"

"Two hundred dollars."

Jerry laughed. "Forget it, Joe. How much you lose?"

"Four big ones."

Jerry paled. "Did you have it on you?"

"Hell, yes; they play for cash."

"My advice: Cut your losses—you are a *dumb . . . stupid . . .*" He stopped. Joe must be suffering enough.

Still standing by the corner of the double bed they shared, Joe persisted. "I got to get back there, Jerry. You like my car, I know. And you'll need one in Chicago. It's yours for two hundred dollars."

Jerry reacted quickly. He bit his lip. "Okay. But I didn't bring two hundred dollars in cash with me. I can give you fifty in cash and a hundred fifty in a check."

"Done!"

Joe reached for the telephone and dialed Richie's room.

"Richie? Joe here. Got hung up for a minute, but don't give me up. Will be with you in no time."

He pulled out his wallet and the registration form for the car, read it hastily, signed his own name as seller, and said to Jerry, "You fill in the rest."

He picked up the cash and the check, opened the door, then turned around, a broad smile on his face. "Jerry?"

"Yuh."

"I'll buy the car back from you tomorrow for two hundred fifty!" He slammed the door shut.

In the dining room the conventioneers were arriving for breakfast, downing their coffee and eggs and cereal, exchanging business cards, and walking off to their cars or buses, or to the railroad station. Joe sat alone, reading the paper. He looked up at the figure who had sat down opposite. It was Richie.

"How'd you get here, Joe? Bus, or somebody give you a ride?"

"Oh," Joe answered cheerfully, "I came down with a buddy. But he's going on south, so I'll be taking the bus home."

"Why don't you let me give you a ride? I go right by your place on the way to the farm."

"Well, that would be just fine. When you want to leave, Richie?"

"In an hour. See you outside."

Richie drove a splendid half-ton, the rear of it equipped as a bedroom/study, complete with toilet and sink and radio and portable library and chicken catalogs. He displayed it to Joe with some pride. "Got all the facilities of a trailer, right, Joe?"

"I think it's *terrific*," Joe said. "Maybe I should get one just like it. Though I'd change a couple of things. . . ."

Richie smiled and went to the driver's door. "Come on around, get in."

On the way, Richie listened to his companion's story of his triumphant chicken farm. Joe was cheerful as ever and confessed that the two nights in Chicago had been the first he had ever spent away from home, indeed, the first night away from his chickens. He asked about Richie's RU-Farm, as it was known. Richie too had begun with nothing but a few dollars. "But I had the advantage of my dad, who

WILLIAM F. BUCKLEY JR.

was retired when I started in. He knew the business and gave me leads. I'm eager to see your layout," he said to Joe.

It was just after eleven when they arrived in Appleton, driving directly to Joe's farm. Richie stopped the truck opposite the chicken shed, got out, and went with Joe into the largest coop.

Inside, he looked about and registered some concern. It was the smell that had got his attention.

"You mind, Joe?" Richie leaned over, grabbed a chicken by the neck, and brought the cleaver from the tool table down sharply, severing the chicken's head. He grabbed the neck and let the blood pour into a glass, throwing the chicken carcass to one side.

"Hang on, Joe, I'll be right back."

Richie returned from his trailer with a foot-wide wooden box. He opened it. There were eight tubes with liquids of different colors, a chart fastened to the length of the box, and a cavity with a dozen cotton swabs. He took an eyedropper and squeezed a few drops of the chemical from the third tube into what looked like a shallow glass ashtray. Now he dipped a cotton swab into the chicken blood and touched it down on the chemical.

The blood, in seconds, turned amber. Richie turned to him. "It's coccidiosis. They'll all die."

Bid hadn't seen him that way, not ever. After hearing the news his father did an unprecedented thing. He drew from the padlocked cupboard his bottle of applejack, measured two ounces into the kitchen cup, poured them into a glass, and offered them to his son.

"Thanks, Dad."

He stared at the glass, then looked up at his father.

"You may as well know I went broke at poker yesterday. Sold my car to Jerry."

Tim McCarthy poured himself a shot glass, and Bid wiped her eyes with the hanging towel. The next morning Joe told them at breakfast that he was going back to school.

Under Wisconsin law, high schools were not obliged to admit any student older than nineteen. Joe was twenty. He sighed on hearing the rule for the first time, this from Miss Hawthorne, tall, stately, her gray-white hair neatly tied in a bun; after thirty-eight years' service, the senior teacher. But the rule was simply one more little obstacle in the life of Joseph Raymond McCarthy. It wasn't as if Joe had caught coccidiosis, he said to himself. He asked for an appointment with the principal.

His encounter with Mr. Hershberger was facilitated by a recent ruling that authorized promotion in Wisconsin high schools for students who showed passing grades on the appropriate exams. Joe would have to take a general test in reading, writing, and arithmetic before being admitted into freshman year. This was obligatory because so much time had passed since Joe had completed eighth grade. He should report at three the following afternoon at Little Wolf High School, Miss Hawthorne informed him.

He thought quickly. "You know, I work, Miss Hawthorne. Work every day at the Cash-Way. They wouldn't like it if I pulled out in the middle of the afternoon. Is there any way I could take the test later in the day—maybe seven, eight o'clock?"

Prudence Hawthorne was impressed by the lanky twenty-year-old's determination to return to school. She felt it only right to encourage him.

"All right, Joe. I'll tell Miss Mackay at the library. It stays open until nine. Complete the test, after you're through seal it in the envelope she'll give you, and we'll get the results."

"My problem," Joe explained to Jerry, who had agreed to give him a ride to the movie house, "is that I'm not so sure I could pass that test. Been a long time since I did grammar and multiplication and that kind of thing. What I *do* know is that when I get instruction I'll whiz along. So, buddy, what I want you to do for me—this is very important to me, Jerry—is to go to Miss Mackay at the Little Wolf library at seven tomorrow and take the test—sign my name."

Jerry was, for a moment, taken aback. He wound a curl from his red hair around his index finger, steering the car with his left hand. He understood about going late in life to school—he would be going to the University of Illinois as a freshman at the advanced age of twenty-two. What the hell. Yes. He'd drive to Little Wolf in his car,

Joe's old car—"I'll drive with you," Joe said. "I'll sit in the car while you take the exam and say a rosary that you do well!"

Miss Mackay was not surprised that it was a young man, not a child, who asked for the sealed envelope. She handed it to him and pointed to an empty desk. "Good luck, McCarthy." She corrected herself. "Good luck, Joe."

Joe's confidence in himself was well placed. He sat down in September with thirty-nine boys and girls aged fourteen; nine months later he was ready to graduate alongside forty seniors whose ages averaged eighteen. Prudence Hawthorne, who administered progressive exams to Joe what seemed every few weeks as he skidded upward to ninth, tenth, eleventh, and now twelfth grade, was deliriously proud of his record, but not happy at the prospect of his leaving, because she loved it when Joe was at school. He was always playing with the younger children, offering to do odd jobs that needed doing, and unintrusively flirting with the younger teachers, and with some not so young. He seemed utterly untroubled by a schedule that had had him working at the Cash-Way from three until eleven and all day on Saturday. But now only graduation lay ahead.

Joe told Miss Hawthorne, passing by her office on Tuesday morning of the big week, that he wanted to have a "date" with her after the school graduation lunch.

"Doing what?" she asked sharply.

"Never mind. Do you promise?"

She promised. And when the time came, after he had kissed his mother and shaken hands with four siblings, Joe guided her to his new car, telling her to hush up.

Twenty minutes later, Prudence Hawthorne was being coaxed into a little Piper biplane. Joe's graduation present to her would be a flight in an airplane—her first. Joe had never himself been up, but promised himself he'd do it soon, after saving money to hire "High-Fly Jim" for a second ride. Meanwhile, he would just watch Miss Hawthorne.

She looked pale when she stepped onto the boarding ladder and into the tiny cockpit. She had no reason to suspect what was in store for her: Joe had arranged with Jim to take her up—and then to do a loop-the-loop.

The whole trip took only five minutes, but when she was helped out of the plane by High-Fly Jim, Prudence Hawthorne was a pale and very irate lady. She said to Joe that she would never speak to him again and would certainly not recommend him to any college. The tirade gave out just about the time Joe's car pulled up at her little cottage. She let Joe take her by the arm to the front door. He took her door key from her, put it in the keyhole, and turned the lock.

"You are a *scoundrel*, Joe."

Suddenly she turned, pecked him on his cheek, closed the door, and rushed to the telephone to call all her friends, one after another, into the early hours of the evening, to tell them about her incredible afternoon, just like Lindbergh.

McCarthy goes to Marquette

It didn't surprise the family and friends of Joe McCarthy that the momentum he had built up would take him on, past high school. In the fall of 1930 he matriculated at Marquette, the large and busy Jesuit-run university in Milwaukee, celebrating, the year Joe entered, its fiftieth anniversary.

He lost no time entering into college life, though his primary concern was the money needed to see him through. His boarding-house, shared with a dozen other students, was four blocks from the campus and charged eight dollars a week for room and board. Joe did everything, including dish washing ("It's okay. Just think about something else"), construction work, and janitorial duties ("I'm going to be nice to janitors for the rest of my life"). He sold flypaper and did short-order cooking in a beanery ("I have become a *very* good cook," he wrote to his mother. And he would volunteer to do the cooking when he visited his girlfriends). Every few months he sold blood, his blood. After a while he fastened on two service stations to which he gave as much as eighty hours of his time during the week ("In a perfect world, everybody would run out of gas once a day").

He paid his way and became something of a money broker. He continued, as ever, to be a gift giver, and anyone who needed a dollar went to Joe, who gave the loan without any regard to whether he would be repaid. As regularly, he borrowed money. At one point he borrowed from his father and brothers. What seemed moments after, he bought another car.

He had a very early disappointment. Applying to the football coach, he was asked, Had he played football in high school?

To the astonishment of his friend Charles Curran ("I'd have expected Joe to say he was captain of the school team"), he admitted that he had not. In that case, the coach said, he could not apply. Joe talked back. "So I haven't played before, how do you know I won't be the best football player in Wisconsin after a couple of months?" The coach told him he'd run that risk, and turned to the next applicant.

He decided to box. He worked at it diligently, and the great day came: He saw his name in print in the *Marquette Tribune*, which recorded that "McCarthy is a husky, hard-hitting middleweight who promises an evening's work for any foe." He worked hard at the sport, and in his second year, when he learned that Marquette's coach had resigned, he applied for the job and held it down for a few weeks, in charge of seventy student boxers. Joe was much taken with his new responsibility and befriended a boxing instructor at a Milwaukee gymnasium. He would stand by at coaching sessions and learn from the points stressed by Coach Fred Saddy. He took these lessons to heart, and toward the end of the year faced a rematch with a heavier competitor who had trounced him the first time out. Joe practiced determinedly, stressing the points Saddy had taught him. He fought now hard as ever, but with finesse, winning the fight. He was so transported by his success that he went early the next day to the gym to find Saddy.

"I want to talk to you about becoming a professional boxer."

The deflation was quick. Saddy sat him down and ended his little lecture by telling him he, Saddy, would rather have a college degree than be heavyweight champion.

Joe signed up to join the Delta Theta Phi fraternity. He was warned by his sponsor that when examined by the admissions board he would be expected to give a five-minute speech. "I've never given a speech," Joe said deferentially to the senior. "Could we just skip that one? I'll do a boxing exhibition if you want. Or maybe milk a cow?"

Dutifully, Joe reported to the debate coach, Hank Razzoli. His first experience was humiliating. When his turn came, Joe stood, looked down at the other dozen applicants, seated, and over at Razzoli, at his desk at the end of the room. Joe stood there, mouth open, but no word was framed.

After a half minute the coach snapped, "Say something, McCarthy. *Anything*. But don't just *stand* there."

Joe stepped away. "Sorry, coach. I'll be back."

Day after day he practiced. He memorized (always easy for Joe McCarthy) Brutus's oration over the dead Caesar and spoke it in whispers when on the bus, and in a loud, declamatory voice in the park at night. He would imagine huge crowds listening to him.

"Is he any good?" Joe's brother Howard asked the debate coach, seated next to him at a football game.

"He's pretty fluent now," Razzoli said to the chatty younger McCarthy, convivial like all the McCarthys, except for father Tim. "But there's a monotone problem. Your brother speaks almost always in the same tone of voice."

"What can you do about that?"

The coach jolted up on his feet to cheer a touchdown. And then replied, "Joe's quick to learn. He's no orator. But anyway, who really cares?"

Joe cared. He cared a great deal. As a freshman he had registered as a prospective engineer. By the end of his second year he had decided that the law was better suited for him: Now he imagined a lifetime of oral arguments and pleadings before juries and judges.

He'd be good at it, he knew. He was persuasive, and everybody liked him. Soon he was a member of the Franklin Debating Club, debating every week. In his final year at law school, five years after his matriculation under the amalgamated curriculum, he resolved to run for president of the Franklin club. This proved painful when, at lunch in the cafeteria with his closest friend, Charlie Curran, he learned that Curran had already filed for the same post. They agreed, in high bonhomie, to vote for each other. The vote was a tie. A fresh vote was scheduled, which Joe won by two votes.

"Did you vote for me?" Charles Curran asked, a severe expression on his face.

Joe smiled impishly. "We were told to vote for the best man, weren't we, Charlie? Well, I did."

The big moment loomed: graduation from law school in exactly one month. Charlie Curran had ruminated with Joe. Most of their classmates planned to take a week's vacation, perhaps even two, then they would line up and try to endear themselves to law firms in Milwaukee and about. "Not me," said Charlie. "I'm going to open my own office."

Joe looked surprised. He would play that game with Charlie. He said he thought it rather presumptuous to do any such thing. Charlie liked that. "Some people are more enterprising than other people, Joe. Never mind; after you hustle for a year or two, come on over to where I'm practicing, and I'll see if I can make room for you."

McCarthy waited until the morning of the graduation on Saturday. Walking down the aisle dressed in academic gown and hat, keeping rough time with the ceremonial organ music, Joe leaned over: "I bet I'll have my own office before you do."

Charlie managed a disdainful smile. "You'll have to open your office before Monday. That's when I'll hang out my shingle."

Joe feigned distress at such a challenge. Then he spoke, quietly, because they were now nearing the stage where the fifty-seven law students would sit for the commencement ceremonies before going to Madison to be sworn in at noon. "I bet you twenty bucks I'm in business before you are."

Late in the afternoon, McCarthy—Bid at his side with her Brownie camera to record the great moment—opened his office, a single room shared with Mike Eberlein, an older friend who was himself excited at going out more or less on his own. Bid could not disguise her elation: two sons dropped out of high school, one son—a lawyer! She went to St. Ambrose church when dark came and prayed out her gratitude for Joe Raymond McCarthy.

His work was routine. There were a lot of title examinations, local people selling their houses and farms, others picking them up. Joe encouraged all his friends to make out their wills if they hadn't already done so, and to revise their wills if they had—if they preferred to pay him only upon death, he would arrange that. He wrote a lot of wills. He wondered about the first client who asked for help in obtaining a divorce—Bid wouldn't like that—but, well, money was scarce, and he couldn't turn down business. He lent himself

WILLIAM F. BUCKLEY JR.

ardently to the enterprise and even performed as a stakeout two nights, opposite the house where his client, Snowbird, insisted he'd get evidence of her husband's impropriety. Joe was disappointed the defendant didn't perform for the benefit of his plaintiff, and confessed to Charlie, who had forgiven him after a few months his duplicity in winning twenty dollars on a sure thing, that he had to think for a minute or two about the moral problem. "There I was, hoping to catch Mr. Snowball, I'll call him, going into that little house to screw the lady. I was disappointed it didn't happen! That's strange, isn't it, Charlie?"

"Nah," Charlie said. "Lawyers always hope the other side screws up—"

"Watch your language, Charlie."

He laughed, but Joe accepted the point, the lawyer's perspective. He won the case for Snowbird and two other divorce cases later. But after a few years of routine activity he felt the tedious exasperations of the country lawyer. He began to notice the surrounding political scene. In less than one week, he had his target, his objective. He was careful not to talk about it until the idea settled, but he yearned for an exchange or two that would accelerate his thinking. He was several times tempted to talk about it to Charles Curran and to brother Bill. On November 16, 1937, he got into his car and drove forty miles to Little Wolf. He had made a date with Prudence Hawthorne.

"Taking me out to lunch, Joe McCarthy! You certainly have got yourself fancy ways. Are you making a lot of money in the law business?" Miss Hawthorne had said over the telephone, and never mind picking her up in his car, she would walk to the hotel from school. Either she had gone home from school before meeting him, or else she had taken to school, to put on for her lunch date, the velvet beret with the royal coat of arms stitched up front and the matching pocketbook. What would she like from the menu?

As they ate, Joe said he wanted to confide in her. He found his law work boring. "It's right, isn't it, Miss Hawthorne, to use whatever talents you have?"

"You have a lot of talents, Joe. You're never going to be a professor; you're too restless. What do you have in mind?"

"Politics," Joe said.

"Well, why not?" Prudence Hawthorne applied her knife to the chicken. "There isn't anybody better than you at getting on. What post you thinking about taking on, Joe?"

"State judge."

Miss Hawthorne paused before taking her fork to her mouth. "State judge? That's for older people, isn't it, Joe? Maybe you should wait before you do that, wait maybe . . . five, ten years?"

Joe impulsively reached out and pressed her arm. "Miss Hawthorne, ma'am, this is what I was *born* to do. I love to mix with people, and people like me and trust me. I haven't told anybody about this, and I have to raise some money, of course. . . . No no no, not from you, I mean, you know, a candidate *has* to have some money, has to get around. But mostly I'll go and call on people. You know, I've done a lot of that, Miss Hawthorne, a lot back when I was selling eggs, and I got a lot of eggs sold, Miss Hawthorne. I'm going to tell everybody how good a judge I can be, you know, somebody who really worked his way up from nothing, you'll agree. . . . No, no, I don't mean Dad and Mom were *nothing,* they've been *wonderful* parents, but you know, there wasn't any thought I'd finish high school — thanks to you, I did — or go to college. And law school? I mean, that was for other people to do, not the McCarthy kids. So I thought, well, that's worth listening to, that's something I can tell them and that the facts bear out. . . ."

Prudence Hawthorne had stopped eating. She just listened. Joe was unstoppable. He gave the details. He would run for judge, run in the Tenth Judicial District, run against the veteran incumbent — Edgar Werner.

Miss Hawthorne resolved to put away her reservations about his age and experience. When they parted she gave him a matronly kiss on the forehead. "I'll vote for you, Joe. But remember something. There are some people who won't vote for you. And some of those aren't going to like what you're doing, competing with a nice gentleman who almost seems to own that job."

"Don't worry, ma'am. People are good sports. They're used to sports. Some people win, means some people have to lose." He smiled broadly and blew another kiss at her. He was right, he thought. He would get the most reliable judgment on his enterprise from Prudence Hawthorne. Because she was an educated woman with a lot of experience and she knew what Joe McCarthy could accomplish. She had seen him through those incredible four years of high school in nine months. It was from her that Joe wanted to hear about climbing steep hills.

For the declaration of his candidacy, his mother and father arrived dressed as they had been dressed at Aunt Bessie's funeral. Tim McCarthy was without his overalls, wearing a scarlet tie with the profile of the state of Wisconsin on the front. Bid's dress was calico, her wide hat a dark blue. Joe's two older brothers sat stiffly, their neckties inconclusively knotted. Miss Hawthorne was there, sitting upright, the same posture in which she was found every day by her students when they trooped into her classroom. Joe's old friends Jerry and Billy wore the jeans and open shirts they wore at school — dressed, with this or that difference, like the half-dozen other high school classmates present, all of them much younger than the candidate. And, of course, there was Mike Eberlein, his law partner, dressed as if preparing to instruct a jury.

They gathered at eleven A.M. in the grand dining hall of the Grand Hotel in Shawano, ordinarily kept closed during the hard winter months to economize on the heating bills. Diners during that period ate on tables set up in the lounge opposite the reception desk. The dining hall's ten heavy wooden tables were cramped together opposite the four large windows, creating a spacious working lounge. Enough chairs were brought in to seat fifty people.

Representing the media was a single reporter, Jim Kelly of the *Appleton Post-Crescent.* Joe and Mike Eberlein, who was now not only law partner but also campaign manager, had done everything they could to promote the announcement. With only twenty-four hours to go, only one of the fifty-odd invitations sent to radio broadcasters, country weeklies, dailies, and scattered celebrities had signaled acceptance. Joe and Mike spent a half day on the two telephones in their law office. They dialed the numbers on their roster, leaving nobody out. Joe — or Mike — would ask whoever answered the telephone: "Is it true that young Joe McCarthy from Appleton is going to oppose Judge Werner in the April election and is going to announce tomorrow?"

Those respondents who were polite would reply, Sorry, they knew nothing about the political race for judge, and declined—thanks-very-much—to take note of where and when the announcement would be made. Other news offices, less indulgent of stray information gatherers, professed no knowledge of Joe McCarthy and registered no curiosity about him.

At a few minutes after eleven, Joe peeked in at the half-filled room. The absence of press confirmed Mike's gloomy forecasts. Still, notice had got out: There were a dozen bodies in the lounge who were neither friends nor family.

The candidate walked in, smiling. The early winter sun shone through the windows on a quiet audience. The family members did not know what was expected of them, so they sat silent. Only Miss Hawthorne applauded, joined listlessly by a few of Joe's schoolmates.

Joe nodded to them all, the bow of the head slightly accentuated when acknowledging Jim Kelly of the *Post*.

He walked to the improvised lectern and read out a speech about the importance of law and of order and of a genuine, up-to-date knowledge by the judiciary of exactly how the world of 1938 worked. He was proud, he said, to have come from a rural background, to have gone into business for himself at the age of seventeen, to have worked his way at a relatively late age through high school, on through college and law school, and now to be launched on a legal career. The incumbent, Judge Werner, was a very nice gentleman, but the seasons come and the seasons go, and—Joe looked up—"little acorns take root," and nature has to make way for youth and for change. When he finished he got a rousing hand from his family, something more perfunctory from his boyhood friends, and, of course, pursuant to protocol (the press is not expected to applaud a political speaker)—nothing from Jim Kelly.

Mike went to the lectern and said that the candidate was ready for questions from the press. Joe scanned the room with concentrated attention, left to right, as if everyone there were representing an organ of the media keen to flash back to his constituency news of Joe McCarthy's candidacy.

Jim Kelly finally broke the silence. His tone of voice was tinged with the tedium of the professional doing his duty. "What gave you the idea of running for judge? You've only been out of law school a few years."

"Well," said Joe, straightening his tie, "I was impressed by the great initiative taken by President Roosevelt just two years ago when he spoke of doing something about U.S. justice. Now, I'm prepared to go along, but the president was *wrong* to try to pack the Supreme Court. Congress was right to turn him down, and the elections last month were pretty conclusive on that point. But," Joe looked up, his expression grave, "I did think the president was right when he said that the country needs new and younger judges. The time comes when elderly judges have to say, 'Well, let's have younger people, maybe more energetic, maybe better informed about what's going on, let's let *them* make a contribution to their country.' I have to agree with FDR on that one, Jim. Hope you agree."

Kelly was suddenly awake, taking notice of this improbable candidate for judge who had so neatly handled the hot quarrel of the political season and apparently emerged with a position congenial to both sides, and, of course, to his own candidacy. President Roosevelt, impatient with a contrarian Supreme Court that had resisted some New Deal legislation, had proposed the previous summer a retirement program for elder judges. *"He tried to pack the court"* was how it was negatively described. He suffered a devastating rebuke when, in November, the voters had sent back to office the same senators—friends of the autonomy of the court—FDR had singled out for defeat. Now Joe McCarthy was having the best of the two positions. Rebuking Roosevelt for his court packing while endorsing Roosevelt's championship of younger judges. Jim Kelly resolved to dig in with his questions.

"Judge Werner is only sixty-six years old; that hardly makes him a . . . rotting old-timer, does it, Joe?"

Joe smiled. "Correction, Jim. That's seventy-two years old, not sixty-six."

Kelly was startled. It had all been a part of local legend for a generation. Edgar Werner had decided to run for district attorney when only thirty-six years old. In order to deflect criticism of his youth, he had given out his birthdate as 1866, when in fact it was 1872. That was a very long time ago, and Judge Werner was now a local institution. At banquets commemorating his years of service he was often teased about his youthful imposture—adding six years to his actual date of birth. But no one took seriously the misstatement of 1916—the misstatement of twenty-two years ago.

"Come on, Joe. You know he's only sixty-six."

Joe reached over to Mike. "Can I have the Martindale, Mike?"

His partner handed him the black-bound volume.

"This, Jim, is the Martindale-Hubbell directory. As you know, it is the official register giving the names and dates of birth of all U.S. lawyers. If you look there, Jim, under 'Werner,' you will read, 'Born, 1866.' This being 1938, that makes him seventy-two years old."

Jim Kelly was astonished. "Joe, you gotta *know* that's a mistake —"

"If it's a mistake, why is it printed in the current volume of Martindale-Hubbell?"

Jim Kelly made a note on his pad. His eyes ran down the McCarthy-for-Judge circular everyone had been handed at the door. He pressed his investigation. "It says here in your official circular that Judge Werner has been paid a total of between one hundred seventy and two hundred thousand dollars —"

"That's right. And that's a lot of money, Jim. I was making just fifteen cents an hour back when Judge Werner was making that kind of money as a judge."

"But what you *don't say* in your circular is that he's been a judge for *twenty years!* If you divide twenty into two hundred —" Jim Kelly looked up, eyes closed for a moment as he did the arithmetic—"that comes to ten thousand dollars a year—less than that. A judge's salary is eight thousand. That's a lot of money, I agree, but it's about what the average lawyer makes in Wisconsin. You make it sound like grand larceny."

McCarthy looked grieved. "I certainly didn't want to give that impression. I just wanted it on record that any man who has taken from the taxpayers over two hundred thousand dollars should be ready to retire and spend whatever is left of his life—four, five years, maybe—I hope Judge Werner lives forever—doing something other than living on the people's money."

Jim Kelly scratched on his pad. He asked no further questions.

Joe looked around the room with the heavy maroon curtains. The noon sun highlighted the dust on the lace.

Did anyone else have any other questions?

Silence.

"Well, let me tell you something," Joe said, "there is no substitute for hard work. I've worked very hard all my life, since I was a boy. And

WILLIAM F. BUCKLEY JR.

I'm going to work hard to give everybody in these counties, in Out-agamie, in Shawano, and in Langlade, a chance to get someone who is young and vigorous. And to let an old-timer get the rest he deserves. Thank you, ladies and gentlemen."

Joe McCarthy moved forward and shook the hand of Jim Kelly, and then the hands of everyone else in the room, giving his mother a furtive hug. One hundred thousand handshakes later, he won the election.

"Nothing to it," Mike Eberlein commented to a booster at the victory party. "All it took was ten thousand handwritten postcards, fifty thousand miles of travel, two hundred speeches—and borrowing money from every human being in three counties!"

What was it like to lose to Joe McCarthy? Many years later, Judge Werner's son would fume that Joe McCarthy had "driven my father to his grave." Joe was sad everybody didn't come to his celebration, but he guessed maybe Miss Hawthorne was right: Some people are just plain on the other side.

But it was more than that. Some people didn't like Joe McCarthy. More than just that. Some people seemed to hate Joe McCarthy. He couldn't understand that.

6

McCarthy goes to war

Captain Joe McCarthy, United States Marines, looked over the photographs for distinguishing features. The photos had been taken on that morning's bombing run of the Japanese installations at Kahili, off Bougainville in Indonesia. It was September 1943, and McCarthy had been at the Espiritu Santo Air Base two months. He was by normal standards buoyant but by his own standards depressed by relative inactivity, day after day, receiving, developing, analyzing aerial photographs. He lived with eight other officers in the tropical heat in a shelter constructed ("I guess maybe it must have taken them two hours," he wrote to his mother) by the Seabees to accommodate eight beds, with mere hints of partitions to permit the privacy officers were theoretically entitled to when living on a base. The Marine Air Force installation VMSB-235 was designed to accommodate forty-six SDB Delta dive bombers, twenty-four fighter planes, and forward repositories for the tanks and light arms — machine guns, bazookas, rifles, ammunition — that General MacArthur had assembled. "I shall return," the general's most famous statement on leaving Corregidor after the Japanese invasion of the Philippines. Well, Captain McCarthy observed in his letter to Charlie Curran, who was on the western front, "if the general makes it back, it'll be us paving the way for him."

Joe was one of twenty-seven nonflying officers, charged with maintenance, provisions, and record keeping. "There is only one objective," he and fellow officer Lieutenant Joyce Andrews had been told on arrival by Colonel Aspill. "It is to keep those airplanes flying, keep the bomb supply necessary to bring off their missions, and be ready to move when General MacArthur tells us to. Come to think of it, be ready to do anything General MacArthur tells us to, and that includes farting."

Joe mingled easily with his fellow officers in the mess hall, the youngest fresh from Officers Candidate School, the elders in their late twenties, with the exception of the senior cadre of four career officers. He tasted that first meal of Spam and beans and coconut in the dining area, the mosquito nets keeping in the heat. He pronounced it awful, and ate it voluptuously. The first few nights he wandered with Andrews about the swampy, insect-ridden half-hundred acres surrounding the airstrip, smiling and gesturing to the native employees in their barracks and makeshift huts. One night, at the far end of the base in close quarters with the dense mangrove forest, a moonbeam darted through the cloud cover, catching the smile of a little girl. She waved at the two officers going by. Joe turned, bowed his head slightly to the mother, and scooped her up, his right arm dislodging her calico skirt under the naked buttocks. "I'm Joe," he said. "Joe."

The girl giggled then turned her face.

"Oh, you have lost . . . twelve teeth! . . ." Joe's appearance was of great shock.

"Looks like three missing teeth to me," Joyce Andrews interrupted. "Come on, Joe."

"What's your name?"

Giggle.

To her mother: "You tell me, ma'am, what little girl called? Er, *nomme?* You know . . . like Chiang Kai-shek, or, er, Horseshit Tojo?"

The mother looked blank.

Joe sighed. "Guess the girl's name doesn't sound like either the big cheese Chinaboy or the little turd in Tokyo. Maybe tomorrow we'll come back with Cheeni."

He was referring to the scrawny young native who looked after their quarters and served as rough translator. An older man emerged from within the little compound hedged in by the jungle and barbed wire. He wore a stringy beard. "Ah . . ." said Joe, "the fabled Hollywood detective Charlie Chan." He had the general aspect of an elderly wise man, the soft voice, quiet and authoritative manner.

"That girl is called Li-la," he said in a singsong English. "She my son's girl. You wish some *pluva*?"

Joe looked over at Joyce. But Joyce deferred: Decisions of this kind were always left to Joe.

"Well, that's just fine, old man, yes, sure."

The grandfather gave instructions, and a young woman materialized with a round tray, its amber surface so highly polished it threw back the moonlight that shot through the clouds idling overhead. There were three miniature glasses. Still standing, the grandfather beckoned his guests to take one. Joyce carefully sipped his. Joe chided him. "What's the matter with you, Lieutenant, you don't take to Indonesian hospitality?" He threw his own drink down his throat and tried to suppress the expression of pain that came to his face. He looked over at Joyce Andrews. His face was still set in the smile he had shone upon the grandfather when he whispered to his junior officer, "*Come on, you son of a bitch. Drink it and pretend you enjoy it!*" Resigned, Andrews closed his eyes, gulped his drink down, and contrived a smile of satisfaction for the benefit of the grandfather.

"That was just fine!" Joe said. "And tomorrow I will come back and bring a present for La-li."

"Li-la," Andrews corrected him.

"La-la," McCarthy obliged.

He looked over at the little girl, now covered by the cloud's shadow. "Good night, dear." He leaned over and kissed her.

Stopping by the PX, he bought some cigarettes for the old man and a coloring book for the girl. "Tomorrow," he said to Andrews. "Remind me."

There was never any question what to do after dinner, not for the officers in VMSB-235. It was poker, Captain McCarthy presiding. They played in a jeep shelter. This meant pulling out the jeep to make room for the players. The jeep was parked right up against the entrance to the shelter, to block light from the gas lamp escaping into the night and attracting the attention of enemy aircraft. The jeep closed in the light, but closed in also the heat. Within the hour the players, sometimes six officers—an absolute limit of eight, Joe had decreed—were dressed only in undershorts and T-shirts. That heat was miserable and also distracting. After a week of it Joe decided to act. The next day he conferred with Cheeni.

The quietest hours of the day at Espiritu Santo began one minute after the last of that day's dive bombers had lumbered down the strip and soared up into the sky. On Tuesday, after the twelfth plane had lifted off, Joe walked to the motor depot. Cheeni was there waiting for him. Joe looked about the pool of trucks and jeeps and signaled Cheeni over to an unoccupied jeep, getting into the driver's seat. He waved at the superintending sergeant. "Mission for Major McClure," he called out. The sergeant waved him on. He didn't much care what officer got what jeep, as long as there was always one in reserve for Colonel Aspill.

Joe followed Cheeni's directions and drove down the narrow row hemmed in by the prehensile jungle. They drove east, away from the main roadway, and six hot, jolting miles later reached the village. Cheeni directed him to one end of it, and, on instructions, Joe drew up beside a very large barrack, as though built for an airplane. The thatched roof was battened down by twine, decoratively applied. The dilapidated walls bore traces of large posters, advertising who or what, Joe could not tell and did not inquire. Cheeni walked to the curtains of netted bamboo and drew them apart.

Joe was astonished by the cavernous sight. It looked like a loading station for an army division, and looked also like a junkyard. Cheeni spoke to the slender shopkeeper. He bowed and walked off to the interior, quickly disappearing in the tangle of wheels, tires, batteries, wheelbases, ammunition cases, and five-gallon cans. Soon he was back, an electric fan in hand.

Then it began. Cheeni would screech out his price, the shop-keeper would pound down his hand on the counter. More shouting. Joe, deciding to get into the act, said imperiously, "Cheeni, let's go back to the base. We really don't need that old thing, you know." He parted the curtains and walked out, Cheeni following; the expostulations came from the shopkeeper, they reversed their direction, resumed bargaining—and after a while, Joe had the fan, and the shopkeeper had Joe's twelve dollars.

It was a big project to run an electrical line to McCarthy's Casino, as it was now called. But that night after dinner, when the players assembled, Joe, seated Indian-style on the ground, looked up as if addressing a native bearer. "Cheeni," he said theatrically, "it's hot in here. Give us some air." Cheeni rose and flipped the invisible switch behind the hidden fan. The air rushed in. Major Stewart's joy was unconfined. "I swear, McCarthy, you deserve a medal. If I'm ever in the line of command and can get you one, by God, I will!" The other men lent their voices in a cheer to Joe McCarthy.

Eight months later, Captain McCarthy had complained one time too many to Colonel Aspill. It wasn't that the camera equipment was all that bad, Joe said, or that the altitude was too high for clear pictures. The trouble was technique. The actual *taking* of the pictures. This time Colonel Aspill turned on him. "All right, goddamnit, McCarthy. You go up tomorrow and show the regular technicians what *you* can do."

That night, after the game, Joe lay in bed. He pondered the day ahead. His first combat mission. The casualties in the bombing campaign hadn't been nearly as heavy as on the European front—they got their *Stars & Stripes* once a week and knew about the terrible attrition there. Still, last week they had lost four planes. Possibly this time tomorrow he'd be . . .

No, no. That wouldn't happen to Joe McCarthy, he thought. Well. He would see. He would, however, make certain to say his prayers. He found himself resisting an answer to the question, *Joe, assuming you come back, and the colonel likes your pictures and says to you, McCarthy, I'm going to alter things, make you a regular combat photographer instead of a photo analyst, would you be glad, or sorry?* He didn't want to answer that question, so he tried hard to think of other things. It was very late when, finally, he dropped off to sleep.

7

Harry Bontecou, age eighteen,
goes to war

One year after Joe McCarthy flew his first combat duty, Private First Class Harry Bontecou faced combat for the first time, in Belgium. One year later, First Lieutenant Harry Bontecou, AUS, 103rd Division, was serving as duty officer at Camp Plattling in West Germany. It was after midnight, and he'd be on duty until six in the morning. Every half hour he would open the heavy wooden door of the one-time farmhouse, converted now for army use, and expose his face to the bitter cold.

He thought back to the night one year ago. He was doing very different duty on his current assignment, to keep guard over refugees from the Soviet military. Then, two weeks after graduating from basic infantry training at Camp Wheeler, Georgia, Harry Bontecou had been in hard combat. Hitler was making his last major play. In mid-December the Germans chose the hilly and wooded country of the Ardennes to launch their great counteroffensive. It came to be called, after the profile of the German offensive across the Belgian border, the Battle of the Bulge. The lights that caught the eye that night weren't the moon's glare and the stars, so vivid tonight. They were the traceries of machine-gun fire. Harry heard now in his memory the confused and confusing orders of his platoon commander, Lieutenant Rothschild. Harry wasn't absolutely certain whether the order had commanded his squad to go forward from their improvised position along the front, or to retreat to yesterday's position. He checked quickly with Pete on his right, but he wasn't sure; neither was Reid, on his left.

Neither of the two commands, however contradictory, would have surprised Private Bontecou. In the last five days they had reversed direction three times as the Nazis bore down . . . then gave way . . . then bore down again. The anxious and harassed Allies fought with counter determination under the dogged leadership of General Anthony McAuliffe. The line went back and forward. It was distorted, it zigzagged, and more than once the men being fired at dead ahead were fellow Americans; or fellow Germans. One morning Harry had heard the captain on the radio barking out the message to headquarters that there was no way to hold on, let alone repel the enemy, without massive air support quickly; instantly. Harry's platoon did retreat, but two days later they were back. Most of them. Not Jesse, nor Coady, Phillips, nor Stimson. Lieutenant Rothschild was gone.

This night Harry Bontecou stayed out in the cold long enough to revive the memory of that other cold a year ago. Intentionally, he overdid it—waited in the cold until the features on his face cried out for relief, the fingers of his hands tingling with pain. Only then would he duck back into the office and luxuriate in the same warmth he'd felt in the hospital, where he woke after the operation on his shoulder.

A sound interrupted his reverie. The telephone rang. The memory clouds quickly disappeared. He picked up the receiver. The duty sergeant's voice came through. "Okay on Gate C, Lieutenant."

"Lieutenant." Lieutenant Bontecou. He mused. The only other Bontecou he knew of was lieutenant governor of New York State and no relation. Harry allowed himself to recall the private pleasure and pride he had taken in the hospital when Major Autrey, a thin smile on his face, brought him the special order. He had been awarded a battlefield promotion to second lieutenant.

He was well in six weeks, and by then they all knew that the Germans had lost the war. Late in a cold March afternoon he heard the short-wave report—the Luftwaffe had run out of fighter planes to deploy against the advancing Allied armies. Why, oh why doesn't Hitler just—call it a day! *Jetzt ist Feierabend.* Now is quitting time. Harry was spending time with a German language book during the long hours in the truck and at night in his pup tent with his flashlight. What *was* this loyalty to Hitler from the soldiers the Allies were killing and maiming every day? He pondered that question with searing incredulity on April 8, when his division opened the gates of the Nazi extermination camp at Gotha, and he learned—and saw—what, in addition to fighting wars on two fronts, was Hitler's other major killing enterprise.

Now, decorated-in-combat First Lieutenant Bontecou was a camp guard. He looked up from his book. He was reading Boswell's *Johnson,* received in the mail from his mother two days earlier and inscribed, "Darling Harry: This will shorten the long hours. Hint: You can always find plenty to read that stands the test of time. This book has never been out of print since 1791, when first published. This edition was published in 1926, the year you were born."

His last day in New York before shipping out to combat duty had begun as usual, as expected. Dorothy Bontecou had given him breakfast and was at the door just after eight, to leave for the subway and her job at the New York Public Library. That night they would dine alone with the bottle of champagne his mother had spoken of; the next day he would go off to war.

On the matter of the information Harry needed, she told him to look in his father's trunk in the office where he had worked in their brownstone on the West Side. "Whatever the insurance company needs has to be there," she called up from the door before shutting it behind her. Harry walked over to his father's dusty office, still crammed with books and papers, the big Royal typewriter jutting out from one hollow of the desk. Harry sat down in his father's chair to gather his thoughts. He had odds and ends to attend to before leaving the country for the first—and last time? he permitted himself to wonder. He had read attentively the morning paper giving the news of the bloody campaign in Belgium. With all that secrecy surrounding his battalion's movements, it was obvious that was where they were headed. But now he needed information on his father for the army insurance form, his serial number in the national reserve. Well, that was for later. Now, to the Metropolitan Museum to see the exhibit of modern Mexican art Miss Yglesias, his Spanish teacher at high school, had warmly recommended in her telephone call yesterday. And he would pick up the course catalog at Columbia and scan it voluptuously.

He lunched at the Automat near the museum and walked back to the house to search out the serial number, dating back to his father's college days. Harry climbed up to the room where his father had sequestered himself most of every day. He opened the creaky trunk and saw what he had expected, great deposits of papers and envelopes. He flipped by what seemed thousands of packets of poetry and lecture notes and lecture clippings and letters from poets and professors. And there, finally, was a scrapbook of his dad's years at Columbia, 1919 to 1923—he must have fingered this book before, because he remembered seeing as a boy the photograph of his father posing earnestly as manager of the tennis team at Columbia. He spotted a folded sheet of paper with a yellow sheet attached, a preprinted form with check marks here and there. Curious, he began reading the letter. It was addressed to his father from a Dr. Homer Babbidge at Lenox Hill Hospital. The text was a single paragraph:

> Dear Mr. Bontecou:
>
> This last, enclosed, is the end of the line as far as medical science has taken us. There are no further laboratory tests to take. Your sterility is, as originally diagnosed, a case of azoospermia, a congenital disorder.

Harry went cold. His eyes froze on the doctor's signature. And then traveled, what seemed inch by inch, up to the top of the page. The date was October 7, 1925.

A year before he was born.

He had begun to sweat as, mechanically, he continued his search for the national reserve number. He stayed seated on the floor, his legs crossed, staring at the trunk. He couldn't think what to do.

He looked over at the photograph of—No. It wasn't his father. All that . . . stuff in the trunk. It belonged not to his father. It was the . . . collection of . . . his mother's husband. He would have to get used to that formulation. He didn't know what to do. He knew only this: He needed right away to leave Eighty-seventh Street. Before his mother got back.

He packed quickly—not difficult for a soldier who, the following day, would embark on a troopship to the western front. The note to his mother he scratched out on the kitchen table read:

> Dear Mom,
>
> Awful. Call from AA company commander's office. Departure schedule moved up. Bad news on the fighting front, I guess. I have to report to the Brooklyn Army Depot by 10 P.M., which means I have no time to lose. Will write the first day I get over.
>
> Love, Harry

Would he have signed off with profuser signs of affection if he hadn't opened the trunk? He supposed so. But she would surely attribute the economy of his closing to the abruptness of his sudden recall, and to apprehension about the future.

Camp Plattling in postwar West Germany was hardly an extermination camp. But there were three thousand human beings in that camp behind barbed wire, forbidden to leave. It was the responsibility of the 103rd Division, of which Harry was an officer, to keep them there until the conquering lions settled the question, Where would they go?

Marshal Georgi K. Zhukov, speaking for no less than Joseph Stalin, had publicly insisted on June 29, 1945, that the Russians among them were to be "repatriated." Zhukov spoke of men (the women and children had been released) who had "treacherously fled their duty." Harry had seen no notice of the Zhukov demand. He was told of it by Major Chadinoff, the fiery regimental doctor obsessed by the evil—"Yes, I mean *evil!*"—character of the fateful deliberations of the U.S./British command.

Plattling, along with a half dozen other U.S. Army camps, detained Soviet citizens who had run, walked, crawled, bribed, lied, or persuaded friends/relations/bureaucrats to give them refuge from the Soviet army. Some had been captives of Hitler who escaped. Most were refugees from the Soviet army. Hitler had run deep into

Soviet territory until he was stopped at Stalingrad. Behind him, over the six-hundred-mile stretch of territory he had overrun, he left scores of thousands of prisoners. In the turmoil and cold and hungry desperation, many escaped the German camps and made their way not to the east, to penetrate the fluctuating Nazi-Soviet war line, but instead went west, seeking relief both from the native despot in Moscow and the German despot in Berlin. They were Ukrainians, Poles, East Germans: men fleeing by whatever means the westbound Communist juggernaut, scurrying past the Polish-Soviet border into central Germany. Captain Pelikan from G2 explained to the officers of Harry's regiment at one of the weekly information sessions that Washington and London were bound by promises made at the wartime Yalta and Potsdam conferences. The Geneva agreement of 1929 acknowledged a right of prisoners of war to refuse repatriation, but these refugees were not protected formally because they were not in uniform. It was widely predicted that Stalin would deal cruelly with the soldiers. Stalin didn't need reasons to send millions to Gulag and death. He had, this time around, reasons that satisfied him and everyone who surrounded him, who labored mightily to satisfy Stalin. It was only left to General Eisenhower and General Montgomery, the principal military representatives of the United States and Great Britain, to maneuver as they could. The sole instrument left to Allies reluctant to send the Russians back home to possible torture and death was what Churchill had dubbed the "apparatus of delay."

"They're trying to find a way out," Captain Pelikan explained. "Meanwhile, we have to keep them here."

Harry wrote to his mother,

When they're sent back, according to Doc Chadinoff, they're declared either traitors for having a) pulled out of the Soviet military, or b) dodged the Soviet draft. Or c) they are people who gave aid to the occupying enemy. Or d) they were Russian prisoners of war who, under Nazi control, were exposed to dangerous ideas.

Whatever. They are enemies of the state and will be treated as such. Out of curiosity, Mom, is anybody over there talking about these people? ". . . What did you do in the war, Harry?" "Well, I helped win it and later made goddamn sure that every Russian I was in charge of would be returned to the Soviet Union. You see, the Russians had unfilled concentration camps and idle executioners." I sound bitter, Mom? Actually, we haven't given up hope. Write your Congressman. Though I guess that won't do much if Vito Marcantonio is still Manhattan's man in Congress. I can't even remember whether in the last election our fellow voters reelected Mr. Communist Party-liner. We'll see.

Yes, Mom, I already told you I sent in the application form for Columbia. We'll know in a couple of weeks. I got to go to chow. Now, in case you forget the aphorisms of Dr. Johnson in the book you sent me, Johnson said, "I look upon it, that he who does not mind his belly will hardly mind anything else."

All love from Harry

He could see her getting the letter and reading it in the hallway of the brownstone on the West Side. (Cold? Probably—heating fuel was still rationed at home, he knew.) He felt a quite sudden, near-mutinous urge to go home, to leave this bloody, disheveled Europe. But he could wait it out. He was scheduled for release in a matter of weeks. Maybe he'd be with his mother for . . . the ides of March? Was he conceived on the ides of whenever it was, nine months before his birthday? It must have been very romantic, the situation back then, Mom and Whoever it was who didn't have a-zoo-spermia. Harry had committed the word to memory, but had to spell it out for himself when, which granted wasn't often, he thought to summon it up. He wondered where that took place. Presumably not at Eighty-seventh Street.

Erik Chadinoff, M.D., Major, AUS, was thirteen years older than Harry Bontecou and enjoyed most about life at Camp Plattling his late-hour chess sessions with the young lieutenant from New York. ("Never forget. I'm from New York too. In fact, Queens is more authentically New York than Manhattan.") They would begin at nine, or a little later if Major Chadinoff had heavy duties at the hospital.

Whenever: Chadinoff would appear with energetic delight ("I shall have back at you after the last time"); they would sit in the officers' lounge, and Chadinoff would bring out of his pocket a medicine bottle, look quickly about him to ensure that the colonel wasn't sitting there staring at this little breach of rules (only beer was served in the BOQ), and pour out his liqueur, a dark Russian concoction— "Riga balsam," he called it—in which Chadinoff delighted. It was a drink served at home, he explained one night, waiting for Harry to make his move. The elder Chadinoffs had arrived in New York in 1915 with their two-year-old son. "My grandmother," Chadinoff explained, stretching out his legs in an exaggerated gesture of fatalism about the length of time Harry would take to make his move, "insisted that my parents leave the country before 'that foolish Czar Nicholas conscripts all the doctors in Russia and sends them west to fight against the Germans.'" Chadinoff's father had enlisted in the army when Congress declared war in 1917. Erik did not remember his father, who did not return from the war. He grew up in Queens. His mother served the Queens Hospital as a nurse and tutored students at Queens College in Russian.

Erik remembered the earnest reading by his mother of all news reports from Russia. He spoke to his mother in Russian and, when he could write, communicated with his grandmother— "I remember the photograph she sent on Easter 1921." But when he was nine, in 1922, his grandmother stopped writing. There was no explanation. Months later, his mother's youngest brother had written to say that the "authorities" had removed the senior Chadinoff lady from her house in the outskirts of Kiev. It wasn't known where she was taken. "She may very well be alive," Uncle Alexis wrote. "We don't ask questions about that kind of thing, though there is no reason why you shouldn't continue to write to her." Erik's mother did. At first the letters were returned, *Addressee Unknown;* after a while, they went unacknowledged or unreturned.

In high school during the American Depression, Erik attempted, but finally abandoned any hope of succeeding, to instruct his classmates on the failed idealism of Communism. Most of the boys and girls in his class were unconcerned with Russia or its ideology. But the few who were concerned, he told Harry, were enthusiastic about the great Soviet social experiment that would teach the world how to avoid such capitalistic blights as the Depression they were now contending with. Erik's frustration led him to attempt a little poetry, first in Russian, then in English. His instructor smiled when she read it and said he had a nice talent for verbal formulations, but he must be careful not to permit himself to be obsessed on the matter of Communism. He had persisted, with Communism and poetry.

Harry didn't ask to see any of the poetry. He reasoned that if Erik wanted to show it to him, he would do so. Erik Chadinoff was decisive in all matters—what medicine to prescribe, what knight to move, what U.S. foreign policy should be.

At the end of the game one Saturday night, Major Chadinoff asked Harry if he would like to meet with one of the prisoners. "Dmitri Usalov is in the hospital, pneumonia. We'll lick it, thanks to penicillin. But he's weak and needs four or five days of beefing up. What's special about Dmitri is that his mother is—was?—he doesn't know whether she's alive—English. His father married her in Copenhagen. She was with the Red Cross, her parents with the foreign service. Usalov was on a Russian freighter that stalled there for over a month during the Russian Revolution—the captain kept getting conflicting instructions from the shipping line and from Soviet headquarters. He met her, they fell in love, got married by the captain, who was frustrated not knowing what to do. Anyway, they sailed eventually on back to Leningrad and went back to Usalov's home near Kiev, where Dmitri was brought up, speaking English, of course, to his mother. How he ended up at Plattling is a story you might want to hear—from him."

Harry met Dmitri on the Sunday and after an hour said he had better leave. "Major Chadinoff will court-martial me if I stay any longer. He said you have to rest. You have to 'rest heavily,' was how he put it."

Dmitri laughed weakly, his bright teeth shining in his bearded face. "Will you come again? I have so much liked talking with you."

"Yes, I can be here on Tuesday. Before I go, when last did you hear from your family?"

"Not since February 1942. Four years ago. On my eighteenth birthday. That was the day I became eligible for the Soviet draft and that was two weeks before the Nazis came. In a little wallet sewn by my mother inside my winter coat I had one hundred twenty British pounds. That would have been more than enough to board a freighter from Odessa to Egypt and Egypt to London, and I had the letter to my mother's sister in Sussex. But I told you what happened." Dmitri closed his eyes, and Harry left, resolved to go back on Tuesday.

He met with Chadinoff for Monday night chess. "He is technically a traitor, right?"

"Yes. He was eighteen, should have stayed in Kiev, should have been captured by the invading Nazis, and if he had survived the Nazis, should have gone into the Soviet army to be killed for Stalin. Instead, he got to Odessa, which was blockaded, and then weaved westward, was thrown into a camp by Romanian Nazis, escaped, worked his way through Poland and now was dodging the Red army, and finally he lands in Stuttgart, where the Nazis use him as an interpreter. He escapes from them and: ends up in the warm embrace of the Allies here at Plattling. All we intend to do, after I cure him from pneumonia, is send him back to Russia so he can be shot or sent to one of those glacial camps—why do I save him from pneumonia now when he will someday soon, thanks to Western diplomacy, die of the cold in Siberia?"

Harry visited with his prisoner-patient on Tuesday, as promised, and again on Saturday before Usalov's dismissal from the hospital. Dmitri was three years older than Harry, but his voice was from another world, the world of Europe, the cradle of political death plots against human beings on a truly massive scale. Harry had known now for the first time, really, someone who had experienced both the great demonic worlds of the century. And was now to be packaged and shipped back to the eastern division.

Late that night in February, Chadinoff was less than decisive in his movements. Reporting to the lounge as had been arranged that morning, Harry sat down at the usual table in the long room with a bar at the corner, a half dozen card tables, and service-model couches and chairs, mostly lit by one thoughtlessly unfocused incandescent light in the middle of the room. Chadinoff walked in, passed by the other card tables and through the thick cigarette smoke. He leaned over to Harry. "I must speak with you. In private. Can you follow me to my quarters?"

Chadinoff led Harry out through the cold, down the roadway to the hospital ward, and into the warmth of his office. He opened his cigarette pack and without thinking extended it to Harry.

"No thanks, Erik."

"Yes, of course. I remember—you don't smoke." He lit his own cigarette and began to talk in high agitation.

"I have seen the orders. They are for two days from now. For February twenty-fifth. We are ordered to round up our Russians, take them to the Bavarian forest beyond Zwiesel, in trucks, and put them in train cars that will be there waiting to take them to Moscow."

"But what about the 'apparatus of delay'?"

"Diplomatic efforts to save the refugees—I insist that is what they are, refugees, not deserters—have failed. Have ended. They are refugees just as my father was—a preemptive refugee, you could call it. The orders call for us to stuff them into trains as if they were German Jews being handled by the Nazis.

"Now, Harry"—Erik's voice was hoarse, and he punctuated his talk with deep inhalations from his cigarette—"this is a moment of great moral weight. There are two alternative roles I have considered for myself—just hear me out: I am not enlisting you, conscripting you, but I want you to know how *I* am thinking of it.

"The first alternative—one way of doing it: Major Erik Chadinoff, on Thursday morning, reports to HQ—regimental headquarters—that he is ill. His illness is of a kind he knows how to treat himself, and therefore he will not be reporting to the sickroom or here to the hospital.

"But that would mean I would be out of action until my health improved. Until Operation Keelhaul is completed."

"They call that malingering, right?"

"That is the word for it. A court-martial offense. Then there is Alternative Two, the other way of doing it: Major Erik Chadinoff, on Thursday morning, reports that he declines to be a part of Operation Keelhaul, that he considers the forcible repatriation of Russian refugees to be a war crime. He will remain in his quarters and await whatever consequences of his insubordination his superiors or the military court consider appropriate."

Harry bit his lip. "Oh, my God, Erik. You can't do that—"

"Hang on, Harry. I have looked at the Military Code of Justice. It is of course very stern on what I propose to do. But there is a graver offense than individual insubordination. It is the stimulation of mutiny by others. What I have not yet decided is whether to post a copy of my communication on the bulletin board, with an invitation to other officers to cosign it with me."

Harry leaned back and closed his eyes. He waited, and then, "What is it you want from me, Erik?"

Chadinoff ground out his cigarette. There was a hint of a resolute smile on his face. "I explicitly decline to urge you to join me in this action. But I want you to know what I will do, either the first step I mentioned, which would be cowardly, or the second. Is there another way to protest this surrender to Stalin?"

Major Chadinoff stood. His hand began a forward motion, as if to shake Harry's hand. He thought better of it. Instead there was a little wave of his hand. "Good-bye, Harry."

Harry went to his own quarters. He slept fitfully. The following morning the orders were given. The next day, Operation Keelhaul would go forward.

"My hands are stained," Harry wrote to his mother on Saturday night, sixty-four hours (he counted) since the 0330 beginning after midnight on Thursday. He did not disguise his feelings and, at age nineteen, he didn't flinch from the theatrical metaphor.

Harry Bontecou had been given a jeep. A sergeant was seated alongside, two enlisted men behind, operating the recording device that fed into the loudspeaker. "It's Russian you're listening to," Major Simcock had explained. "It's just to tell them they will be moved to another camp."

"Another camp where?" Harry asked.

"Oh. West Germany."

Lieutenant Colonel Henry Cooper was in charge of the operation. He convened the company commanders and the platoon leaders at five on Wednesday afternoon. They got their orders and assembled at 0300 on Thursday. A tank battalion was in formation at the other end of the hill on the east end of Plattling. At 0515 it was still dark. Harry ordered his four squad leaders toward the refugee barracks he had been assigned to. Someone in the squad directly ahead of Harry made a noise. He could hear now, at some remove, the purr of tanks on the move. A second later, the sound of the tanks and the brilliance of their searchlights roused the entire camp.

Companies A, B, and C sent 180 armed soldiers through the camp gate to their preset stations, encircling the barracks individually and comprehensively. Slipping out of his hut, one Russian saw the column of American tanks approaching with their searchlights. Harry spotted him and detached a soldier to approach him and give him instructions. The GIs were wearing heavy-duty rubber-soled shoes; at the gateway there was a whispered pause while they took up the long riot clubs issued to them. They had been warned to expect violent resistance. The soldiers divided into separate companies and moved stealthily through the shadows to the dormitory huts. Harry banged open the door of Barracks C10. Inside there was darkness and confusion. Light came in through the windows from perimeter searchlights. The crouching silhouettes dodged and wove about. Harry shone the beam of his light, scanning the room. The soldiers from his platoon filed in. Two GIs were assigned to every bed.

Suddenly, at Harry's nod to the communications corporal, who relayed the signal, the stillness was broken. There was a shrieking blast of a whistle. Those who were still asleep woke. "They looked all around, as if it was a nightmare," Harry wrote to his mother.

> But then they sized it all up, and there were yells, yells from everywhere. Some of the Russians refused to get out of bed, so we had to prod them with our clubs. I lifted my right hand and stretched out my fingers, five — five minutes to pack, I pointed to the bags in front of their beds. We prodded them to the camp gates. The trucks were there, a long row of them, engines humming. They were loaded into them, and the trucks drove off.

The convoy clattered and swayed down the darkened roads. Harry was silent. He declined to order the Russians in the truck he commanded to be quiet. At the end of the road, twenty miles distant, there was a hasty transfer to a train.

Under way, the train rattled on toward the east, a pale, cold light appearing now in the sky. Near the Czech frontier, beyond Zwiesel, the train halted in the stillness of the Bavarian forest. The Russian troops waiting for their cargo were wearing blue caps.

> We shook hands. There was an interpreter. We didn't say much, didn't want to say anything. I signed the human invoice and got a Russian invoice in return. The Russians were shepherded down by the railway track. I could see them down at the end of the platform. Mostly they were trying to keep themselves warm. We got back into our train, to go back to Plattling. I looked back, Mom. I saw Russians there waiting to be pulled to Russia, to go to the prison camps and the execution squads.

The tumult of Thursday and Friday left him no time, but on Sunday morning Harry rang the hospital telephone extension. "Major Chadinoff, please."

"Major Chadinoff is not here."

"Where is he? This is Lieutenant Bontecou calling."

"I don't know," the attendant said. "I mean I don't know where he's gone, but he's no longer at Camp Plattling." Harry went to the door and opened it into the cold. I have known a real hero, he said to himself. If Chadinoff was gone, that meant he had elected Alternative Two: formal, public resistance. Harry asked himself, Why wasn't he there, alongside him, saying—doing—the same thing?

He went listlessly to the mail room to dispatch his letter to his mother. There was a letter waiting for him. It was from the registrar, admitting him to the Class of 1950 at Columbia University.

8

Alex, Lord Herrendon,
reminisces

Alex, Lord Herrendon, was proud of his mastery of the computer. "I suppose it's obvious you know and use it, Harry?"

Yes, Harry said. He had in fact brought his own laptop from America and had it in the office provided for him. The two men met for lunch and, four or five times a week, for dinner. First in the "garden room," which was English boarding-room cold year round; the evening meal in the small formal dining room that eased away from the very large dining room, whose table—for twelve? twenty?—was covered by tablecloths. On top of it were photographs and, as their work progressed, more and more piles of file material.

"Lovely quarters you have for me, Alex."

"It's a nice place," Lord Herrendon said. Most—lordly manors— are, Harry thought. Not that he knew the insides of many such, though he had had a professional look at several in Germany when he did the research on the Victorian cousins.

Herrendon walked Harry about in his impressive library, with volumes of material in varied folders. There were books, manuscripts, transcripts of hearings, congressional records, Hasards. Harry had asked the first day, "Do you have a record of the Senate hearings, the McCarthy hearings?"

Herrendon led him to a corner shielded from the sun by the heavy window curtain. He pointed to a dozen bound volumes. "I have here the Tydings hearings on McCarthy, the Gillette-Monroney hearings on McCarthy, the Army-McCarthy hearings, and over there the McCarran Committee hearings—he pointed to eight volumes. "And here," there was a touch of pride in his voice, "are transcripts of the two trials of Alger Hiss. In those three volumes there—" these were large volumes, suitable for filing newspaper clippings—"are reports on the work of the Communist underground, beginning in Los Alamos and going through preliminary revelations of the Venona files, the archive recording Soviet radio activity in and about America during the Second World War. Did you have a chance last night to look over the outline of my proposed book?" It was the book Alex Herrendon dreamed of writing. An account of Communist activity and public opinion in the West. How much was Western indifference traceable to manipulation? How much to ignorance? How much to moral fatigue? How much to—insouciance?

Harry nodded, drawing up a chair from the long table with books scattered over it to the side of his computer desk. "In the two pages with chapter headings having to do with McCarthy, I notice the 'George Marshall Episode.' I know a lot about that."

"I supposed that you did. Let's talk procedure here. At our next meeting, we can hope to get down to work. . . . If you don't object, I will bring the recording device—it is very good, very sensitive, you don't need to hold a microphone to your lips, nothing like that. But I will sit by your side and question you, rattle your memory, which I suppose is very keen—like mine." He gave a sly smile. "Depending on the volume of material, the transcriptions will require one or two days. We can be on to other matters while they are being done. But shouldn't we take first things first?"

Harry smiled too. "I was going to say. I'd like to hear what it was that drew you—Alex—to the Communist Party and what it was that drew you away from it."

Alex Herrendon was the only son of Lord Herrendon, who had been made a hereditary peer in the last days of Queen Victoria. The first Lord Herrendon had been active on several civic fronts, stressing the education of poor children in major British cities. As a young man he went to South Africa and, together with a partner, prospected, with marked success, for diamonds. In young middle age he withdrew completely from business, selling his holdings and joining the Socialist Party. He became a trusted friend and benefactor of Sidney and Beatrice Webb, the two leading Fabianists, who devoted their long lives to bringing socialism to Great Britain without revolution. He contributed substantially to the Labour Party and was rewarded with a seat in the House of Lords by Ramsay MacDonald.

Herrendon's opening speech was widely noticed, causing amusement in some quarters, curiosity in others, sheer rage in some. He said he would devote his career in the House of Lords to abolishing it. Every year he submitted a fresh bill. They got nowhere but marked him as a regicidal character, in one sense the godfather of Willie Hamilton, who won a seat to Parliament a generation later. But Hamilton had raised Herrendon's ante, calling for the abolition not only of the House of Lords, but also of the monarchy.

"My father informed me—he never consulted me, he always informed me—when I was in my last year at St. Paul's here in London that I was to go to America for my higher education. He had just acquired this castle. There wasn't that much home life to be sorry about, on the matter of going to the United States for college work. My mother had died, and Father did not remarry. He crossed the Atlantic frequently, and on one visit to New York befriended Fulton Chapin—you know the name?—"

Harry nodded. "The American millionaire socialist."

"Chapin had attended Columbia and easily persuaded my father to send me there. One month after I arrived in Morningside Heights I was delirious with joy over my circumstances. I had a comfortable two-room apartment—Father didn't practice socialism, he preached it. I had total liberty of movement for the first time in my life. I was aflame with my father's socialist cause. I made several friends. I was worldlier than the average freshman. By the time I graduated, I had had two experiences that greatly influenced my life. One was with a woman, the other with a student four years older than I. His name was Whittaker Chambers, and when I was twenty, he took me—a dramatic journey involving your subway and then a long walk—to a little office, the business and the dwelling place of one Ben Mandel. He was a party functionary. He wrote out a Communist Party card for me and told me that, pending the decision of my superiors, I was not to divulge to anyone—even my own father—the step I had taken."

Harry looked up. "You knew Whittaker Chambers!"

"I must suppose that you did too."

"I saw him just once, traveled out to his farm with Joe McCarthy. But we had a warm correspondence after that. I can't imagine at that age—he was, I guess, fifty—he died at fifty-seven—what he was like when you knew him."

"Whittaker Chambers was twenty-four, muscular, good looking, quick to laugh, teeming with excitement over the last book he had read, which would have been the one he picked up two hours before. I learned—mostly from him, in fact—of endless troubles at home, eccentric father, alcoholic brother, the whole thing. He had decided to quit Columbia—he got into some kind of trouble, carried off a bunch of books to his house in Long Island. The last time I saw him was, I think . . . 1925. He just disappeared.

"But I got a postcard a year or so later, just as I was nearing commencement. It was sent, I remember, to 'Alex Herrendon, Class of 1926, Columbia University, New York.' But it reached me. A couple of sentences. Hoped-I-was-okay. He-was-keeping-busy. 'Upholding the cause.' There was no return address. I stayed in New York. My father got me a posting as assistant to the British consul on Third Avenue, on the Upper East Side. I was there four years, then back to London four years, then to Washington, with my—American wife and daughter—"

"Yes," Harry interrupted. "I know about that. You will of course be writing about what you did in the underground for the party. And I'm here to answer your questions. You wanted to know about Joe's—I still think of him as Joe—about McCarthy's attack on Marshall. The background is curious."

"May I turn on the recorder?"

"Of course."

Harry Bontecou goes
to Columbia

A week before the Christmas holidays at Columbia, the *Spectator,* the student daily, held elections. The eight-week competitive ordeal had been stiff and time consuming. The student contenders for posts on the paper, by tradition, reported to the managing editor at John Jay Hall on Monday through Friday at one P.M. to receive their assignments. They had also to go out and sell advertising, the *Spectator*'s principal source of revenue. Harry Bontecou and his roommate, Tracy Allshott, were eager competitors. This proved convenient, both because of the camaraderie of joint exposure to the rigors of the contest and because there were no complaints from one roommate to another about lights being kept on late. Both needed to work extra hours on their studies after completing the *Spectator* assignments.

Tracy's reserve was perhaps traceable to his absorption with the *Spectator* challenge, Harry conjectured. When his mother suggested inviting Tracy for lunch or dinner on Sundays, which Harry spent at home, he said he thought it wise to put off the invitation until after the competition was completed. "Maybe later on in the term, Mom."

She looked up from her book. "You do *like* him, don't you Harry?"

"Yes. I do." Without great conviction.

Dorothy Bontecou could tell that the answer was ambiguous but knew not to ask for more. And of course she knew that if there was festering incompatibility there, Harry and his roommate needed only to wait until the end of freshman year to make other rooming arrangements. She would not make any further reference to Tracy Allshott.

But Harry, it turned out, *did* want to talk about him.

"I wish I had a picture of him. I don't, but there'll be one in the freshman yearbook they'll be distributing next week. You know, Mom, I think maybe Tracy is, well, practically an albino. He doesn't look absolutely bleached, but I mean his hair is so blond it's almost white. He's very good-looking, imposing. Blue eyes, of course, maybe one hundred seventy pounds—a little shorter than me, very intense, yet very—vague. Last week he was up all night reading up on Chaucer."

"Is Tracy—disoriented?" Mrs. Bontecou had reached for an inoffensive word.

"I don't know. Just plain have no idea. I think he meets all his deadlines on the *Spectator*. He's from Iowa. I know—Des Moines. But he's never said what his father does. I know he has connections, otherwise we wouldn't have a telephone in the room. There's something like a year's waiting time for phones. He was in the Pacific theater but got only as far as Honolulu when Hiroshima happened. He did tell me, somewhere along the line, that he wishes he had declared himself a conscientious objector. Of course I had to ask the obvious question—was it *this* war he objected to, or all wars? His answer was kind of queer. He objects to all wars, get this, that aren't 'civilizationally conclusive.'"

"Did you ask what he meant by that?"

"What I did, Mom—look, that's how freshmen who are war veterans deal with each other: If it has to do with the war, you give a guy a chance to say what's on his mind. If he wants to, fine. If he doesn't, fine. So I didn't say, 'Tracy, tell me exactly what you mean by civilizationally conclusive.' I didn't even say, 'What *is* civilizationally conclusive?' What I said was: 'Oh?'"

"Did he come up with an explanation?"

"No. He just nodded his head a bit, a bit condescendingly, actually. Did I tell you he was terribly bright? Well, he is. And he's been around. He has a girlfriend he talks to over the telephone. In *French*. And he served in the Pacific, so I guess he didn't pick up French there."

"Is his lady French?"

"No. No, no. He starts and ends the conversations in English. I've heard a lot of French spoken in the last couple of years. I suspect it was maybe his first language; he's that fluent. And oh: He subscribes to a classics quarterly and does their crossword puzzle in Latin."

Mrs. Bontecou sighed.

". . . I'll keep you posted, Mom."

She was amused by Harry's way of telling her that he didn't want to pursue the conversation ("I'll keep you posted"). Jesse Bontecou used to do the same thing, using almost the same words. Maybe it's genetic, Mrs. Bontecou thought roguishly. She hoped not all her late husband's attributes were transmitted. She comforted herself that Providence had given Harry her husband's good looks, his curious eyes, his diffident but room-illuminating smile.

Some time late in the *Spectator* competition it crossed Harry's mind that Tracy, for all his skills, might actually fail to accumulate the points necessary to put him in the winning circle. The *Spectator*'s rules were explicit. Contenders would be given points for whatever they accomplished, epochal or trivial. An article about a planned rise in tuition might earn 500 editorial points. Double that if the student dug up the story himself. Fetching a Coca-Cola for the sports editor would get you 10 editorial points. Fetching a Coca-Cola for the business manager, 10 business points; bringing in a semester's ad schedule from Lucky Strike, 1,500 business points. No student was permitted to give his time exclusively to editorial or to business. The students' credit points were meticulously tabulated by the assistant managing editor and kept from view in a locked desk. At the end of the eight-week period the senior editors would meet and review the totals of points earned. They were at liberty to draw the line where they chose—to elect none or all thirty of that competition's aspirants. What they were not at liberty to do was to pass over a student with a higher score in order to elect a student with a lower score, never mind that they thought the lesser scorer a better potential writer or editor, or that they preferred his company. If they wanted K, perforce they had to elect A through J.

At their election meeting in the *Spectator*'s single formal room, with its wood paneling and bound volumes of eighty years of the daily, the senior editors called out their opinions of the competitors, going down the line beginning with the highest scorer. When they came to Tracy Allshott, they all agreed that he was a gifted student with marked, if erratic, writing skills. But his scorecard was not impressive, this very much owing to the extensive time he had given to his ambitious but ultimately unpublishable series on the (imputed) corruption of the Gardiner Trust. Tracy was "a little disconnected," was how the features editor, Henry Bevan, put it.

"We'd go broke if we had to depend on him for ads," the business manager contributed, commenting on Tracy's low score at the business end. To elect Tracy, who was tenth in overall points, the editors would have to elect the students whose points ranked eighth and ninth. The editorial board voted to draw the line at eight.

Harry Bontecou came in first. He knew he was doing well, but he dreaded the traditional alcoholic extravaganza only at the end of which the elections were announced. The party convened at five in the *Spectator* offices. Twenty-three student competitors (seven had dropped out) were present to hear the results, to the extent they could hear or understand anything after they (with some help from their seniors) had consumed six pitchers of dry martinis, chugalugged and passed from victim to victim to the metronomic beat of the managing editor, who served exuberantly as master of ceremonies.

Harry did what he could to sip the booze slowly but was roundly jeered for malingering and egged on to do better. During drinking time his eyes were on Tracy. When Tracy's turn to chugalug came, Harry was surprised, as were the junior—and senior—party goers, to see someone so self-disciplined swallow down, to the mounting cheers of the assembly, what seemed like a pint of gin. Finally, the editor called for silence. Two hours had gone by. Half the competitors were lying in various postures on the floor, two or three of them sound asleep.

Abe Rosen read out the names of the successful competitors, in order of precedence. Bontecou . . . Jelway . . . Hesse . . . Aubrey . . . Shapiro . . . Carton . . . Ilsen . . . Shevitts.

Silence. And then: "*Congratulations!*" The editor led the applause in which the senior staff joined. Gradually, shaken from their torpor,

WILLIAM F. BUCKLEY JR.

the winners joined in the applause, applauding themselves, actually, applauding also those among them who had scored higher. Then came the applause from those who had not made it, were awake, and had taken in the proceedings. That applause—the good-sport applause—was perfunctory. The hurt was too great and the anesthetizing of the event too dulling.

Now, Harry thought, after being congratulated by what seemed twenty classmates, *I have to go back to Wallachs Hall.* He had kept his eye on Tracy during the felicitations, hoping he would slide away from the party room. If so, after an interval, Harry too could go back to their quarters, perhaps even to find Tracy asleep. But Tracy lingered there in the large boardroom, propped up against one of the bookcases, an empty glass in hand, his blond hair hiding one eye and most of his forehead.

Harry braced himself. He walked over to him. "Sorry about how it went for you, Tracy."

"Congrashulations, Harry."

"Tracy, shall we go get something better to eat than the junk they gave us? Or shall we just . . . go back and . . . sleep it off?"

"We go back, yes," Tracy said, achieving his balance with some difficulty, then setting out through the thinning crowd toward the door.

Harry extended his hand discreetly to Tracy's glass, removed it from his hand, and put it down on one of the trays. Without appearing to do so, he tried to give Tracy the balance needed to effect the walk down the staircase of the *Spectator* offices in John Jay Hall. They walked in tandem in the mercifully bracing December air, across the frozen and silent quadrangle to Wallachs Hall. Harry had to help him up the first two flights of stairs. Tracy was prepared to end his climb at the second-floor landing.

"Shall we just ask them if we can shay here tonight?"—he pointed to the marker beside the door on which the names of the students in that room were printed.

"No, Tracy. We have only one more flight to climb and we can sleep in our own beds."

"Awright, Harry. After all, you won. You give the orders, I say Yesssir."

Tracy fell into his bed fully clothed and was asleep in one minute.

Harry wanted badly to sleep, but he would not disappoint his tense mother. He reached her on Tracy's telephone and gave her the good news. Dear old Mom, thought Harry. What *else* would proud mother Dorothy Bontecou say?

"Of course, I'm not *surprised*, darling."

10

Trying out

It was the Wednesday after Monday's editorial elections. In the little space reserved for in-house bulletins directly under the Columbia *Spectator*'s masthead appeared the notice: "Senior editorial meeting called for 5 P.M."

The senior board comprised six officers. The editor in chief, Abe Rosen, plus the deputy editor, managing editor, assistant managing editor, the features editor, and business manager. Joe Benedict, the assistant m.e., had left word that he would be late. He was on a story — out covering the United Nations meeting at Flushing Meadows. The UN was scheduled to vote that day on whether to make New York City the permanent capital of the organization. The *Spec* had run two spirited articles from senior editors, one of them favoring the idea (he was a Californian), the other (a New Yorker) opposing it. Benedict's note to Abe Rosen said he would check the *Spectator* office on his return; if the meeting was still going on, he'd step in.

At 6:35 the meeting was very much alive. Rosen summarized for the benefit of Joe Benedict, who had just come in, the purpose of their assembly. Rosen wore a khaki shirt left over from his army days, his Zeta Beta Tau fraternity tie loosely in place. Cigarette in hand, he told Benedict, "What this's all about is Allshott." He peered through his glasses to the penciled score sheet in front of him. "In the elections, Allshott came in tenth. Joe, we've been sitting here going over Allshott's complaint. It's six pages long, and the appendices are"—he looked down at the paper folder in front of him—"twenty-three pages. Here it is in a nutshell. Allshott says his six-article exposé on the Gardiner Trust was turned down by George"—he pointed to the managing editor—"because it leveled charges against several powerful people, one of them a trustee. What he's saying is that George chickened out, scared of the consequences of running the series."

He turned to Benedict. "Joe, did you also read the pieces when they were submitted?"

"No. I think I remember George saying something about them. That they were . . . unsubstantiated?"

"The actual text, the articles he wrote, make up the appendix of the complaint, and we've been reading them here, before you arrived. Only George and Henry"—Henry Bevan was the features editor—"read them when Tracy submitted them just before Thanksgiving. So . . . tell us, George, why you turned them down."

George Stillman was a solemn twenty-two-year-old, stocky and tidy. He was headed for law school and already inclined to the use of formal language. "It's just this simple: There wasn't *any* hard evidence of the kind of skulduggery Allshott alleged. Here's the situation"—he took the pages from the business manager, quickly refreshing his memory.

His recital was orderly. "The Gardiner Trust is presided over by John Heather, son-in-law of the old man, Henry Taylor Gardiner, Columbia, 1892. Heather apparently runs the trust, even though there are six other trustees. Over the last ten years Columbia has received four or five gifts from the Gardiner Trust, from ten thousand dollars—that was for a museum purchase—to one million, pledged for a chair in the political science department. When the poli sci chair was set up last year, a faculty committee of three was appointed to look for someone to fill it. The chair is for Russian studies." George Stillman lifted his head from the folio and spoke on.

"Allshott's article says that the faculty committee recommended Professor Pierre Enfils—you heard of him? Big deal at Johns Hopkins. Well, Allshott says Enfils has written a couple of books which are friendly—'objective' is Allshott's word—to the Soviet, uh, enterprise. And—I'm quoting from Allshott, understand—when Big-bucks Heather heard about it he raised holy hell. He went right to the president at Hamilton Hall, says Allshott, and Hamilton Hall backed down. In doing so, it violated the sacred faculty independence that Columbia University et cetera, et cetera, et cetera."

"Well, that sounds pretty raw," Rosen said.

"But where was the proof?" George's eyes went back to the articles in hand, scanning the last two. "Allshott didn't interview John Heather. Heather isn't even quoted. Only one of the faculty committee was quoted, and he wouldn't permit the use of his name. Why didn't he check with the other two? They wouldn't see him, he said. Allshott's inquiries to Hamilton Hall yielded nothing, but Allshott here attributes the vagueness and the silence of the three or four people he tried to get information from to a conspiracy of silence.

"I told him: Tracy, look, we can't run six pieces by you on this business unless you can back them up, and you simply *haven't done that.* He was sore and argued that the evidence—I like this—the evidence in the articles 'is incandescent.' I finally told him, Tracy, it's my job to decide whether an article merits publication."

"Now," Rosen took over again, "Tracy says that if the six articles had been accepted, the points he'd have been awarded from them would—he is certain—have lifted him into the winners' circle. By the way," he said, now addressing Joe as assistant managing editor and bookmaker in charge of the competitors' score sheet—"is that in fact the case? How many points would he have earned if we had run with his series?"

"A lot. They were his idea. His research. His writing. Figure fifteen hundred points each: nine thousand."

Rosen looked down at the large paper spread, three stiff sheets of paper Scotch taped together, listing, after the name of each applicant, the number of points earned in editorial, in business, and then the totals, in descending order.

"Let's see. We did elect Shevitts. He came in number eight, with 47,526 points. Allshott wasn't ninth just behind Shevitts. He was tenth, with 39,800 points." He looked up. "The answer is: Yes. With nine thousand extra points he'd have come in ahead of Shevitts.

"Allshott doesn't know that with nine thousand extra points he'd have been elected. We haven't yet sent the score sheet out for framing. It has to be ready for the Christmas party, when our board presents it"—he reminded his colleagues—"to the winner. It becomes his souvenir."

George said: "You're talking about Bontecou. As winner, he gets the score sheet, right?"

Rosen nodded. "Yeah. Harry."

"He *rooms* with Tracy Allshott!"

Rosen paused and then said out of the blue, it seemed, "Anyone know anything about the Civil Rights Congress? Allshott says here he is sending a copy of his complaint to the Civil Rights Congress." He looked around the table. He reached over to the coffee table and picked up the phone. "I'm calling my father," he said as he dialed the number. "He's an expert on this kind of thing.

"Dad, I'm at an . . . important meeting here, the *Spectator*. A student who didn't make it on Monday—that's when we elected junior editors—is saying we cheated on him and he's sending a copy of his complaint to the Civil Rights Congress. Who are they? You got any idea?"

He listened.

"Thanks, Dad." He hung up the phone.

"The Civil Rights Congress, my father says, is a Communist front. It takes on complaints by pro-Communists."

There was silence.

Then George said, "You know, I think it would make sense, in our situation, to check with counsel, as the lawyers say. Bill Bradbury is a trustee of the *Spec*. He was editor sometime before the war; 1938, I think. He's with Coudert Brothers."

"What do we do in the meantime?"

Rosen took off his glasses and stuffed the papers back in the manila folder. He announced his decisions. "One, we hold up the score sheet. Lock it up. Two, I'll check out the legal scene. Three, then I think it makes sense for me to call Harry on over, see if he can help figure it all out. Next item, four, is chow."

Harry Bontecou walked from the *Spectator* offices to the Butler Library. To do so he had to cope, as he had got used to doing, with the renowned irregular bricks modeled after the famous School of Athens. Reaching the library, he brought up the book *Shadows of*

WILLIAM F. BUCKLEY JR.

Change, by Pierre Enfils. It was published in 1945. He ran his eyes over the text, a history of the Soviet Union beginning with the "October" uprising. He scanned the chapter summaries. They told of events Harry was first told about by Erik Chadinoff at Plattling during his discourses on the perfidy of the Communists. He had told of the John Dewey Commission, and later Harry had read about the famous commission and its exposé of the 1938 Soviet "show trials." In 1937, the philosopher John Dewey agreed to head up a commission of inquiry to examine the great trials in Moscow. His pretense back then was that he was searching out collaborators of the despised Leon Trotsky, exiled from the Soviet Union in 1928. Stalin, two years after the trials, consummated his hatred of Trotsky by arranging for his assassination in Mexico. The show trials had been followed by the execution—for alleged treasonable activity—of a large number of what had been the Communist cadre in Moscow. The ruling of the Dewey Commission was emphatic and conclusive: The so-called confessions from high Communist functionaries had been fraudulent, coerced, contrived.

Chadinoff had stressed, in his winter seminars at the Plattling BOQ, the importance of the Dewey findings, "especially since Dewey was a man of the left. It was a terrible blow for the left intelligentsia who were fellow travelers."

Returning to New York, Harry's summer reading had included Malcolm Muggeridge's *Winter in Moscow,* Freda Utley's *The Dream We Lost,* and Arthur Koestler's *Darkness at Noon.* Now, Enfils's book in hand, he turned to the chapter on the show trials of 1938. Professor Enfils stressed that it was naive to assume that the trial's defendants were innocent, nothing more than Stalin's victims. This paragraph in particular caught Harry's eye.

The commission to investigate the trials was headed by the prominent philosopher and educator John Dewey. He assembled a jury of distinguished academic figures. What they had in common was a virulent distrust of Soviet policies. Many of them, like Professor Dewey himself, had ten years earlier sympathized with the socialist ideal. Many turned away from an understanding of Soviet policies after the break between Stalin and Trotsky. It was evident from the language in which Dewey brought his indictment that the Soviet Union was being dismissed without an appropriate sense of the vicissitudes of historical evolution. It is characteristically American to apply whatever its own standards are as instantly paradigmatic for other societies. Thus if America writes a Hatch Act in 1939 protecting the political freedoms of public servants, all other societies must have a Hatch Act. What truly happened in 1938 was that evolutionary Stalinism felt the need to excrete men who were basically antagonistic to Soviet ideals. In the United States, a President Jackson could find other ways of getting rid of John C. Calhoun. But it is naive, and self-deceiving, to repudiate Joseph Stalin for exercising procedures which have been routine throughout Russian history.

Harry left the library and went to room 302 of Earl Hall, the office of the Columbia Young Progressives. He found Tom Scott, the Progressives' twenty-three-year-old president, tall, brown-haired, tousled, wearing thick steel-rimmed glasses, at his desk pounding a typewriter. Behind him was a huge poster of Henry Wallace, former vice president of the United States under President Roosevelt, and until only a few weeks ago secretary of commerce under President Truman. The small room's broad shelves were crammed with brochures and pamphlets.

It was Tom Scott who, in March, had led the student protest against the awarding of an honorary degree to Winston Churchill. Churchill had delivered his "Iron Curtain" speech in Fulton, Missouri, denouncing Soviet practices and deeply antagonizing those who favored an accommodationist foreign policy. It had been arranged that on the way back to Great Britain, the former prime minister would stop at Columbia in order to receive a degree. The Young Progressives amassed a remarkable 1,700 student signatures protesting the degree. They were directed to retiring Columbia president Nicholas Murray Butler.

Asked to comment on the student protesters, Churchill, accepting his degree, jocularly urged Communists, "wherever they are," to read up on the life of the "white ants" — "termites which lead a life of slavery." He then pledged "all the moral and material forces of the British Empire to strengthen the United Nations and maintain the peace."

Scott looked up at Harry. "What can I do for you?"

The telephone interrupted him. He conversed with the caller

about a joint rally with Hunter College soon after the New Year. While they spoke, Harry looked at the brochures being offered by the Young Progressives, pocketing two or three.

"Can I do anything for you?"

"Yes. The *Journal American* said in an editorial last week that the Civil Rights Congress was a Communist front. Can you enlighten me on that?"

"It's a lie, of course. I hate to put it this way, but there are fascist tendencies in Washington, and they're applauded, of course, by people like William Randolph Hearst and the warmongers."

"But what about the Civil Rights Congress?"

"It's an organization devoted to the civil rights of everybody, Negro, white, Jew, Christian, Communist. It is being reviewed by the the attorney general with the obvious design of listing it officially as a Communist front—in order to appease the ultrarightists in Congress. It's just not true that Attorney General Tom Clark is a reliable liberal. He's a Red scare demagogue who likes to list organizations that disagree with government policy as Communist fronts."

"Are they all innocent? I mean, all those organizations he has listed?"

Scott was slowed down. "Innocent of what?"

"Innocent of taking orders from the Communist Party?"

Scott leaned back in his chair, lit a cigarette, and said, "Look,— what's your name?"

"Harry. Harry Bontecou."

"Look, Harry, the Communists have certain ideals in common with other people who aren't 'Communists.' They oppose imperialism, nuclear proliferation, inequality, and fascism. I can't speak for *all* the outfits on the attorney general's list, because I don't know enough about them, but I *can* speak for the Civil Rights Congress. I am all for it, and I have their literature." Scott reached over to one of the stacks in the bookcase. "You'll see. Pretty important people back the congress. Including academics, artists, scientists."

Harry pocketed the brochure. Scott's phone rang again. He picked it up, listened for a moment, then cupped the mouthpiece with his hand, looked up at Harry, and said, "This call is going to keep me busy for a while." Harry gave a half wave with his hand. "Thanks. I'll look the material over. See you."

He left the building and walked to the offices of the *Spectator.* He didn't want to review the material he had collected back in his room, with Tracy looking over his shoulder. He turned first to the brochure on the Civil Rights Congress. He spotted, in the roster of sponsors, the name Pierre Enfils.

He had had enough. He felt a rush of indignation and a hot rage. He felt he knew from Camp Plattling what kind of a world threatened. He walked back to his room. Tracy was there, typing those punchy strokes Harry had got used to. Harry sat down at his own desk at the other end of the room, facing Tracy.

"Can I interrupt you for a minute?"

"Yeah." Allshott edged his typewriter toward the wall.

"Tracy, do you know Professor Pierre Enfils?"

Tracy was surprised. "What do *you* know about him?"

"I've read your articles on the Gardiner Trust."

"Oh? I didn't show them to you, of course—we were in competition. What did you think of them?"

Harry's jaw tightened. He looked directly into Tracy's eyes. "What I think, Tracy, is that if it's true that Enfils was intercepted on his way to a chair in the history department of Columbia, I say: *Good* for whoever did it—the Gardiner Trust people—President Butler—whoever."

"So much for academic freedom, Harry?"

"There is also freedom to react against distortion. I'm asking you again. Do you know Professor Enfils?"

Tracy was silent.

"Did you get the Gardiner Trust story from him directly? Or maybe from the Civil Rights Congress? Do you know Enfils's position on the Moscow trials?—"

Tracy stood up abruptly. He slammed shut his desk drawer, grabbed the book on the sofa, and strode from the room.

Harry's heart was pounding. He took the material from the Young Progressives office and the notes he had made in the library. He put them in a manila folder and walked from their little two-desk study into the bedroom, upper and lower bunks, he shared with Tracy. He opened the door to the clothes closet and reached for the briefcase with the combination lock his mother had given him in September. He put the folder in the case and twirled the lock. His heart was still pounding. He had a feeling that he had met the enemy at very very close quarters; different, yes, from when he was fighting in Belgium, cheek by jowl with the enemy, but he felt something of the thrill and danger of the reconnaissance scout, identifying the enemy at close hand.

11

McCarthy runs

In the seven years that had gone by since McCarthy had served as judge, going then to the Marines in the Asian theater, he wrote regularly to his mother. In one letter he let it out of the bag. "The war isn't going to last forever, Mom. And you know what I'm going to do when I get back home? Well, if you *promise* not to tell, I'm going to run for—" Joe then listed a half dozen political offices.

"Scratch all of these out except one—your choice. Whichever one you choose, that's the one I'll go for, what I'll do for you and Dad." He had written down, "District Attorney . . . Mayor . . . Congressman . . . Governor . . . Senator . . . President."

"Joe is always teasing us," Biddie McCarthy said to Tim, showing him the letter. But she kept it, and reread it the day Joe filed for the United States Senate in December 1945.

Joe McCarthy was still in uniform when he made the decision to run in the earlier 1944 Senate race. He had planned the campaign even before his resignation from the Marines in December 1944. It amused him that he had a year earlier communicated his intention to his mother, however enigmatically. It had been nothing more than a family joke. Captain McCarthy's last six months on duty were spent back in the United States on various mainland bases. From wherever he was stationed, he rattled such political floorboards as he had established in his race for judge and during his career as judge. He submitted his name as a candidate for the Senate against incumbent Senator Alexander Wiley, by way of warm-up, five months before he left the service. He had designed that campaign, which would never get off the ground, with the single purpose in mind of getting his name before the public. His political line boiled down to a widely distributed postcard:

Stand by for the return to Wisconsin of Joe McCarthy—
Circuit-Judge-to-Captain-in-combat with the Marines!

That campaign was playtime. This campaign, aiming at November 1946, Joe McCarthy insisted, was serious. Joe McCarthy wanted to go to the Senate. On this point he was resolute even while still stationed in the Pacific. He had told Joyce Andrews he knew how to bring it off. Andrews, recovering slowly from a shrapnel wound after he had ditched his plane near Bougainville, was skeptical. "Joe, they don't elect people like us. We got no connections, no money, no—nothing."

Joe reminded Joyce that he had been elected judge against long odds. "And now I have a Silver Star. That's not nothing."

"Okay, Joe. You run for senator. If you're elected, I'll run for president."

Joe just smiled. It was impossible to discourage Joe McCarthy, and after a while his friends stopped trying.

All hands at the hotel reception could see that the campaign was beginning to hum. The target was the renowned Senator Bob La Follette, incumbent, populist, legendary son of Bob La Follette of Wisconsin, founder of the Progressive Party. McCarthy had hoped it would be a three-man race, but the Progressive Party was disintegrating and being wooed by the Democrats. La Follette had decided instead to rejoin the Republican Party, listing himself as a candidate to return to the Senate on the Republican line. That meant that McCarthy needed to fight not only in the general election against a Democrat, but in the Republican primary against the formidable La Follette. When La Follette registered, all Republicans except McCarthy put aside their hopes for the Senate.

There had been a hint of trouble ahead on the matter of the war record. At the press conference before Joe's dinner speech a reporter from the *Madison Capital Times* rose and asked Joe why it was that his citation from theater commander Admiral Chester Nimitz didn't specify the nature and cause of his leg injury.

Joe chuckled and answered that perhaps Admiral Nimitz had other things to do. "You know, Mike,"—as ever, Joe used reporters' first names—"we hadn't won the war yet."

Joe turned then amiably to the young woman with the recording mike in her hand—a new device used to capture spontaneous exchanges and interviews for later broadcast over the radio. She read her question from a written note.

"Judge McCarthy, you were discharged last December after only sixteen months' service."

"Eighteen months," Joe interrupted. "And I wasn't 'discharged.' I resigned."

The reporter, her rhythm broken, stared down at her notes. "Uh, eighteen months. . . . That was a year ago. Then we were facing a—a costly—Nazi offensive in Belgium, and our casualties at Iwo Jima were very high. But instead of sticking to your unit in the Marine Air Force you came home and campaigned against Senator Wiley. How did you get an early discharge?"

There was a murmur of curiosity from the audience.

"I told you, dear, I resigned. Resigned my commission. Why? I had been hospitalized. And anyway, remember that draft regulations exempt sitting judges. I never had to go into the armed services in the first place. I was a volunteer. And I'm glad I did serve, and I'm proud of the work I did as an intelligence officer and tail gunner in action."

The host for the dinner to follow, the congenial Malcolm Aspic, president of the Elks Club, raised his hand. He saw nothing to be gained from more of the same. He called an end to the press conference even though there were two reporters with their hands raised. "Come on, guys, ladies. Let the candidate go. There's a *hundred* people in the next room waiting to shake his hand. You all come on in with us and have a drink." He turned to Joe and mock-whispered: "*We'll* never tell on them if they go to the bar instead of paying more attention to the business of politics, will we, Joe?"

Joe waved his hand at the four press and radio representatives, bowing his head submissively. He was telling them he had no alternative but to oblige his hosts. Y'all know how it is. . . . His wave conveyed that he would have preferred to stay and answer more questions

The first person to accost him in the crowded lounge where the drinks were served wasn't an Elk, it was a visibly agitated Richie O'Neill. "How'm I doing?" he said to Richie. He motioned Joe to follow him to the corner of the room. Joe agreed to go, "But only if you get me a drink."

"*Bourbon and soda for the judge*" — Richie shot the directive briskly to the nearest human body. The mayor of Fond du Lac, taken for the waiter, received the bar order with some amazement, delegating it coolly to the young man on his right. Richie O'Neill's attempt to arrest Joe's attention was blocked by a large, bearded guest, who, drink in his left hand, put his right arm around Joe's shoulder. "Joe, what I have to tell you is *really* important." The solicitor began on the subject of the Potsdam Agreement of the preceding August and the opportunities forfeited by President Truman at the diplomatic table. It was at Potsdam, three months after the death of Hitler, two weeks before the Japanese surrender, that the great force of adamant Soviet diplomacy was experienced. On the subject of the lost freedom of Poland and other misfortunes that flowed from Potsdam and, before that, the Yalta Agreement, the guest was fluent and vociferous and impossible to shut down.

Richie sighed with exasperation and managed to get across only the sparest message, whispered in the candidate's ear. "Joe: Right after your speech come to my suite. Number four twenty-four. Ollie will be there." Joe managed to hold the geopolitical strategist at bay long enough to express his genuine surprise.

"Ollie here? How come?" Ollie Burden had been scheduled to do some money raising for Joe's campaign at a gathering of friends of Wisconsin tycoon Tom Coleman. Why was Ollie, all of a sudden, in Madison, missing so important an opportunity? But there was no way Joe could hear Richie's explanation in the commotion and the sound of the cocktail hour.

Richie O'Neill had been a friend since Joe's chicken-farming days and, ever since the campaign for judge, a dollar-a-year political adviser, now campaign chairman. O'Neill was glumly resigned to Joe's quite extraordinary capacity to polarize. His public was not now numerous: Joe's statewide race against Wiley the year before had been a mere formality, never arousing the interest of the Wisconsin public. His successful race for judge seven years earlier had been in the Tenth Circuit, comprising only three counties. But within that small circle, his friends and admirers were ardent. They found him attractive, earnest, yet never boring or fanatical, courteous, and thoughtful, a life lover who animated all situations in which he involved himself. They never doubted he would move up the political ladder.

But the stamina of his critics was at least as enduring. They had coalesced early, as critics of the tactics Joe had used in his race against Judge Werner. Miles McMillin, of the *Madison Capital Times,* was an early and adamant critic. "To go around and pretend that Edgar Werner was seventy-two when McCarthy knew goddamn well he was sixty-seven was infamous and unforgivable," he said at a public gathering of Friends of Bob La Follette. The resentments festered as McCarthy prospered. The anti-McCarthy forces consolidated in their determination to block this latest effrontery of the chicken grower, his bid for an august Senate seat. The heaviest concentrations of his critics were in the editorial offices of the *Madison Capital Times* and the *Milwaukee Journal,* and now the *Journal* was set to blow a very loud whistle on Judge-Captain-Candidate Joe McCarthy.

The after-dinner speech went well. The preliminary routine was well established. For maybe the fifteenth time since he had declared his candidacy thirty days ago, Joe sat while the master of ceremonies, alongside, read out loud the citation from Admiral Nimitz. It didn't matter if the masters of ceremonies had entirely different introductions in mind. Joe—or Richie—or Ollie would instruct them: This is the way it goes. And this was the citation that prompted the emergency meeting in Richie's suite: Ollie had an advance copy of the next day's *Milwaukee Journal.*

At the hotel suite Joe quieted down, but only after campaign manager Richie O'Neill demanded a stop to his animated but disjointed conversation. "Look, Joe, we're here to listen to Ollie, who has something very important for us to hear. So let's give him a chance, okay?"

Ollie Burden had reached the hotel in Madison just before Joe's speech began. Ollie's base was eighty-two miles away, in Milwaukee. There, in the morning, he had got wind of the *Milwaukee Journal*'s scheduled "exposé," as the paper would label it, of Judge McCarthy's war record. It was urgent to plan a response, so he had driven non-stop to the hotel in Madison.

McCarthy's primary attention getter was a photograph: Captain Joe McCarthy, United States Marine. He was dressed in flying gear. Tall, handsome, earnest but with a twinkle in his eyes. Clean shaven (he had eliminated his beard). Under the photo in his campaign brochure, in bold print, was the citation from Admiral Nimitz.

Ollie reached into his briefcase for the newspaper galleys and began reading.

Joe listened for a moment or two. Then he reached up to the overhead lamp that shone over the table and their tight little circle. He turned the light off. Ollie's voice stopped abruptly. Joe turned the light back on. What he had done was as striking a gesture of irritation from Joe McCarthy as anyone present had ever seen. Joe *was* irritated, a lesser cause of that irritation being Ollie's cigar smoke, which was getting at Joe's sensitive sinus. Mostly he was irritated by the story he was being made to listen to.

"Ollie, that kind of thing *always* gets said about political candidates. Why're you so *red hot* over this attack? And could you aim the cigar at Richie for a change?"

"Because," Ollie said, stamping out his cigar, "this story is different. They quote *two* Marine officers who say that your war wound was the result of an accident on a boarding ladder at a drunken equator-crossing initiation ceremony off New Guinea. How're we going to *answer* these people?"

Joe reached into his pocket and drew out the campaign circular featuring his citation. He leaned back in the armchair and took a swallow from his whiskey glass. "Okay. Let's take it bit by bit. . . . I'm quoting. 'He'—that's me, right Ollie? Or is the *Journal* saying I wasn't the Captain Joe McCarthy the citation was written about?—'He obtained excellent photographs of enemy gun positions despite intense anti-aircraft fire, thereby gaining valuable information which contributed materially to the success of subsequent strikes in the area.'

"Anybody saying that's not true?"

Joe went on. " 'Although suffering from a severe leg injury . . .' "

Joe stopped, raised his right pants leg, and pointed at the three-inch scar. "Okay?" His voice was now singsong, as though he were giving a speech. "'. . . he refused to be hospitalized and continued to carry out his duties as Intelligence Officer in a highly efficient manner. His courageous devotion to duty was in keeping with the highest traditions of the naval service.'"

Joe turned to Ollie. "Makes me blush, Ollie."

Ollie banged his fist on the coffee table. "*I'm* not doubting you, Joe. But the story quotes *two* guys who say they were *there!*"

"So they were there when we had that little fun party on shipboard. Maybe they weren't there when I got the scar from the Jap flak. So who's going to say they're the only guys who were ever around when McCarthy got banged up in the Solomons? Let's have another drink."

He continued without a pause. "I got here"—Joe went again to his jacket pocket—"a list of political positions I'm going to run on. We've got to do something about veterans' housing. That's an A-Number-One priority. We have to figure out a way for the United Nations, if it's going to amount to anything, to have some kind of military force at its disposal. And we've got to keep our eyes on the Soviet Union. Last month they took over the Hungarian oil fields at Liège, including the big Standard Oil play. There was a fellow there tonight gassing on about Potsdam. But he had a point. Looks to me like we gave away the show there."

Ollie looked over despairingly at Richie. Suddenly he brightened. What he thought to reserve to say privately to Richie he found himself saying in front of Joe: "Richie, it's just possible—it suddenly occurs to me—that Joe knows more about political communication than we do."

"So?" Richie asked.

"So maybe Joe's right. Maybe we should just—have another drink."

They did, and many, many drinks later, it was champagne, toasting the election of Joseph R. McCarthy as United States Senator from the state of Wisconsin.

WILLIAM F. BUCKLEY JR.

12

Senator Joe McCarthy
goes to Washington

Joe McCarthy arrived in Washington on the train, early in the morning. His arrival was in sharp contrast to the excitement of his departure. In Milwaukee there was a cheering section of his supporters, an improvised band, and something on the order of a farewell address: McCarthy would leave now his home state and dwell in Washington, looking after the affairs of the whole country.

He didn't exactly expect a parade when the train came into Union Station. What he got was nothing. No one greeted him and his aide, Victor Johnston. Their entourage was one porter, who carried on his trailer Joe's large bag, containing his entire wardrobe and a briefcase, and Johnston's three bags. But at least the junior senator knew where to go, what address to give to the taxi driver. He had sent ahead Ray Kiermas, who agreed to act as McCarthy's office manager. Better, Ray and his wife rented a two-room house and turned one of the rooms over to McCarthy. Joe would live with Ray for three years, until he got his own apartment.

Ray had been a great success, a high school dropout who worked as a milk grader and then leased a dry-goods store from his father-in-law for fifteen dollars a month. He prospered and during the war opened a locker plant. He had intended to start a real estate–brokerage business when in 1946 he was lured into the McCarthy campaign by Tom Coleman, a friend and a commanding Republican figure who had decided to help Joe McCarthy out. Ray Kiermas had been given a single commission: to supervise the mailing of a personally addressed postcard to every voter in Wisconsin. On one side, a picture of Joe McCarthy. On the other, the addressee's name and address and the handwritten sentence, "Your vote will be greatly appreciated by Joe McCarthy."

"Well, Ray," McCarthy was lugging his suitcase into the house, "there are no signs here—yet!—that *Washington* greatly appreciates Joe McCarthy." Ray's wife, Dolores, whom Joe had also hired for his senate staff as a clerk, unpacked Joe's bag, surveyed its contents, and delivered the first of what would be successive lectures over a period of six years on his perpetual disarray. Joe would wear dark blue double-breasted suits, buying them four at a time only after the first set was entirely frayed. Joe responded by tickling Dolores under the chin and sitting down on the chair at the card table he'd use as a desk. To Ray he said: "Let's call a press conference. Tomorrow at three."

It surprised Joe, but gratified him, that there were twenty-eight members of the communications industry there in the President's Room of the Senate, with its tall windows, high ceiling, leather and velvet appointments, and scrubbed and polished tables. Senator McCarthy, junior senator from Wisconsin, was thirty-eight years old, the youngest senator serving. It had been a Republican landslide, and the GOP was in charge of the House and the Senate for the first time since 1931. The demoralization among the Democrats had been such that Senator Fulbright actually suggested that President Truman should acknowledge the tidal wave in sentiment, appoint a Republican secretary of state, and resign his office. By the rules of succession that then obtained, the secretary of state would succeed him to the White House—"and we can have a Republican government, which is what the people apparently want," said Mr. Fulbright, loyal Democrat.

McCarthy joked about the Fulbright proposal as he opened his first press conference in Washington. But his affability didn't immobilize everyone in the room. One reporter asked, "You're a new man here. Why did you call a press conference?" Joe McCarthy said he felt he should comment on the strike by the United Mine Workers. But his recommendations on how to cope with the strike were garbled. He cited the need for authority, of the kind exercised by the military, if the situation was one of military necessity; but he disapproved, he added quickly, of the effort made in the preceding year by President Truman to nationalize the steel industry in protest against the steel strike.

Did the senator know to which committees he would be appointed? He did not know, but he hoped to serve in the Senate Foreign Relations Committee. McCarthy ended the brief conference by shaking the hands of all the reporters. "He's that way," Sam Tilburn from Indianapolis said to a colleague as they walked out. "I've read up a little on him in Wisconsin. He knows everybody and likes everybody. But not everybody likes him. Bill Evjue and Miles McMillin over in Madison, they *hate* him. They were nicer to Hitler."

Joe McCarthy was sworn in with a lusty cheering section in the galleries—two Pullman cars full of supporters who had traveled overnight from Madison. Joe loved it all, and loved the life of Washington. He bought an off-the-rack tuxedo and happily attended the parties he was regularly invited to by hostesses who were drawn to a young, handsome, sociable bachelor senator who, they liked to whisper it, had not so long ago been a chicken farmer.

And McCarthy continued, to the continuing dismay of Vic Johnston and Ray Kiermas, to be simultaneously a pauper and a spendthrift. He never had any money and was never without money. He loved to entertain, and soon after arriving, when Ray had temporary access to an apartment whose owners were gone for two weeks, McCarthy invited eight women members of the Senate press detachment to dinner, cooking his beloved steaks, while Dolores, acting on only an hour's notice, brought together what she could to make a more complete meal. But that night McCarthy went back to his little room to make notes for his maiden speech.

There are hangovers after wars, when people prowl to shed light on the activity of the Merchants of Death. Joe McCarthy was not lured by the historical revisionists who thought the Second World War unprovoked, avoidable, and opportunistic. But McCarthy felt strongly that it was right to investigate profiteers. An investigation to that end had been authorized by the Seventy-ninth Congress, but now the National Defense Program Investigating Committee was scheduled to close shop. Senator McCarthy, before his press party, had spent three hours at Walter Reed Hospital chatting with veterans. He told the Senate about one of them, a Marine with both legs missing who claimed that many of his comrades had died because of "the graft and corruption which the Senate proposes to investigate." He quoted a second veteran as saying, "What are you gentlemen there thinking about? You are the body who voted us into war. Now why do you object to investigating the graft and corruption which occurred *during* the war?" McCarthy lowered his voice: He did not speak, he told the chamber, on behalf of the fifteen million men who had fought in the war, "but I speak as one of them." The Senate voted forty-nine to forty-three in favor of continuing the committee.

McCarthy was not named to the Foreign Relations Committee, but he was assigned to the Committee on Banking and Currency and given a seat on the Committee on Expenditures in the Executive Departments, a committee McCarthy would make famous.

13

President Harry Truman
gives 'em hell

President Harry Truman was hopping mad. Except that he was in the Oval Office when he read the news report he'd have loosened his tie, which was a habit he had when his dander was up. Henry Wallace, his secretary of commerce, had gone and given one of those goddamn speeches about how we needed to be friendlier to the Soviet Union, and this just one week after the Soviets conscripted 400,000 teenagers, making now a total of 1.2 million, into the army.

On top of that there was the whole sense of . . . order. Actually, yes, the whole sense of protocol. Harry Truman believed very firmly in protocol. The buck stops here — he was proud of having said that. Well, you can't exercise the responsibility without having the authority. It's the president, goddamnit, who makes foreign policy, and he doesn't need speeches from a Cabinet member telling him what to do. On top of that, it was a dumb political move, he explained to Clark Clifford, his close confidant and legal expert, whom he had summoned for compassionate company. "Half the country thinks we've been too sweet with the Soviet Union and that's the reason Stalin continues to score, civil war in Greece, threats to blockade Berlin, Polish purge, the business in Turkey. . . . And while we work on the big scene, my own Cabinet officer goes and does it again, another of those valentines to Joe Stalin."

Young Clark Clifford had an easy grace, and it worked well with

Harry Truman. Truman knew what it was to work under an Absolute Boss: He had been schooled under the severe political tutelage of Prendergast in Kansas City. With Boss Prendergast you could be informal in your language but never really relaxed. At the relatively young age of forty, Clark Clifford was both informal and relaxed in the company of the supreme U.S. boss. Relaxed, but never, ever suggesting that his loyalty to the president was secondary. Clark Clifford could negotiate with the president, and sometimes did, but only in the sense of suggesting alternative treatments, never pleading for them. The president paid close attention to what Clifford said. What he said now was rather startling, but only because it was absolutely correct: "On the other hand, Mr. President, I guess we should all be grateful to Henry Wallace. Except for him, you wouldn't be sitting where you are. Henry Wallace would be sitting there."

Truman didn't welcome references to Roosevelt-Wallace. He liked it when people referred to FDR's bold action in 1944—enjoyed hearing about how FDR had got shed of Wallace as vice president, giving the nod to Senator Harry Truman. He liked to hear it because it was great historical drama. What he didn't like was to reflect that his presidency was, in an odd sort of way, the doing of Henry Wallace. In the sense that but-for-Wallace-having-antagonized-FDR, Truman would not now be president of the United States. He would hope that history would say that toward the end of FDR's third term, the president, that great and prophetic man, knew that he was ill and might not finish out a fourth term, and for that reason faced the responsibility of getting the best man possible to succeed him. And the very best man possible meant—Harry Truman.

All he said to Clark Clifford was, "Maybe it's safe to say God was smiling at the United States when the president made that decision. Meanwhile, I've got to do something to clam Wallace up."

Clifford agreed. He recalled the conversation in 1946, on the presidential train bound for Fulton, Missouri, when, late in the night, he had shared the company of the president and Winston Churchill. Churchill was out of power as prime minister, but as leader of the Opposition and heroic wartime figure, he remained the dominant voice of the English-speaking world. They had been playing poker, along with Admiral William Leahy, chief of staff; Harry Vaughan, military aide and presidential companion; Charlie

WILLIAM F. BUCKLEY JR.

Ross, press secretary; and Colonel Wallace Graham, White House physician. Churchill would shoot out a breezy little political essay as the cards were being shuffled. "You remember, Mr. President," Clark Clifford said, "he was talking about political realism, and we knew he was going to drop that bomb the next day at Fulton, saying that there was an Iron Curtain between the Communist world and us. Back in Washington, General Marshall was a little upset, remember? And Churchill said that politics viewed in the laboratory might justify dealing with Stalin with conciliation and understanding, but politics at another level argued against it—the people would lose their 'weights and measures' was the phrase he used. A nice expression for basic freedoms, I thought."

"Yup." Truman nodded his head. One of Clark Clifford's strengths was that he never misunderstood a presidential signal. The signal said that their session, Clark Clifford and President Truman, was now over. The president had heard him approve of the need to do something about Henry Wallace. Now he could leave.

Former vice president Henry Agard Wallace had not enjoyed the hour—the half hour. (Could it have been only fifteen minutes?) *Before that afternoon, Henry Wallace hadn't set foot in the Oval Office for months!* Secretary Wallace, just to begin with, wasn't used to being treated that way. FDR had simply ignored him. That was one thing: Wallace had known it would be that way when he was tapped for vice president back in 1940—Wallace with his Midwest agricultural following could add a little strength to the Democratic ticket. He had already served FDR, as secretary of agriculture, and he had a broad populist appeal. So it hadn't surprised him when, on taking office, there wasn't much to do: His name on the ticket was what FDR wanted from him, nothing else. That kind of thing just *happens* to vice presidents. The historical literature is full of it, he had often consoled himself—get elected vice president and history runs out on you.

There are exceptions, of course. He looked up at the bookcase. His eyes focused on the volume on Teddy Roosevelt by Henry F. Pringle. But of course What's-his-name, the anarchist, had shot President McKinley, and Teddy woke up to find himself president. Nobody had shot FDR between 1940 and 1944. Now Harry Truman was president. One thing to be ignored as vice president, quite another to be ignored as a member of a Cabinet serving a president.

Henry Wallace looked up absentmindedly when young Trevor came in. Trevor always came by before leaving the office, just in case the secretary of commerce had any afterthoughts about work undone, which, in fact, he never did. Mr. Wallace never left work undone; it was not his fashion.

No, the secretary motioned with his hand—"Nothing more, thank you, Trevor." Just that, and a routinely spoken good night. Henry Wallace wanted to stay in his office. He wanted to brood a bit.

As he proceeded to do, for a full half hour. He decided at last to share his misery over the presidential session with Carl. Granted, by doing so he'd be letting a third party in on what had happened in the Oval Office. Theoretically, at least, nobody—as of this moment— knew about what had happened. Wallace had been alone with the president, and the president had said he planned to tell *nobody* about their meeting.

But, really, there was no such thing as guaranteed privacy at such a stratospheric political altitude. Drew Pearson, that pestilential political gossip columnist, nationally syndicated, would probably publish an account tomorrow of what had happened, president to commerce secretary. The hell with it. He'd call Carl, tell him everything. He would feel better, sharing this with his friend.

He picked up the telephone. The duty officer at the switchboard responded. "Yes, Mr. Secretary?"

"Ring Mr. Pforzheimer."

A minute later Carl was on the line.

"Carl, I want you to know about it. I met with the president this afternoon. He summoned me. That's what it was—a *summons.* Usually his appointments lady chats it up with my secretary—'Is that a convenient time for the secretary' kind of thing."

"How was it this time?" Carl asked.

"The gal just told my gal the president would see me at three forty-five."

"Did he . . . talk about the speech?"

"Carl. Did he talk about the speech? *He chewed my ass about the speech.* About *your* speech. He didn't want to hear the other point of view. Just didn't want to *listen.*"

"That's the kind of attitude that makes for world wars, Henry." Carl had been instructed to address Henry Wallace as Henry, even back when Wallace was vice president.

"I *know* that. And on top of everything else, I don't even know that he *read* the whole speech. Probably he just saw the American Legion–type headlines. Those people go crazy if you say anything about the Communists, except to denounce them. You can't even say they fought well at Stalingrad. You wouldn't think it was subversive to say—which is really all we *did* say—that it pays to *consider* the Soviet point of view. Which obviously it does. Stalin lost fifteen million dead; the whole country is gutted. They set out in 1917 to attempt a really dazzling thing, change the whole nature of modern materialist society—I don't need to tell *you.*"

"Of course, Henry."

"But Carl, it's pretty bad. Harry Truman is a *very* direct guy. He's been president what, a year and a half? And he's become cock of the walk. With FDR it was never that way. FDR was, well, naturally the boss, as though he had grown up sitting at the head of the table. *This* is very different. When Truman sits in that chair he's the guy who was just an hour before elected president of his high school class and he wants you to know it."

"That's how small men behave, Henry. It would have been different with . . . well, with you sitting there."

Wallace didn't like it when friends brought up his humiliation in 1944, when FDR dumped him in Chicago—ditched him as vice president. But right now he didn't mind Carl's bringing it up. He let himself say it out loud.

"Yes. It *would* have been different, Carl. What he doesn't realize—what so few people realize—is that post-Hiroshima we have to think the whole thing over again, the international order. It's what the Russians *also* really think, or at least that's my idea—*our* idea—about it. That's what we have to take advantage of, fresh thought, and that's what we said—hinted at—in the speech. And it's not possible to do that unless we try to understand *why* they behave as they do."

"I'm sorry you got hit so hard. Prophet-without-honor business—"

"I'm not feeling sorry for myself. I guess it's true that I'm sorry history turned out just as it did. Imagine. FDR died on April twelfth. If he had died *one* year earlier, I'd have turned the whole thing around—"

"And on top of that, shortened the world war, I'd guess."

"*And* shortened the war. Well," Wallace stopped himself. "I'm not sure exactly how we'd have shortened the war, though maybe I could have persuaded Stalin to move sooner against Japan. . . ."

"You've got a feel for history, Henry. And this is a critical time. Did the president say anything that sounded, well, sounded like an ultimatum? He didn't say you weren't to give any more speeches, did he?"

"Carl, you don't know Harry Truman at close quarters. He doesn't *say* things like that. He says things like, *What you said yesterday was so stupid I know you will never say anything like that again because nobody says such stupid things twice.* . . . You call that an ultimatum?"

"Well," said Carl, "it does *sound* a little . . . threatening. If he— acted. If he—replaced you, you wouldn't just go back to"—Carl laughed derisively at the mere thought of it—"farming, would you, Henry? With every peace-loving American behind you?"

Henry Wallace drew a deep breath. "I haven't thought that far ahead, Carl. But I'll tell you this, goddamnit, I'm not going to retire to Iowa and let the Democratic Party lead the country back into another war. Over my dead body!"

"Mustn't talk that way, Mr. Secretary." Carl was now the solicitous father, consoling the wounded son. "As long as you're around, the right things will get said."

"Well, I appreciate that. And I don't want you to think you're to blame for anything. Everything in that speech needed to be said, and I don't know any student of foreign affairs who can pull things together the way you can, no one, and I read them all. Did you see *Life* on Togliatti in Italy? I wouldn't be surprised if he made it to prime minister by 1948. Head of the Communist Party and prime minister of Italy. Imagine!"

"I know you have a world view on these things, Henry. You're quiet, and you're retiring by nature. But nobody ever doubted your genuine curiosity about how the world really *is*. You figured out how the world really *is*"—Carl allowed himself a little admiring chuckle—"in the agricultural world. Thanks to you we have a revolution in hybrid-corn growing."

Wallace corrected him. "In hybrid-corn *breeding*, Carl."

"Well, they'll never take that away from you. Uh. Henry, what tack do you want to take for the speech in Fort Wayne?" He laughed sympathetically. "Want to talk about the history of corn growing?—corn breeding?"

Wallace paused.

Carl waited.

"Let me think about that. That's three weeks away. I know how fast you can put together a first-rate speech—"

"A speech that catches the presidential eye!"

Now Henry Wallace laughed. He didn't laugh very often. He felt better.

"Thanks, Carl. I'll be in touch."

Two days later, Valysha Ordoff, first secretary of the Kremlin's U.S. Intelligence Division, brought the long, decoded message to the foreign office. Dmitri Bibikoff read it and picked up the telephone. He was put through to Foreign Minister Molotov.

"President Truman gave Henry Wallace hell for the Wednesday speech. Carl thinks he will probably be fired. Truman wants to appease the militants. He very much wants to be reelected in 1948."

"You are keeping a close eye on Carl?"

"A *very* close eye, Vyacheslav Mikhailovich. Very close eye."

"If Wallace is fired, Carl is no longer very useful to us, is he?"

"Permit me to correct you, comrade."

"You are telling me that the confidant and speechwriter for a *former* vice president, a *former* secretary of commerce can continue to be useful to us?"

"Perhaps"—Dmitri spoke the words as if letting out smoke from a choice cigar; slowly, sensually,—"perhaps he can be useful to us as the confidant and speechwriter for a candidate for president of the United States."

Molotov paused.

Dmitri knew better than to go any further, to stay on the line and chat now, or gossip, or speculate. Not with Molotov. "More on the subject when there is more to report." He signed off. The conversation was over.

Molotov put down the phone. He thought for a moment.

Should he take the news to Stalin? Better not. He might find in it a crazy reason to purge Dmitri.

14

The students debate, 1948

At the end of December 1947 Henry Wallace announced by radio from Chicago that he would run for president. The Progressive Citizens of America immediately disclosed its plans: The political organization that for two years had promoted socialist domestic programs and a pro-Soviet foreign policy would forthwith dissolve and reincorporate as a national political party—the Progressive Party. It would schedule a national convention in Philadelphia in July for the purpose of naming its own national candidates.

On his return to Washington from Chicago, candidate Wallace spoke to a crowded press conference and gave his political agenda. The primary aim of his program, Wallace stressed, was the search for a diplomatic solution to differences between East and West. A photograph of Henry Wallace at his press conference appeared in the Columbia *Spectator*. Seated at the far end of the second row of journalists facing Wallace was Tom Scott, president of Columbia's Young Progressives Organization. Identified among others, seated to the candidate's left, was Professor Pierre Enfils of Johns Hopkins.

As chairman of the Progressive Party of the Columbia Political Union, Scott was very active. The campus hummed with political life, led—in organizational energy and scheduled activities—by the Young Progressives. They were unencumbered by such dissipations of political purpose that trace to factional strife. The Young Progressives were united—for Henry Wallace. Campus Democrats, by contrast, were restless under the national leadership of incumbent president Harry Truman, who had polled only 20 percent support from Columbia's student Democrats asked whom they would favor as the presidential candidate in 1948. The Republicans were braced for hard primary campaigns ahead, waged by Senator Robert Taft, the Republican leader in the Senate, beloved of orthodox Republicans; New York state governor Thomas E. Dewey, who had run for president against FDR in 1944, popular with moderate Republicans and with the Time Life publishing empire; and former governor of Minnesota Harold Stassen, with a huge following among young Republicans and GOP Midwestern populists.

The Columbia Political Union's nine hundred members were enrolled in three parties—Progressive, Liberal, and Conservative. At Miller Theatre partisans collided at their weekly meetings, debating the disputes of the day. They quarreled over the recently proposed bill that would criminalize membership in any organization committed to the overthrow of the government. They debated Senator Taft's proposed reforms in labor law, the projected Taft-Hartley Act. They argued over how much authority should be given to the United Nations, now formally ensconced in Manhattan.

The typical debate featured a visiting speaker who would plead the posted resolution for twenty minutes (sometimes the president had ever so gently to gavel him down when he seriously overran the time he was given). He was followed by three student speakers, one from each party. Inevitably they divided on house resolutions, one or two speakers in favor, one or two opposed. Rising from the floor, members would then direct questions to the speaker and contribute their own comments. ("If we vote in favor of Taft-Hartley we are identifying ourselves with a movement that wants to castrate the labor union movement!" "The speaker clearly hasn't read the act. Why deny to workers, *just because they are union members,* the right we have— even as students.") At the close of the session, often after heated debate, came the vote on the resolution.

The union's executive committee met early in January to make up a schedule for the spring semester and decide whom to invite and what resolutions to debate.

Tom Scott had twice argued in the *Spectator* that the Communist

Party U.S.A. should be treated as simply another American political party, not as a subversive organization. In a guest column written for the *Spectator*, he argued that the Bill of Rights and the protocols of democratic practice required the recognition of the Communist Party "at every level, as a voluntary organization, promoting its own positions, set forth by its own officials and candidates."

It didn't surprise the executive committee members, seated around a table at Hamilton Hall in a classroom used for seminars, when Tom Scott, cigarette in hand, proposed inviting Gus Hall, president of the Communist Party, to address the Political Union. Harry Bontecou, as vice president of the Conservatives, objected forcefully. "The Communist Party U.S.A. is *not* an independent party. It's an agent of the Soviet Union. If it *were* independent, we'd go along."

Scott replied fervently that there was no firm evidence of any such link. "And if it's an open question — 'Is the CPUSA independent or isn't it?' — the business of a politically interested body like ours — after all, that is what we are, the Columbia *Political* Union — is to — *inquire.*" The format of union proceedings provided "ideal auspices" for open discussion. And who was better equipped to stand up to such questioning than Gus Hall? "Let him have his say. Is that a pro-Communist position, to permit somebody to speak?"

Bontecou argued his position tenaciously. "That which is known should not be approached as if it were unknown." It was *known*, he insisted, that the Communist Party was a Moscow-run operation.

After a half hour, Ed Tucker, the president, suggested an alternative. "Why don't we schedule a debate on the question 'Resolved, That the Political Union should invite Gus Hall, the head of the Communist Party of America, to address the Political Union'?"

Scott asked for a five-minute adjournment to consult with his colleagues. He and his lieutenants went into an adjacent room. Harry turned to Chris Russo, seated on his left. They spoke in quiet voices, out of hearing of the president at the other end of the table. Russo was Conservative Party president.

"What do you think?"

"We'd obviously lose. All they have to do is bring up the First Amendment and stroke that violin good and hard — and we lose the house."

"So?" Lionel Spitz, the party parliamentarian leaned over, "We can still get the important things said. What's *important* is to bear down on the Wallace movement, stress its subordination to the party line."

"We don't have the votes in the executive committee to block the debate. So let's think about the guest speaker. Maybe invite one of the senators or congressmen supporting the Mundt-Nixon Bill outlawing the Communist Party." Spitz listed a few names: Senators Pat McCarran—Howard McGrath—James Eastland—Herbert O'Conor—"

"What about going with a faculty speaker? Willmoore Sherrill would be great," Harry said.

His associates agreed. "Let's hold out for that. We had two Progressive speakers last fall, and one of them was Emerson"—the reference was to an ardent Progressive from the law school faculty.

Conservative Party president Russo called out to Tucker at the end of the long table: "We'll go along with the resolution," he said—"provided we get to name the speaker."

The Progressive cadre returned. Scott sat down, lit another cigarette, and announced in grumpy tones, "We'll go along with the resolution." Confronted by the Conservative claim to precedence in naming the speaker, Scott froze. *Nothing doing.* The wrangling went on into deadlock. Tucker called for a lunch break and an opportunity for the principal antagonists—the Progressives and the Conservatives—to caucus.

"Here's an idea you can take with you to lunch," Tucker said. "Cancel the visiting speaker. Let the whole evening be handled by student speakers." An hour later, returned from the break, the parties agreed. Scott would speak first, Bontecou next.

The debate was scheduled for March 18, 1948. On March 10, Foreign Minister Jan Masaryk of Czechoslovakia, son of the republic's founding father and the voice of Czech resistance to operational Communist control, was found dead, three floors down from the apartment he occupied in the Foreign Ministry Building.

That was the end of such resistance as the traditionalist liberals had been able to maintain against the colossus of postwar Soviet power. Masaryk was dead! Who was left to lead opposition to Communist control?

The coalition government was dissolved. The Communist Party now exercised undisputed power. The purge of the opposition began. The "Czech coup" had taken place: Czechoslovakia was now behind the Iron Curtain. Ten years after the Nazis had asserted claim to the Czech Sudetenland and, a few months later, to the entire Czech Republic.

Sentiment at Columbia was preponderantly critical of the fake suicide, but opinion was not undivided. Scott issued a press release from the offices of the Young Progressives urging a calm view of the Czech drama. He warned against jumping to "warmongering conclusions." He asked whether anyone could presume to pass conclusive judgment on the Czech development without first investigating the charges, "widely circulated in Europe," that Masaryk had been found in collusion with neofascist elements to engage in repressive counterrevolutionary activity. There was heated talk in Congress. Outraged members dismissed as transparently unpersuasive the hollow Soviet claim that Masaryk's defenestration had been his own doing.

Two days after the coup, the Political Union convened. Anticipating the heavy demand for seats in the heated political atmosphere, the secretary declined to admit nonmembers until five minutes before the program was to begin. Membership cards were examined as students filed through two entrances to the hall. At both doors Young Progressives handed out a pamphlet, with excerpts of spoken and written views of prominent Americans, mostly academic figures, who had spoken out against the projected prosecutions of the Communist American leaders under the Smith Act, which forbade conspiracy to overthrow the Constitution. The students made their way to their seats with excited anticipatory chatter. But quickly they fell silent. The large hall was packed. Two dozen nonmembers stood in the rear of the hall.

Only a few minutes behind schedule, President Tucker called the house to order. He read out the resolution, written and punctuated according to high Oxford University debate protocols: "Resolved, That this house should invite to speak the president of the Communist Party of the United States."

Ed Tucker was from Georgia. When he was speaking to more than three people his Southern accent deepened. He was affable, relaxed, and quick witted. "We figgered it's our problem, not any outsiders' problem, to talk about who we want to inviyate to speak. So we're going to hear from students of Columbia, not from outsiders." First, he said, the president of the Progressives, Tom Scott. Then, for the Conservatives, vice president Harry Bontecou. "I don't really care *who* wins this debate; I think we're going to have a *great* evening. Tom, you all go ahead. Ten minutes."

Tom Scott devoted the first half of his time to recalling American figures who in their day had been thought alien and seditious. He reminded the audience of the terrible Alien and Sedition Act passed under President John Adams. He spoke of efforts attempted before the Civil War to silence those who took unconventional positions. He spoke of the persecution of the Wobblies before and after the First World War. Of the Palmer Raids in 1920. He cited the prominent civil-rights scholars who opposed any disqualification of the Communist Party to participate in the great national debate, to compete for the opinions of free men. And concluded: "Do we want to do that bit all over again?"

He turned finally to face Harry Bontecou, sitting in the front-row right, spokesman, that night, for the hundred-odd Conservative Party members.

"I do believe, Mr. President, that after we are through with this debate tonight with the antidemocrats, we ought to schedule a debate for the next session.

"I am convinced that the arguments for illegitimizing the Republican Party," he said, just a trace of a smile on his face, "are every bit as convincing as those that would forbid the Communist Party." There was laughter. "No one seriously doubts that the GOP is engaged in class warfare and that its policies are substantially, perhaps even critically, influenced by the all-powerful munitions makers who lust for another world war." There was scattered applause.

Scott was staring him in the face: "I call upon Mr. Bontecou, whose subversive demagogy you are fated to hear, to make his fascistic case."

That was tough language, even for the PU. The applause was more tepid than Tom Scott expected, more robust than the Conservatives thought tolerable.

　　　　　　　　　　　WILLIAM F. BUCKLEY JR.

Harry Bontecou was pale. The applause from the Conservative ranks was tentative, apprehensive. When he began speaking there was a strain in his voice. Student speakers were permitted, under union rules, to consult notes, not text. Harry scanned his notes briefly.

He began by recounting what had happened one year earlier at Berkeley, in California. A student political organization announced two scheduled events. The first was to feature George Hamilton Hughes, the self-proclaimed Nazi, the founder, in North Dakota, of the "U.S. National Socialist Party." At the succeeding session, the speaker would be Gus Hall, president of the Communist Party.

Harry's voice matured into a more stable pitch, the tone becoming forceful but never strident. What happened—as Harry told the story to the packed, attentive house—was that soon after hearing the news of the invitations, John Meng, the chancellor of Berkeley, released for circulation in the university an open letter to the student body.

Dr. Meng had begun by saying that he would not interfere with the students' right to invite whomsoever they chose to come to Berkeley, but that—Harry consulted his notes—" 'to accord these undistinguished visitors anything more demonstrative than a shudder of polite disgust would be to attribute to their presence a totally fictitious importance.' "

Harry told how Chancellor Meng had then called on the faculty of Berkeley to join with him in making an appropriate demonstration on the day that Hamilton Hughes arrived: Faculty and students would remove to a synagogue to participate in a memorial service for the millions of victims of Nazism and Communism.

"You have read what Mr. Gus Hall said about what happened in Czechoslovakia last week," Harry reminded them. " 'A counterfascist victory.' " Harry asked the assembly whether they expected to hear anything from Mr. Hall they did not already know a Communist official would say.

He turned his head up slightly, looking now at the heavy Gothic woodwork above the head of the presiding president. "Communists in America or elsewhere, whether native or Soviet, come to recapitulate their dogmas, to press their drive to coopt the moral slogans of the West, and to practice their science of confusion. Yes, we of the Conservative Party concede that Communists are fit objects of curiosity, but only for practicing social scientists"—some boos were heard—"who inquire into the darker mysteries of the human temperament. This organization isn't a psychological laboratory."

He asked whether one could expect to satisfy political and, indeed, intellectual curiosity when inviting to speak someone whose views were entirely synchronized with the "unflinching even if erratic" will of Joseph Stalin, who "only nine years ago declared his friendship with Adolf Hitler." What service was being performed by inviting the head of the Communist Party to speak if he could say nothing attributable to any thought that originated with him? An invitation to a self-proclaimed Communist served "only an extrinsic point—the affirmation of the students' administrative right to invite whomsoever they choose. But that right is not being challenged at Columbia any more than it was at Berkeley."

He closed solemnly: "And yet they are human beings. Few of us are practiced at giving that 'shudder of polite disgust' recommended by Dr. Meng. How then do you treat a Communist we have ourselves invited? We can jeer him. Some may treat him with that terrible coldness that says that we can't, at our level of attainment, take seriously a man who seeks out and works for an ideological kingdom which it is the very purpose of our education to know to despise. Why then bring him here, if no purpose can be served by doing so, and if the only result can be that we will humiliate ourselves and him?"

Harry looked now at the Chair. "Fight him, fight the tyrants everywhere; but do not ask them to our quarters merely to spit on them, and do not ask them to our quarters if we can't spit on them. To do the one is to ambush a human being as one might a rabid dog; to do the other is to ambush ourselves—into breaking faith with humanity."

The hall was in an uproar. There were jeers and catcalls but also wild applause. President Tucker struggled a full two minutes to get silence. Succeeding speakers tried but did not succeed in recapturing attention.

The vote that night detonated on campus the next day when news of it got out. The verdict—to deny Gus Hall an invitation—was a story in the *New York Times.*

Two days later, Tom Scott announced that the Columbia Young Progressives had extended an invitation to Gus Hall to appear on campus under the Progressives' sponsorship.

WILLIAM F. BUCKLEY JR.

15

Underground maneuvers

"Dell?" The phone rang in the corner office rented only ten weeks ago and awash with campaign posters and buttons and brochures and yesterday's paper coffee cups.

"Yeah, this is Dell. Victor?"

"Dell, you are a *true* asshole."

"Stop making love, Victor. I'm spoken for. What you want, boy?"

"I'm talking about the list of convention speakers published in the *Times*. So we put you in charge of the Arrangements Committee in Philadelphia and who do you line up to nominate Henry Wallace? Humberto Stover!"

"What's the matter with Humberto?"

Victor put down the telephone and lit a cigarette. He needed a breather, even a few seconds. "*What's the matter with Humberto Stover?*" Was it possible the dumb sonofabitch didn't *know*? "Stover is— was—a paid-up party member. Yes, we know all about our neat little party-member ploy. So do most people seriously involved in our business."

The Communist Party had made an internal move attempting lightly to frustrate the FBI and others in search of Communist Party members. The new rules were: Any individual membership was automatically rescinded if anybody got officially curious. Vaporized! "Nobody, except maybe Gus Hall, is documentably a 'member of the party.' Oh, yes. And Stalin, of course. Dell, you know what I could lay my hands on, with only maybe ten minutes' research?"

"What, Victor?" Dell's voice was quieter.

"I could give you the party *card number* for Humberto before it was deactivated. It's just *that* dumb what you did. I can't believe somebody else, some journalist, isn't going to come up with Humberto's party record. The FBI—*somebody*—will leak it. The press is moving in on our Philadelphia convention, and now you give them as lead-off nominator for Henry Wallace somebody who is—was—is—what the hell—a member of the Communist Party U.S.A.!"

"Victor, I was wrong, I know. But Stover is tops with labor unions, tops with the academic set, fought in Spain, I mean he's Hollywood made for that first speech. And anyway, it's too late to change, Victor." Dell sounded truly repentant, waved away the volunteer clerk who had tried to come in to take something from the file. ("*Shut the door!*" he hissed out at her.)

"*I know it's too late to change,* Dell. Michelangelo Dellabocca. Should have called you Bocca, not Dell. Look. There is one chance in about one thousand that nobody will pick it up. Humberto has a following and moves in good circles. So the first thing: Don't mention his party background to *one living human being.* Don't even mention it to Gus. He likes to think he knows everything about what's going to happen in Philadelphia, but he's left the program part of it to us. Yes, he's the boss, and the platform will be checked out through Gus. But—again, it's just a *possibility*—he may just not happen to *know* about Humberto. The other guys you picked to second the nomination are okay. Usual types. Well, let us pray."

Dell could begin to feel the morning heat in New York in this room without fan or air conditioner. But he picked himself up enough to be able to say, jocularly, "Let us *what,* Victor?"

"Fuck you, Dell. No. I should pray? Okay. Lord, will thee please *fuck Dell?* I'll call tomorrow."

Victor put out his cigarette and placed another call. It was Sunday—only two weeks to go before the convention opened in Philadelphia. The Wallace team worked every day—and Max would be home, safely out of the way of the House Committee on Un-American Activities, where he worked, blissfully undetected as a clandestine Communist.

"Max? Victor. . . . Fine, fine, thanks. She's fine. Now Max, I want you to do me another favor. It's a pretty simple one. You still get to see the committee files when you want to? Yes? Well look, I want to know just one thing. In the file for Humberto W. Stover, S-t-o-v-e-r, do they have his card number? 'There is no party member.' But I happen to know that Humberto Stover's number was floating around just a couple of years ago, and maybe one of your HUAC people got hold of it. I know, I *know* it's risky. What the hell, Max, we're in a risky business. World revolution isn't for sarsaparilla types. *I* take risks, *you* take risks. I really want this information, Max. Okay? . . . Great. Good man, Max. We really appreciate what you do."

Harry was at home at Eighty-seventh Street, seated in the great armchair that had belonged to his father, drinking coffee, when the Saturday afternoon paper came. It gave the text of the Progressive Party platform for 1948. It would be ratified, the story said, in Philadelphia on the first day of the convention, a week from Monday.

Harry was astonished by the platform's planks. "I mean, Mom, what's surprising is how they *almost* succeed in avoiding doublespeak. I mean, it's all right there—the Communist Party platform on foreign policy is the platform policy of the Progressive Party—allegedly a United States–driven political movement. Its only consistency is that it favors every plank of Soviet foreign policy." Dorothy Bontecou, protected by an apron, was kneading dough while her eyes focused from time to time through her eyeglasses on a recipe pinned by a thumbtack to the cupboard above the work area. But she looked down to answer her son.

"What's in it, Harry?"

"Okay. Sit tight."

"I can't sit tight when I'm making a pie, Harry."

"Listen, Mom. I'm quoting. The Progressive Party wants 'Negotiation and discussion with the Soviet Union to find an agreement to win the peace.'"

"What's the matter with that?"

"Mom. Please. Next, 'Repeal of the peacetime draft.' Next. 'Repudiation of the Truman Doctrine and an end to military and economic intervention in support of fascist regimes in China, Greece, Turkey, the Middle East, and Latin America.'"

"Next. 'Abandonment of military bases designed to encircle and intimidate other nations.' Then, 'Repeal of the National Security Act provisions which are mobilizing the nation for war, preparing a labor draft, and organizing a monopoly militant dictatorship.'"

He paused and looked through the doorway at his mother.

"So Harry Truman, Mom—in case it escaped your notice—is 'organizing for a monopoly militant dictatorship.'"

His mother didn't comment.

"More. 'Repudiation of the Marshall Plan and in its place creation of a UN reconstruction and development fund.' They want 'destruction of existing atomic bomb stockpiles. . . . Support of all colonial peoples throughout the world for independence, including Puerto Rico, Africa, Asia, West Indies, Korea.'"

"Isn't that right, Harry?"

"The point, Mom, is they don't talk about freedom for Poland or Bulgaria or Romania or Czechoslovakia or East Germany."

"Will they get anywhere, Harry?" Mrs. Bontecou was now in the kitchen doorway, wiping her hands with a washrag.

"Wallace isn't going to win the election, if that's what you mean. But the Progressives are predicting ten million votes. What hurts is the high-profile people they've got backing the party. Professors, scientists, artists, critics." He ran his eyes down the news story. "Everybody's in the picture. Academics from NYU, Harvard, Yale, Williams . . . These are *educators*."

"What are you going to do about it?"

He broke the news to her. He and Chris Russo had made their plans. "As soon as we get out of class in June, we're going to do research on the people who are running the Progressive Party. Do you know who Sidney Hook is, Mom?"

"Of course."

"Well, on top of being a well-known philosophy professor, he's been a very active anti-Communist. He served on the Dewey Commission exposing the Moscow purge trials. Listen to this, I found out that last week he went to Princeton and spent two hours with Einstein. You know Einstein is a backer of the Wallace movement? Well, Chris Russo's father knows James Burnham, the professor—he was also at NYU—who wrote *The Managerial Revolution*. He's a superinformed anti-Communist, and he told Mr. Russo—Chris's father—that Hook pleaded with Einstein to get out of the Wallace movement."

"Did he make any progress?"

"Einstein listened. He admires Hook. But apparently Hook couldn't get Einstein past the basic problem, which is that Moscow is a socialist society and Einstein is a socialist, so why shouldn't he be pro-Russian? But of course Sidney Hook is a socialist too. What I imagine Hook said to Einstein was that what's important about the Soviet Union isn't that they have nationalized the sources of production and exchange, to quote from the socialist kindergarten. It's that they suppress human freedom and torture and imprison and kill. What has to be done is get to the key people—the intellectuals, I mean, the intellectuals who are making the mistake. Talk to them and get them when they look at Moscow to look through the socialist state to the repressive state. Erik Chadinoff—you remember him? at Camp Plattling? the doctor who was court-martialed and did six months in the brig— has promised to come down to Philadelphia for the convention. He's a magnetic guy. I wish Einstein could talk with Chadinoff."

The doorbell rang.

"That would be Elinor," his mother said. "You can get your mind off politics."

Harry got up and went to the door. At the end of the room he turned suddenly.

"Mom? How do I look?"

"Dazzling."

Harry gave a little yelp of joy as he opened the door to Elinor.

16

Herrendon and Harry comment

Herrendon had gone over the material Harry had given him, saved from his college years. He turned to Harry, "You had an intimate experience there, I know, with fellow traveling, back when you were a Columbia student. I knew Enfils. Very bright. When he wrote that book he was less cautious than later on. Ten years later, he'd have watched his step in talking about the show trials that way."

"Was he a party member?"

"I don't know. And, really, it never greatly mattered. The party sometimes wanted some of its . . . friends to take membership—it gave the party a more disciplinary hold on them. And some friends of the Soviet enterprise wanted to be members of the party in a comparable sense of some people wanting to be priests or monks—to identify themselves plainspokenly with the cause. Enfils—I don't remember what came of him—was useful to the party, up through the Wallace years."

"Wallace, yes. Henry Agard Wallace. His campaign was the loftiest you people ever got. But finally it was a fiasco; or was it?"

BOOK TWO

PART TWO

McCarthy at Wheeling

Joe McCarthy never ducked the political party speech assignments. Lincoln's Birthday was a great ritual day for the GOP, just the right day for political oratory, poignant, fiery, nostalgic, orotund, challenging, the more of everything the better. When the GOP chairman made out the roster for Lincoln's Birthday, 1950, he was careful to stroke lobbies scattered about the country that clamored for special attention.

The year was heavy with political passion. It was generally thought that Harry Truman's victory in 1948 had been something of a fluke. Republican pols agreed that they had lost the White House because, as Representative Everett Dirksen put it with characteristic color, "We were hit by a concatenation of forces." What had happened was a spunky performance by Truman, who denounced the "do-nothing Eightieth Congress," summoning the legislators back to the sweaty capital to stare, poutful but noncompliant, at Truman's agenda.

That and (Everett Dirksen would concede in private conversation) a self-indulgent, vapid campaign by challenger Thomas E. Dewey of New York. "The future lies before us" was a Dewey line much quoted by the derisory legions left desolate by his failure to recapture the White House for the GOP, which went now for the *fifth* consecutive time to the Democrats.

Internationally, Europe was slowly rebuilding, but the looming figure was Joseph Stalin. He had lost his bid to win Italy in the 1948 election, but Communism continued to threaten, there and in France; and the captive nations, as they were now regularly referred to, despaired of liberation. In New York City there were clots of Romanians and Bulgarians, Poles and Lithuanians and Latvians, Estonians and Czechoslovakians who did what they could, which was not much, to keep a candle lit in memory of the forgotten purpose of the war declared by Great Britain against Germany on September 3, 1939—to maintain Polish independence. All liberty or prospect of it had been forfeited to an Iron Curtain.

There were Republican activists in the House of Representatives. Joseph Martin of Massachusetts, the minority leader, had a long memory. California's Richard Nixon was the rising star who had played the critical role in the House Committee on Un-American Activities' development of the historical case against diplomat-bureaucrat Alger Hiss, now convicted of perjury or, in effect, of treason. That case, the most prolonged and dramatic in American postwar political history, had decisively divided the community, the common man persuaded of his guilt, much of the academic class and the social elite committed, in the name of the integrity of the New Deal, to his innocence.

But mostly, Lincoln's Birthday cities put in to hear a GOP senator. It was the job of the GOP chairman to match postulant cities to individual senators. It was in the first week of February that Senator Joe McCarthy learned that he was to speak at Wheeling, West Virginia.

"Where is Wheeling?"

"Well, Joe," Mary Haskell responded. She was his gray-haired, no-nonsense office manager, with the wry smile. "Wheeling, West Virginia, is about eight hundred miles east southeast of Appleton, Wisconsin, and about the same size."

"You have a nice way of clamming me up, Mary."

"I wish I could patent it."

"I guess the date is absolutely fixed?"

"It is absolutely fixed. You gave your word in January you'd accept whatever assignment the GOP gave you. West Virginia is Democratic country and in 1948 went for Truman. Tom Sweeney is a peppy Republican chairman in Wheeling, and the newspaper will give you good coverage."

He was met at the airport in Wheeling by Tom Sweeney, a business-man who had run unsuccessfully for the Senate and now served as local GOP head. He ushered McCarthy into his Buick Roadmaster and, driving off, asked what he was going to talk about. He had two speeches in his briefcase, the senator said, one on public housing, the second on the loyalty issue.

"Do you talk about Fuchs in the loyalty speech?"

"Yes," said McCarthy. He made reference to Klaus Fuchs, arrested early in the month for stealing atomic secrets from Los Alamos and passing them to a Soviet spy ring. Four days earlier, President Truman had announced his intention to build a hydrogen bomb. The Soviets had got off an atomic explosion in August the year before. "Is there any secret left that hasn't been stolen from us?" Sweeney wanted to know. And added quickly, "Did you see the polls, Senator?"

Joe: "Which polls?"

"A *Fortune* poll says ten percent of the U.S. think the Communist Party is close to wielding decisive power, that there is nowhere we can effectively stop them anymore."

"Ten percent isn't many. Only what, twenty-four, twenty-five mil-lion?"

"No, but thirty-five percent think the party is growing and that Communists are exercising control in key government posts."

"My speech on the loyalty issue charges that there are Commu-nists in government, known to the secretary of state to *be* Com-munists, who were nevertheless undischarged."

"That's the speech you got to give us, Joe. And station WWVA is ready to broadcast it. Have you got a spare copy?"

They pulled into the hotel. McCarthy plopped his briefcase on the registration desk and, while Sweeney was checking him in, pulled out a thirteen-page speech.

He didn't immediately release his hold on it. "This is very impor-tant stuff, Tom. I thought maybe of holding it for Reno—that's actu-ally Lincoln's birthday, Thursday."

"I'd really like to have you give it tonight. It's an important day for us."

McCarthy loosened his grip on the manuscript. What the heck. The people in Reno wouldn't know he had already given it in Wheel-ing. And vice versa.

He went up to his suite. He had got used to being given a suite when he spoke here and there — the way to treat a senator. Different from what he had got used to *running* for the Senate, let alone for judge! He welcomed the difference as he took off his shirt and, in his underclothes, fiddled with his manuscript. He found it providential that, above his king-size bed, there was a framed photograph of Abraham Lincoln, looking dolorous as ever. An appropriate expression, McCarthy thought, for February 1950. A hundred years ago all they had to worry about was slavery and the Missouri Compromise. But it was time to go to work. He dressed, and soon the phone rang. They were ready for him.

His talk was written out in rough draft, thirteen pages, just under a half hour. But he spoke grave words, and he felt the lift of the audience, at once that of alarm and that of satisfaction at being told what it was that would explain it all. He had a sense of it, that his message, this time around, would resonate.

There would be very long and heated debates over exactly what he said that night. The radio station that broadcast his talk erased the tape the next morning, routine practice. Nobody questioned the thrust of what he said. "I have here in my hand a list of — [205?] — [57?] — a list of names that were made known to the secretary of state as being members of the Communist Party and who nevertheless are still working and shaping policy in the State Department." Later, Joe McCarthy said he had spoken of "loyalty risks." Whatever the exact wording, his speech to 275 members of the Ohio County Republican Women's Club in the Colonnade Room of the McClure Hotel charged that United States foreign policy was being affected by the operations of men and women disloyal to the United States and tolerated by their employers.

Joe McCarthy's Eastern Airlines DC-4 wouldn't arrive back in Washington from Wheeling until just before noon. He'd have twenty-four hours before leaving for his two other Lincoln Day speeches, both in Nevada. From his hotel room he called Mary Haskell at the office, just after nine. She told him he had several calls, mostly from reporters. "I'll give you the call slips when you come in. But you may want to call back Tom Coleman, maybe from the hotel before you go to the airport."

"Tom always gets priority."

"Yes. But he pays for it, dear Tom," Mary said. "Your number one Wisconsin backer, Tom. He put the call in himself. He's at home. Got the number?"

Joe said he did, and put in the call. It was the first time he had submitted to an interrogation concerning last night's speech. He'd need to practice saying it more succinctly, he reflected fifteen minutes later.

"Yes. Yes, Tom. I did say that. I said there are Communists—loyalty risks—in the State Department and almost certainly everywhere else. I have the list. . . . I actually have *two* lists. One list is made up of people acknowledged by Jimmy Byrnes—yes, when he was secretary of state, 1946—as loyalty risks but haven't been fired. . . . What? Right. Right. They hadn't been fired when Byrnes wrote that letter— . . . Are they fired now? . . . Yes. I *know* it's been four years. But we know how the State Department is, especially under Red Dean Acheson— . . . Yes, the other list is more current, Bob Lee's list. Bob is with House Appropriations— How do I know they're still there? Tom, Tom, you *do* remember that Truman in 1948 froze all congressional investigations into executive personnel—denied us access to *all* the security files. So the assumption is they're all *still there.* . . . Yes, I'll make that clear. I'll be talking in Reno tomorrow, same general pitch. . . . Good, Tom. Give my love to Josephine."

One week later Joe was back in his office. It was Marge on the switchboard, yet again, maybe the tenth time since he had come in. "Mr. Tom Sweeney, Senator. Says you told him to call you."

McCarthy sighed—he had been interrupted ten times in the hour he had set aside to read the three morning papers.

But he liked the excited pep in Sweeney's voice, and reacted to it by saying, "How'm I doing, Tom?"

"That was a shot heard 'round the world, Joe."

"You're telling me, Tom. It's total war."

"And we've got to win this one, Joe."

"Yeah, we do. But you know what, Tom, I got to sign off. Another phone's ringing, and I got to take that call." It was only Mary Haskell, but she plopped a dozen phone slips on his desk.

18

J. Edgar Hoover calls McCarthy

Immediately after he had landed in Washington, Joe McCarthy began to walk toward the baggage room behind the airport's ticket counters. A man stepped in front of him. He was tall, of middle age, and wore a heavy winter coat and a fedora. He extended a card in his hand. "Excuse me, Senator. I'm Agent Danielson, FBI. I've been instructed to hand you this letter. Director's office."

McCarthy nodded and put the letter in his pocket. "Thanks. I'll read it in the cab." Joe took the envelope and shook the hand of Agent Danielson.

"Dear Senator McCarthy," he read as the taxi drove off with directions to take him to the Capitol.

> It is most important that I speak with you concerning the speech you gave last night at Wheeling. I will need 1–2 hours with you. I suggest we meet at an address I will subsequently give you either between four and six, or, if you would care to have dinner, between six and eight. Please confirm with Miss Lalley, at DUpont 4226.

Joe McCarthy had never laid eyes on the legendary head of the Federal Bureau of Investigation. But he knew something of the director's singular power and prestige. Everybody knew of them. Through Hoover's office every security file was processed, though the State Department and the National Security Agency had their own investigators. "And whatever you do," senatorial colleague Karl Mundt from South Dakota had told him when first Joe checked in to Washington as a freshly elected senator, "don't cross J. Edgar. Yes, he's a great American. We all know that. But there isn't anybody in town he can't make trouble for, and that includes" — Mundt doffed his hat to the White House as, driving down Pennsylvania Avenue, they passed it by.

Joe confided the summons to his office intimates, Mary Haskell, aide Jean Kerr, and assistant Don Surine. He would go, of course. He wondered which of the options to take.

"Why not go for dinner," Mary said. "For one thing, he'll give you a drink at six, but he certainly wouldn't at four."

At 5:40 the car and driver were waiting for him at the designated spot. McCarthy hadn't inquired where exactly they were going. Some restaurant, probably. But he was driven to a modest brownstone in the Georgetown area. The driver parked the car, opened the car door, and led him to the entrance, opening the door for him.

The director, in double-breasted navy blue blazer, a tiepin holding up his tie knot, his ebony cuff links conspicuous, extended his hand to greet McCarthy. Hoover took his coat and led him into a small drawing room. The heavy door closed. "Can I get you something from the bar, Senator?"

"Thanks. Maybe a bourbon and soda?"

Quickly the director got him the glass, bent down, and lit a fire. McCarthy stayed on his feet.

"Senator, you are onto the most important challenge in the history of the United States."

The director went on through the cocktail hour, through dinner, and for an hour after dinner. He spoke of the loyalty/security problem in the federal government. That was of course basic, he said. But it went beyond loyalty/security. "I can tell you this right now, Senator" — McCarthy had not invited the director to address him as Joe. If he had, that would have implied a reciprocal invitation to address Hoover as Edgar, and Joe could not imagine doing any such thing (like calling the pope Pius, he told Jeanie the next morning). "What was the incidence of Americans who voted for Henry Wallace, one in fifty? I'd wager a year's salary that among federal employees in the State Department it was one in five. What that suggests is an attitude. And it's that attitude that's killing us in China, Korea, Germany, Turkey, Greece—and in Soviet nuclear-development laboratories."

He looked McCarthy directly in the eyes. "You have the message. I felt it when I got the report this morning. Pickups on your speech were placed on my desk throughout the afternoon. You're going to have the ear of the American public. The people out there know what's at stake. They have a sense of what has happened to eastern Europeans, what goes on every day in the Soviet Union. But *our leaders* don't have that intuitive sense. Senator, you may be the critical man of this decade."

Joe McCarthy was driven back to his apartment. When he got in the door he opened a bottle of bourbon. He sat at his desk and closed his eyes. After a few moments, he got up and walked over to his briefcase, removing the text of his Wheeling speech and Don Surine's suggested revision for Reno. He opened the large research folder detailing information on the Bob Lee list of 108 federal employees. He pondered the first on the list, *Esther Brunauer*. He ran his eyes over the data. His eyes traveled down to *Owen Lattimore*. Finally he lay down in his shorts and T-shirt. He recited his mother's prayer. It closed, ". . . and make me, Lord, worthy of thy designs. Amen."

Wheeling Plus Two—for a while McCarthy and company used the term *Wheeling* as the military historians used *D-Day*—called for a speech in Reno. The night before, ABC News had made a brief mention of McCarthy's speech at the Ohio County Women's Club two nights before. The national stir over the Wheeling speech was building. By the next day it was a large national story. When Senator Joe McCarthy deplaned from United Airlines at Reno, Mac Duffie, his host, was at the gate with a telegram received one hour before. He handed it to the senator at the baggage counter, where they stood waiting for his two bags. Joe opened it. It was from Deputy Undersecretary of State John Puerifoy. He turned to his inquisitive host, who quivered with curiosity.

"Department of State," Joe said. "Puerifoy. He wants me to give him the *actual* names of the Communists I spoke about. I mean, the loyalty risks I spoke about. . . . You know—the people I talked about night before last at Wheeling."

The rhetorical shuffling missed Mac Duffie. From "Communists" to "loyalty risks." Months and years of fighting would take place: Which of the two terms had McCarthy used in his Wheeling speech, which had not been recorded. Mac Duffie didn't much care. "That was one hell of a speech, Senator."

"Well, they had it coming."

"How many Communists did you list in that speech? Was it two hundred?"

"God knows how many are there, Mac. There's two sets of people we're after, it's not just 'two hundred and five' and 'fifty-seven.' It's a complicated story. But I don't blame John Puerifoy for being nervous about it. I'll have to cable him a reply. . . . I've got an hour or so in the hotel before the reception, right, Mac?"

"Yes, sure, Senator."

"Call me Joe."

"Sure, Joe."

"I'll need an hour or so. I'll be sending a letter to the president."

"A letter to President Truman?"

"Yes. I'll dictate it to my office. It can be delivered to the White House."

This was very big time, Mac Duffie told himself. He would call Tom Zurkin at the *Reno Gazette-Journal* the minute he dropped the senator off at the hotel.

Joe was taken to his suite, Mac left tactfully, and Joe placed the call to his office. The telephone call to Don Surine seemed endless. Don Surine was a former FBI agent, in his early thirties, dark haired, sturdy in build, serious in manner. He had just joined up with McCarthy. He was tenacious but also fastidious, and he wanted to know exactly how to handle, now, the confusion over exactly what his employer had said at Wheeling. Surine knew that McCarthy often departed from texts, improvising freely. He simply did not know exactly what figure he had used or the exact wording of his charge. The most stringent version was that Secretary of State Dean Acheson continued to head up a State Department where 205 employees were members of the Communist Party. The most moderate version was that 57 employees of the State Department were loyalty risks.

"We got to get it straight on the numbers. Let's decide which of the lists you want to stick with, Joe. What's the figure you're using in the speech tonight?"

"Fifty-seven."

"Should we stick with that, Joe?"

McCarthy was a little irritated. "The place has got to be crawling with them. We've seen Bob Lee's report. And he was talking about just the State Department. My guess is they're all over the place. We've just scratched the surface on this question. We now — finally — have some idea why our side is losing all over the world. Because the let's-go-easy-on-the-Communists people are influencing policy."

"God knows I agree with you, Joe. But what're you going to do about Puerifoy? His telegram was leaked to the *Post*."

"I'm going to reply directly to Truman."

"What're you going to say?"

"Put Mary on the line. I'll dictate to her. I've got it written out here. She'll show it to you. Send it by messenger to the White House. Okay?"

"Okay. Here's Mary."

Joe began to dictate. He described his list and said, "This list is available to you, but you can get a much longer list by ordering Secretary Acheson to give you a list of those whom your board listed as being disloyal and who are still working in the State Department." He went on to say that only 80 out of 300 State Department employees certified for discharge had actually been let go. He added, ". . . presumably after a lengthy consultation with Alger Hiss." He interrupted himself after dictating that line.

"Like that, Mary?"

"Yeah, Joe. And the president will of course love it. What's it been, three weeks since Hiss was convicted? Two years since Truman said the Hiss case was a red herring?"

McCarthy finished his letter by requesting the president to revoke his 1948 order sealing the loyalty files. That famous presidential order, issued under executive authority, forbade any interrogation of executive personnel by legislators. Truman had reacted against efforts by the House Committee on Un-American Activities to probe the security files of State Department and other personnel. If he refused to revoke that order, President Truman would be labeling the Democratic Party "the protector of international Communism."

"Why not make that 'the bedfellow of international Communism,' Joe?"

"Good. The 'bedfellow of international Communism.' Now put me back to Don, Mary."

He came on. "Don? Look, the other side is playing pretty dirty. You knew about Puerifoy's letter to me before I actually read it. Let's show them we can play that game too. Let's release my letter to the press."

"Anybody in particular?"

"We want instant action on it. AP."

"I'll give it to George Backer. Know Backer, Joe?"

"Hell, yes, he was in the marines."

"Get wet crossing the equator?"

"Fuck you, Don."

"Will do, Senator."

19

McCarthy defends
his Wheeling charges

At 9:45, carrying a bulky manila folder, Senator Joe McCarthy opened
the door of his office to begin the long marbled walk to the Senate
chamber. The day had come, just eleven days after the Wheeling
speech, when the full Senate would hear out "McCarthy's charges"
and decide how to proceed. The august body seldom moved so fast,
but there was a national clamor: Investigate McCarthy's charges.
Majority leader Scott Lucas interrupted the calendar. McCarthy
would make his charges to the entire body.

Don Surine and Mary walked with him as far as the elevator.
There Surine extended his hand. "Give 'em hell, Senator." Mary
angled herself for a quick kiss on the forehead. She had sneaked a
folded handkerchief into his vest pocket. "Try to dress up our Joe just
a little bit."

"Never used one of these before, Mary. I was saving it for when I
get married. Now they'll confuse me with Cooper." Joe's reference
was to John Sherman Cooper, the picture-perfect solon from Ken-
tucky, conspicuous as a natty dresser.

"No one will confuse you with Senator Cooper," Mary said, backing away from the elevator door as it opened.

Waiting at the lobby were a half dozen photographers and as
many reporters. One middle-aged woman in a long skirt, her hair

tightly contained in a bun, writing pad in hand, came to within a few feet of the senator, walking alongside to keep pace.

"What are you going to tell them, Senator? You got any new names?"

"Excuse me, ma'am, but I've got to get to the chamber. You'll hear everything I have to say."

A voice from another reporter overrode. "You got anything on the White House, Senator? On President Truman?"

He succeeded in catching Joe's attention.

"He's made some mistakes. But—" Joe was rescued by his colleague, Senator Homer Capehart, approaching the chamber along with a dozen other senators.

"Let's get along, Joe. There's plenty of time later." Senator Capehart had had long experience with importunate reporters. He smiled, brushed them to one side, and propelled Joe McCarthy down into the Senate subway.

A few minutes later, they entered the sacred chamber. It was very nearly full. Joe sensed genuine anticipation. The smell of it brought both drama and spice. The constant routine, the aides in their neat jackets and ties buzzing about silently with their folders and messages, the little drone from the press gallery, like an orchestra tuning up. He passed by the desk of Senator Wherry, who caught his coat sleeve and said, "Let's hear it all, Joe. I'm listening." Joe smiled broadly, tapped his manila folder. "See you later, Ken."

A young newsman seated next to Sam Tilburn, veteran reporter for the *Indianapolis Star,* leaned over in the press gallery to his fellow reporter. "What I don't *really* understand, Sam, is why so many senators are obviously on McCarthy's side. Do they know he's right about Communists in government? Do they hope he's right? What is it?"

"They like the sound of him, they like the national support he's getting. They like it that Truman and Acheson and the liberal bureaucrats are hurting. I mean, it's only ten days since he gave that speech in Wheeling and he's become a national celebrity."

"So it's got nothing to do with anything he's proven?"

"Nothing. He hasn't proven *anything*—yet."

The aged vice president was in the chair and gaveled for the start of proceedings. The Senate chaplain said a prayer. It included an appeal for divine protection against the enemies of the state. Joe's bowed head looked up, registering apparent surprise. Vice President Alben Barkley then acknowledged the majority leader.

"Mr. Lucas has the floor."

Senator Scott Lucas, senior senator from Illinois and Democratic majority leader, rose. He was tall, dignified in bearing. That day he was in good humor, not always the case. He leaned heavily for expert opinion on how to conduct his high office on Senator Russell of Georgia, the member most conversant with Senate business, lore, and indeed arcana. Senator Russell's desk was in the same row, a few desks removed. Russell eyed his protégé expectantly.

Lucas's opening speech was relatively brief. He made three points. The first, that everyone agreed that maximum protection against Communist agents was critically important. The second, that President Truman and Secretary Acheson were very well aware of this and had made every effort to protect the government against penetration by "the enemies of true government, who are friends of tyranny." The third, that the junior senator from Wisconsin had leveled very grave charges against the security system and very direct charges against the security program in the State Department.

"There is some question about exactly how many Communist spies . . . or just plain Communist Party members . . . or loyalty risks whose names the senator says he has, are still in the State Department. I myself have heard 207, 81, and 57. But let's start at the beginning and ask our colleague what it is that makes him allege any such delinquency in the State Department. Sir, will you inform us?"

Joe McCarthy rose. He did not appear to be ill at ease. He had been four years a senator and had engaged in many debates, some of them spirited, one or two acrimonious. With deliberation he opened his folder and began to talk.

When Joe McCarthy was reading his remarks, the voice was monotonic, the speed a little faster than ideal for listening. It was different when he was interrupted. His speech then became lively. An interruption came a few minutes after he had begun his historical description of loyalty/security procedures in the State Department. Senator Benton, the quick-witted, erudite, verbose senator from Connecticut, broke in.

"Can the senator from Wisconsin inform us why the Communists

WILLIAM F. BUCKLEY JR.

have made available only to *him* their roster of agents in the State Department?"

The spurts of laughter from the floor and the galleries broke Joe's rhythm. Lips tightening, he looked over at Benton.

"Maybe under the Truman administration the Communists have become so cocky they figure it doesn't matter *who* they inform about their people, nobody will bother them. Only from now on, the senator from Connecticut may be dismayed to know, they are *not* any longer safe. I," he paused for a moment, then thought to look about the chamber, to share the credit, "and my colleagues—and the American people—will not let it happen. We're going to ruin their day. . . . Now let me get on with it. I have here . . ."

McCarthy's formulation would be imitated for months and years by late-night comedians and talk-show hosts and, indeed, the whole derisive community—"a photostatic copy of—"

Senator McClellan of Arkansas broke in to ask for the history of the State Department's loyalty procedures.

"I was coming to that. I was interrupted by the senator from Connecticut, who wanted to say something reassuring to some of his constituents in Connecticut." A little frown of dismay crossed the face of Senator Knowland of California. It was not lightly suggested, on the floor, that any senator had constituents to whom he pandered, let alone Communist constituents.

McCarthy continued reading again. He sought, he said, to "refresh the recollection" of his colleagues by giving a little of the background of "U.S. efforts to protect itself."

In 1938, "twelve years ago," Congress had passed the McCormack Act, ordering all agents of foreign governments to register with the Department of Justice. That act, said McCarthy, was designed to "blow away the pretenses of American Communists, who were taking their orders from the Soviet Union."

The Hatch Act of 1939, McCarthy reminded the chamber, forbade federal employment to members of any organization that advocated the forcible overthrow of our constitutional government.

"Even though there was a military honeymoon during the war, when Stalin and FDR fought the same enemy," McCarthy went on, "in 1942 the Civil Service Commission came through with loyalty criteria supposed to govern federal agencies in determining whom to hire. That commission set up the criterion of 'reasonable' doubt as to an applicant's loyalty. If reasonable doubt as to the applicant's loyalty and reliability was found, he couldn't be hired." That criterion, McCarthy said, was very important. Yet the Hatch Act had simply been unenforced.

"Whose responsibility is that?" Senator McKeller of Tennessee wanted to know.

"The attorney general, Senator, is supposed to enforce the laws we pass."

The senator nodded. McCarthy continued. He gave an example. "The American League for Peace and Democracy is universally recognized as a Communist front," he reminded them. "It was never anything else. It had been so declared by the attorney general. Yet 537 members of the American League for Peace and Democracy were still in government."

"*Were* still in government, or *are* still in government?" Senator Hubert Humphrey of Minnesota asked.

McCarthy hesitated. He came in with the more dramatic alternative. "*Are* still in government."

"How did you get that number, 537?" Senator Benton wanted to know.

McCarthy flushed. "From the Encyclopaedia Britannica, Senator." Benton was chairman of the board of Encyclopaedia Britannica. The laughs now were at his expense.

However, McCarthy explained, mark this loophole. The Civil Service reasonable-doubt criterion applied only to applicants for government employment, not to those already *in* government. Frustrated by different loyalty/security standards being applied by the departments of the federal government, the attorney general in 1942 created an "Interdepartmental Committee on Investigation."

But it was ineffective, McCarthy said. "It never got its act together." And besides, under its permissive criteria an applicant could not be excluded "unless he personally advocated the overthrow of government by force and violence.

"Gentlemen, Senator Smith," McCarthy said—Margaret Chase Smith, junior senator from Maine, was the only woman in the Senate—"I'm not sure that by using Interdepartmental Committee standards you could exclude anybody. That committee said nobody could join government who was in favor of overthrowing our government

WILLIAM F. BUCKLEY JR.

by force and violence. I mean, is it all that easy, if you're a security officer trying to make a case against an employee or an applicant, to pick up a document that proves that a particular person once said, '*I believe in overthrowing the government of the United States by force and violence*'? I'm not one hundred percent sure you can find that statement signed by Joe Stalin.

"Okay," McCarthy went on. "You think I'm exaggerating. However latitudinarian the Civil Service Commission, in fact its exertions did block access to federal jobs to some Communist employees. With what result? A protest from the Communist-dominated Federal Workers Union.

"Did anybody pay any attention to this protest, a protest from a Communist union? Yes: the Bureau of the Budget. It cut the funds required to implement the loyalty program. And the result was that Communist after Communist worked his way into the assorted wartime agencies."

But the most important development, McCarthy told his colleagues, was the presidential order of March 13, 1948. President Truman's executive order instructed all federal departments to deny to any congressional investigating committee access to loyalty/security files. "The president looked down on Congress and said: 'Go away. We don't want you around messing with our business.' Well, the Soviet Union has been messing with government business, and I believe it is time for the Congress of the United States to assert its responsibility to monitor the executive branch."

Senator McKeller spoke again. He wanted to know what proof there was that Communists had actually *remained* in government since wartime. He was seated next to Senator Benton, who spotted immediately the danger of his colleague's formulation, but before he could enter the exchange in an effort to distract from it, McCarthy pounced.

"*Proof?* The senator from Tennessee wants proof! Senator, are you aware that Alger Hiss was convicted by a federal court as recently as *six weeks ago*? Did you not know that the State Department *and the White House* were *twice* informed about Alger Hiss? Mr. Adolph Berle relayed Whittaker Chambers's report on Hiss to his superiors in 1939. In 1943, Chambers spoke with the FBI, which, we have to assume—is that fair to say, Senator?—passes along the information it gets about subversives to the government officials who employ them. The FBI must have passed its information, dating back to *1939,* to the State Department. How do you account for that, Senator? Well, *I* have an explanation. There are people in the State Department who take the same view in these matters as Paul Appleby, not so long ago an employee of the Bureau of the Budget."

He paused. Waiting for a reaction to the name Paul Appleby. He got none.

"You know what he said? Mr. Appleby? He said—it's in the *Congressional Record,* July 18, 1946—he said, 'A man in the employ of the government has just as much right to be a member of the Communist Party as he has to be a member of the Democratic or Republican Party.' What do you think of that statement, Senator?"

Senator Benton raised his hand and began to speak, but McCarthy did not pause. "And Chambers didn't give just the name of Alger Hiss. He spoke of Lee Pressman and Nathan Witt and John Abt and Charles Kramer, among others. Some of them were still in government; *all* of them have been in government. None of them was ousted from government. Why didn't the loyalty/security division of the State Department catch them? The State Department not only didn't catch Hiss, it *promoted* Hiss. It was Hiss who presided at the opening session of the United Nations!"

McCarthy looked about him. Two of the senators were reading their mail. But most of the rest were listening, and were silent. ("There are two kinds of silent senators," McCarthy later told Jean Kerr at dinner. "There are the senators who are silent because they aren't talking. And there are the senators who are silent because they are actually listening.")

He completed his discussion of Hiss and the State Department. "If an Alger Hiss can slip through the fingers of the State Department with that kind of incriminating evidence sitting around since 1939, maybe we shouldn't be surprised that there should be other Alger Hisses. How would we know?"

The Senate recessed for lunch and resumed its session at two in the afternoon, to adjourn, finally, just before six.

———

Sam Tilburn picked up his telephone in the Senate press gallery and dialed his boss, the editor of the *Indianapolis Star*. The *Star* was a part of the Eugene Pulliam chain. It had been cautiously receptive to McCarthy's charges after Wheeling. Ed Reidy's lead editorial had said,

> Intelligent Americans will simply deduce from the deteriorated position of the west that our policies have been misguided. Who guided them? We mean, obviously, below the glittering surfaces, where one deals with Presidents and Secretaries of State. Did any of our senior counselors have other motives in mind than the advancement of western interests? We believe that this is at the heart of Senator McCarthy's contentions.

Reidy had received a Pulitzer for reporting from China, ten years before. In those reports, which centered on the great Japanese aggression against China, Reidy had emphasized the critical dependence of Japan on its supplies of oil. When President Roosevelt imposed the boycott on selling oil to Japan, Reidy prophesied that Japan would react violently. His story was filed on July 26. Five months later, the Japanese attacked Pearl Harbor.

Reidy was anxious to sustain his reputation as a reliable analyst, and now he gave instructions to his Washington reporter.

At age thirty, Sam Tilburn was a skilled Washington hand. He had lost a leg in a car accident when still a boy (his father, at the wheel, had been killed) and so did not have to give up his post as a young reporter for the *Star* to serve in the army. He spent the war years at his desk, in Washington. Reidy's orders now were to stick to the McCarthy story "until the Communists and their sympathizers are run out of Washington, or until Joe McCarthy is."

"It's going to be a long haul." Tilburn held the telephone mouthpiece close to his lips to make way in a room with twenty reporters using twenty telephones. "I mean, the business of sticking to McCarthy until he shoots them or they shoot him."

"What about today?" Reidy was impatient. "All we got on the ticker was that he had named two suspects. Why didn't he name more?"

"The Senate voted to set up an investigating committee. McCarthy said he would give the names to the committee 'in an orderly manner'"—already Tilburn was skilled at imitating McCarthy's nasal monotone. "He blasted the living hell out of the State Department, Truman, Acheson, and of course Alger Hiss. The arch enemy on the floor was Benton. If there is an early kill, it will be Benton or McCarthy, one or the other."

"Who'll head up the investigating committee?"

"They're talking about Millard Tydings."

"I forget, Tydings. Bright guy?"

"Yeah, and knows his way around. There's no *way* he's going to be Nice-to-Joe, though he certainly isn't going to say he's indifferent to Communists in government. He's up for reelection in November. Joe McCarthy—you know this; we talked about it during his senate race four years ago—has this thing about him: Give him ten minutes with six people, and if they're not already committed, he'll end up with three ardent fans and three guys who want to kill him."

"Did they land any heavy artillery?"

"Not really. Except to insist that McCarthy had nothing *new*—Benton said it, also McClellan, also Douglas—that McCarthy's cases were old stuff, that they had been reviewed and rereviewed. But Joe said, 'Why're they still around, then?' Big crossfire on whether 'they' *were* still around, and of course we didn't have the dates. . . . The whole thing after a while was pretty hard to follow, who they were talking about, what their numbers were on Joe's files, how many files there were. We're going to have to wait and see."

"I can wait and see until seven-fifteen, which is when my editorial for tomorrow is set in type."

"I know, I know, Ed. Just nurse a few ambiguities, I'd advise. On both sides. So that your faithful readers won't be surprised if, next week, Acheson confesses he was a Communist all along. Or Joe is exposed as a total fake, resigns, and goes back to chicken farming. Anything more, Ed?"

"No. Thanks. Will you be at the office if something comes up?"

"Till seven-sixteen," Ed answered.

At 7:16 Joe was in his office, eating sent-in fried chicken with Mary Haskell and Ray Kiermas and Don Surine. Jean Kerr brought in the food and, having laid it out on the senator's desk for him and the participants, moved back to the door. She was a relative newcomer and hadn't been invited to the royal feast. Joe spotted her.

"Jean? Jeanie?"

"Yes," the tall brunette answered, still facing the door.

"Where the hell you going?"

"I thought I'd let you alone, unless you need me, Senator."

"Need you, Jeanie? I can't live without you, can I, Ray? Can I, Mary? You should know—you hired her because I spotted her and told you I couldn't live without her. Right, Mary?"

Mary came through with the expected chuckle. But she added, chicken in mouth, "He wants you in here, Jean. Grab some chicken."

Jeanie sat down, and Joe continued. "I had them on the run, right, Ray? Especially Benton. I think he'll be careful from now on. Thing is, they don't really know what I have, what we have—"

"Easy, Joe," Ray Kiermas said. "We're not so sure what we have, what you have."

Joe McCarthy paused. "Look at those files! Hot stuff in all of them we've opened!"

"Yes, Joe," Surine interrupted. "But what we don't know is: How many of them are still employed? We just *can't* track down those names."

"Yup. But we have certain contacts in certain places—" Joe ostentatiously crossed himself, which always meant he was thinking about J. Edgar Hoover. "And guess who I'm going to visit on Monday." Silence. McCarthy liked to orchestrate silences in his staff.

"Whittaker Chambers."

There was something like a gasp.

"Who's going with you?"—Ray finally broke the silence.

"I thought I'd take Jeanie along"—he caught her surprised smile with enormous pleasure. "I'll want to take notes. Granted, I have to clear that."

"Through whom?"

"Through Richard Nixon. Congressman Nixon. The guy who backed Chambers from the start. He's running for the Senate in November. He stays close to Chambers, who trusts him." Joe turned to Kiermas. "Did the Lucas people tell you when we'd be notified?"

"Hester—Hester Ogilvie—told me the Democratic leadership was going to caucus tonight. Probably at the end of that session they'll officially announce it: the formation of a committee to investigate the charges of Joseph R. McCarthy. Chairman—Millard Tydings. We think."

"I don't care who it is," Joe said, pushing aside his plate and opening a second bottle of beer. "I didn't care today who asked the questions. Did I, Mary?"

"You did all right, Senator." She wouldn't call him Joe when others were in the room.

"How'm I doing, Ray?"

"Good, Senator. Good, Joe."

"How'm I doing, Don?"

"Okay. But it's going to be a long, hard road ahead."

"I'm used to long, hard days at work. At the farm I got up at four."

"Sometimes," Jean was now heard from, "it's better to stay in bed."

McCarthy looked up at this gorgeous Irish creature. Where *had* Mary got her? And the three other people needed to handle the mail since Wheeling. That was a strange remark to hear. Maybe he assigned more meaning to it than he should have. "I didn't get up too early the day I gave that speech in Wheeling, Jeanie."

She nodded her head.

20

The Senate acts

"How'm I doing?"

Jean Kerr knew exactly what Senator McCarthy intended when he said that. Some people ask that question—How'm I doing?—when halfway through an exercise. The pitcher looks smilingly over at the coach after striking out six in a row. He mouths those words right through the chew on his gum, in search of a valentine. The lawyer at the hasty lunch before court resumes preens for the approval of his partner and his client: "How'm I doing?"

Joe would say those three words no matter what he was in the middle of. He might be cooking a steak (on his beloved outdoor grill). But it wasn't as though the words were undirected, given purely as punctuation. When he asked "How'm I doing?" he was acutely aware whom the words were directed to. It mattered a whole lot what he then heard back in some cases. If it was Don Surine or Mary, Joe wouldn't notice what they said, how they responded. He'd have expected—he'd have gotten, from friends and entourage—an affirmative of some kind, variously expressed. The words sounded the same when addressed to Jeanie, but they were differently intended. He was saying, Hey, I'm Joe McCarthy, junior senator from Wisconsin, war hero, lawyer, judge, the hottest political numero in America, and I want to know what you think of my performance.

There were tourists out there, on the driveway outside the Capitol, looking for any recognizable face. Nobody's picture, except for General Eisenhower's, had appeared more often than Joe McCarthy's in the past two months. He had mesmerized the whole country. What he charged in that speech in West Virginia was that the terrible troubles America was having all over the world were in part because enemies of America were influencing decisions. Specifically, Communists. Now he had to prove he knew what he was talking about. The Senate had voted a special investigation and named Millard Tydings of Maryland its chairman. Tydings loathed McCarthy, it was that plain. It had been a tough day at this hearing, three weeks after they began.

Jeanie was seated on McCarthy's right, Don Surine was driving the 1948 blue Chevy; the Senate Office Building seemed stark against the gray sky, a few drops of cold rain drifting down. Jean Kerr would not be bulldozed by the ritual call to affirm that Joe was doing just fine. Tall, beautiful, statuesque, she was very emphatic in her judgments. She had been with McCarthy only a few months, but in the office everybody knew by now that what she thought mattered most.

"You're holding your own, Joe. But Tydings isn't going to let you get away with the waffling."

"On the numbers?"

"On the numbers."

"Hell, Jeanie, that's a phony. We've gone over that. Okay. So on one of the lists Esther Brunauer is number one. On another list she comes in as number twenty-seven. On *my* list she's number forty-four. What Tydings and Cabot Lodge — when he's not asleep — want to talk about isn't, Should somebody like Esther Brunauer, who joins a Communist front every two weeks —"

"Every two years, Joe."

"All right, every two years — does *that* matter? How many Communist fronts have *you* ever joined? They're so dumb, those liberal Commie-smoochers. No. That's not right, Jeanie, some of them, yes. But some of them know exactly what they're doing."

McCarthy waved at the man with the camera, jittery with excitement at having spotted Senator Joe McCarthy himself driving out of the senators' parking lot.

While still waving, McCarthy instructed Don Surine not to stop for the tourist and his camera. "He already got a picture, Don. Just go ahead. Slowly."

He turned to Jean. And said absentmindedly, "How'm I doing?"

"It'll be another long night, Joe."

She opened the briefcase on her lap. We've got one *hundred* files to look at, and we don't know which names Tydings is going to ask you to talk about." She looked up from the file on her lap. "Joe, I'd cool it at the press conference. Don't *feed* ammunition to Tydings."

"Tydings! . . . Baltimore blueblood, Jeanie. He'd have sided with Benedict Arnold." Joe was an accomplished mimic. He began with Tydings's cracked voice. He went on. Now Jean and Surine were listening to McCarthy's version of the Grotonian accents of Dean Gooderham Acheson, Secretary of State. 'Senator McCarthy, are you aware that General Arnold has a distinguished military record and that the charges you bring up against him are based on nothing more than *rumor* and that these facts have been scrutinized—' notice, Jeanie, how he says *scrroo*tinized? '—Senator McCarthy, by five different loyalty/security boards?' "

Don Surine's laughter was welcome. McCarthy began now to imitate the voice of Drew Pearson on the political gossip columnist's weekly television show. But Jean Kerr stopped him.

"Joe. *Listen* a minute. What you're going through—three weeks behind us and God knows how many weeks ahead for us—isn't a political after-dinner roast in Appleton. This isn't one William T. Evjue or one Miles McMillin of the Madison, Wisconsin, *Capital Times* you're talking to—"

"Evjue? McMillin? Why *would* I talk to them? To wish them happy May Day? To congratulate them on the latest Communist putsch?" McCarthy laughed. "You know something, Jeanie, if somebody like, say, Dorothy Kenyon called the AP tonight and said, 'I, Dorothy Kenyon—distinguished lawyer, former municipal judge, former appointee to a United Nations commission on the status of women— have decided I can't live with my conscience any longer. I want to come clean, admit that for twenty years I have done work for the Communist Party. It was me who put the sleeping pills in Dean Acheson's drink before he gave the statement about how Alger Hiss was the greatest American since Abraham Lincoln—"

He interrupted himself, raising his eyes to look up at the driver's seat. "Don. Turn the radio up—"

The newscaster's words flooded the car.

"*. . . repeatedly asked for the floor. Senator Tydings at one point gaveled Senator McCarthy into silence and instructed him not to continue to interrupt the committee's proceedings. Senator McCarthy said he was not going to participate in 'star chamber' rituals. He said, 'This isn't a Communist trial.' A staff member reported that Senator McCarthy was then heard to say to an aide, 'Not yet.' Senator Tydings gaveled him down again and called a five-minute recess. Meanwhile, a State Department spokesman revealed that Esther Brunauer's file had been inspected as early as 1947 and that no security question had been raised when she was reappointed—*"

"Turn it off, Don. Where was I?" He chortled. "Oh, right. Evjue. McMillin. And now Drew Pearson and Jack Anderson and Herblock and the *Washington Post* and the *New York Times* and CBS and—you know, Jeanie, I'm asking you, Were they *this* upset when Stalin exploded an atom bomb last September? Of course not! They feel now—thanks to McCarthy, Jeanie; yes, thanks to me—that their whole show is somehow in danger."

He started to laugh again, then stopped: "Only it's not a laughing matter, Jeanie, is it? How'm I doing?"

The car pulled up to the Hilton Hotel. He would speak to the American Legion Convention at five, after his press conference.

"You check out my speech?"

She nodded, handing him the manila folder.

He turned to her. "You're so beautiful, Jeanie, I mean, on top of everything else. One of these days I'm going to make you marry me."

He slid his hand under her thigh and quick-squeezed her. "We'll get the pope to fly on over and preside! Wonder if the State Department will give him a visa?" He winked. The mischievous wink that had helped to make him, according to the recent national poll, the second most admired man in America, after General Dwight D. Eisenhower, who was waiting in the wings to challenge the Democratic candidate for president to succeed Harry Truman in two years.

The doorman opened the door. McCarthy stepped out and held the door open for Jean. Three delegates from the American Legion were waiting excitedly for him. Joe McCarthy was, for them as for much of America, already Mr. Anti-Communist.

WILLIAM F. BUCKLEY JR.

21

Factional politics

"I swear," Harry Bontecou said to Jean coming into the office on Monday, the day that marked the beginning of the ninth week of the Tydings investigation, "I never saw anything so *freighted* with politics as what's going on."

"Welcome to Washington, Harry. Didn't you know it would be like this?"

"Jeanie: Why isn't it *this* simple? Senator Joseph R. McCarthy has charged that the loyalty/security machinery of the federal government is *not working.* And his net goes wider: He says there are a lot of people around who don't really *want* to prosecute the Cold War. Well: Can't at least the *first* of these allegations be *investigated*?"

"Sure." Jeanie was sorting mail as she talked. "But it's also *this* simple. At the end of this year there are congressional elections. At the end of 1952 there is a presidential election. The Democratic leadership wants to *quiet things down.* Joe's not a tranquilizing type. Besides, he's onto the major personnel scandal of our time. So what they want to do is: discredit him, keep things quiet, and win the elections."

Am I really that naive? Harry thought as he sat down at his desk. The phone rang. It was George Backer, Associated Press. He had met Harry at a cocktail party, introduced by Jean, who had whispered, "We leak some things through George. Nice guy. Also very useful."

"Have you seen the *Indianapolis Star*?"

"No," said Harry.

"Get it," George said. "Got to go." He hung up.

Senator Richard Russell, the august Democratic Party elder and chairman of the Armed Forces Committee, was in Paris on one of his periodic inspection visits of NATO. He was staying at Rocquencourt with NATO chief General Dwight Eisenhower. An aide handed him the cable from his office. It gave the text of the article.

The *Indianapolis Star* story spoke of a leadership conference the Friday before at which the majority leader had addressed ten senior Democratic senators. Russell read on with dismay.

> The *Star* has learned that at that meeting Senator Lucas reported that the "Red scare" is a hot issue and the Republicans "want to run with it in 1952." He said that the GOP wants to get back in the White House after twenty years, and in control of Congress after twenty-four years. Senator Lucas is reported as having said, "We got to take the whole McCarthy chapter and turn it around. Show the public there *never was* any reason for a Red scare." Senator Lucas was not available to a reporter from the *Star.*

The *Star*'s story was bylined by Washington reporter Sam Tilburn. The cable quoted the *Star*'s accompanying editorial. It was entitled, "Dems Prepared to Vaporize Red Scare."

Richard Russell winced on reading the first paragraph:

> Our source in Washington advises us that Majority Leader Scott Lucas has instructed the Democratic senators he appointed to investigate Senator McCarthy's charges to come up with a finding that there never was a Red scare. Perhaps the Majority Leader will advise the Chinese people that the takeover by Mao Tse-tung last year was a hallucination. Since he is a thorough man, he should advise our military that the explosion of an atomic bomb by the Soviet Union last year was really nothing more than a May Day fireworks display. And yes, the massing of the North Koreans in the last two weeks threatens nothing at all on the southern side of the fron-

tier. We should be grateful that there is no reason to be scared by
Red activity.

Senator Russell was naturally cautious, and his responsibilities to
the armed services enhanced that reserve. He did not cable Scott
Lucas—cables get seen. He went into the "bubble," the glasslike
igloo in NATO headquarters, similar to the facilities in U.S. embassies, designed to shield conversation from the electronic curiosity of Soviet bugs or interceptors. From there, on the secure line, he
telephoned Senator Lucas.

He gave his counsel in a calm voice. "You can't unsay what you
said, Scott. Just say at this point—if the press pushes you on it—that
you meant to convey that the Democratic leadership is resolved to
make any Red threat '*futile*.'" He went no further.

Scott Lucas wasn't the sharpest man in the world, but Russell
himself had okayed Lucas's designation as majority leader and now
he had to live with the situation. He was surprised that Lyndon Johnson from Texas, one of the ten Democratic senators at the meeting,
hadn't been shrewd enough to reformulate Lucas's language. All
he'd have had to say was "*What you mean is, Scott, that we're doing our
job and are very much alert to the Communist problem.*" Some son of a
bitch in that room, the senator said to himself, should have known
that with two dozen staff people present there was *always* the proba-
bility of a leak.

Senator Russell was on very close terms with General Eisenhower,
and at their private dinner that night, in the lustrous candlelit dining
room with the famous tapered sconces, preserved from the period
when it was built for the free-spending natural son of Louis XVI, he
said, "Ike, you may be hearing about the fuss kicked up by the *Indianapolis Star* report." He told him the story.

Ike shook his head. "The *Star* talks about the Republicans hoping
to get into the White House in 1952. Imagine anybody thinking there
might be a Republican president elected in 1952!"

Russell laughed, raising his glass. It wasn't easy to tell whether
he was laughing at the prospect of a Republican president in 1952,
as if conforming with General Eisenhower's ingenuous remark; or
whether, as a Democrat renowned for his political savvy, he was rais-

ing his glass to his private hope that the Republican candidate for president in 1952 wouldn't be his host at dinner that night.

McCarthy was both outraged and elated by the *Star*'s scoop. Instead of moving directly to his next security case at the Senate hearing he decided to have a little fun with the chairman.

"Senator Tydings, before I take up the next case on the agenda today, I think we should put on the record the comments of your leader, the distinguished senator from Illinois, to the effect that your job isn't to investigate my charges but to prove they're insubstantial—"

"Oh, please, Senator—" the chairman's voice was strangely conciliatory. "All you have is an unverified report in an Indianapolis paper of remarks perhaps never even made by the majority leader and certainly misinterpreted by the so-called informant." He continued to talk about the gravity of the charges and the committee's conscientious efforts . . .

McCarthy looked down at the note Harry passed over to him.

Harry had worked up a modus operandi: a) McCarthy is asked a question, or is made to suffer a point, by one of his Democratic taunters. b) Harry has a bright idea how McCarthy can answer that point or quote from material that makes an answer effective. But c) Time is required for Harry to scratch out his idea or to come up with the file or clipping from the material in front of him. d) While he is doing this, McCarthy has to stall however he can—say he didn't hear, say he needs a parliamentary clarification, yield to a senator on the misunderstanding that that senator wanted the floor—whatever. Just so it would consume twenty, thirty seconds, perhaps one minute. e) As fast as possible, Harry would slip onto Joe's desk surface, unnoticed except by superobservant press men, the useful document. . . . It worked, and Joe now had the note.

His eyes on it, Joe said, "I happen to have here, Senator, a copy of the *Indianapolis Star* article." Joe was now reading through the corner of his eye Harry's text. It was brief. Without difficulty he improvised the verbal bridge: "What Senator Lucas said, Senator, is borne out by what *you* said on March eighth at the beginning of these hearings. You said—" he brought Harry's paper closer to his eyes "—what you said was 'You'—that's me, McCarthy—'are going to get one of the most

WILLIAM F. BUCKLEY JR.

complete investigations ever given in the history of the republic, so far as my abilities permit.' Well, Senator, I greatly respect your abilities. You have certainly devoted a lot of time to investigating McCarthy, though there is no record of my being a loyalty or security risk—"

The chairman raised the gavel, but he did not bang it down. Not this time. He had lost the polemical round. He said simply, "Proceed with case number forty-five."

"All right, I'll do so. But let me remind you, Mr. Chairman, for maybe the what—fiftieth time?—that it was *you*, not *I*, who insisted that the names of these cases be read out. I was prepared simply to give them by case number. But no—and the majority leader was also very insistent on this—you *insisted* the names be read out. All right. Case number forty-five is one J. Daniel Umin."

Democratic Senator Brien McMahon of Connecticut, a skilled attorney and former head of the Criminal Division of the Department of Justice, leaned back. As ever, he took notes.

The third Democrat, Theodore Francis Green of Rhode Island, eighty-two-year-old Democrat, former governor of his state, had the habit of closing his eyes when concentrating on proceedings. He did so now, but managed also to reach for his notepad.

Bourke Hickenlooper, Republican senator from Iowa and by now staunch supporter of McCarthy, liked to peek over at the two dozen reporters (television was not permitted) with their notepads. They appeared to be concerned to record the highlights of what was going on. They would, of course, get the transcript of the day's events from the Senate reporter, but not until later in the evening. By then they'd have filed their stories for the day. Hickenlooper looked over at Sam Tilburn of the *Indianapolis Star*, whose sensational story of what had been said at the Democratic caucus had raised all the fuss. You owe me one, Sam, Hickenlooper said to himself. He had called Tilburn and whispered to him the scoop on the Lucas meeting. "Hicks," as he was called, had in turn been tipped off by a Democratic staff member who was at the closed meeting and owed Bourke Hickenlooper a return for a very big present: no less, sponsorship of the informant's son into West Point three years ago.

Henry Cabot Lodge, the other Republican on the Tydings Committee, leaned back in the semireclining chair, somehow managing to keep his dress immaculate. His face was impassive. He spoke infrequently at the Tydings-McCarthy hearings. Though of course a loyal Republican, he managed to communicate to the reporters a certain chemical distaste for Joe McCarthy. Lodge was an unregenerate patrician. His appearance alongside McCarthy dramatized the contrast. Murray Kempton, the New York columnist, had a week or so before described McCarthy's blue suit: "It looked as though it had been washed in clam chowder." Senator Lodge, by contrast, dressed in formal gray with a trim white shirt. He wore a vest even in the hot summer.

On the major issue before the committee—Had government loyalty/security agencies been negligent?—Lodge was careful to be receptive to Joe's arguments, even if they did not inflame him. He knew already who would be running against him two years later in Massachusetts for reelection as senator. He'd be facing Congressman John F. Kennedy. A great deal hung on how the Tydings Committee finally ruled. If McCarthy's case was indefensibly empty, the whole GOP would be hurt, including him. If McCarthy made a case of some kind, the Democratic, Catholic, anti-Communist voters of Boston would look kindly on the Republican senator who had been in on the investigation supporting the heroic senator from Wisconsin.

Senator McCarthy opened the file.

"J. Daniel Umin, who was born in 1909, is by training an attorney. He worked in the State Department's legal division until October of 1949.

"Mr. Umin, on leaving the Yale Law School, managed to evade the draft. He then went to work for the Federal Workers Union. That was in 1939. The FWU has opposed loyalty/security measures steadfastly. You will remember, Mr. Chairman, that in my initial statement on federal loyalty/security practices, back on February twentieth, I identified that union, the FWU, as the union that made a dead letter out of the Civil Rights Commission's directive when it tried to set up uniform loyalty standards during the war.

"In 1944, Mr. Umin—I do not have the information, Mr. Chairman, on just how he evaded the draft—"

Tydings interrupted. "Maybe he has only one leg, Senator?"

There was a titter from the gallery.

"Yes," McCarthy shot back. "And maybe the Communists told him he was more valuable doing what he was doing than merely serving as one of the troops, like me."

A sound of approval from the gallery.

"Anyway, as I was saying, in 1944, Mr. Umin was hired by the State Department. You will ask—I know, Mr. Chairman—two things. You will wonder what this has to do with loyalty/security. I told you he worked for the Federal Workers Union. And then—as I was about to tell you—he joined the National Lawyers Guild. You'll ask: Is that presumptive grounds for disqualification as a security risk? Well—"

"Senator Green." Chairman Tydings acknowledged the raised hand of his colleague.

"How many lawyers," Green asked, "are members of the National Lawyers Guild, Senator?"

McCarthy looked to his right. Harry leafed open a page from his file. He whispered to the senator, who then said, "Three thousand eight hundred and ninety-one."

"Are you saying, Senator, that no member of the National Lawyers Guild qualifies to serve in any branch of government?"

"I think this, Senator. If you join the National Lawyers Guild either you are openly sympathetic to the Communist cause, or else you haven't figured out that it's a Communist union. If the first, you are presumptively disloyal. If the second, you are presumptively dumb. In either case, you should not serve in government."

Tydings: "Is that the whole of your file on Mr. Umin?"

"Oh, no, Senator. In 1948, Mr. Umin left the State Department. We don't know whether he was fired. But we do know that there had been an investigation, and that it had been initiated two years earlier. This committee should be interested to find out: What was *going on* during those two years? The *first* of those years, Alger Hiss was still in the State Department. What was in Umin's file, other than what I have been able to come up with, his membership in a Communist union?—"

Senator Green: "You didn't establish that the Federal Workers Union was a Communist union—"

"What do you want me to give you, Senator? A carbon copy of instructions to the FWU from Moscow?"

"You said it followed the party line. But for all we know, J. Daniel Umin opposed their doing so."

"And joined the National Lawyers Guild to protest *its* adherence to the party line? Come *on*, Senator."

Senator Green pursed his lips and reached for his notebook.

"What is Mr. Umin doing right now?" Senator Lodge came in.

The chair: "Point of order, Senator." Tydings reproached Lodge. "We do not discuss the current activities of ex-employees whose case histories in government we are examining; we don't go into their private lives—"

McCarthy was back: "Do you call it a private activity when Mr. J. Daniel Umin, in 1948, turned up as head of the Boston committee for the election of Henry Wallace as president of the United States?"

There was a brief silence. Although it was ten minutes before the scheduled lunch hour, Senator Tydings brought down his gavel. "The committee will reconvene at two-thirty."

Sam Tilburn, immediately after adjournment in the afternoon, put in the scheduled call to Ed Reidy. He began, "That was a nice edit you did this morning."

"Thanks for the scoop." Reidy's delight with a scoop that made the *Star* the most quoted paper of that day was huge. "And tell whoever leaked it to you that if Scott Lucas ever uncovers who ratted to us, he/she—I know you're not going to tell me who the informant was—can have a job at the *Star*."

"Yeah. Well, my . . . anonymous . . . friend is a—valuable friend. Now you want to know about today. I mean about this afternoon—I gave you the morning rundown on the McCarthy hearing at lunch. Well, there was three more hours, same kind of thing. Wrangle, wrangle, wrangle. Joe was pretty deft today. Kept the Democrats a little off balance. Did you succeed in getting somebody to track down J. Daniel Umin?"

"Yup. He's a lawyer in Boston, low profile since 1948. Ziggie has a contact on the *Christian Science Monitor* who went through their files. They don't have any notice on a Umin since the 1948 campaign. God, what a mess. Anybody else's name come up?"

"No. They spent at least two hours going back to the Lattimore case, even after two weeks. That's Joe's big hit, in my book. The Umin case brings up the reasonable-doubt business. And of course the eternal question: Did Joe at Wheeling use the term 'two hundred and five members of the Communist Party' or did he use a lesser figure—as he claims—and more indirect language?"

"Anything come up on that front?"

"Something pretty funny. The critics—Senator Benton, especially—have been relying on a copy of McCarthy's speech that he gave to the broadcasting station. McCarthy said that was just draft notes. Benton says a technician insists he read the text exactly. Joe replies:

"'Here is a copy of the text you said I read from. Here is a sentence from that text: "Today less than one hundred years have come under Communist domination." Did I say that, I ask the honorable junior senator from Connecticut? Before he answers, let me ask him if he thinks I read the following words, another sentence in that text: "Today, only six years later, there are eighty million people under the absolute domination of Soviet Russia—an increase of over four hundred percent. On our side the figure has shrunk to around five hundred thousand. In other words, in less than six years, the odds have changed from nine to one in our favor to eight to one against us." Does the honorable senator hold that up as a reliable text of anything anybody *ever* said?' That got a laugh, at Benton's expense. But the serious talk had to do with loyalty/security *standards*."

"That's crucial."

"You going to write about it?"

"I'm going to try to go one day without writing about McCarthy. Might kill me. If so, was good knowing you, Sam."

"Requiescat in pace, Ed."

22

A professor tries to understand

"Who is this guy McCarthy? You keep your eyes on the Washington scene, Harry. Tell me about him."

Willmoore Sherrill paced his Fellows' suite and addressed his protégé. Harry sat comfortably in one of the armchairs, a bottle of beer in hand.

Willmoore Sherrill taught in the political science department. He was in his late thirties, nattily dressed in a tweed coat and gray trousers, his close-cut hair graying. He was renowned for his ability to infuriate his colleagues and to engross his seminar students. Born in Oklahoma, he was raised as a child prodigy by his father, a blind Methodist minister. Beginning at age five, Willmoore read to his father for several hours every day. He graduated from the University of Oklahoma at age sixteen and two years later was awarded a Rhodes scholarship. At Oxford he concealed his surreptitious marriage, but not his political position — Sherrill was a socialist. His dissertation, written subsequently at the University of Illinois, was on John Locke. It focused on Sherrill's endorsement of majoritarian supremacy. He believed in the relevance of the general will to democratic government. When in 1946 he was appointed associate professor at Columbia, with tenure, he had left socialism, becoming a Truman Democrat.

"McCarthy's certainly onto something. There's a raw nerve out there, Willmoore, and I think McCarthy is pressing it. It's a hot public issue, I think. People are fed up. They sent Henry Wallace packing. He got what, just over one million votes? But my sense of it is that McCarthy is becoming a very big deal. His talk in Wheeling was a detonator."

"Yes, that's pretty plain now. What I'm asking you is, Do you know anything about Joe McCarthy that hasn't been in the newspapers every day for the last two weeks? What is it about him that makes people vibrate? Is it only what he says, or is it the way he says it? Why are people listening to him who haven't paid all that much attention to, oh, Senator McCarran, or Walter Judd, who've been generals in the anti-Communist movement for years? Do you know anything about him personally? Have you ever run into him, at the Political Union or anywhere else?"

"He was on campus last winter. He gave a talk. It was unusual. . . ."

Harry got up from the chair and leaned back on the brick where the mantelpiece ended. He was giving fresh thought to an episode entirely trivial, he'd have thought. But perhaps no longer so, he reckoned, since the infamous Senator McCarthy was featured in it.

"We got the call from the senator's office on a Wednesday afternoon in December. His secretary, or whoever, said that the senator would come to us—the next day, Thursday. He was giving a speech somewhere around here the night before, so it would be convenient. —You probably don't know how the PU operates. We send out invitations in September and again in December to just about everybody in the news. McCarthy was on the general list of people we invite to speak—the list includes practically every sitting senator. That way, by inviting everybody, we get three or four. Of course, we put in a special effort to bring in the big names, which did not include Joe McCarthy. Anyway, his office said the senator could talk to us at two-thirty. We got a bulletin into the *Spec* that morning. The union execs got on the phone. We called a bunch of people to show up. We were pretty apprehensive—late announcement, unknown senator.

"He arrived by cab at the theater. Gerry Fillmore—he's the president—and I were there to meet him. He got out of the cab, about five feet ten, on the heavy side, big, pleasant face, big grin, big ears, hard handgrip. He paid the cab, picked up his briefcase, and said, 'Well, gentlemen, where's the crowd?'

"We took him to lunch at the faculty club. He ordered a minute steak and a beer and talked—you know, Willmoore, I don't remember *what* he talked about—yes, it was about veterans' housing. There were six of us, and we just bantered about this and that. Then we walked over to Miller Theatre. It was embarrassing."

"Nobody there?"

"Practically nobody. Maybe twenty guys. But WKCR"—the student radio station—"sent a reporter, and he had the lectern wired in. McCarthy's speech went out on the air."

"What did he talk about?"

"Again, vets' housing; there was some stuff on the Malmedy massacre. Nothing that stuck in the memory. The next day the *Spec* gave the speech about two inches of space." Harry paused.

"There was one amusing bit. He was winding up his talk. WKCR had obviously allocated exactly a half hour. McCarthy didn't know that, of course. He was just winding down. He began the closing bit. 'I believe in God'"—Harry imitated the senator's high-pitched monotone—"the student announcer's voice came in. He had earphones on and was speaking in a real low voice into the mike, but everybody could hear it, '*The views you have heard do not represent the views of station WKCR.*' Everybody broke out laughing. Including McCarthy. He finished the I-believe-in-God sentence, going on to flag and country. He was very polite, good-natured about the turnout. Left no impression, except—a nice guy."

Sherrill took it all in and made one of his characteristic turns, famous among his seminar students: turning from the recounting of an event in the news to theoretical speculation. Sherrill had moved politically since his strenuous opposition to the Wallace movement in 1947 and 1948. That opposition had led him not so much to the Republican Party as to a defiant conservatism centered on his respect for the general will. When two years later ten Communist Party leaders were convicted for belonging, as Communists, to a movement that sought to overthrow the government, Columbia's political science department scheduled a faculty meeting to deplore and protest the verdict and, indeed, the Smith Act itself. Going around the table, one after another of the tenured professors expressed grave concern over the Smith Act. When it was Willmoore Sherrill's turn to comment, he had said (the word spread quickly), "There's an old colored gentleman who looks after my Fellows' suite. He said to me this morning, 'Professor, is it true there's people who want to overthrow the government by force and violence?'

"I said, 'Yes, that's true, Jamieson.'

"He said, 'Well, Professor, why don't we just run them out of town?'"

Sherrill turned to his distinguished colleagues. "I think Jamieson has a more sophisticated understanding of democratic theory than any of you gentlemen."

"My guess"—Willmoore Sherrill was pursuing the theme over a second glass with his talented student, "is that Senator McCarthy is going to cause a hell of a row."

At his seminar the next day, Professor Sherrill encouraged a discussion on the theme of what he called "clear and present objectionability." He asked the students to consider the question whether, under a bill of rights, a society could satisfactorily formulate language that allowed the majority to say to an unassimilable minority: "'*We don't want you in our society.*' We can tinker with ways of saying *why* we don't want you—the clear-and-present-danger business. But the problem is like obscenity—how do you define it? Answer: You can't define it. But a free society isn't satisfied if there isn't any language around to convey what it is it *doesn't want* to tolerate. Communists and fellow travelers," he told the students, "are urging something the people don't want. How do they talk back conclusively? Isn't that what Joe McCarthy is saying: that the Communists are *illicit* members of the American society?"

"Through something like the Smith Act?" Harry had ventured.

Professor Sherrill predicted that the language of the act wouldn't hold up in the long run. "Society's managers will say: 'Prove it. *Prove* that the society is wobbly enough to get overthrown.' But what the people are saying is they don't want a society that tolerates people who might succeed in making society wobbly, or even want them in the American tent. My guess is that Senator McCarthy is saying something—trying to say something—like that."

The objections in class were heated and varied. Willmoore liked it that way.

23

Harry applies for a job

They had been to the theater to see *Antony and Cleopatra* and walked now up and across town toward the Stork Club. Harry had been there only once, also with Elinor, that notable time, one year earlier. They had dined, danced, and drunk moderately and taken great joy from each others' company. Harry had never, ever missed the company of anyone in quite that way. He teased himself. "You missed the company of Erik Chadinoff back at Plattling, didn't you, Harry, my boy?" Sure. He loved those evening sessions with Chadinoff, playing chess and listening to him work off his knowledge of Communism and hatred for it. . . . He missed his mother, sure. He even missed Willmoore Sherrill, what the hell.

Was it possible? He had fallen for her? She was oddly, provocatively inattentive. He said to her only a month ago, "Has it *ever* occurred to you to pick up the phone and ring me — I've had a phone now for over a year. I don't need to rely on the phone I used to use when Allshott was my roommate."

How had she handled that? She giggled. But Harry knew that there were a lot of contenders for her company. Obviously the Stork Club wanted her (them?) back because —

When on that visit a year ago Harry called for the bill he had been told by the head waiter that there was no bill; it was all "courtesy of Mr. Billingsley." Harry got the news, said nothing, then laughed. For a preposterous moment he was—jealous! As if Mr. Billingsley—

He was the legendary owner of the Stork Club. He cherished the patronage of beautiful people. A beautiful person, in the eyes of Sherman Billingsley, was either an influential reporter, a gossip columnist, a tycoon, a movie star, or J. Edgar Hoover. Or . . . a truly handsome young couple. Once or twice a week Billingsley himself would tour his fashionable club and signal with his eyes to the head waiter, indicating, when time came for the bill, the lucky couple. When he asked for the bill, the young man would be told, "Courtesy of Mr. Billingsley."

That night Billingsley had not hesitated when he looked over at the corner table and spotted the laughing couple, Harry Bontecou, the trim and poised and handsome young man with sensual lips and lively eyes, rapt in the company of Elinor Stafford, tiny, perhaps the size of the queen of England, dark, and alluring.

Tonight was young, young as the tragic Cleopatra. "And this is our twenty-fifth anniversary," Elinor said, for once forswearing her traditional giggle. "The twenty-fifth time we've gone out together."

"Yeah, well, I'm a monogamous type," Harry said, affecting great pomp and giving her hand a squeeze. They strolled across town on Fifty-third Street, talking and laughing.

"Look!" Elinor said. "The Stork Club!" They had decided to walk to it but not to enter it.

Suddenly, from Elinor: ". . . Why not?"

They paused. Harry frowned. It would be abusive to patronize the Stork Club too soon after their free ride. "Too soon? It's been over a year. And, Harry, presumably Mr. Billingsley gives free rides in order to stimulate regular business. We can go ahead in without giving the impression he's going to pick up the tab again. In fact, maybe it's, you know—sort of *polite* to go back again."

She laughed—"I know what! We'll go in, eat and drink wildly, and if the bill comes, unpaid by Billingsley, we can make a scene! Walk out in a huff!"

"You've spent too much time with Cleopatra tonight. She owned the world too!"

They went in and were seated. They were in no hurry, and the Stork Club never seemed to close. The music was just right, quiet, energetic but not convulsively so. In honor of Kurt Weill, who had died early in the week, they played "September Song" and something from *Lady in the Dark* that Elinor recognized, Harry didn't. They danced after the first course and then, back at the table, Elinor brought up the implications of the letter Harry had received that morning from the army reserve. It was to celebrate that letter's message that Harry had pulled away from the campus on a weekday to have an evening on the town.

The army reserve's claims on First Lieutenant Harry Bontecou had hung over him since he had received the notice in March that his reserve unit was now on standby for reactivation. Notices from army reserve commanders (or draft officials) were never discursive on the subject of world affairs. The reserve notice made no mention of Korea, but of course the projected remobilization was traceable to the brewing crisis there. Harry had been considering law school or perhaps graduate school, to which Willmoore Sherrill was so ardently beckoning him. But he was in no mood to start in on three years of school from which, at any moment, he might be yanked away by the army.

They were seated, as it happened, at the same table, by a corner, at which they had sat a year before. They ordered wine. The notice they were celebrating had come in that morning, a letter from Major Reuben Holden, in command of Harry's reserve unit.

> In answer to your letter of March 22, 1950, requesting resignation from the Army Reserve, your application has been reviewed. Resignation is denied. But because you were wounded in action on January 12, 1945, you may apply for a one-year exemption from further military service under U.S. Military Code 801.1 effective May 15, 1950.

"So what does that mean, Harry? That we can dance all night up till midnight, May 14, 1951?"

"They do make things sound that way, don't they? I suppose a lot depends on what happens in Korea. If the North Koreans back down in the negotiations going on, then it's over and out, crisis ended. If there's a war and South Korea overwhelms North Korea, then it's also over and out. If there's a war and North Korea overwhelms South

Korea—again, over and out. If there's a war and north and south are fighting it out every day, then who knows whether, on May 15, 1951, they'll decide they need the services of First Lieutenant Harry Bonte-cou, 01334961, B.A., Columbia, 1950."

"Doesn't make for a stable . . . career move, Harry."

"No." He laughed. "I like that. A career move. Then one day Edward decided to make a career move and proposed marriage to Mrs. Simpson." Elinor joined him in laughter. He put his hand on hers, under the table. She returned the squeeze. They had finished their wine. The time had come. Harry withdrew his hand and reached into his inside jacket pocket, bringing out a single sheet.

"I sent this off this afternoon."

Elinor maneuvered the letter to read it in the Stork Club's candlelight.

Dear Senator McCarthy:

Your speech yesterday spoke of the crowning challenge of the free world to resist Soviet claims on our freedom and to expose the agents of servitude and surrender.

I served in the war in the 103rd Division. I was decorated with a Bronze Star, received a battlefield promotion during the Battle of the Bulge, and was discharged as a First Lieutenant in the spring of 1946.

At Columbia, my academic major has been in history and political science. I am Phi Beta Kappa. I fought the presidential candidacy of Henry Wallace in New York and at his convention in Philadelphia. I was elected editor in chief of the student newspaper, the *Spectator*, and served as editor beginning in junior year. I was active in the Political Union as vice president of the Conservative Party. I met you when you spoke for the Union. There is obviously no reason for you to remember this.

In the last period of my service I was stationed at Camp Plattling. My final duties were to guard Russian refugees pending their forcible repatriation into the Soviet Union. I resolved, after my experience at Camp Plattling and many hours talking with one of the detainees, that the highest calling of our time is to contribute to the anti-Soviet cause. To this end I apply for service on your staff. If you consent to interview me, your office should ring New York,

BUtler 8-0337. My mother, Mrs. Bontecou, will take the message. Or you can write to Apartment #3, 12 West 87th Street.

Hoping to hear from you, and with sincere congratulations on your work and your courage,

Harry F. Bontecou

Elinor put down the letter. "I'm not surprised, Harry. That's the way you feel about things. If you're not fighting in Korea you'd want to be fighting here."

"That's right." Harry had spoken to Elinor a month ago about the McCarthy investigations initiated after his speech in Wheeling in February. "The whole idea is to find out whether the State Department et al. have been so sleepy they don't really ask the right questions."

"What are the right questions?"

"The right question is: Does this policy forward the interests of the United States, which includes a concern for human liberty, or does that policy mostly add up to giving in to Soviet pressure, as we did in 1945–46, when we repatriated those Russian refugees."

"Those are the loyalty risks?"

"It's not easy to draw a clear line between one category of people who shouldn't be working for the State Department and another."

"They're mixed up together as far as I can see," Elinor said. But her point was inquisitively phrased. Harry took her up on it.

"Sure. There are four divisions, roughly. The first is the kind of thing Alger Hiss has apparently been caught up in. There are—spies, saboteurs. Americans who work for the Soviet Union. We've got Russians who work for America. It's standard, the difference being that our people are working to free Russians who have been enslaved since 1917. Their people are working to advance the fortunes and the leverage of the Soviet empire. Now, they are, really, beyond loyalty 'risks.' They are agents of the enemy.

"A loyalty risk is a federal employee who has left a trail—policy recommendations that add up to siding with the Communists on one Cold War issue after another. If you come across an employee who belonged to the Soviet American Friendship League or to the Civil Rights Congress or to the National Lawyers Guild—or all three— and there are dozens and dozens of Communist-organized and -dominated organizations—you have 'reasonable grounds'—important term — to question whether continuing them on duty is wise. They are, Elinor, 'loyalty risks.'

"Now, beyond that, let's say you have someone who gets drunk too often, maybe carries state papers home against the rules. Maybe he's a homosexual and is frightened of exposure and susceptible to blackmail. . . . People in that category are security risks. That's the kind of thing that makes up security risks. They oughtn't to be in government this side of the post office. Anyone who is a loyalty risk is automatically a security risk. But a security risk isn't necessarily a loyalty risk. . . . Is that too complicated for you, honey?"

"Hey. Don't be condescending."

He laughed. "Let's have some more wine. A half bottle?" She nodded, and he signaled to the waiter.

"The point is, a lot of people are hung up on the distinction." He gave a couple of illustrations. She listened. He watched for a tug from her, resisting his decision to apply for a job in Washington. He didn't feel anything. On the other hand, her curiosity on the public question stopped, abruptly. Elinor knew that Harry didn't want to be removed from the center of anti-Communist action. "He seems to want to acquit himself of the burden of Operation Keelhaul," she told her roommate the next day.

But some time later that evening he did touch again on the subject. "Washington — if he takes me — isn't so far from New York. Tell you what. I'll manage to be in New York a lot. I'll persuade McCarthy to investigate Barnard, make sure in your final year you're not corrupted. Like Cleopatra."

"She wasn't corrupted. It was Mark Antony."

"As Mark Antony said to Cleopatra, 'Do we have to talk about world affairs tonight?' "

They got up to dance, and two hours later Mr. Billingsley overrode their protests and sent them home once more with wallet undiminished.

The letter from Harry arrived in the office of Senator McCarthy on the same day that the Senate voted an appropriation for him. Twenty thousand dollars were voted to hand over to the junior senator from Wisconsin to defray the costs of preparing his case on the delinquency of the loyalty/security practices of the federal government. McCarthy's office kept a file for applicants for jobs. Most of these were precipitated by the post-Wheeling publicity; a few—usually from Wisconsin—came in from routine job seekers whose applications arrived with a covering letter, affectionate, admiring, paternal, from a Wisconsin judge, alderman, state senator, or uncle. The office had ready a we're-so-sorry form reply on which Joe would scratch out a handwritten sentence aimed at stroking the sponsor.

Ever since Wheeling, screening and sorting the incoming mail was taking more than one hour. Mary Haskell paused over the letter received that morning from Harry Bontecou. Impulsively, she walked into Joe's office with it. "I think you should read this."

He proceeded to do so.

"Hot stuff from the Ivy League, eh, Mary? Well, I tell you what: You answer it; you tell him to come on down to Washington, and you interview him." Joe smiled and resumed his examination of a huge folder.

She didn't tell Mr. Harry Bontecou, when she called him on the phone, that it would be she, alone, who would be talking to him. She thought to be diplomatic by setting up the interview for Saturday morning, when the office was officially shut and the senator was elsewhere. It was more tactful that way. If the boss who has declined personally to interview the applicant is during the interview sitting at the other end of the office, feelings get hurt. Giving him the impression that he would meet and be interrogated by the senator, Mary told Harry that Saturday morning would be a very good day, "less hectic for the senator."

As arranged, Harry arrived at eleven. There was plenty of activity in the Senate Office Building. Young men and women, usually carrying large briefcases, scurried back and forth, a few of their seniors entering and leaving offices, dodging men and women with their cleaning materials. It was only May, but the temperature was summerlike, and Harry felt gratefully the refreshing coolness of the Senate's air-conditioned office building, the envy of the occupants of the legion of federal office buildings not yet equipped with that postwar luxury.

He went by elevator to the second floor and walked down the hall to office number 212. On the outside of the door he examined the polished brass plate.

MR. MCCARTHY

WISCONSIN

Should he knock, he wondered? He did, but got no response. He tried the door. It was not locked. He walked in. There he saw a wide expanse of desks, each with typewriter and telephone. On four or five desktops vast piles of papers and manila folders were stacked. Two large sofas, the state flag of Wisconsin woven on the upholstered back of the larger of the two, were placed near the entrance door, in front of them a coffee table. Copies of Senator McCarthy's recent speeches and of editorials commending his activities lay on the table. Harry could hear a typewriter clicking away behind a partition at the far end of the big room. He was beginning to walk toward the sound when, from the recessed alcove, Mary Haskell appeared, her reading glasses held around her neck by a slim yellow band, her gray hair slightly tousled, two pens attached to the pocket of her yellow blouse.

"You're Harry Bontekow?"

"Yes, ma'am. It's Bonte-KEW."

"Sorry. . . . I'm Mary Haskell, the senator's office manager. Let's go over to the sofas. Nobody else is here to bother us. I'm sorry to say that the senator is at the State Department; emergency meeting. But he will listen closely," Mary smiled reassuringly, "to what I have to say. You won't be wasting your time."

She sat down and positioned her glasses over her nose, her secretarial pad on her lap, and said—"Let's begin, all right? Where were you born?"

Mary Haskell wrote in shorthand, so there was little delay between answers and queries. Harry was surprised by the thoroughness of the interview, and later gratified by it.

"Father?"

"Jesse Bontecou, deceased."

"Profession?"

"He was a . . . scholar. But unattached to any university."

"How did he make a living?"

"He wrote. Articles, reviews, and books. His field was poetry."

"When did he die?"

"1943."

"Of?"

"Heart."

"Surviving family members?"

"Widow and one child. Me."

"Sources of family support?"

"Poetry."

"*Poetry?*"

"My father published a book called *Poetry to Live By.*"

Mary Haskell looked up. "I read that book in school."

"Fortunately," Harry smiled, "most people since 1937 read that book in school."

"Other sources of income?"

"None."

"Did your father's estate provide for your schooling?"

"My father left no estate. Just the property in his book. The revenue from it goes equally to my mother and me. Most of my schooling was paid by the GI Bill."

"What is your annual revenue from the book royalties—you understand, Mr. Bontecou, we have to ask a lot of questions other senators wouldn't have to ask. We use the same preliminary interview form as the CIA. I was asking you about income." She returned to her pad.

"Last year, 1949, the royalties were just over twenty thousand. So my half was ten thousand."

A half hour later, taking notes assiduously, she was questioning Harry about his activities at Columbia. A voice came in from the other end of the long room, beyond her own office.

"Hey, Mary?" the voice called out.

Joe McCarthy had entered through the private entrance.

She rose quickly to intercept him, but McCarthy was halfway to them, charging in in characteristic stride, shoulders weaving to one side then the other.

"Joe—Senator, this is Harry Bontecou. . . . I already apologized to Mr. Bontecou, Senator, for your absence because of the State Department meeting."

Mary Haskell had worked for Joe for four years. She knew how to flash signals to him. "We were just talking about his activities at Columbia, after his service in the war and on Operation Keelhaul. It's good that you were able to get away to meet Mr. Bontecou personally. He's down from New York."

Joe caught all the pointers. He had been told by Mary 1) the name of the young man (three times). She had told him 2) what excuse she had concocted to account for his absence. And that 3) young Bontecou had served in the war and attended Columbia.

Joe McCarthy off stage was pleasant by nature, and uninhibited. He took the hand of Harry, shook it vigorously, and plopped himself down at the end of one of the couches. He looked at Harry but addressed Mary.

"Catch me up, Mary."

"Mr. Bontecou, Senator—"

Harry interrupted. "I wish you'd call me Harry, Mrs. Haskell." Harry smiled informally. At ease. "After all, Mrs. Haskell, you know my life story."

Joe smiled his own approval.

"Harry has graduated from Columbia, where he was editor of the student newspaper. He was very active in fighting the Wallace for President movement in sophomore year." She was scanning her notes. "He graduated with honors, won a battlefield commission in January 1945, was wounded, decorated, and closed out his service by prodding the Russians—by sending them back to the Soviet Union. You gave a speech about that, Senator."

Joe interrupted her. "You believe in my cause, Harry?"

"That's why I'm here, Senator."

McCarthy trained his eyes on the young man, hesitated for only an instant, and then,

"Harry, let's go to lunch."

Joe spoke with animation about the trial ahead. He would need to convince an antagonistic Senator Tydings, chairman of the investigating committee, that the loyalty/security situation in the State Department was "lousy" and "dangerous."

"What you need to remember, Harry, is that what's important to Tydings isn't whether that's so. What's important to Tydings is to discredit McCarthy. He's figuring: If McCarthy is right, then that damages the Truman administration and McCarthy's critics."

Mostly, Harry listened. But he interposed occasionally. He asked, "On your two hundred–odd cases, Senator, is there evidence at hand that ties these people to any particular *deed*? I mean, to a memo obscuring reality to the benefit of the Communists, or obvious delinquency in passing up damaging information—I mean, obviously, some activity this side of actual policy espionage."

"In some cases, yes. In most cases, no. And of course there are two kinds of policy corrupters. The kind that says, Don't sell arms to Chiang Kai-shek because he's a lost cause. And the kind who delay the delivery of authorized weapons to Chiang Kai-shek. We've got to get both kinds."

Harry nodded.

Suddenly McCarthy said, "Did you ever hear of Owen Lattimore?"

"State Department?"

"Not quite. A professor by background, Far East specialist. Never mind. You'll be hearing a lot about him." He paused. "You know we're losing the struggle, don't you Harry?"

"I know we've had a lot of setbacks."

McCarthy looked up at him and chuckled. "Yes, that's right. A lot of setbacks is different from losing."

He looked at the tall young man with the light brown eyes, dressed in a white shirt and light gray suit, a hint of a reciprocal smile on his face. "When can you come to work for us, Harry?"

24

McCarthy meets
Whittaker Chambers

Jean walked into his office carrying a file. She intended to wait until Joe finished his telephone conversation but became impatient. She wiggled her fingers in front of him. It worked:

"Hang on a second, Dick, Jeanie's trying to tell me something." McCarthy put his hand over the mouthpiece. "What is it, Jean?"

"Tell him Mother's out of town and her big, roomy old Packard is sitting in the garage. Harry and I will pick you up, and together we can go to the Senator's, pick him up, and I'll drive you all."

McCarthy lifted his hand from the receiver. "Jeanie says let's stop fightin' about who will pick who up in what car: She's going to pick us both up."

The date was made, after two postponements, and at eleven on Saturday morning, Jean Kerr at the wheel, Harry alongside her, Joe McCarthy behind, the car stopped at an apartment house on Gunston Road in Alexandria, Virginia. She stayed in the car while Joe went out and rang the buzzer. Harry opened the door and stood by. The audiophone sounded. "It's me, Dick. We're downstairs."

Five minutes later Richard Nixon walked out, dressed in a light summer gray suit and wearing a fedora. He had already met Harry, whose hand he shook.

"We've been instructed to sit in the backseat," McCarthy said.

Harry will sit up front with Jeanie, who knows the route. Chambers wrote me giving directions."

"Hell, I know the way," Nixon said. "I practically lived there during the Hiss trial."

Whittaker Chambers—his story was by now very public—had joined the Communist Party in 1925 and, during the thirties, served as an espionage agent for the Soviet Union, acting as courier for a ring that included Alger Hiss of the State Department. In 1948 he had given testimony before the House Committee on Un-American Activities, identifying Hiss as his coconspirator ten years earlier, when Chambers had broken with the party and joined *Time* magazine, where he became a senior editor. Hiss had sued Chambers for libel, and a trial was held in New York, the point of which quickly became less whether Chambers had libeled Hiss than whether Hiss had engaged in espionage. The jury was divided, and a second trial ordered. This time, the jury found against Hiss, and the superliterate Chambers became the hero of the anti-Communist community. He had exhibited his great learning as an editor, dared to challenge a bastion of the diplomatic establishment, and prevailed in a judicial contest against dogged and well-financed forces that thought the vindication of Hiss necessary to the validation of the New Deal. Chambers, dismissed from *Time,* had retreated to his farm in Westminster, declining almost every invitation to leave it or to receive visitors.

The two legislators talked in the backseat. Jean chatted with Harry. Occasionally McCarthy would consult Jean, who drove evenly and waved at the cop guarding the crossing near Baltimore. She did not conceal her excitement over meeting the now-legendary figure. "He's supposed to be very polite," she reassured Harry, who felt his own heartbeat accelerate as they neared Westminster. Joe, seeking some show of approval from Chambers, as also perhaps his advice, had taken the initiative. He didn't want to appear as the guest of Richard Nixon, but he thought it wise to make him a part of the delegation. In his letter to Chambers seeking permission to visit, McCarthy suggested that Nixon, who had stood by Chambers during the ordeal of his congressional testimony and the suspense and agony of two trials, might like to be present at their meeting. Might he come, and might he bring Jean Kerr and Harry Bontecou of his staff with him? "She is very good company and can take notes if ever you want notes taken. And Harry is only twenty-three but has fought the wars since he was a lieutenant in Germany."

Whittaker Chambers wrote back quickly. Yes, he said, do come with Miss Kerr and Mr. Bontecou. If Congressman Nixon can join you, fine; if he is busy, come anyway. He enclosed driving directions. Jean had enjoyed their exactitude, and gave Chambers's letter to Harry, to read sentence by sentence as time came to turn onto different highways or roads.

"Let me tell you how to get here from Washington," Chambers's letter read.

I assume you will drive. Drive out Wisconsin Avenue to Bethesda. From Bethesda to Rockville, from Rockville to Gaithersburg. Then to Damascus, Mt. Airy, Taylorsville, Westminster. A road map will give you the route numbers. Route 140 is Main Street, Westminster. Drive out 140 (towards Pennsylvania) for three miles beyond Westminster. There a concrete road comes in to 140, but does not cross it. This is Route 496, the only concrete road you will meet above Westminster. Drive out 496 two and 7/10 miles. We are there, on your left, we are back from 496 on a hill; you have to turn left down a dirt country road for a short distance; then right at the mailbox into our lane. At the corner of 496 and that country road there is one of those metal Guernsey Cattle Club signs which says: <u>Chambers</u>. In addition, anybody in the county can tell you where we are. I look forward to seeing you.

It was warm and sunny when they emerged from the car in Maryland farm country. Esther Chambers, slim and ascetic, her gray hair austerely brushed back, opened the door of the farmhouse. She kissed Nixon, who introduced her to Jean Kerr, Joe McCarthy, and Harry Bontecou.

They heard a "Hello!" It was Chambers, coming from the red barn. Of medium height, pronouncedly heavy, his face round, his lips parted in a smile of formal greeting. He wore khaki work pants and a loose white sport shirt. He was perspiring heavily. He wiped his face and hands with a handkerchief, shook hands, and asked them in to the comfortable living room. "I think we'll need the fan." He went to turn it on.

They sat around the large old coffee table on a sofa and three armchairs in the book-crammed living room, the foliage in the surrounding trees and bushes now dimming the window light. On the mantelpiece were photographs of the two Chambers children, the girl, Ellen, a student at Smith, the boy, John, attending high school locally and working on his father's farm. Esther Chambers asked who would like coffee, or tea?

They stayed through a lunch of potato salad and ham and mixed fruit. Chambers asked Nixon about Korea: "I don't have my private wire into the hotboxes anymore, and the people at *Time* don't exactly keep me posted, but from the news I get it looks bad."

Nixon confirmed that his own contacts were pessimistic about the scene there. "Kim Il Sung is anxious for an opportunity to be bloodied in the Communist wars, that's what I think."

Chambers then turned to McCarthy. "What do you know about Oliver Edmund Clubb, Senator?"

McCarthy had tried earlier in the morning to persuade Chambers to call him Joe. Chambers had nodded quietly and, rather than rebuff him by addressing him as "Senator" in the next breath, used neither the formal nor the informal address; but now, at lunch, he slipped back into conventional habits. McCarthy knew better than to protest.

Clubb's was one of the names given by McCarthy to the Tydings Committee. "Did you bring the file on Clubb with you, Jeanie?" She had brought a large briefcase in the car. "No, but I can remember." She spoke to Chambers. "Clubb was an important China hand in the State Department. Born in Russia, came over in the thirties, I think, and was chief of the China desk in 1950."

Chambers puffed lightly on his pipe. "Yes. I knew him slightly, met him in 1932 when he came into the *New Masses*." Chambers's reference was to the Communist monthly he was briefly associated with.

"Did he come in to the magazine as a party type?" McCarthy asked.

Chambers laughed. "Or do you mean, Was he just calling? . . . That was eighteen years ago. I don't remember. The reason I asked is the FBI came around a week or so ago with some names, and he was one of them. On the Korean business—I spotted Clubb's name in a quarterly"—he pointed to a large pile of magazines on a stand in the corner of the room. "He was writing about Korea from the perspective of Peking."

He looked at McCarthy. "They are giving you a very hard time. I wrote a chapter for my book yesterday, Wednesday, whenever. I wrote of the quite extraordinary spontaneous mobilization of all the people who want to believe that it is problematically un-American to spy for the Soviet Union, but it is certainly un-American to call attention to it." He put down his pipe and chuckled. "Now, Senator, you are not to say to anybody that Whittaker Chambers informed you that Oliver Edmund Clubb was spying for the Soviet Union."

Everybody laughed. And Nixon said, "I assume *everything* we talk about here is off the record, as usual, right, Whit?"

"Yes. Of course."

Chambers dilated then on his favorite theme, the corruption of the West, documented by its failure to rise adequately to the Soviet challenge. Nixon insisted it would soon be different. Truman was a lame duck, as also Dean Acheson. In two years it would be different.

"In two years, the cow will jump over the moon," Chambers remarked. And then he asked, "Who will it be when the Republicans meet?" Chambers peered over at Nixon.

Nixon cleared his throat. "I don't have any party secrets on that point, Whit. I don't think there are any party secrets, but it's plain that a movement for Eisenhower is forming."

McCarthy said he'd be more comfortable with Robert Taft.

Chambers said, "Esther and I saw him on television two or three days ago. We found him terribly stiff, didn't you think, Esther?"

"Yes. Stiff, but decent. And I'd guess strong. Strong on the important points." She rose. Everyone responded to her signal. Time to go, to leave Chambers alone, whether to go back to his work or to rest for a bit. But Chambers sensed that there had been a neglect of Senator McCarthy's young aide. "Wait one minute," he said to McCarthy. "I'd like to introduce Mr. Bontecou to my son, John; he's probably over by the shed." He smiled at Harry, who bounced from his chair and out the door Chambers held open.

They walked together in the direction of the barn. Chambers chatted, asking about Harry's background. Harry spoke quickly, compressing it all into the minute or two they had. He added this, that he thought Chambers's trial and the little he had written about it moving and memorable. "I think the whole world is waiting for your book, Mr. Chambers."

They had reached the barn door. Chambers opened it and called out, but John was not there. Chambers turned to Harry. "I can see that you are close to the senator. He has grave responsibilities. I know you can help him. Do not hesitate to write to me if you need—anything." Harry was bowled over. An invitation, evidently sincere, to stay in touch with the poet—Harry thought Chambers just that—the poet of the Western resistance to Communism. "Thanks so much, Mr. Chambers. I really appreciate that."

Chambers smiled, and they met his guests coming out of the door. Extending his hand, McCarthy looked Chambers directly in the face. "I really would like it if you would . . . think of me as Joe."

Chambers smiled, nodded, and said quietly, "Yes. Thank you, Joe." Then he narrowed his eyes. "Be careful. Be very careful."

Back in the car they were silent. After a while Jean turned on the radio. The broadcaster spoke of 500,000 East Germans carrying Lenin banners who had marched that afternoon in Berlin. He commented that the demonstration was an obvious answer to the 500,000 West Germans who had marched early in the month in protest against the Communist government in the eastern part of the city.

"You got to hand it to the Communists," McCarthy commented. "If they want a mass demonstration, they get a mass demonstration."

"Yup. And some of them, we got to believe, believe in what they're cheering," Nixon observed.

25

A covert messenger

On June 4, several weeks into the Senate's scheduled debate on McCarthy's charges, the telephone rang at his apartment, two blocks from the Capitol. A month after his return from what forever after would be referred to in his office as "Joe's Wheeling week," McCarthy had unlisted his telephone number. He had heard the phone ring every few minutes for days on end, bringing calls from newspaper reporters, radio interviewers, agitated citizens, and what he referred to, in the office, as "the spook patrol." ("We got enough spooks of our own," he commented to Mary Haskell. "We don't need somebody on the telephone prepared to dictate the names of three hundred fifty homosexuals in the Bureau of Weights and Measures.")

McCarthy, dressed in shorts and T-shirt, a half-consumed cup of coffee in hand, picked up the phone that now rang only when dialed by the few who had his new, secret number, leaving him secure in the knowledge that whoever was calling was an intimate.

The voice wasn't one he had heard before. It was a refined voice, a man whose words were soft-spoken, the syntax poised, his message intriguing.

"Senator, I'm not permitted to tell you on whose behalf I am calling you. And there is no way you can, over the phone—or for that matter in person—verify my credentials because I cannot give you any credentials to verify. I'd like your permission to come to your apartment and to take fifteen minutes of your time. It doesn't matter what time of day, if you consent to see me, but you should know that my message is urgent and may lead to information useful to you in the Senate investigation. May I come?"

"Hang on." McCarthy put down the receiver and looked at his watch. He reached into the inside pocket of his brown tweed jacket, lying over the couch, and pulled out his appointment book. He scanned the schedule.

He picked up the telephone again. "Is what you want to tell me something one of my aides can listen in on?"

"Under no circumstances. I am authorized to give my message only to you."

Joe hesitated. "How soon could you get here?"

"Five minutes."

Joe said, "Make it ten minutes. When you call up from downstairs, say it's Henry calling. I'll ring the door release."

He hung up and dialed his office. "Hello, darling," he greeted Marge, the telephone operator. "Put me through to Don."

"Don? Joe. Look, it's nine-oh-five. Go down, right now, to the delicatessen across the street from me. Yeah. That one. They have a pay phone there. Now, I want you to ring my number here at exactly nine-twenty. I got somebody coming in. I don't know anything about him, but I have a hunch about it so I'm having a look. When I answer the phone, if I say, 'Don, I'm running late,' then that means everything is okay—go on back to the office. If I say, 'Okay, I'll be right with you,' that means I want you to use your key and come to my apartment as soon as you can make it, which I figure should be like twenty-five seconds. Got that? I hope so; I don't have time to say it again."

"Got it, Joe."

He opened the door to a short man, neatly dressed in a dark blue suit, white shirt, and regimental tie. His hair was full, carefully parted, and there were signs of gray. He wore tortoise-shell glasses and carried a briefcase. Slung over his right arm was a light tan overcoat he had evidently removed in the hallway.

"May I put down the coat?"

"Yes, sure," Joe said. "Give it to me. Er, coffee?"

"No, thank you, but I will sit down."

McCarthy indicated the chair at the other end of the room. He positioned himself by the telephone, behind the coffee table.

"So what's up, Henry?"

The stranger made only the slightest effort at a smile at the reference to him as "Henry."

"Senator, you may pretty soon infer who sent me, or try to do so. Do me the favor of not suggesting who you think it is, as I can say nothing on that score."

"Okay, Henry. So go ahead."

"A woman who was for six years active in the government and served as a Soviet agent has turned. She has a very detailed story to tell, we have reason to believe. She recounted to her interrogator the names of two people who worked closely with her. One — there is reason to believe — is still in the government. The relevant people have tried to persuade her to tell the whole story to the FBI or to the loyalty board of her government . . . division. At one point we thought she would. Then she changed her mind. A few days later she left her lodging. May I smoke?"

"Sure."

"She disappeared. Until yesterday we were afraid she might have left the country, or maybe — had an accident. Yesterday, almost four weeks after we were last in touch, she telephoned — to a number — a number she had been given. And what she said was that she would be willing to tell the whole story, but would tell it only to 'Senator Joseph McCarthy of Wisconsin.'"

McCarthy was a good listener. But a lifetime of poker playing had taught him not to reveal what he felt. He looked on, impassive.

"We asked if we ourselves could come by. She said she was not giving out her new address, but would give it to Senator McCarthy. She did say that she is an hour's driving distance from Washington. You can probably guess what else she said, but I have to repeat it. She said that if she hears from anyone — anywhere — anything that she thinks traces to her initiative, no one will ever hear from her again."

The telephone rang. Joe picked it up. "Yeah, Don. I'm running a little late." He put the phone down. Don Surine could return to the office.

He turned back to his visitor. "What does this lady want me to do?"

"You're to tell me yes or no. If the answer is yes, you're to say when. 'When' means — she warned — that you've set aside a minimum of four hours. One hour driving each way, two hours with her to hear her story. If you say yes, we'll tell her. She'll call her special number twice a day until she gets the word. When the time is set, one hour before you're ready to go, she calls our number and gives us driving instructions. I then drive you out."

Joe said nothing for a few seconds, then stood up and walked to the stove nearby. He filled his coffee cup.

"Y'know, Henry. I'm just wondering what the FBI — this is hypothetical, of course — I know you've got nothing to do with the FBI — or the CIA — but suppose I am a trainee at either of those places and the training officer takes me through a security exercise.

"Situation: A nice guy comes to the door of a page-one hot senator, says interesting things, and Page-One Hot Senator is invited to make a date with this nice stranger, step into his car, and disappear . . . for only four hours, of course.

"I'm wondering what my instructor would say if I answered, 'Sure, why not?'"

"You would be dropped from the trainee section and sent for work at some other part of the organization," McCarthy's visitor said matter-of-factly. And then quickly went on, "But you know, Senator, that's the problem with categorical rules. Any rules. They just don't cover every situation — like this one, for instance. And there is, in this situation, a very special lure. We've looked at the two people the lady told us about. If it's true they're Communists, and worked for Soviet intelligence, then they're headline-making material. Page-one hot senators don't mind headlines."

"Listen, Henry. Sure, I don't mind headlines. That's how politicians get votes and how they lobby for their policies. I'm also interested in doing something about a country that just lost a world war, know what I mean? It was a free Poland that the war was all about, back in 1939."

"I don't deny your sincerity, Senator. I'm simply saying that in the hypothetical situation you're describing, the trainee should also be told that the page-one hot senator is looking very, very hard for the

kind of information that the nice stranger says he can lead him to—
if he'll make the date and reserve four hours."

Joe McCarthy always thought instinctively, and acted impulsively.

"Okay, Henry. I'll scrub other appointments for this afternoon.
Tell me where to be at two P.M."

26

McCarthy meets an informant

Senator McCarthy did exactly as requested. He got out of the car at Sequoia and Fourth and told the kid (a volunteer driver doing a paper in Georgetown) to wait until he returned. He didn't tell him to keep his eyes away from where McCarthy would then walk to, but he didn't feel he needed to do that. He walked west ("away from the Liggett's drugstore") one block, turned left, and found himself at the specified address. He gave the shabbily dressed doorman a name, "Joseph McPherson," and, after a quick phone check, was told to go to apartment 6M. She opened the door.

McCarthy correctly assumed that the woman who let him in wordlessly was the object of all this feverish curiosity. The apartment was neat and sparely furnished. Perhaps it was rented as a furnished apartment. She motioned him to an armchair, and he could see that her arm was shaking. She wasn't old, but she looked fragile, and her voice sometimes broke. She asked him if he wanted tea; he shook her hand and said, "Coke all right?" She produced it, sat down, and they talked for two hours.

"She's an aristocrat, Jeanie. With sad, sad eyes, and not much of a smile. But she knows how to tell her story, the part of the story I got. There's apparently a lot more. And she cares a lot."

"Who is she?"

"I won't write down her name, not anywhere. I'll refer to her as—Ouspenskaya. Madame Ouspenskaya."

At the office everyone who knew about her adopted the name quickly. "Maria Ouspenskaya." Joe rolled the name about his tongue. He *loved* it! and spoke with near proprietary expression about Hollywood's venerable character, the slightly mysterious old lady with the long, mellifluous Slavik name—oo-spen-SKY-ah—who was featured in film after film playing character parts, the classic lady-not-to-be-crossed.

"I found her an authentic lady," he told his inner staff, Don, Harry, Jean, and Mary. "She's fragile, you can tell. She talks with just a slight accent—Russian, Czech, something like that. But there's grit there, and her story is completely, well—composed. The background isn't all that unusual. It was her husband, he's dead, who joined the party. She strung along, became a true believer, stayed on after he died. She did some courier work for somebody called 'Allan,' and in 1944 was told that two of the people working in her division, one man, one woman, were fellow agents. She knew the man—a code clerk. The woman she knew only by her secret agent name. They collaborated on one operation. After that she was told not to be in touch with her again."

"What turned her?" Mary Haskell asked.

"Czechoslovakia. Masaryk was her—'devoted friend' is how she put it. They were in college together and stayed friends till she came to America, fifteen, twenty years ago."

"Has she told the FBI her whole story?"

"No! That's *their* point. *Her* point. She's waiting for us. Waiting for McCarthy to weigh in on the problem. She's suspicious that if all she does is tell it to the FBI nothing will happen except that she'll be in danger. She's waiting for McCarthy, for me, to give her case to the Tydings Committee as one more example of system failure, but I think there's a surprise coming. The FBI are, excuse me, Mary, excuse me, Jeanie, pissing in their pants. She wants to tell it to everybody and decided to do it to the Tydings Committee."

Joe had tried to get Ouspenskaya to go further with him than she had been willing to go in her first encounter with the FBI. She had explained:

"I called the FBI in March. That was two years after the Czech coup. I dreaded it, dreaded it. But couldn't put it off any longer."

McCarthy didn't comment.

"But I decided to be very careful. I gave the FBI one folder of coded documents passed by me to Allan from our . . . code clerk." She didn't offer his name.

"What did you expect the FBI to do?"

"I asked them to test the documents. To establish that they were top secret and that the . . . clerk had had access to them."

"Why did you do that?"

"I wanted to find out if the FBI could verify my story. If yes, then I'd consider giving them more. Giving them the whole story. If no— if they weren't persuaded by the documents—then I'd just have to face it, face whatever prison they put me in."

"What happened?"

"They moved quickly. By April they authenticated it. The documents told of results of tests conducted as late as January at the Aberdeen Proving Grounds. Tests on antisubmarine detection devices and correspondence with British scientists. The FBI moved quickly, but not as quickly as the code clerk. One day he was gone. Obviously he found out. And I would guess that he knows who informed on him. I had one more conversation with my FBI contact. He said not to worry about the clerk. He said Mr. Hoover wanted a 'comprehensive counterintelligence' operation. That would mean I'd have to stay right where I was and just answer questions on the side for the FBI. That was when I knew I had to move quickly. I didn't want that, to sit there doing my job when somebody—I think I know who it is—sitting above me can play with me like—matchsticks." She picked up the matchbox, then thought to light a cigarette. She took a deep puff. "I want the whole story known. I saw you on television. It was when you spoke about Jan Masaryk and the alleged suicide that I decided that you were the man. Your talk about Czechoslovakia—"

"St. Louis, in May."

"I don't remember where. But I remember thinking that you would do the right thing and get the public attention."

———

WILLIAM F. BUCKLEY JR.

"That," McCarthy told the story, "was when she got really scared, when she figured the FBI planned a full-scale program built around her staying in place, in her job at Commerce. So she packed her stuff and moved to . . . the new address. Didn't tell anybody.

"Well." McCarthy rose from his desk. "Tomorrow morning I'll talk about her to the committee, tell about the code clerk spy, about 'Allan.' Then I'll reveal her real name. In the afternoon session, she'll come in person and testify about the slipshod security practices and how the code clerk got away even after she had given his name to the bureau. And the woman spy who's still there. And who knows what more. *That* should prove some of the points we're trying to make."

"You got hot stuff there, Joe," Don Surine said.

"Yeah. I want to hear whoever is in charge of security at Aberdeen Proving Grounds and related clients to explain Maria Ouspenskaya and her little network."

"Maybe it was a big network, Joe?" Mary put in.

"Naw. The Communists don't operate that way. They try to keep down the number of people who can be exposed by any one defection. You know that, Mary."

"Well, Whittaker Chambers named a dozen, Elizabeth Bentley more than a dozen."

"True. Well, we'll see. Tomorrow."

That night McCarthy and Jean Kerr worked late. "What do you want from Calder's?" she asked—Calder's was the delicatessen that delivered (excellent service for senators, good service for congressmen) to Capitol offices.

"BLT on rye, with chips and coleslaw. And honey, order up a bottle of wine."

"Chianti okay?"

He nodded and resumed writing on the legal pad that never seemed to give out, because when Mary saw it was running short, she'd bind in a fresh one.

Two hours later he said, a note of weariness in his voice, "Jeanie, come sit by me for a bit."

She affected a reluctance to get up from her work, but soon sat in the chair Mary used to take dictation. Joe reached for her hand.

"Do you realize, Jeanie, the importance of tomorrow? Ouspen-skaya—her real name is Kalli, Josefa Kalli—was never caught. She worked with this guy Allan. Then this code clerk comes in and out and does his bit. The bureau has documented that the files she stole were high-security stuff. We've got the equivalent of the same proof Whittaker Chambers had against Hiss, traceable secret documents. Both she and Allan sailed through security even though Ouspen-skaya's husband was a declared Communist. We're getting deep down now, Jeanie, deep down, and tomorrow is going to get the senior sen-ator from Maryland hopping."

"Joe, what's the *matter? Why* don't our people catch your . . . your Ouspenskayas?"

Joe took his hand from hers and stood up. "It's one part because there's sloppiness out there and one part because their immediate superiors *don't think it's such a big deal.* You heard Senator Green. He said—in effect—Well, there are over three thousand lawyers who belong to the National Lawyers Guild, so—so what?"

She looked at him, then tilted her head, her lips slightly parted. And then, "Joe, do you think after the Tydings investigation is over you can just, well, move into something else?"

He sat back down on his chair and took her hand again. "It's rough. . . . I'm not sure it's ever possible to back away, not from this one."

"I hate to look at the papers in the morning. What they say about you. They'll say *anything.*" She pulled a handkerchief from a side pocket and turned her head. She wasn't the crying type, she said to herself. Joe caressed her shoulders from where he sat. "We've got to get it done, Jeanie. And the Ouspenskaya lady, she'll make a lot of dif-ference, putting her case on the record. She'll be, well, *our* Whittaker Chambers. You know we've got to see it all through, Jean."

Through her sobs, he made out the words. "I know. I know."

As usual, Joe took lunch back in his office during the two-hour recess of the committee. Even the cool, disdainful Tydings, he thought, had been impressed—and visibly disconcerted—by what he had heard about one Josefa Kalli—McCarthy had that morning given out her real name, as agreed. There was quite general apprehension about what she would say, what experiences she had had with the security system so ardently defended by Senator Tydings and the Truman administration. Two reporters, hoping to get more details on what the witness would be exposing that afternoon beginning at two, followed the senator from the committee room to his office. McCarthy, as always, chatted affably. But—he told them—he had given the committee that morning all the information he was at liberty to give out. They would have to wait until two "for the fireworks."

He was sipping on a beer with his fried chicken, eating at his desk, running over the list of questions he was preparing for Mrs. Kalli. His mouth was full when Mary's voice came in over the little speaker.

"I know you are lunching, but he says it's a major emergency. All he gives is the name 'Henry.'"

Joe picked up the receiver and heard the report. He was less than one minute on the phone. He rang for Don. "Come quickly."

Surine opened the door to the office and closed it behind him. He remained standing. Joe said: "She's committed suicide. They just found her. They'll investigate the possibility of foul play, but right now they think the pistol that was aimed into her mouth was put there by—Maria Ouspenskaya."

McCarthy managed a wry half smile.

Neither of them spoke for a moment.

"So, Don. She was a nice lady, I thought. Well . . . we have fifteen minutes before we go back and chew the rag with Senator Tydings."

"What you going to say, Joe?"

"What is there to say? 'Just a little infield practice, Senator.'"

But the shock was very real, and all the office felt it. And it was fueled by frustration and rage. But rage at, exactly, whom?

"Has the bureau given anything new out since four?" Ed Reidy wanted to know.

"Yeah. Just a half hour ago their press guy said that she died between eleven and eleven-fifteen. No one heard the shot. On the other hand, there wasn't anybody in the apartment next door, or the ones above or below. She had been to the post office, and in her purse was a receipt for a registered letter that went out with the mail at noon—"

"To anybody we know, Sam?"

"Yeah. Get this. It was mailed to Senator Joseph R. McCarthy."

"Well . . . I'll . . . be . . . *damned!* So maybe Joe gets the last word? Has the bureau intercepted it?"

"Interesting question, Ed. But now just think for a minute. a) There's no way to do it, not for sure. The letter's en route from Baltimore, could be by mail truck, could be by train—could even be by airplane. The post office uses all three, Baltimore-Washington. b) The FBI would need a court order to intercept a private communication, and since there is no evidence that Josefa Kalli committed a crime, the court would have to be persuaded there was immediate cause for taking possession of somebody's privately addressed letter—"

"And privately addressed to a senator."

"Let alone a letter addressed to Senator McCarthy," Sam topped him. "I figure there's no way the letter is going to say that McCarthyism is the reason why she decided to end it all. That's going to ruin the whole week for Drew Pearson. He's already filed copy, my good friend who will be nameless told me"—Sam Tilburn—Ed Reidy had got used to it—had tipsters everywhere—"for his column tomorrow, blaming Joe for causing her to commit suicide."

"Oh, sure. That's what he'll write about. 'McCarthyism Caused Old Lady Suicide.' You can bet he's not going to write, 'McCarthy Finds Former Communist Spy Who Commits Suicide Before Testifying.'

"What do you imagine she wrote him, a couple of hours before— biting the bullet? Poor, poor Josefa. We got to do a big story about her. But what did she have to tell Joe? Apologies?"

"I don't know, Ed. Maybe she said she couldn't bear to live in a society with two hundred and five Communists in its State Department."

"Ha ha. Fun*nee.* . . . You're certainly helpful today, Sam. . . . Well, I'll write something."

"You always do, Ed."

"Good night, Sam."

"Good night, Ed. Ed?"

"Yeah."

"Say a prayer for that poor lady."

WILLIAM F. BUCKLEY JR.

27

Owen Lattimore

On the opening day of the meeting of the special Senate subcommittee, Chairman Tydings had surprised McCarthy by asking him to reveal the names of the suspects.

McCarthy said that he thought it wrong to give them out in a public session — "Some of the material associated with some of the names might prove wrong, or outdated." But the chairman, sustained by the three-Democrat majority, wanted names, and McCarthy edged in, releasing the name of the man he dubbed the "top Russian spy" in the United States, Owen Lattimore. What's more, McCarthy said he would provide a witness who would identify Lattimore as a Communist wielding great influence.

Coming to testify, McCarthy said, would be Louis Budenz, now an assistant professor of economics at Fordham College. Budenz had been a party member for ten years, reaching the commanding post of managing editor of the *Daily Worker*. He had defected in 1945 and given testimony concerning four hundred U.S. members of the Communist Party.

On the day that Budenz was to appear, five hundred people were crowded into the Senate hearing room. "Excuse me," Joe said, approaching the table set up for him, facing the examiners. He needed to step over the legs of a photographer attempting a floor-based angle shot of the full committee seated at the long mahogany table opposite: Senators Tydings, McMahon, Green, representing the Democratic majority, and Lodge and Hickenlooper, the minority.

"Sorry, Senator"—the photographer, lying on the floor, bent his knees up toward his chin, allowing the senator to slide up to his seat. McCarthy propped his briefcase on the table and sat down. A flashbulb went off directly in front of him, and klieg lights from newsreel cameramen blazed on. On his right, on his left, and behind him were tables fully occupied by news reporters.

It was a scene packed with bodies and with drama. Senator Tydings banged the meeting to order, and instantly Senator Hickenlooper put in for a point of order. He advised the chairman that the minority wished to have counsel of its own during the forthcoming proceedings. Tydings denied the request, banged down his gavel again, and to everyone's surprise turned to McCarthy, "You will kindly stop interrupting the proceedings, Senator."

Everyone was surprised, inasmuch as McCarthy had not opened his mouth since sitting down. He looked over at Hickenlooper with bewilderment. The senator from Iowa merely shook his head.

Louis Budenz was sworn in. It was achingly hard to get his story because he was interrupted ever step of the way.

Budenz: It was then that I met with Frederick Vanderbilt Field.

Ed Morgan (committee counsel): How do you spell the name?

Budenz: F-r-e-d-e-r-i-c-k V-a-n-d-e-r-b-i-l-t F-i-e-l-d. Mr. Field, of course, is well-known as a Communist—

Morgan: Mr. Budenz, we are not going to take for granted such charges as—

McCarthy: Mr. Chairman, Mr. Chairman. If you can't say Frederick Vanderbilt *Field*—is a Communist, you can't say Harry Truman is a Democrat—

Tydings (his gavel pounding down): I remind the junior senator from Wisconsin that I am presiding over this hearing—

McCarthy: But Senator Tydings, Senator Tydings, I mean, would we have to prove that *Stalin* was a mem—

Tydings (renewed use of the gavel): If the senator does not obey the rulings of the chairman, we will call a recess—

McCarthy: All right. All right.

Tydings: Counsel may resume.

Budenz was shaken by three hours of this. "What's happened," he said as they walked out together at the lunch recess, "is obvious. They're on the public record about Lattimore. He seems to be very special for Tydings. They've all lionized Lattimore. What's that all about?"

"It's all about McCarthy," Joe volunteered. "I said on the Senate floor—you know—that my case would stand or fall on Lattimore. That means they've got to take good care of Lattimore."

Owen Lattimore was a professor at Johns Hopkins, a specialist in Far East Studies. When asked by a student journalist what he had to do with the State Department, his answer had been, "Nothing." Then the student asked, Why was his name brought up to begin with, if indeed he had nothing to do with the State Department? Lattimore commented, "I've told everybody, Senator McCarthy is crazy if he got me mixed up with the State Department. I have never been in the State Department." At the third session Tydings informed the committee at large that he had checked with the State Department and indeed there was no record of Lattimore's having served.

Budenz had never met Lattimore. He had learned of Lattimore's commitment to the party from party faithful Frederick Vanderbilt Field. "Why didn't you mention Lattimore in your article in *Colliers* magazine last year when you wrote about Communists in government?" Tydings asked. Budenz replied that *Colliers* had not wanted him to name Lattimore for legal reasons, but that he had in effect named him when Budenz complained of the Communist authors who wrote for *Pacific Affairs,* a journal edited by Lattimore. Budenz said he could not there and then document the leaning of all the articles published in *Pacific Affairs,* but that Lattimore was its editor and no one would deny that the journal was pro-Communist in its direction.

"Was he the top Soviet agent?" Senator Tydings asked.

"From my own knowledge, I would not say he was a top Soviet agent."

The headline in the following day's *Milwaukee Journal* read, "Budenz Says Lattimore 'Aids' Reds But Refuses to Call Him Communist." The testimony of Budenz was largely discounted. "Budenz has been around the ring once too many times," the *New York Post* article read, making reference to Budenz's numerous appearances on the witness stand. "Most probably he's just making it all up, to help Joe."

The following day, Tydings called the committee into executive session, no press allowed. Executive sessions were generally attended only by the committee's executive members, though all were reportedly notified, and entitled to attend.

At the start of this session, Budenz was asked to give such other information as he had about Communists in the State Department. At just that moment, Senator McCarthy opened the door and entered the room. It was the first meeting of the committee in executive session, and he had arrived late. At the door of the chamber he had bumped into Minority Counsel Robert Morris, who told him that, moments before, Tydings had ordered him to leave the room, on the grounds that minority counsel would not be permitted at executive sessions. Joe angrily shut the hearing door and strode to his seat.

Tydings: "The junior senator from Wisconsin is not a member of the investigating committee and will leave the room."

McCarthy sizzled for a moment, then stood up and wheeled around toward the door. But then he stopped to peer down at an alien presence sitting to one side at the end of the table.

He would give many a speech, telling and retelling it: that at the same executive session to which minority counsel was denied admission and Senator McCarthy was denied admission, there sat—Owen Lattimore, accompanied by his lawyer.

That evening they spent at McCarthy's office. Ray Kiermas, Jean Kerr, Don Surine, Mary Haskell, and Harry Bontecou. Harry had begun work only the week before but had been assigned from the first day to the Lattimore case.

Joe drank a bottle of beer and munched a salami sandwich. The staff had Coca-Cola with their sandwiches. "I'm going to say tomorrow, on the floor, that maybe I was wrong to say about Lattimore that he was a top espionage agent. But the way the hearing's shaping up, nobody thinks Lattimore has done anything except study and write books. Yeah, Harry?"

"I pulled out Lattimore's book. There's a revealing blurb on the jacket. Want to hear it?"

"Yeah, go ahead."

"It says, 'He' — Lattimore — 'shows that all the Asiatic people are more interested in actual democratic practices such as the ones they can see in action across the Russian border, than they are in the fine theories of Anglo-Saxon democracies which come coupled with ruthless imperialism. . . . He inclines to support American newspapermen who report that the only real democracy in China is found in Communist areas."

"Holy *Jezus!*" McCarthy dropped the sandwich on his plate. "You got to be kidding, I mean, show me the book."

"They wouldn't let me take it out of the library. I wrote out the blurb."

"Mary. Send someone to the library tomorrow and get a photostatic copy of that jacket. Harry, did you read the book?"

"No, didn't have time. But I called a professor of mine who knows the publishing business and asked him whether a blurb would ever appear on the jacket of a book if the author of it didn't approve."

"Answer?" — Joe was impatient.

"All but inconceivable in such a situation as this. That means to me not only that Lattimore argued those positions, but that he was proud to advertise them."

They spent until eleven in the office. "Your real problem, Joe," Jeanie said, "is you can't do any thorough exposition of the points you are trying to make, the way Tydings is running the show. I think you've got to try to put it together in a speech —"

"Tydings wouldn't like that," Don Surine interjected. To give a speech in the Senate about something that is currently being investigated *by* the Senate — no, that's not right. Not only Tydings wouldn't like that. The Southern gentleman wouldn't like that. We wouldn't want to alienate Senator Russell." It would not do to antagonize Senator Richard Russell of Georgia. He was not the majority leader, but he was senior in almost every other sense of the word. The tribune of Senate practice, custodian of procedure and protocols.

McCarthy mused. "Yes. Maybe I should give it as a speech?"

They bandied that about. But that too might appear—would appear—"contumacious." McCarthy the lawyer supplied the word. And went on. "Maybe we should get somebody else to give the speech."

"—or write an article," Jean said.

"An article wouldn't see print for a couple of weeks. Don't we need to move faster?"

"What about this: We could feed the information to Larry Spivak, maybe. Maybe get him to invite Lattimore on *Meet the Press* and ask him a couple of questions."

"That would mean giving Lattimore a very big audience when he hits you over the head. He's probably pretty good at it."

"Still," Joe said, "let's sleep on it. If we decide to go with it, I'll call Spivak tomorrow."

"He's not all that friendly." Mary Haskell never missed *Meet the Press* on Sunday mornings.

"He's above all things a journalist," Jeanie said.

McCarthy got up, grabbed his briefcase, and stopped. He put his arm around Jeanie. "How'm I doing?"

"Not too good, Joe."

"We'll see what we can do about that."

28

Herrendon and Harry dig in

Harry Bontecou and Lord Herrendon worked now every morning in the library of the country estate, Hanberry, not a villa as vast as one gets used to, visiting titled tycoons in England. "My father never cared much about space when he didn't use it. But there is the farm down there, and we have quite enough acres—forty, when I last looked at the tax bill. The house itself is very old, Georgian, eighteenth century. And ample for six scholars, let alone two. You will be comfortable."

They met for three hours before midday in the library, and for three hours late in the afternoon, after taking exercise and a rest. Alex's computer sat on the table and lit up a large screen at the end of the room, a pedagogical device recently developed. He worked studiously in his notes on Western capitulation to the Soviet Union in the matter of the prisoners-refugees.

"Operation Keelhaul was not a heavily documented operation. American and British files are incomplete. We don't have that genetic German compulsion to record everything, no matter how heinous."

"Yes," Harry concurred. "I know what you mean. In the summer of junior year—"

"You were in Nuremberg."

Harry was no longer surprised by his host's detailed knowledge of Harry's life. The long article in *Contemporary Authors,* published after his Pulitzer-winning biography of Bismarck, had brought Harry Bontecou his fifteen minutes of fame. The article had recorded in some detail the historian's year-by-year itinerary, beginning with his wartime duty. It was, except for the war years and the immediate post-college years, the life of a sedate historian.

"I, er," Harry had not yet devised a workable name for Lord Alex Herrendon. Though he yet been urged to do so, he found it difficult for more reasons than age and rank to call him Alex. He'd get used to it. But meanwhile — "I was about to tell you that I had a firsthand experience with that aspect of German historical punctiliousness we're talking about. I worked that summer vacation from Columbia in the War Crimes Office — I was in Germany to study the language, but I was earning my own vacation money. The honcho I worked for asked me one night if I wanted to know exactly what happened to the men who tried to assassinate Hitler on July twentieth."

"But of course you knew what happened to them, didn't you? Lowering them live onto the meat hooks?"

"Sure I knew. I still shiver. Yes, Stauffenberg had to guess that if he didn't succeed in killing Hitler with a bomb on July twentieth, Hitler would find something more painful than a bomb to punish Stauffenberg and his collaborators with. When I visited Berlin I found out there what actually took place. The executions. What Captain Rothstein showed me was something I didn't know existed."

Alex killed the computer screen and looked over at Harry. "I guess I don't know what you're talking about."

"There is a — movie of their executions. I asked Captain Rothstein to stop the screening after I viewed Stauffenberg lowered onto the hook. Hannah Arendt was talking about the Holocaust when she coined the phrase 'the banality of evil.' But you can't see that movie and believe people could get used to it. But then, that's what you — are working on."

"Yes, though at some remove. I'm not talking so much about how torturers go to sleep at night. Though it's good to remember that professional hangmen in Britain during the last century couldn't find anybody to drink a beer with them after work. What I want to look at is: How is it that societies estrange themselves from huge-scale systematic brutality? Hitler-Stalin, of course. But Pol Pot? Strenuously unnoticed. Did the movie you saw part of—I didn't know it existed—get any kind of circulation?"

"No, I gather not. It was suppressed even by the Nuremberg tribunal. . . . Mildly interesting development: The filming was intended for showing to the führer, to give him personal satisfaction in seeing the . . . the treatment of his would-be assassin, so to speak, in the flesh. It was in a fine European tradition. You've read about the public torture of Guy D'Amiens, for trying to kill Louis XV. Anyway, for whatever reason, Hitler never got around to viewing the film.

"What a waste," Harry spoke grimly. "I don't know whether your people—your then people—went in for protracted torture of that kind—"

"No. Well, no unless you count Gulag as protracted torture, and there's a good argument for saying that is exactly what it was. But when the idea, for the Bolsheviks, was execution, the shot in the back of the head in the Lubianka was the routine. Granted, Gulag—I repeat myself—is torture, as is starving to death in the Ukraine. . . . But we're a far cry from what you engaged in at Plattling. The men you helped to round up to return to Russia were in many cases shot, or sent to Gulag. What I was saying," Alex relit the screen, "is that I am anxious exactly to trace the events of February 25, 1946—exactly what happened to the repatriated Russians. And I have come up with material that wasn't available to early historians like Nikolai Tolstoi. I've loaded my computer with six photo shots of what I think was Plattling; I'm wanting your confirmation of this—" he called them up on the screen, one after another.

"Yes, that's Plattling," Harry said, his voice husky. "That's definitely Plattling. You can see off at the corner—at eleven o'clock—where my company headquarters was."

"And I have this one. I need to know if it harmonizes with your memory of that morning."

The photo was taken from a hundred yards outside the camp, looking in at an angle on the main gate. There was scattered snow and a heavy congregation of soldiers on both sides of the gates. At the left, one tank was visible, facing the gate.

"Is that it?"

Harry examined it carefully. "At least I can't find my own face among the U.S. Army contingent." And after a pause, "I can't say. I can imagine other situations where there'd have been a lot of GIs and Russians on the scene, and tanks here and there weren't rare. . . . Tell you what, Alex. As a historian I'm careful about these things. You can say that the photograph is of Camp Plattling and in no way contradicts what happened on February twenty-fifth, and is probably authentic."

Alex, as usual, was writing down on computer Harry's answers to the questions put to him.

They went on to pictures of the Bavarian forest, where the Soviet soldiers had picked up the refugees. Once again there was the question of absolute identification. Indeed it was a picture of a train loaded with men with indistinct features, once again a picture of what might have been on February 25, 1946, beyond Zwiesel, near the Czech frontier. "Does it really matter?" the historian asked his host.

"I would like to fortify a personal narrative. The pictures would make that possible."

The balance of the week was spent reviewing the long textual narrative of U.S. and British appeals against the Soviet demand for repatriation of the refugees.

"You know something," Harry said at the end of a long day. "If Truman and Churchill had been as resolute as Stalin, they'd simply have said: No. 'No, Marshall Stalin. You can't get them back. So what do you want to do about it? Go to war?' But they really abandoned that kind of language at Teheran and Yalta. They hoped Stalin would come around; FDR was ill and Truman new at the game, Churchill beleaguered by the British rejection of his government, Attlee relatively green and concerned mostly about domestic socialization—"

"Yes. And Stalin's obduracy, I think we both agree, was a great strength. I was certainly impressed by it. I saw Stalin staking out his position: the Marxist-Leninist position. Everything else was derivative. Like Saint Thomas on God: If He exists, then you have a postulation, and nothing that you see or experience can undo that postulation. It just exists—and is permitted to exist by the divine order. I'm writing about why the West wasn't as convinced about *its* position as Stalin was about his. And I'm asking why Stalin appealed to so many, in so many forms. God help me I'm qualified to write about that. It is vulgar to forget, which so many people in fact do, the high appeal that Communism had for so many."

"Maybe I was too young to come across that appeal."

"Come now. Do not pretend to be unfamiliar with the story. I know you are not. I marked here, I took it from a manuscript, unpublished, of letters to Ralph de Toledano, the American author and journalist, from Whittaker Chambers. It is a paragraph that for reasons hard to understand was omitted from his great book, *Witness*, apparently at the urging of his editor. Chambers was apparently remonstrating to a friend who wonders that Communism's idealistic net could ever ensnare the sophisticated. Here, let me read it to you. I like to *hear* the sound of Chambers, and his reproach here is arresting."

He picked up the book and read.

"'Now, in the light of its late sundown, you tell me that you took one look at Communism and knew at once that it was a fraud. My friend, you are mistaken. In the terrible decade, 1915–1923, you scarcely knew the word Communism. You did not know that, for multitudes, Communism hung, like a star-shell, lurid, but casting the only steady light into that bleeding, dark and ruined world. It is only now that you know that Communism is a fraud. You only know now that, of the ways of saving the world, Communism is not one. I know that too—now. I learned it in another school. I learned by trying, in the day of disaster, to do something, and doing the wrong thing, because I did not see what else to do. Life has been more gracious to you—or perhaps your judgment is better. For you did nothing at all.'"

"Of course I understand, but then it's true I didn't live through that decade Chambers is talking about. My decade, 1938 to 1948, tilted me, and most others, in a different direction. But we're to talk about all that."

"Right, Harry. And to get down to a little business. I need to know some details of your life that were not reported in the *Contemporary Authors* biography of 1986. What did you emphasize when you served in the National Endowment for the Humanities?"

29

Meet the Press
with Lattimore

Public attention to Josefa Kalli quickly ebbed. There was a memorial service in Baltimore, attended by a half dozen of the men and women she had worked with at the Commerce Department. There was no family, and no one stepped forward asking to be put in charge of burial arrangements and the final service. The assistant secretary of commerce then stepped in and ("I've never done this before. What exactly do I do?") asked his personnel director for help. What had to be done was pretty routine. Police . . . mortuary . . . cremation. "But there is one less-than-routine thing I'd do if I were you, Mr. Secretary."

"What's that?"

"I'd call Senator McCarthy and ask him please not to attend. He'll understand why. If he comes, the whole tabloid community will be there and a lot of stuff will get said that won't exactly—well, you know, help our own . . . personnel situation."

Donald Sutherland said he understood.

He put in the call. He didn't want to ask for Senator McCarthy personally. For one thing, the assistant secretary was in no mood to chat with the senator about the reasons for Kalli's behavior. The operator put him through to Mary Haskell. "You understand, Mrs. Haskell, if the senator wants to speak to me I'd be absolutely delighted to do so. But I thought perhaps this business was better handled at . . . this level."

"I understand," Mary said.

And Joe understood; in fact was grateful to be excused. His only knowledge of Josefa Kalli, after all, was what he got from his two-hour interview with her. He had filed inquiries about her record, but he knew they would be of no effect: He would bump into the 1948 executive order that barred legislative inquiries into personnel security records.

"So, Mary, I had two hours with her and"—he drew it from the drawer he had placed it in—"this letter, which you've seen." The letter spoke of Josefa Kalli's fright, her despair, her reluctance to reveal names, and her decision to end it all.

"I got the hundredth request for a copy this morning. Do you intend to give it out?"

McCarthy sat back. "No. Let them speculate—and worry—about what's in it. Let's let the poor lady alone."

"What if Mr. Hoover asks to see it?"

"That's different. But if the FBI asks for it, tell them to have the director call me."

Kalli was forgotten, but the tempest over Owen Lattimore heightened. McCarthy moved forward on his idea.

Harry had worked hard on the research, and Don Surine drew on his many sources. Joe brought in some data without saying where he had got them. The whole package was sent to Lawrence Spivak, editor of *Meet the Press* and its principal interrogator.

The TV program was heavily advertised: Owen Lattimore on *Meet the Press*. McCarthy had said early on in the Tydings investigation that his case stood or fell on the correctness of his identification of Owen Lattimore as a Soviet agent. McCarthy retreated on the matter of his being the "top" agent, but Lattimore remained, week after week, the dominant figure in the Tydings investigation. It would be an important half hour.

• Millard Tydings, spending Sunday in his ample house in Baltimore, told his houseguests to be quiet, even though it was only 10:55 and the television program didn't begin until eleven.

• Dean Acheson had come into the imposing secretary's office at the Department of State. He had been meeting with political advisers on the matter of Korea, but ten minutes before the hour he said, simply: "Look, gentlemen. I have to see the Lattimore program on *Meet the Press.* It is very important to me, and very important to the department. You may join me in the Red Room or disport yourselves as you please until eleven-thirty. All seven joined the secretary of state in the adjacent room with its brand-new twelve-inch television.

• The First Baptist Church, on Sixteenth and O Street, was the church of the Reverend Edward Pruden, and his Sunday services began at ten o'clock. President Truman and Mrs. Truman were regular congregants. There was this problem, namely that the Reverend Pruden tended to deliver substantial sermons, with the result that services ended approximately one hour after they began. On the Friday before, a White House aide — Posi Casertano — had met with Mr. Pruden. If he could manage to end the service this next Sunday at 10:50, the president would be grateful to go from the church to the rectory next door in order to watch *Meet the Press* on Mr. Pruden's set. No publicity, just an impromptu call by the president on his minister.

The clergyman was delighted and winked at Miss Casertano. "I'll make certain the last hymn ends at ten-fifty. On the other hand, I shall certainly make it a point not to end the service *too* early. That would give the president time to return to the White House, and I wouldn't want that! I'd be honored to have him as my guest, even if it is only for a half hour."

• Don Surine had suggested the entire staff view the program on the senator's set in the office, but Joe said no. He didn't want the press to sniff out that McCarthy attached that much importance to it.

"You watch it here. I'll watch it at Jeanie's house. At Jeanie's mother's house." He turned to Harry. "Want to come?"

Harry nodded. "Wouldn't miss it. I don't have a television set."

• Ed Reidy called Sam Tilburn from Indianapolis. "You going to watch it at home? So am I. Give me a call after it's over, okay?"

— Good morning, ladies and gentlemen. This is Larry Spivak bringing you *Meet the Press.* Our guest today is Professor Owen Lattimore. Mr. Lattimore, as everybody knows, has been the principal target of Senator Joe McCarthy, who two months ago charged that there were two hundred and five Communists in the State Department. There is a dispute over that figure, but he did charge that there were a number of loyalty and security risks in government, and he named Owen Lattimore as his primary target.

Mr. Lattimore is a Far East specialist, teaching at Johns Hopkins. He is the author of many books, including *The Desert Road to Turkestan*. Our panelists are four journalists who will be introduced later.

Welcome, Mr. Lattimore.

—Thank you, Mr. Spivak. I am glad to be here.

—Mr. Lattimore, you said on February fifteenth that you had no association with the Department of State. You also said, "I am the least consulted man of all those who have a public reputation in this country as specialists in the Far East." But Mr. Lattimore, in 1941 President Roosevelt appointed you personal political adviser to Chiang Kai-shek, then head of state of China, and you remained in Peiping until 1942. What is your comment on that?

—Well, Mr. Spivak, that was a special appointment and it was outside the, the purview of the State Department.

—But surely the State Department was concerned about what you reported on China?

—Well, we like to think the State Department is aware of *everything* that goes on that can in any way affect foreign policy.

—Mr. Lattimore, after you got back to Washington you were made the chief of Pacific Operations for the Office of War Information. Surely that is one, well, one front of the State Department?

—The Office of War Information was created after Pearl Harbor, Mr. Spivak, and it would be incorrect to think of it as a part of the State Department—

—In 1944, Mr. Lattimore, Vice President Henry Wallace made his famous visit to Siberia and to China. That was the trip about which he wrote, representing forcefully the Soviet position on the issues of 1944, having to do with bringing the war to an end and planning the peace. You accompanied Vice President Wallace on that trip. Would you not call that an official connection? Surely the State Department was concerned with the diplomatic impact of the trip of the vice president of the United States?

—Well, Mr. Spivak, I have—I'm not denying it—a, er, considerable professional reputation in my own field. And the vice president obviously wished to have one or more people in his entourage with whom he could consult on historical and cultural matters, Russian and Chinese—

—Mr. Lattimore, in 1945 President Truman appointed you as a member of the Pauley Reparations Mission to Japan—

—Look, Mr. Spivak, that was a purely technical assignment—

• "*I* didn't know that," Harry Truman said, "about Lattimore and the Pauley commission. Why the hell didn't somebody tell me that? Make a note to find that out. Make a note for me to call Mr. Acheson as soon as I get back."

"Yes, Mr. President." Presidential Assistant Ellery Grew took out his notebook.

—Mr. Lattimore, in 1949 you attended a State Department conference on China policy. And—wait just a minute, Mr. Lattimore—yet you have said, I quote you, again, February fifteenth, "I have never been in the State Department." Mr. Lattimore, I have a photostatic copy of a letter signed by you and directed to Mr. Benjamin Kizer, dated June 12, 1942. The last paragraph of that letter reads, "My home address is as typed above, and my home telephone is Towson 846-W. I am in Washington about four days a week, and when there can always be reached at Lauchlin Currie's office, Room 228, State Department Building; telephone NAtional 1414, extension 90. Yours very sincerely, Owen Lattimore."

• "God almighty," Dean Acheson pointed his finger at his aide, ignoring the seven senior officers grouped around the television set with him. "Lauchlin Currie's office! Lauchlin Currie isn't just a McCarthy target. He was FDR's administrative assistant for foreign affairs *and,* we now know, a member of the Silvermaster spy ring!" He stopped. He wanted to hear.

—Mr. Lattimore, my information is that when Mr. Currie went away for a period of time he would ask you to take care of his mail at the White House. That question was raised during the Tydings investigation. You have most vehemently denied this. But I have seen a letter, I have a copy here, written by you to Mr. E. C. Carter of the Institute

WILLIAM F. BUCKLEY JR.

of Pacific Relations. The date on that letter is July 15, 1942. The first paragraph of it reads, "Dear Carter: Currie asked me to take care of his correspondence while he is away and in view of your telegram of today, I think I had better tell you that he has gone to China on a special trip. This news is absolutely confidential until released in the press."

—Well, er, I have to admit my memory lapsed on that particular point, Mr. Spivak—I think I was doing Mr. Currie merely a personal clerical favor—

• Senator Tydings was absolutely silent. His wife watched him. Even his guests playing dominoes stopped, turning their attention to the little man with glasses asking all those questions and the other man with the little mustache, sitting opposite, answering them.

—Mr. Lattimore, the reason Senator McCarthy has leveled his accusations is of course that he charges you with being a Communist— No no, *I'm* not asserting this, Professor Lattimore. I'm not asserting that you are or have been a Communist. I'm asking you questions. And of course the question most people have been asking about you is: Are you, or were you, pulling an oar for the Communists, in the Soviet Union and in China? I have here one of your books, *Solution in Asia*—

• "That's *my* book!" Harry said excitedly. "The book I told you about—"

"*Quiet, Harry!*" Joe stopped him. "Listen."

—The book carries—here, on the jacket—a blurb. A brief account of what's in the book. My information is that such accounts are provided by the book publishers but that their content is always okayed by the author. Now this blurb reads, "He"—that's you, the author—"shows that all the Asiatic people are more interested in actual democratic practices such as the ones they can see in action across the Russian border, than they are in the fine theories of Anglo-Saxon democracies which come coupled with ruthless imperialism. . . . He"—that's you, Mr. Lattimore—"inclines to support American newspapermen who report that the only real democracy in China is found in Communist areas."

• Dean Acheson stood up, walked to the set, and turned it off. There was silence. One counselor said, "Don't you want to hear what Lattimore says?"

"No," Acheson said. "Bloody fool. And he has greatly strengthened the hand of that terrible . . . man. Let's get back to the subject of Korea. We must continue our efforts, gentlemen, and I am sure they will be successful, to prevent any military action there."

• Ed Reidy's phone rang. "Gee . . . *whiz!* Sam. That was human slaughter. Do you figure Lattimore bailed out at all in those last ten minutes?"

"He did as much as you can do, Ed, with those half dozen arrows sticking out of his chest."

"What will the Tydings people do?"

"They've got a problem. But they can't drop Lattimore. They'll have to try to smother the whole thing with academic tributes and testimonials and hate-Joe-McCarthy talk. There's no way they can just hand Lattimore over to Joe McCarthy."

"Sam, have you dug into Lattimore's articles and books, especially in the last year or so?"

"I've poked about. What're you especially interested in, Ed?"

"I'm wondering whether he's made recommendations on the Korean scene. It looks real bad over there. Might be good if you poked into the *Readers Guide* or some of the professional journals."

"Will do, Ed."

At Mrs. Kerr's house the telephone rang. A few minutes later it rang again. The press had tracked down Joe McCarthy.

Jean came in from the kitchen with a bottle of champagne.

30

JUNE 25, 1950

The North Koreans
invade the South

At five A.M. Korean time, on June 25, 1950, the North Korean Army invaded South Korea. Two hours later, at 5:45 P.M., New York time, the United Nations Security Council met, petitioned to do so by President Truman's ambassador to the United Nations, Ernest A. Gross. By a stroke of luck for the U.S., Soviet Ambassador Jacob Malik was boycotting the Security Council that week in protest against the Nationalist Chinese occupying the China seat—it belonged, the Soviets insisted, to mainland China, which Mao Tse-tung had conquered in the preceding year. When Secretary General Trygve Lie, after giving an up-to-the-minute report on the military crisis in Korea, initiated his resolution, Ambassador Malik was not within reach and could not therefore exercise the veto the United Nations Constitution had awarded to Russia, France, and England, along with the United States. The delegates endorsed the secretary's cease-and-desist resolution against the North Korean Communists and in successive sessions voted a) to resist the invasion by military means, and b) to request all members of the United Nations to assist in the military effort.

That was on Monday and Tuesday.

On Wednesday, Senator Joe McCarthy issued a statement to the press. He charged that the terrible, disastrous war—Seoul, South Korea's capital city, had fallen to the Communist invaders on day four—was the result of inept diplomacy by "two men, a secretary of state, Dean Acheson, and a former secretary of state and special emissary, General George Marshall."

These men, "informed and perhaps guided by" the Institute of Pacific Relations, which "for a long time has been a Communist-directed operation," failed to support the Nationalists in China, "losing that great subcontinent to the Communists in October." And now, "less than a half year later," the Communists in North Korea—"a lethal finger of Joseph Stalin—have pitched the world into war, one more time, a mere five years since our great struggle of 1945."

The press everywhere featured Senator McCarthy's comprehensive indictment of the Truman administration's foreign policy. Telegrams poured into his office beyond any capacity of Mary Haskell to handle them—she had to enlist the help of her retired brother and his wife to cope with more than five thousand messages. McCarthy instructed Harry to call the administrative assistant of Senator Tydings to request one week's postponement in the Tydings hearings until the Korean crisis could be assimilated; he pointed out that a moratorium would give individual senators the time to be briefed and to arrive at whatever recommendations they wished publicly, or indeed privately, to urge on President Truman.

Senator McCarthy now found photographers and reporters stationed during all business hours outside his office. Their assignment: to cover every public movement of the senator—the whole country seemed now to want to follow, hour by hour, Joe McCarthy.

Throughout the barrage of questions regarding his criticism of the Truman administration, nobody brought up the name Forrest Davis, and McCarthy kept his secret to himself.

The meeting with Davis had been three weeks earlier.

They all knew Forrest Davis, a talented and scholarly journalist associated for many years with the *Saturday Evening Post*, now coeditor of the conservative fortnightly *The Freeman*. Davis was in his late sixties. He was balding and wore what one fellow journalist described as "a little sprig on his chin." He was happy and relaxed at the cocktail party given, that Saturday evening early in June, by Frank Hanighen. Hanighen was editor and publisher of *Human Events,* a weekly conservative newsletter-essay, four pages of political briefs by Hanighen followed by one four-page essay, usually written by educator Felix Morley, alternating with French essayist and philosopher Bertrand de Jouvenel.

Forrest was much at ease in the company of fellow conservatives. The headliner at that party was of course Joe McCarthy, who arrived accompanied by his young aide, Harry Bontecou. Ralph de Toledano and Karl Hess were there, the little conservative enclave in *Newsweek* magazine. Henry Regnery, the publisher of conservative books, modern and classical, based in Chicago, chatted and nibbled on a cheese cracker; he was a patron of Frank Hanighen's *Human Events*. Regnery had brought along young Bill Buckley, freshly graduated from Yale, whose projected book on the ideological vectors at his alma mater Regnery had agreed to look at. C. Dickerman Williams, chief counsel for the Commerce Department, had been a law clerk in 1925 for Chief Justice William Howard Taft. He was discussing the uses of the Fifth Amendment, on which he was an authority, with Ben Mandel, former Communist official — it was he who had written out the Communist Party card for applicant Whittaker Chambers, then twenty-four years old, in 1925. Mandel was now a researcher for the House Committee on Un-American Activities. And there was Freda Utley, the British journalist, a naturalized American, author of an exposé *(The China Story)* on the loss of China, published by Regnery. She was talkative, affectionate, a little deaf. She had a lit cigarette almost always, often between her lips, even when she spoke.

Forrest Davis was enjoying his fourth vodka and tonic. He was a warm friend of anyone he liked and could be suicidally generous when inflamed by wine with a love of the world, which was much of the time.

Davis was also in arrears to Putnam's, his publisher. Putnam's, approving his outline, had advanced Davis three thousand dollars to write a book-length, critical account of the career of George Catlett Marshall, chief of staff during the Second World War, special presidential delegate to China, and secretary of state for two years beginning in January 1947, during which time he helped to launch the Marshall Plan. That important initiative called for immediate and abundant economic aid to western Europe to help it revive after the world war.

Working on his Marshall biography in the summer and fall of 1949, Davis ran out of time (he was several months behind on delivery date) and money. He was desperate and thought to gain a little leeway by enticing Doubleday to take an interest in the book. He approached an acquisitions editor, sending him an outline of his proposed book. He did this without consulting his agent, let alone Putnam's. He asked for, and got, five thousand dollars. He intended to repay Putnam's forthwith its three-thousand-dollar sum, but the press of immediate debt caused him to defer this. Still, he was confident that — his book completed — the royalties from sales would earn him more than enough to repay Putnam's advance.

McCarthy, drink in hand, approached Davis in a corner of the noisy room. They greeted each other and Davis winked, mentioning that he had seen Joe in the clutches of Freda Utley during the past fifteen minutes.

"Yes," Joe said, brushing off his jacket flamboyantly, "Freda breasted me" — he moved his own chest forward in near-body contact with Forrest, imitating Utley's intimate aggressions when struggling through her deafness to hear cocktail chatter. "And she managed to spill her cigarette ashes down my coat."

Joe chuckled, patting the lapels of the jacket, then said, "But who can get mad at Freda? After what she's been through."

As a young woman in England, Freda Utley had joined the Communist Party. She traveled to Moscow, met and married Arcadi Jacovelevitch Berdichevsky, a young Soviet official, and bore him a son, Jon. One night in 1933, at three in the morning, came one of those legendary knocks on the door of their apartment. Arcadi opened the door to two men in civilian clothes. They told him he was wanted "for a few hours" to give vital information.

From that moment on, Freda never heard from him or of him again. She waged a five-year international campaign, persuading illustrious pro-Soviet British intellectuals to participate in her effort to persuade the Kremlin to disclose where her husband was. To no avail. What came then was her renunciation of Communism and her influential book, *The Dream We Lost*. She was now an icon in the anti-Communist movement.

Their host, Hanighen—orderly, finicky, acerbic—had joined McCarthy and Davis in their reclusive corner. He advised Joe, with a

WILLIAM F. BUCKLEY JR.

straight face, that there was one other version of what happened in Moscow that night in 1933, namely that her husband had been *relieved* when the knock came, sparing him more time with Freda. McCarthy laughed heartily. He and Davis reached out to the waiter for replenishment of their drinks. Hanighen was called away by another guest.

Davis suddenly said, "Joe, follow me, just a minute, into the next room."

They took their drinks into Frank Hanighen's study and sat at a card table. McCarthy stretched out his legs. Davis leaned over to him.

"Joe, I think the fight you're engaged in is the most important fight of the postwar years."

"Well, yeah, Forrest. I *know* it's important, but glad to hear from you you think the same, though I've known you did."

"Well," Davis's eyes were brimming with solicitude and affection, "I want to make what I think will be an important contribution to your fight. I want to give you my story on George Marshall."

"I know you've been working on a book, Forrest. But what are you suggesting, a speech based on your material?"

Davis drew himself back. He looked now, with his goatee raised slightly, his eyes drawn down, his hands raised about his waist, like a Chinese emperor bequeathing a whole province to one of his sons. "I propose to give you the whole thing. The entire manuscript. As if you or your staff had written it. It is dynamite, Joe, an explanation of the person primarily responsible for our diplomatic problems, from Yalta to the present."

At eleven the following night the telephone rang in Harry's apartment. "Joe here, Harry. I want you to come over to my place right away."

"You okay, Joe?"

"I'm okay. But I got something I want you to read. Something vital. You're young, it's *early*, not even midnight."

Harry, at twenty-three, was indeed young, he reflected as he pulled on his pants, though he needed more sleep than McCarthy, whose legendary indifference to sleep his staff could admire, even if they did not have the same stamina.

He found Joe excited. "This tells it *all.* Marshall kept Roosevelt ignorant of critical intelligence reports at Yalta. Kept the generals' military advice away from FDR. He opened the critical pass to the Chinese Communists so they could make contact with the Russians." Joe was now consulting his notes. "He couldn't 'remember' where he was on Pearl Harbor. Couldn't *remember*—chief of staff, on the day of the worst military disaster in history! Went to China and in effect starved Chiang Kai-shek to death, making the Communist victory possible."

"Are you saying, Joe, Forrest thinks Marshall's a Communist?"

"He never says that. But he says he is responsible for our collapse in the Pacific theater, with who knows what's ahead for us in Korea."

"You want me to read it now?" Harry looked down at the bulky speech folder. "Gee. This thing must be fifty, sixty thousand words."

"I *know.* I spent all afternoon with it. I thought I'd use it as a speech, schedule it for day after tomorrow. But I wanted you to look at it."

"Sure. But, Joe, what's the—hurry?"

"I think you'll know what's the hurry after you've read it."

"Okay. I'll do half of it tonight, half tomorrow morning. Check with you by noon."

"Good man, Harry. How about a nightcap?"

"What I'll need is strong coffee, Joe."

"You won't be sleepy after you start reading this."

"Good night, Joe."

Harry called at exactly noon. "It's a troubling story, Joe. A real icon shatterer. But how the hell are you going to read that manuscript to the Senate? It kept me reading until three, then from eight to eleven."

Joe was never much interested in details. "Oh, well, I'll read fast. You agree it's terrific stuff?"

"Forrest Davis is a fine writer and very scholarly. But Joe, it's not going to be easy to pass this off as just one more speech by Joe McCarthy. It's got references to works by Churchill, Cordell Hull, Henry Stimson, Robert Sherwood, Sumner Welles, Hanson Baldwin. There are sentences in it that don't, well, don't *sound* like you."

"Everybody knows busy senators get help with their speeches."

"I know. But senators try to *sound* . . . authentic. There are some sentences here that . . ." Harry turned to the manuscript. "Listen:

"'I am reminded of a wise and axiomatic utterance in this connection by the great Swedish chancellor Oxenstiern, to his son departing on the tour of Europe. He said: "Go forth my son and see with what folly the affairs of mankind are governed."' I mean, Joe, that's just not going to sound like something cooked up in the office—"

"Even with a Phi Bete assistant like you?"

"Even with a Phi Beta Kappa assistant. This sounds like a dissertation."

"Harry?"—Harry knew what was coming: McCarthy had made up his mind. When that happened—the mind was made up.

"Harry, I've decided to give it as a speech. Now, is there anything in particular you want to tell me about it?"

"Yes. As it stands, there isn't *one* sentence in the book that says that General Marshall is a Communist sympathizer or agent. *That's got to be preserved.* Don't let *anybody* push you across that threshold, into saying Marshall is a Commie."

"Right, right. Well, get the manuscript here real fast, first thing after lunch. We'll need the whole thing retyped. I've already warned Mary. She's lining up a couple of extra hands."

For the next two days, the office was chaos. McCarthy wrote a letter to every member of Congress to advise that he was going to review at some length the whole Marshall record. The press was cued, and when he took the rostrum on June 14 the galleries were packed. Jean Kerr and Don Surine and Harry sat on a couch at the rear of the chamber. McCarthy began by acknowledging the heroic endeavors of his staff. "I believe most of them are in the gallery today. I salute them; they worked eighteen, nineteen, and twenty hours a day in getting the documents together."

Harry listened with agonized intensity as Joe began. His heart fell when he heard the opening words, words he had not seen in the Davis text. McCarthy told his colleagues, and the world, that he would talk now about a "mysterious, powerful" figure who was part of "a conspiracy on a scale so immense as to dwarf any previous such venture in the history of man. A conspiracy of infamy so black that, when it is finally exposed, its principals shall be forever deserving of the maledictions of all honest men."

After reading for almost three hours to an all but empty Senate chamber, Joe signaled to the Senate reporter and gave him, to enter into the record, the balance of the speech. He looked back at the couch, but Jean, Don, and Harry had left. Don and Jean, when he entered his office, pleaded the press of work as having required them to leave the Senate chamber and return to the office.

Harry wasn't there. He was home. He sat at his desk and stared in frustration at his notes of three nights before. He dialed Willmoore Sherrill in New York, but there was no answer. He pulled out Elinor's number in Amsterdam. She greeted him joyously. He tried to banter with her.

"Harry, you're upset. What is it?"

"Oh, I'm fine. I was just worried a little."

"Worried about what?"

Harry knew he wasn't getting anywhere. He was, really, talking to himself. "Worried about the tulip crop."

"Okay, okay. But really. Anything going on?"

"Oh, just a little setback in the office. Nothing to worry about. How are the dikes? Holding?"

The conversation loosened up, and Harry blew her kisses. He put down the telephone and started to dial Sam Tilburn, but thought better of it. He had become a friend, and Harry could talk with him about McCarthy and the entire scene absolutely confident that Tilburn would betray no confidence; confident, also, that Tilburn would listen, and advise, and—sympathize.

But he didn't ring Sam. There wasn't anything further to say, he decided, than that there are good days, and bad days.

The speech was commercially published a few months later by Devin-Adair, Inc., as a 169-page book, *America's Retreat From Victory, The Story of George Catlett Marshall,* by Joseph R. McCarthy.

31

Acheson reflects,
Did he give the wrong signals?

Dean Gooderham Acheson sat in his office in the State Department—old wood, brightly varnished; oil paintings of a few of his predecessors; fine crystal and gilt; the Chippendale desk, at the right corner of which flew the little American flag crossed with the Great Seal of the United States. His penetrating eyes went over the briefing paper prepared by his press aide.

His press aide was his young nephew, Ezra Black. He sat at the desk in the corner, assembling papers for his fastidious employer. Mr. Acheson had the habit of emitting little grunts, barely audible, when he read material in which he or his policies figured. It took close-in experience to distinguish a grunt that marked Mr. Acheson's approval of what he had read from one that marked his disapproval. But Ezra had been on board over a year and knew which was which. This morning the four or five grunts were all negative, emphatically negative. Ezra had no difficulty guessing why. The secretary of state was reading a digest of remarks made the day before on the floor of the Senate that related very directly to the policies of the State Department.

Acheson tilted back his great leather chair, mounted on the brass swivel base, and twirled his full, immaculately groomed mustache pensively. Without turning actually to look at him, he addressed Ezra. "It was perhaps not wise for me to say what I did in January about

Korea. *Correction. Concerning* which remarks, certain deductions were made about Korea. Correction. Certain deductions were made about Korea by certain people."

"They're certainly hitting you for it, Mr. Secretary."

"Do you have the exact words there? The digest does not give them all. Senator Ferguson is merely quoted as saying that the— I quote him—'boys' are dying in Korea because—I quote him again—'a group of untouchables in the State Department sabotaged the aid program.'

"You will remember, Ezra, that the distinguished junior senator from Michigan, Mr. Ferguson, early in the spring, denounced our— I quote him—'wanton waste'—in sending, quotes, 'everything to everybody.' But here . . ." the secretary raised his voice slightly and attempted the flat Midwestern tones of Homer Ferguson, "but here he is angry because we did not send *everything* to *everybody*. He says, according to the digest, 'He told'—Secretary Acheson told—I told—'the world the U.S. would not interfere in Korea.' . . . You have it there, Ezra, my actual text?"

Black was flipping through a loose-leaf notebook looking for the speech at the National Press Club. It was in January, five months before.

"What you said"—Black had found the digest—"was that Japan, the Ryukyu Islands, and the Philippines were within the defense perimeter of the United States and would be defended. Your omission in that speech of Korea—and Formosa—was immediately picked up by the press."

"Hmm. But of course I was correct. To describe the *defense perimeter* of the United States is not to say that we are not *interested in,* do not *care* about, *will* refuse to help, will *fail to defend,* a particular country or geographic area outside that perimeter in particular circumstances. I am not a military man, Ezra—I don't think of you as one, even though you were in the army during the war—"

"Navy."

"Navy during the war. A defense perimeter is a boundary within which a country *has* to act in defense of itself. The Philippines are our westernmost base in the Pacific. That does not mean we would not defend, say, Okinawa."

Ezra Black was silent, his head cocked just a hair to one side.

WILLIAM F. BUCKLEY JR.

Acheson waited. Then: "Do you have any problem with that?"

"Well, no, sir, not as a theoretical point. And the president did in fact immediately decide to oppose the North Koreans with military force."

"Yes. And I fully concurred in last week's decision. We are resisting a specific act of aggression. This obviously would not be the time to do so, but I would expect that at the National War College and other military-academic sanctuaries free from one of Senator McCarthy's informants—if such exist—the distinction would be observed between a place the United States *has* to defend, lying as it does—I cite Guam as an example—within our defense perimeter, and a place which we *do not* have to defend in order to defend ourselves but which we may *elect* to defend for a number of reasons, in this case, our commitment to oppose aggression, as also to affirm our psychological and diplomatic obligations."

Again Black was silent.

Acheson's eyes went back to his press briefing. He spoke as he read. "Did I never give you the illuminating observation by John Stuart Mill? He said, I think I have it correctly in memory, that all stupid people are conservatives, which means that the conservative party always tends to be large."

He returned to his briefing papers. "Mr. Wherry of Nebraska, with characteristic finesse, observed that the 'blood'—again, of our 'boys'—lies on my shoulders. And the *tricoteuses*—do you know who they were, Ezra?"

Black nodded.

"Well, I should hope so—the bloodsuckers—better, the *bloodlustful*—had help from our friend Senator McCarran." This time the secretary did turn his chair around to face his aide. "Why doesn't Senator McCarran leave the Democratic Party and join the Republican Party, Ezra? Or, for that matter, the Flat Earth Society, if they will have him?"

He swiveled to the front of his desk, where the digest lay. "The senator says we—he is referring to *us*, Ezra—'produce statesmanship at the level of the psychopathic ward.' That is a dull-witted remark." Again he paused. Once more he swiveled.

"Ezra?"

"Yes, sir."

"Your silence has got to mean something."

"Well, sir, I understand your thinking, and your foreign policy. After all, I'm by your side day after day. But the Republicans—and at least one Democrat—are raging mad. Whether they really blame you—blame the Truman administration—or whether they're just making political hay, I don't know. But I do think they have a very plausible political case.

"Look." The young aide seemed now almost to be pleading. "The secretary of state gives a talk in which he describes the western military perimeter, and people look at the map of the Pacific and say, '*Korea's not in it.*' Therefore it follows that the United States will not defend South Korea.

"Therefore Stalin feels it's safe to push that button, and four days after he does it, the capital of South Korea is captured."

"Yes, yes, Ezra. I know a little about advocacy. Ask Covington and Burling. I was their chief litigator for many years, you may remember."

He swiveled the chair right around, and now Black could see only the back of his head. His nephew feared the worst. That came when the secretary was especially riled. He now was especially riled and expressed himself fully.

"I believe I am as alert as anyone to the great tensions of the day. I am perhaps more sensitive than any but a very few—"

Black's pencil scratched out on his pad, almost involuntarily. Oh, shit! he thought. Here we go.

"—to the special dangers of a nuclear-armed world of mortal antagonists—"

The telephone gave the special tone buzz. Acheson picked it up immediately. Ezra Black rose quickly—he was expected to absent himself when the president telephoned. His hand was on the doorknob when the secretary of state said, "Yes, Mr. President?"

Ten minutes later the limousine emerged from the State Department garage and headed for the White House.

WILLIAM F. BUCKLEY JR.

Harry writes to Elinor

Dear Elinor. Dear, *Dear* Elinor:

You can't be *serious*. Come visit with you in Amsterdam "for a couple of weeks in July and August"? There is no *way* I could get away from Washington for two days, forget two weeks. The Tydings Report on Joe will be released sometime during those two weeks. We don't know exactly when, but we do know it will be tough. The Tydings people are fronting for the entire Truman administration (my apologies to the ambassador! your eminent father). Everything we bring up they are prepared to shoot down, or try to. You've read about Owen Lattimore? They're prepared to pass *him* off as a disinterested Oriental scholar. The operative premise is that, really, *nobody* is a Communist. Sometimes, listening to Tydings or Morgan (Ed Morgan is the committee counsel) you get the impression that Joe McCarthy made a speech in Wheeling last February charging the State Department with failing to root out all the duck-billed platypuses (platypi?) in the State Department. They really all but assume that Communists just don't *exist*. Oh sure, they'll have to acknowledge Alger Hiss, and the Gouzenko people up in Canada, and Klaus Fuchs—sometimes the evidence is just plain un-ignorable, especially if the person, like Fuchs, goes to live in the Soviet Union. (But don't get too mad at him. All he did was give Stalin the atom bomb.) They just won't *focus* on the reasonable-doubt crite-

rion I told you about at our final (I hope not) Stork Club dinner—
or was trying to tell you when the great Sherman Billingsley took
over. I *know* you didn't ask him to sit down with us, but you hardly
drove him away. I reconstruct . . .

Billingsley. "Well, it's nice to see you two again."

You. "We've *loved* it, every time."

SB. "What's that, little girl, a tear in your eye?"

You. "Well, we're going away. My father and I."

SB. "Going where, little girl? Your name?—"

You. "Elinor—"

SB. "Going where, Elinor?"

You. "Amsterdam. My father is the new ambassador. My mother
died—very suddenly—in April. So I've pulled out of Barnard to be
with Dad."

Well, talk about sympathy for the bereaved! Before we were out
of there we had champagne and a quickie cake with a little Dutch
flag on it—where in the *hell* did he come up with that? Wonder what
he'd have done if you said you were on your way as ambassador to
Tibet? Elinor, how you gabbed with him, darling. I'm surprised you
didn't go on and tell him—after all, you wrote a paper on it—all
about the Peloponnesian War. . . .

Oh. Sorry darling, but life here is really . . . *distracting.* We've
got support in the Senate, but only one rock on the committee,
Hickenlooper. Henry Cabot Lodge woke up one day and denounced Joe. Well, not exactly denounced, but did a lot of equivo-
cating. From outdoors, Lattimore fires off at us every day. So do
Jessup and Acheson. So, as a matter of fact, does the President. And
the State Department security head, General Conrad Snow, who
doesn't know his — oh, the hell with it. And, of course, mistakes are
made by Our Joe — I didn't mean Your Joe! The Honorable Joseph
Stafford, Ambassador to The Netherlands from the United States
of America. Your father is an appointee of Harry Truman charged
to keep Holland from sinking. — No co-optation ("Our Joe") permitted. Know that word, honey? Co-optation? Well — *look it up!*
(I'm teasing. It means putting someone into your camp without,
really, consulting him.)

It's a madhouse here. Momentous event I know you've read
about. The lady who was going to testify. The FBI verified prelimi-

narily that she had been feeding information to two other Soviet agents. Well, as you probably know, the day she was coming in to testify, she committed suicide. Everybody blamed Joe! She wrote him a letter just before pulling the trigger, took it to the post office to mail. It was very pathetic. She said that she had worried all night about giving testimony, she knew it was the right thing to do, but in doing so she would have needed to "identify" an old friend. She said she knew she should do that but couldn't bear to do it — so she was "going to take the problem to my maker."

The Drew Pearson types said McCarthy drove her to suicide. They'd never say the Communists drove anyone to suicide. . . . I'm going to try to find a Communist to investigate at Columbia so I can get up there and have a session with Willmoore. I need to *talk* to somebody about what this is all about. But one thing I know, the people out there are *our* people. The same ones who saw through Henry Wallace. Good night, love. Let me hear from you. Send me a tulip.

Love, Harry

33

Hoover calls McCarthy
to his lair

Just after noon, Mary Haskell opened the door to Joe's office, opened it just wide enough to permit her quiet but resolute voice to get through to him even when he was talking on the phone, which was most of the time.

Every hour or two, depending on the special density of the telephone traffic she fielded, Mary would enter his office, her telephone-message pink slips Scotch-taped to a legal-size clipboard. These were records of the telephone calls that had come in during the interval between her last visit to Senator McCarthy and this one. She tried to assign callers the same priority she thought, if he had time to be deliberate in the matter, he would assign them. Favorite journalists; important senators; obliging government officials; generous political campaign donors; key political supporters; family; close friends. Mary knew who Joe a) needed, b) liked, and, roughly speaking, c) everyone's rank within those headings.

Mary's sorting of the calls helped, but not always. Sometimes McCarthy would coast by Mary's office and run his eyes over the master row of pink slips thumbtacked to the huge cardboard surface behind her desk, a tiny corner of it reserved for a picture of Hilda, Mary's daughter, when she was nine.

"Mary, why didn't you tell me Jack Weinkopf had called?"

"Who is Jack Weinkopf?"

"Aw, come on. He is maybe my closest friend."

"Joe, don't *play* with me that way. I know your closest friends from one to one hundred, and Jack Weinkopf isn't one of them."

McCarthy grinned, patted her on the back, pulled the pink slip free from its thumbtack, went back to his office, and put in a call to the soft-spoken, retiring young man, editor of the student paper at Marquette, who had interviewed him in the car a few months ago on the way to the airport.

Today Mary opened the door slightly and resolutely called out his name. Joe cupped his hand over the telephone mouthpiece. "What is it, Mary?"

"He calls himself Henry. Says you'd know that it was important."

McCarthy lifted his hand and talked into the receiver. "Jack, this is an emergency. Sorry. Will call you back. But not till tomorrow." He nodded to Mary. "Put . . . Henry through."

Henry spoke, the usual calm voice. "Just confirming our date, Senator. At six-oh-five I'll be parked directly opposite the entrance to your apartment building. I'll be in a Buick Roadmaster, dark blue."

"Okay."

"Will any reporters be following you out of the Senate building, Senator?"

"I can shake them. See you at six-oh-five."

He elected to sit in the passenger seat, next to Henry, who drove carefully but with dispatch. Henry was prepared to discuss with McCarthy anything McCarthy wanted to talk about—except for his assignment. McCarthy chatted about this and that as, grateful for the air conditioner, they made their way out of Washington. But soon McCarthy was silent. Leaning over into the windshield pillar, he closed his eyes, his lips parted slightly. Joe McCarthy was asleep.

Henry watched him closely as he approached Fredericksburg, in Virginia. He was pleased to have to nudge him awake after he had parked the car in the garage. Otherwise he'd have had to request him to put on the eyeshade for the duration of the last ten minutes of the drive to the hideaway.

McCarthy woke quickly. He walked out of the garage and looked up at the house, well separated from the houses on either side. He felt a sudden chill. He was surprised. He wondered: Was this fear? Odd. He hadn't had this kind of apprehension since the day he looked up across the boxing ring at Marquette at the huge black opponent his coach had decided to humble him with. He hadn't felt anything when he saw the flak on the exposed bomber run over Bougainville. But he felt it now and knew it was not just trepidation. *You must be crazy, McCarthy, to have got into this.*

"Please follow me, Senator."

Henry walked ahead. McCarthy followed him by a step or two. When they reached the door he saw the number 322 on the side in polished brass. The door opened from the inside, Joe stepped in and saw a middle-aged man, formally dressed, who looked at Henry and exchanged nods with him.

"Upstairs, please, Senator," Henry said.

McCarthy followed him. At the end of the hall Henry put his hand into his jacket pocket. McCarthy thought he heard a faint buzz. The door opened. Henry beckoned him in. He walked into a comfortably appointed office, a small sofa on his left, small sofa on his right, scenic lithographs on the walls, and J. Edgar Hoover sitting behind the desk, in shirtsleeves.

The director came around, dismissed Henry with a spare flick of his fingers, shook McCarthy's hand, motioned him to the couch, and returned to his desk. He came immediately to the subject.

"Sorry about the ruse. I had to lure you here. And I had to do it in a hurry.

"Joe, I've given you quite a lot of help through channels in the past few months since our initial meeting. Now you've got to do something for me. I think I better put it to you straight, Joe. I *require* your cooperation."

McCarthy began to bristle. He was in awe of the power of J. Edgar Hoover and the FBI, but he was too confident of the sway he now had over the entire country to be treated like a—plebe.

"Edgar," he said, venturing into territory very few others had penetrated. Who else called J. Edgar Hoover Edgar? Since schooldays? "You know what I think of you. And I am very indebted to you. But I have the pulse of the American people on this business, and they look to me—"

"Joe. Stop. I know all that. I was the first person in Washington to recognize your special effect on the American people. But listen to what I have to say. First, we're sitting, right now, in this room, inside an electronic bubble. It's constructed just like the bubbles in the embassies, except that this is decorated to look like a regular office. No bugging can go on here, and nobody sees who comes into the office. No human being knows what you and I are talking about. Nobody will know."

"So where we going, Edgar?"

"We have informants. You know that. Chambers, Hede Massing, Elizabeth Bentley. You know all that. We had the goods on Julius Rosenberg, on Alger Hiss."

"I don't get it. If so, why did the president refer to the Hiss case as a red herring?"

"President Truman obviously didn't think Hiss was an agent."

"I still don't get it."

"The situation is that bad, that serious. The president doesn't believe the Communist infiltration is that deep."

"You're telling me the president doesn't believe Chambers and the rest?"

"How do *you* read it? It helps to remember that the president never met a Communist until he went to Potsdam. He does not know how difficult the security question is."

"Why are you telling *me?*"

Hoover paused. Then lifted his eyeglasses a fraction of an inch.

"Because there were two men on your list last Tuesday who must not on *any account* be pursued by you. They are Ted Levinson and Michael Gazzaniga. You are to cease any further mention of them, and you are to direct your staff—in such a way as not to excite suspicion, I hardly need tell you—to discontinue *any* interest in them."

McCarthy looked up at the director of the Federal Bureau of Investigation, his chin brawny, his fists tightly closed. Instinctively he transposed the scene. It was a heavy-deal poker game. He and J. Edgar Hoover were players, with great stakes moving here and moving there.

He crossed his legs. "I understand, Edgar. But it's right for me to say: What are you offering me in return?"

"Silence."

"Silence on what?"

"Silence on Mary."

"Mary . . . Mary who?"

"Mary Haskell, your principal secretary. She is a security risk."

"Mary Haskell? *My* Mary Haskell, who runs my office?"

"She was a member of the party when you hired her."

When Joe McCarthy left the house, he and "Edgar" had a deal.

Though Mary Haskell was an intimate figure in Joe McCarthy's operations, she was never a part of his informal life. That was simply the
way it was, and that was the way Mary wanted it to be. At the end of a
long, tiring day in the office she'd return to her apartment a few
blocks away and mostly just let the air around her still her nerves.
There were a lot of books on her shelves, and she regularly brought
home diversionary reading, in particular modern novels, from the
library around the corner. Early in July, Mary had acquired a small
television set, but she would turn it on only at hours when she could
be certain she wouldn't be staring at Joe McCarthy or his enemies. Or,
for that matter, his friends.

At one corner of her library she kept her college textbooks. At the
end of sophomore year at CCNY in New York she had married,
become pregnant, and quit college. During the day she nursed Hilda,
at night she attended secretarial school, learning Gregg shorthand.
Her husband, Igor, was a typesetter at 30 Union Square. He was
employed by the *Daily Worker*. She and Igor divorced when Hilda was
nine.

There were no suitable jobs to be had in New York, but in Washington the expansive federal government of President Roosevelt created a considerable need for secretarial help, so she and Hilda moved
there in 1931. Hilda was grown and married when Mary went to work
in the office of Wisconsin senator La Follette in 1942. The defeated
senator rose above the bitterness of his humiliation and offered his
successor guidance about staffing his office. "I can make your office
life significantly smoother and happier. What you do—Joe—" Senator La Follette found it hard to call him "Joe"; on the other hand, he
found it harder to call him "Senator" "—is take on Mary Haskell, age

forty-five, skilled in shorthand and the smoothest, ablest office manager in town. And a very nice lady."

McCarthy liked her instantly. She became his den mother, amanuensis, expediter of all enterprises and overseer of problems coming in from whatever quarter. She appeared to have no other life, though she kept the picture of her daughter prominently displayed. The office seemed to be her life, and its tenant, her special charge.

Today she was surprised to find the handwritten note on her desk from Joe. He must have scratched it out and left it there when she had gone out for a quick lunch. Joe McCarthy communicated with Mary Haskell thirty-five times every day, mostly over the intercom: Why a written note? It said simply, "Mary, I need to see you alone. I'll go from my television date at WRC-TV to the Phoenix hotel. If I don't hear back from you, that means you're okay to meet me at the bargrill at 6:30. J."

He had to have found her out. She held her breath. . . . Either that or Joe was going to tell her he was dying of cancer . . . or—but no. If he had cancer, he'd have been told it by a doctor. If he had gone to a doctor, Mary would have made the appointment, and that hadn't happened. It had to be the other.

Oh, my goodness. (Mary never used the name of the Lord in vain.) After all these years.

To her surprise, Joe was punctual. He gave her a fleeting peck on her forehead. "Well, what'll it be for you, Mary? Your usual Singapore sling?"

"My usual Coke, Senator."

Joe ordered a gin and tonic and a Coke. He spoke of his experiences on the television interview with the CBS Washington anchorman Gus Attlee. "Okay guy, Mary. We must be nice to him. He's a youngish guy—"

She interrupted him. "Joe, what's on your mind?"

He drank. "Mary, were you a Communist?"

"Yes." She twined the paper napkin around her fingers. "I joined up sophomore year at college. Married a Communist; he worked for the *Daily Worker*. We had Hilda, got divorced in 1931, came to Washington. Igor went to Spain to fight against Franco. He was captured and shot. I never heard again from anyone in the party."

"When you were in the party, what did you do?"

"Mostly I passed out leaflets at student meetings. We distributed a lot of them in November, at election time."

"That's sort of—all you did?"

"Yes, Joe. I didn't try to influence foreign policy." But she regretted the crack. "Sorry about that. You asked the right questions. . . . You going to fire me, Joe?"

He leaned across, put his hands on either side of her head, and kissed her on the cheek.

"No. But I want you to do something for me, Mary. I want you to write me a letter describing everything you did as a Communist, when you became one, when you quit, why you quit."

She nodded.

"But Mary, here's the most important thing. I want you to date that letter to me December 1946." He winked at her. "You know, Mary, I always run a thorough security check on everybody I hire."

"Of course, Joe. That's always been your rule. Joe," her smile was weary but affectionate, "how'm I doing?"

"You're doing just great, Mary. You *are* just great."

34

The Tydings Committee
reports its findings

The finding of the Tydings Committee surprised no one, but the language used surprised everybody. The report read not like conclusions to an investigation but like a bill of indictment against the senator who had brought the charges.

The committee report was made public on July 17. McCarthy's office had received page proofs only twenty-four hours before. He called out from his office through the open door to Mary when the package of page proofs arrived. "You all go ahead and read it first. Just tell me this. It's not unanimous, right?"

Mary called back. The report had the signatures of the three Democratic senators. "Hickenlooper and Lodge weren't even shown it. Naturally, they've refused to sign it."

When a half hour later Mary brought it in, he looked up at her. She turned her face away.

"That bad?"

She walked out of the room.

As agreed, Sam Tilburn telephoned Ed Reidy in Indianapolis after he had read the report and made a few phone calls.

"Let me give you the tone of it, Ed, by reading you two sentences. McCarthy's campaign is, quotes, 'a fraud and a hoax perpetrated on the

Senate of the United States and the American people . . . perhaps the most nefarious campaign of half-truths and untruth in the history of this republic. For the first time in our history, we have seen the totalitarian technique of the "big lie" employed on a sustained basis.' Unquote."

"Sam, how they going to get away with language like that?"

"Hickenlooper and Lodge have already renounced it. Lodge wants a brand-new investigation of McCarthy's charges and the whole loyalty/security picture. As an example of distortion, all you have to read is the section on Owen Lattimore. But what comes from it is just . . . a smell. A plain old cover-up."

"A brand-new investigation! What I tried just now over the phone was a sigh. Did you pick it up?"

"Yes, Ed, I know, I know, nightmare time. But it seems to me your editorial lead is obvious. The Tydings Committee didn't investigate the charges—they completely cleared Lattimore, by the way—they set out to reject McCarthy's charges. The full Senate will have to vote on whether to accept the report. I doubt we'll see a single Republican voting in favor. And let's see what kind of a public reception Joe gets tomorrow—he's making a big speech in Baltimore."

"Call you back after I read the wire-service report."

Harry got an extra copy from Andrew Ely, Senator Taft's administrative assistant. He took it home, and on the way to his floor, scooped up his mail. There was an airmail from Elinor.

He sat down and looked at his watch and took a minute to survey the scene. A one-bedroom apartment, a living room that looked more like a study than a lounge. It funneled into the tiny kitchen. To economize on space, Harry had the newly bought television in the kitchen mounted on a lazy Susan. He could swivel it and watch it sitting at his desk or on one of the two armchairs—or while preparing a meal. He had three photographs plopped about: one (his mother, his father, Harry at age ten) on the desk; a second (Harry at Columbia, sitting as editor of the *Spectator,* his first day in office!) on a bookcase; the third (Elinor boarding the *Nieuw Amsterdam* with her father) also on the bookcase. He thought to himself: If ever he got two days in a row with nothing to do, and could come up with a loose two hundred dollars, he'd probably spend the time and the money replacing his boarding-house khaki–colored curtains, which reminded him of Camp Wheeler.

The news would come in at six. He turned on the television set to CBS and turned down the sound. He'd turn it up when the news he especially cared about today came on. He put the report down on one side of his typewriter, which he kept on the coffee table where he liked to work. He opened the letter. After he read the first paragraph, he put it down, went into the little kitchen, and poured himself some bourbon. He looked about in the freezer compartment for some loose ice, but there wasn't any. He didn't have the energy to pull out the tray and disgorge the cubes. He took his glass, brought it to the table, and sat down.

The television images turned to the news and flashed a photograph of Joe McCarthy. Harry didn't turn up the sound. He stared at the typewriter, the letter on one side, the report on the other. Which should he go through first?

What the hell, he'd go first with Tydings. The first paragraph of Elinor's letter said she had become engaged. He could wait to read the closing paragraph of the letter.

At the Admiral Fell Inn in Baltimore, Senator McCarthy faced a full house. He was speaking not to the American Legion or to the Veterans of Foreign Wars; this was a hotel-keepers convention. There were a half dozen reporters and a television news camera there. How would he respond to the historic rebuke of the Tydings majority? How would the crowd respond to him?

After dinner he rose to speak.

"I'm glad to be in your company tonight. A perfect night to celebrate shelter!"

There was a big laugh.

But quickly McCarthy got serious. "The words we most remember about Pearl Harbor were President Roosevelt's. Recall, he spoke of a day that 'would live in infamy.' Well, today was an infamous day in the Senate of the United States."

McCarthy denounced the committee findings. They constituted an "invitation" to Communists and fellow travelers to come into the government or stay in the government without any fear that there would be action to uproot them. He itemized the backgrounds of some of his targets, and contrasted their treatment by the "Democrat report" of the committee. He felt the listeners tuning in on his indignation. His speaking voice as ever in monotone, even so he passed on his mounting scorn and bitterness. Toward the end, the assembly of professional hotel keepers and their wives, much excited that their dinner speaker was the same man featured on the front pages of every newspaper in the country, were rallied to McCarthy's banner.

"When things get very bad, ladies and gentlemen, very, very bad, then we have to pay for grave mistakes, pay with the blood of young American soldiers, which is being shed this minute, while we speak, in Korea. We won a great world war just four and one-half years ago. We defeated enemies on both sides of the globe. We developed a nuclear weapon. Four and one-half years under the leadership of President Truman and Dean Acheson and the State Department. What have we got? We have lost Poland and Bulgaria and Czechoslovakia and Romania and East Germany. The Communist Party threatens to take over in Italy and to paralyze France. China, almost one billion people, has been taken by the ruthless Communist dictatorship. The Soviet Union has got the nuclear weapon, stolen by spies right from American laboratories. In Korea, I say, they are dying. And in Washington, three senators invited to investigate these colossal events end up—talking about the sins of—Joe McCarthy."

The applause was huge, beginning in indignation with the committee, changing gradually to sympathy for its victim, their speaker. The occupants at the first table rose to their feet clapping. In a minute all 450 guests were standing.

McCarthy told the television interviewer that the voters in Baltimore had one very direct opportunity to speak back to Millard Tydings. He was Maryland's senator.

"They can vote him out of office in November."

In November the voters did just that.

Harry reflected. Joe is riding high, he thought. It was *stupid* of Tydings to write a report so egregiously distorted. Would he complete the reading of Elinor's letter? He turned to the last paragraph. Nice, warm, but, really, formalities. He knew he had to write her back, and made his way to the typewriter. He began to stroke out a few words, but quickly he stopped. He'd have to wait.

How long? An hour? A day? Two?—before he got her out of his mind, the girl-of-his-dreams while at Columbia. He had thought the separation would be intolerable, but he had lived McCarthy minute after minute after hour after hour after day after month. He thought back on her calm invitation to go to Holland to spend—a few weeks, was it? Perhaps his letter then had caused that little—tectonic shift he had felt in the ensuing weeks, the phasing down of letters that in June had been coming three or four times every week. There had been more space spent, in the last few weeks, on public affairs. That meant she was progressively disinclined to talk about herself—or about Harry. He thought she too was distracted, by diplomatic life, even as he was distracted by political life. But Elinor was not the kind of girl who could do without a real boyfriend. In New York, though they had dated continuously, he had never got her so to speak full-time. What she wanted, needed, was a full-time boyfriend. Had she found someone in the American Embassy?

Or was it a Dutch boy?

He closed his eyes and began typing, with sure fingers. "Dear Elinor." Not "My darling Elinor," not this time around. "I was stunned//// I was shocked//// I was surprised and saddened/// I was shaken by your letter. You must write and tell me more about the wretched young (?) man who has taken you away from me. What can I say? Would you like me to write you a speech about—what? But I could write a speech about how you are the most entrancing girl in New York. In Holland. You are in my thoughts. All love, Harry."

He went back to his whiskey bottle, but this time he paused to shake out some ice.

He was surprised, and comforted, to find his mind wandering a bit, wandering from Elinor—and wandering from Joe McCarthy. He looked over at his bookcase. He'd do a chapter from Gibbon's *Decline and Fall of the Roman Empire*. It was always, *always* instructive.

HANBERRY, 1991

Alex and Harry
discuss espionage

"The criticism"—Alex Herrendon addressed his colleague Harry Bontecou—"is generally to the effect that McCarthy did not uncover espionage—"

"Which is true," Harry said. "But that doesn't mean espionage wasn't going on—"

"I know. I engaged in it."

Harry leaned back in his chair. "You can imagine, Alex, that I want to know about *that*. I don't think it's clear yet whether it belongs in your book about Western innocence/indifference to Communist cruelty. Or in mine about Joe McCarthy."

Lord Herrendon cackled. He rang the buzzer for tea. "I suppose we can fight over it, but if you resisted me that would be—what? Parricidal?"

"Maybe you can shed light on this episode. I learned of it very very late, and only accidentally."

"Did it have to do with Khrushchev's ultimatum on Berlin?"

"No. It had to do with Korea."

Two Soviet agents
meet in Pennsylvania

The farmhouse nestled in the rolling farmland outside Hanover, two dozen miles from bloody Gettysburg. The little house near the barn was looking old, though not so old as to disclose its true age. It and the larger building were built just after the war of 1812. Then it was a dairy farm, and in 1950 it was still a dairy farm, though the efforts of Floyd Dunn to maintain it were listless, or had become listless since the death of his wife and the departure of his two children, from both of whom he was estranged. There were six cows and twenty acres of corn, a tractor, a prewar truck, and, in the main house, a kerosene heater and a winter's supply of corn liquor. Floyd Dunn kept a picture of Madeleine, none of Bobby and Sara. He tried, every now and then, to train himself to blot them from memory, but he was cursed by the vision of them playing in the courtyard, or waiting for the school bus, or toiling over their homework before exams.

Then—it was as if it had all happened in one moment—suddenly Bobby went off to war. According to the letter from a fellow soldier, also a patient at the hospital, written to Floyd at Bobby's request, Bobby was not coming home. "Not ever, Bobby says to tell you. So don't look out for him."

Floyd deduced that Bobby had been blinded, because a P.S. had been added by his friend (no name or address given). Bobby, the amanuensis wrote, had been "badly disfigured" when the explosive went off at Okinawa. Floyd Dunn figured that Bobby had not seen the P.S. written after the bitter dictation of the short text.

Mrs. Dunn was in the hospital at the time, dying of cancer. Floyd did not show her the letter, or tell her of it. Madeleine, in turn, had never spoken of Sara, not after Sara left home with "Little Bill," as they used to call him (son of "Big Bill") — after forging her father's name at the bank and drawing out everything he had saved in ten years.

When Andy, his tenant farmer, died, Floyd was too old and tired to find another hand and start out all over again. He decided to quit. Floyd asked Cornell, the druggist in Hanover, his friend and everyone's counselor, if he knew of anyone who might want to rent the little farmhouse. Cornell suggested Floyd place an ad in the weekly paper, and it was to that ad that Ned had responded.

Ned Johnson was young and athletically built. He had a brand-new car and arrived in it at the farmhouse to meet with his prospective landlord in the summer, without jacket or tie. But Floyd sized him up, knew instantly that Ned Johnson was a city dweller. Ned didn't disguise this, but said he liked to "get away" to the countryside. Floyd guessed what that meant, and he was right. After they made the deal, Ned started coming in for weekends, often with the one girl, often with a different girl. But he came sometimes with a male friend. Sometimes he stayed over the weekend; occasionally he would appear and leave on the same day: Floyd didn't care, and they didn't see much of each other, but the check for forty-five dollars came in regularly, at the end of every month.

On this cold Monday in December, Ned drove in as Floyd was leaving the cow barn. They waved. An hour later another car drove in. Floyd looked hard at this friend of Ned's, a tall, well-built man wearing a thin mustache. He wore a fedora and a heavy brown overcoat. Floyd's memory flashed back to 1942, to the head of the draft board, who had checked Bobby in at the post office in Hanover that day, to catch the bus to the induction center. Wasn't this man the head of the draft board? If so, might he know something about Bobby?

Impulsively, Floyd intersected the visitor.

" 'Scuse me. Were you, I mean, back in 1942, just after Pearl Harbor. Were you the head of the draft board? I thought I'd just ask something—"

"Sorry," the visitor said. "That wasn't me. I'm—from out of town."

That was clear. Floyd had addressed someone with an English accent. "Sorry," he said.

The visitor nodded his head with a quick smile and knocked on the door.

Inside, Ned had fired up the kerosene heater. He was stoking the log fire when Gabe opened the door. Ned greeted him, took his coat, and motioned him to the chair opposite. Gabe accepted the glass of sherry.

Ned had placed beans and sausage in the skillet and now put sliced bread in the toaster. Gabe moved his chair toward the fireplace. "You got something for me to read while you cook, Ned?"

Ned left the stove and drew from a briefcase two sheets of paper. They were stamped EYES ONLY TOP SECRET. The first was a memorandum from the president of the United States to the secretary of state, the second to the chairman of the joint chiefs.

The language was spare. Army prose, Gabe thought as he looked down the page. But in an instant his mind was engrossed by what the spare prose communicated. He was reading a precis of a meeting and decisions made by the president intended as an ultimatum to the Chinese Communists.

If they did not yield in their offensive against South Korea, the United States would resort to "maximum force, not excluding the use of a nuclear weapon" to repel the aggressor.

The final page was devoted to the need to keep the president's decision utterly private.

"The likelihood of success in this major maneuver," the president instructed the secretary of state,

> depends on a direct communication of our ultimatum to the enemy, to whom we'll speak using our access in Moscow, not our access in Tokyo. Our strategy here requires that there be no pressure on the White House either from our allies or from the public. Such pressures would build quickly and undermine the force of the ultimatum.

Gabe poured himself another glass of sherry.

"Jee-*sus,* Ned! I shan't ask how you got ahold of this . . . steamer."

"That's right, Gabe. Don't ask." Ned brought over a plate of sausage and beans, a tomato, and two pieces of dry toast. He placed them at the end of the little table, getting a second plate for himself. "And *I'm* not going to write down how I got a copy of that memo, except maybe at Sing Sing the day before my execution. Speaking of which, you think they got the goods on the Rosenbergs?"

The reference was to Julius and Ethel Rosenberg, arrested for stealing nuclear secrets as agents of the Soviet Union—a capital offense.

"Yes. I think they'll, to use the picturesque American expression, fry. A risky business we're in. The conviction of Alger Hiss in January stirred things up, all right, and McCarthy knows how to take advantage of it. The *Meet the Press* program with Lattimore didn't help. . . . But the important thing: This memo has to get to our people right away."

"Gabe," as he was known to Ned, paused to think about strategy. He spoke as if to himself. "A counter-nuclear-threat campaign has got to build up *before* this threat is actually issued by Truman. Pressure— publicity—diplomatic pressure. If necessary, public pressure. That's what we need to scare Truman off. We need pressure right away, *right away.*"

Ned was silent. Gabe would make that decision. Gabe was in his mid-forties. He had years of experience in diplomacy, in the manipulation of pressure. Ned waited for him to say more.

"What I'm thinking is, Shouldn't *we* leak it? Like right away. Like—I'm serious—tonight? Moscow would take a day or two to act, and what they'll do, obviously, is pass the word around and help crank up world opinion and public pressure. 'TRUMAN PROPOSES NUKING CHINA.' "

Gabe stopped. He thought through alternatives. Ned did not interrupt him. ". . . We could—tonight, I'm thinking—leak it to Paris and London, which is exactly what Bibikoff is sure to do—what Stalin is sure to tell him to do. But that would take two days minimum. There's no way of knowing, but it's possible Truman would deliver the ultimatum in *less* than two days."

Gabe paused again. He knew that Ned would have to concur in

WILLIAM F. BUCKLEY JR.

the decision. Gabe was senior, but in this situation, nothing could be done to jeopardize the man who came in with the secret. His own security as espionage agent was an overruling priority. But Gabe continued. "On the other hand, leaking it ourselves does have risks. I put it to you: Are you confident there's no *way* they can connect you up in this, Ned?"

"To get that memo I took a chance I wouldn't ordinarily take."

"Well, on that point: Where are you supposed to be, like right now?"

"I'm theoretically meeting this afternoon with . . . someone at ECA. I got cover there."

"Where did you develop the film? Usual way?"

Ned nodded and put a fork to his beans. "I don't know, Gabe. No point in mailing it on over. It would take three days to arrive. We *could* radio it using SamVox, delivery tonight. Bigger risk, but it's an *awfully* big item."

They were both silent. Gabe spoke up. "My recommendation is that we use SamVox in Brooklyn. I can't be away for the length of time it takes to get—him—to make the contact print, get to Brooklyn and back, and give instructions. We'll have to use a courier. I can get this to Basil by," he looked at his watch, "six. He can be in Brooklyn at eleven. SamVox can have it in Moscow, Moscow time, at dawn."

Ned agreed. "That's the way to go. And it gets done outside of Washington, which suits me just fine."

The beans and conversation were on Monday. On Wednesday afternoon, Her Majesty's Government announced that Prime Minister Attlee would fly from London on the following morning to confer with President Truman.

The morning of Attlee's flight, reports appeared in Stockholm, Paris, and London that President Truman was considering a nuclear ultimatum to China designed to contain its offensive in South Korea.

There was immediate speculation that the purpose of the unscheduled Attlee trip was to dissuade President Truman from threatening any use of the atom bomb in the Korean conflict. The whole of the intelligentsia of the Western world mobilized overnight, it seemed, in a chorus opposing any use of atomic weaponry: "Not even as a hypothetical threat," Walter Lippmann, the premier American solon, wrote solemnly in his syndicated column.

Attlee's plane had taken off from London at noon—seven A.M., Washington time. At ten A.M. the president was asked at his regular news conference to comment on reports that he had threatened the use of the bomb.

Truman said that while his deliberations with his generals were private, he could certainly say that no such alternative had ever been considered.

37

The GOP Convention
nominates Eisenhower

General Eisenhower didn't like it at all when he was shown the speakers' roster for the 1952 GOP Convention. What he especially did not like was the positioning of McCarthy for a prime-time speech. He addressed his complaint to the manager of his campaign, Sherman Adams, governor of New Hampshire.

"General," the gruff New Englander said to him, "you don't control the Republican Party. Maybe you will a week from now. But between now and then you have to defeat Senator Taft for the party nomination. Right now, Taft controls the party—and the convention, and he okayed McCarthy."

Dwight Eisenhower was prepared to make critical concessions in return for securing the nomination. He had cleared the choice of Senator Richard Nixon of California as running mate. Richard Nixon's identification with the party faithful was as: the man who flushed out Alger Hiss. As such he had been the premier anti-Communist in Congress, until Joe McCarthy came in. Eisenhower could hope, with Nixon on the ticket, to carry California and the mighty Midwestern states so much alive to the Communist issue.

The keynote speaker was to be General Douglas MacArthur, the august hero of World War II and the Korean war, dismissed by President Truman in April of 1951, an act of enormous political consequence. MacArthur was the greatest living American orator, and his speech was greatly anticipated. "The Democrats want to see how he's going to play the Communist question," Adams told Ike, who, as a major, had served as personal assistant to MacArthur in Manila in 1939.

MacArthur was not ambiguous in his keynote address on the matter of U.S. diplomacy. He denounced "those reckless men who, yielding to international intrigue, set the stage for Soviet ascendancy as a world power and our own relative decline."

Eisenhower, in his hotel suite with a half dozen of his staff, watched intently the following day when time came for McCarthy to address the convention. He was introduced by temporary convention chairman Walter Hallanan of West Virginia.

"Ladies and gentlemen of the convention," Hallanan said, "the Truman-Acheson administration, the Communist press, and the fellow travelers have all joined hands in a gigantic propaganda campaign to discredit and destroy an able and patriotic United States senator because he had the courage to expose the traitors in our government." Applause. "Let us make it clear to the country here today and now that we turn our backs on Alger Hiss but that we will not turn our backs on any man such as that fighting marine from Wisconsin whom I now present to this convention, the Honorable Joseph McCarthy." Great applause.

Eisenhower turned to Adams. "You say Taft controls the convention. Looks like McCarthy controls it."

The Eisenhower contingent watched the big television screen as McCarthy entered the convention hall, walking slowly to take and shake proffered hands. The band played "On Wisconsin" and the marine corps hymn.

On the platform, Senator McCarthy lost little time in hitting his theme. The Truman administration, he told the convention, was trying to hold back Communism "in the Acheson-Lattimore fashion of hitting them with a perfumed silk handkerchief at the front door while they batter our friends with brass knuckles and blackjacks at the back door." The crowd cheered and yelled. It was a minute and more before McCarthy could resume his tongue-lashing of the administration.

"Wait till you hear his closing lines," Adams warned General Eisenhower, an advance text of the speech on his lap. "They're powerful."

McCarthy preceded his peroration by introducing on the floor Robert Vogeler, who as an executive of the International Telephone and Telegraph Company had been arrested by the Communist government in Hungary on bogus charges of spying and kept in jail for seventeen months. Mrs. Vogeler, who had been a beauty queen in Belgium, had petitioned for intervention by the secretary of state. She arrived at Mr. Acheson's office, but was not given a hearing. She coped with this bureaucratic intransigence by reappearing every morning at nine A.M., filing her petition with the receptionist, and staying until the office closed. She did this for several consecutive months until her visitation became a news event. The great diplomatic machinery began finally to clank, and Vogeler was let out of jail. But there were other Americans detained by Communist governments.

"Mr. Truman says there is nothing wrong in the State Department," McCarthy went on. "He says everything is just fine; he has actually said that if anyone hears of anything wrong, just call him collect and he personally will take care of things."

The pause was dramatic. Where was Senator McCarthy going to take that opening?

McCarthy's voice was suddenly thunderous, demanding, frustrated. "Mr. Truman, your telephone is ringing tonight. Five thousand Americans are calling, calling from prison cells deep inside Russia and her satellite nations. They are homesick, Mr. Truman. They are lonely and maybe a little afraid. Answer your telephone, Mr. Truman. It will be interesting to hear what you have to say. Some of them haven't heard an American speak for years.

"But, Mr. Truman, they are getting a busy signal on your line. They will call Washington again; they will call again when the American people are through with you, Mr. Truman, and through with the Achesons, the Jessups, and the Lattimores."

This brought on an eruption from delegates transfixed by what they heard, their great resources of indignation over Communist practices tapped. McCarthy's closing had, word for word, been heard by everyone who had heard him speak in the past two years. It was his standard closing. It began, "My good friends, I say one Communist in a defense plant is one Communist too many." And ended, "And even if there were only one Communist in the State Department, that would still be one Communist too many."

McCarthy received a standing ovation.

Everyone in the suite looked at Eisenhower for his response.

"That was a pretty good speech, in my judgment." He turned to Hagerty, his press aide. "Jim, what's the scoop on those Americans detained by Communists? Get that researched and let me have it."

"Yes, General."

"Oh, and let me have a briefing on my breakfast tomorrow with the Texas delegates." Their support for Eisenhower was critical.

On Wednesday they came over to Ike's rolling bandwagon, and the next day Dwight David Eisenhower was nominated for president.

38

Enter Robin Herrendon

Lincoln McNair, his seersucker jacket loose to let in what comfort he could in the heavy summer heat, leaned on the branch of the birch tree, his long arm outstretched. He'd have taken off his jacket anywhere else. *Anywhere* else, but not here, not at a White House party. He was chatting with Andrew Ely, administrative assistant to Republican majority leader Senator Robert Taft.

"I swear to you it's true, Andrew, the day after the Korean war began — June 25, 1950 — I looked down at the schedule for the next week and thought, Oh, my God, we've got to do something about *that*. A White House party while we're at war? I put a note on President Truman's desk and stayed in the room. He liked that — I know, I know, the guard has changed, but I can still say it was great back then. Mr. Truman liked to have a note summarizing your message, where that was possible. What I wrote was, 'Sir, should we off-load the Fourth of July party on account of Korea?' He raised his head and snapped out, '*Don't anybody here suggest eliminating the Fourth of July celebration. Pass that word out.*' So here we are, three years later under another administration, and I still get invited even though I work now for a lowly senator. Speaking of lowly senators, Andrew, why in the hell don't you people curb that madman from Wisconsin? I mean, he's been driving everybody crazy the whole time."

"I accept that you people are crazy, Linc. Then you accept that our people drove you people out of the White House. What's wrong with that? . . . What did you get to eat with Mr. Truman?" He swigged on his beer bottle.

Lincoln McNair was also drinking beer. "If FDR could serve hot dogs to the king and queen, Mr. Truman said in 1945 at his *first* Fourth of July party for congressional staff, I can serve beer in bottles. Now nobody thinks about champagne anymore."

Andrew Ely accepted the challenge, if belatedly. "McCarthy has an, uh, emphatic way of putting things. But, Linc, if you will forgive me, you people screwed things up something awful, and it's almost a relief to think that maybe some of that screwup was intentional. When cuckoo things happen, and under your ex-boss, at Fourth of July time, the North Koreans had all but swallowed up South Korea. The Red Chinese were egging them on—our European partners are all but ignoring us—Stalin's successors are continuing to provision North Korea, in case the war resumes, using a lot of hardware *we* gave *Stalin* to fight a very different war with—. As I say, it would almost be a relief if we could figure out that somebody *wanted* it that way."

"Good thing I've known you since Andover, Andrew. I might otherwise take offense. You've been reading too many of McCarthy's speeches, is my guess. They seem to encourage Americans to believe that when things get bad it's because we Democrats want them to get bad. But—to change the subject sharply: How's Alice doing?"

"She really appreciated your note. Oh, Linc, have you met Senator McCarthy's star aide, Harry Bontecou?" They hadn't met. Harry extended a hand.

"Lincoln McNair, former administrative assistant to the president, administrative assistant to Senator Kennedy—Harry Bontecou, administrative assistant to the junior senator from Wisconsin." McNair drew himself up from his slouch against the tree and extended his hand.

"How you doing, Harry? Better, I hope, than your boss."

"My boss is okay; he isn't so busy." Harry grinned. "He hasn't had to mobilize an army to cover for his mistakes." The Korean war had quieted down, though peace negotiations continued.

"Hey, hey, kids, cut it out," Ely interrupted. He spotted a friend. "*Robin.*" He signaled to the girl in yellow with the light brown hair.

"Robin, you beautiful thing with the light brown hair, come here for a bit and keep these two brawlers separated."

She was introduced, and her smile lit up the players, and soon they were talking and laughing together. Harry observed Robin with wonder. The sheer freshness, he thought—how to manage that in such heat! She didn't have a beer bottle in her hand. Somehow such a combination was unimaginable. She had a Dixie cup with something dark in it. Coke, probably. "Let's sit down for the fireworks," she suggested. Lincoln McNair wandered off, looking for his wife at the far end of the Rose Garden.

"I got to get back to Alice," Ely said. He blew a kiss at Robin, and nodded at Harry.

"Guess it's you and me." She smiled. "Okay?"

"Very okay."

They sat down on two of the four hundred garden seats and saw the fireworks light up on the South Lawn, a twenty-minute display, the marine band playing Sousa music, rounds of applause as the firework sequence reached more and more exuberant heights and splendors. And at the end of it, sudden momentary dark. Quiet. Peace.

"Are you free for dinner?"

"Yes," Robin said. "I feel very, wonderfully free."

39

McCarthy vs. Kerr

Jean Kerr opened the door to Joe's office. It was seven-thirty and he was conferring, collar open, tie askew, with Don Surine and Harry. The whole of five-foot-ten Jean Kerr, made even taller by her six inches of upswept bouffant hair, came into the room. She strode to Joe's desk, slammed her folder of papers down, reared back, placed her hands on her waist, and hissed, "That's *it*, Joe McCarthy. I told you what, *ten* times? *Fifteen* times that we had to be at Bazy's at seven? But you can't be there at seven because you have to find one more Communist in the Department of—of—Weights and Measures. I'll call Bazy, tell her we're not coming. While I'm at it I'll tell her never mind being a bridesmaid at our wedding because *there will be no wedding!*"

She turned to Harry. "Hear that, Harry? Hear that, Don? *There will be no wedding!* Don't you smile at me, Joe McCarthy. Go marry the Statue of Liberty, or whoever was your last informant. Go marry Freda Utley. Go marry—Mother Bloor!" She left the office, slamming the door.

"Oh, dear," McCarthy said. He leaned over, picked up the phone, and roused the stand-in office operator.

"Midge, ring Mrs. Tankersley at home."

Bazy Tankersley, the young niece of Colonel McCormick of Chicago, was the publisher of the *Washington Times-Herald*. That paper was a property of the Tribune Corporation, owners of the *New*

York Daily News and the *Chicago Tribune.* The papers were presided over by maybe the country's most indomitable right-winger, Colonel Robert McCormick. He had refused to back Eisenhower for president on the grounds that Eisenhower was too much of an internationalist, a liberal, an Anglophile.

"Hang on a minute," Joe instructed Don and Harry as his phone rang.

"Bazy? Hello, doll. It's Joe. Bazy, something's come up, not something I'd want to discuss over the telephone—"

He paused to hear Bazy out.

"Well, Bazy, I can't answer that, not for sure—I appointed J. B. Matthews chief committee aide because he's a good man. Now, Bazy, listen, what happened is I'm here with my staff working on the deadline tomorrow, and Jeanie comes in. And Bazy, she is *very* upset because she told you we'd both be over there with you at seven. Now I could be there at eight-fifteen, but the *problem*, Bazy, is that Jeanie came in just now and she's *awfully* sore. I can't say I blame her. But you know, she's all Irish, like her husband-to-be—"

He paused. Then,

"I know, I know, I'm really looking forward to married life with Jeanie, only there's this problem. She said just now she's not going to marry me. . . . Well I *agree* that's silly. You know I adore your dinner parties, Bazy, but just because I'm late for one of them shouldn't mean my wedding is off, you think? . . . What can you do about it? Well, Jeanie lives only two minutes from here. Maybe if you could call her at home, and say . . . you know what to say, Bazy. And tell her I'm coming to your house direct from the office—I know you, Bazy. You'll make everything okay *before dark*. Whoops! It's dark already! Before midnight! Big kiss, Bazy."

He leaned back in his chair. "We'd better wrap it up. Don, you pull together the J. B. Matthews business. Just stress the line I told you. Just because Matthews said in his article that the Protestant clergy were the—what words did he use?—"

Surine spoke the sentence.

What seemed like the whole Senate was in an uproar over the article by Matthews published in the *American Mercury.* The Republican sweep of 1952 had made McCarthy the chairman of the Government Operations Committee, and now he had nominated J. B. Matthews, the veteran expert on Communist front activity, as chief of staff. "What he wrote," Don said, "was, 'The largest single group supporting the Communist apparatus in the United States today is composed of Protestant clergymen.' How do you want to handle it?"

"Just stick to what I said. Stress this: J. B. didn't call any single Protestant minister a Communist. What he said strikes me as just plain *obvious*. A lot of people—well, not a lot of people, but some people—support socialism because they think it's going to, you know, eliminate poverty, starvation, war, et cetera, et cetera. So they end up supporting Communist fronts. I mean—Harry, you probably saw this at college. I did: You start up a committee in favor of peace, and the pacifists and Protestant ministers flock in by the carload—"

Surine, ever patient, but resolute, interrupted him. "We know all that, Joe. I'll get the statement ready for you in the morning."

McCarthy got up. "Well, I've got a little diplomacy ahead of me tonight. Mary still here?" He pressed a button. Mary Haskell's voice came in on the speaker.

"You keeping tabs on the wedding, Mary?"

"Yes, Senator."

"Did Dulles accept?"

"Allen Dulles did, not John Foster."

"Nixon?"

"Nothing yet."

"He'll come. . . . Miles McMillin?" He laughed.

"Joe," Mary called him Joe when there was nobody else around. "You might want to know about Ross Biggers—Biggers. You know him, Fort Worth? Well, he is giving you and Jean as a wedding present a Coupe de Ville."

"Hey, that sounds great. I never even drove a Cadillac."

"But get this. He has paid for it by taking donations from his employees. It says here some gave twenty-five cents, a few one hundred dollars. It'll be here when you get back from the honeymoon."

"That's really wonderful! I'll tell Jeanie. If she decides to marry me!"

He clicked off the speaker and got up. "Good night, folks."

"Good night, Joe."

Don Surine took a deep breath. "Long day." He picked up the intercom. "Mary, come on in here. We boys are yearning for a little female company and a deep breath of—deep breath of what, Harry?"

"Deep breath of Joe-absence!"

Mary had come in, sat down, and lit up a cigarette. She laughed. "Ray"—Don's assistant was Ray Kiermas, office manager and Joe's oldest friend in town, who had stopped by on his way out—"how many days since you stopped smoking?"

Kiermas, with his pince-nez glasses, tightened his tie and looked very solemn. He replied, "It depends, Mary, on how you count the days. Some people would say 205, others 81, others 57."

They all laughed. Harry said to Don Surine, the former FBI agent, industrious researcher, utterly loyal to Joe and his cause, "Don, is it true you worked once for Senator Ralph Flanders?"

"For about three weeks. I was just out of the army, and you know, I'm from Vermont. I had to do something for the month I had before reporting to the bureau. The morning paper had a profile on Senator Flanders, said his Burlington office was immobilized because his aide there had a ruptured appendix. So I thought—why not? Arrived there at ten A.M., and he hired me at ten-fifteen."

Ray: "Didn't he ask you if you were a Communist?"

There was more laughter. But Mary decided the time had come to be stern. "Now cut it out, boys. This is serious stuff we're into." She was afraid she had sounded the schoolmistress. "I know you're joking. Was Senator Flanders, well, you know, normal?"

"Wouldn't think so after the kind of thing he says about McCarthy. But, to tell the truth, he was only in Burlington for two days during the few weeks I worked for him. I don't remember his smiling ever, come to think of it."

"He's a mean man. I wonder if anybody ever told the junior senator from Vermont that Joe isn't a mean man?"

"Well," Harry smiled, "Jeanie thinks he's a mean man."

Mary got tough again. "Now, nobody here say anything about Jeanie except that you love her. Kiermas?"

"I love Jeanie."

"Don Surine?"

"I love Jeanie."

"Harry Bontecou?"

"I love Jeanie."

"Okay, Mary." Don yawned. "We've passed our loyalty tests. I'm going to the cafeteria for a sandwich or something. Anybody want to come?"

Jeanie was there, but when Joe walked in she most conspicuously did not greet him. At dinner for twelve she was seated, following her request to Bazy, as far from him as the table would allow. The conversation was animated and collegial. All ten guests were ardent backers of McCarthy, and Betty Lee, who was scheduled to be maid of honor, spoke excitedly about the event on September 29. "I bet the whole *world* will be there, Jean."

Jean flushed and nodded her head aimlessly, without looking over at Joe.

So it went. By eleven o'clock Jeanie had cooled down, and at eleven-thirty, McCarthy drove her home. He promised he would tame his schedule.

"You always say that."

"Well, but you know as well as anyone, Jeanie, the kind of things that come up. I mean, like the J. B. Matthews business. That's taken *hours and hours.*"

"I love J. B."

"And I love Ruth." McCarthy spoke of Matthews's scholarly, beautiful, and devoted wife.

"So you see how it is, Jeanie?"

"Do you *really* want to marry me?" Jean asked.

Joe knew the best way to answer her. He leaned over, left hand on the steering wheel, and kissed her fully on the lips.

Herrendon and the security check

Alex Herrendon found it hard to believe. As press aide to the British Embassy he regularly attended State Department briefings on trouble spots around the world, a courtesy extended to Washington representatives of all NATO powers. Now the letter, brought in by the ambassador, advised him that the privilege of attendance at these meetings was suspended, pending a more thorough investigation of Press Attaché Herrendon's security file.

If Herrendon wished to appear at the security hearing about himself, he was, as an accredited diplomat with the British Embassy, entitled to do so. The first paragraph of the State Department letter was clearly standard. The second said that Herrendon would be asked, specifically, to account for his association with the National Consumers League.

The National Consumers League! . . . He dimly remembered. It was sometime in the late thirties. Thirteen, fourteen years ago. His neighbor across the street in McLean—what *was* his name? *Pacelli!* "Same name as the pope," he would tell you—was indignant over the cost of electricity and went around the Drury Park neighborhood collecting signatures for an organized consumer protest group against monopoly utilities. He had signed that paper for Pacelli in 1939. During the war, Herrendon did intelligence work for the War Ministry in London. It was after that, posted again to America, that he noticed—

quite accidentally—that the House Committee on Un-American Activities had listed the National Consumers League as a Communist front. Herrendon's reaction, as given to an associate at the embassy, had been: For all I know, that's what it was—a Communist front exploiting consumer resentments.

But of course that was pre-McCarthy.

He wasn't exactly alarmed, but he was troubled. It would take a little time. Probably, for the hell of it, he should fish through his files to see if there had been any communications from the consumer people—the Communist consumer people—to whom he had paid no more than cursory attention. Which was a mistake.

But Alex was advised by Simon Budge, the British congressional liaison officer, to consult a lawyer. They spoke in his office, and Budge had a most visible hangover. The day before, he had married off his daughter to an American—Alex was at the wedding and had toasted the couple extravagantly.

"McCarthyism is a booming industry, Alexie-boy. It may become a major field of study in American law schools. Specialty? 'Defense of federal employees or security-cleared foreigners who once belonged to a Communist front.'

"But—" Budge was now the negotiator "—the point is there are lawyers in town who specialize in this kind of thing. They know what questions are going to be asked. And they have a keen nose for smelling out whether the case is likely to metastasize to congressional committee investigation proportions. You've got a special problem, you know: You've got a high security clearance—and you were at Yalta."

"Yes. Perhaps I was with Mr. Churchill's staff to help him persuade Stalin to give better care to Russian consumers. On behalf of the consumers union."

"I know, I know, Alex. But this is 1953, and McCarthyism reigns." Budge put his hand theatrically over his mouth. "I mean," he reduced his voice to a whisper, as if frightened to be overheard, "this is 1953, and McCarthyism reigns."

Alex Herrendon laughed. "Very well. I'll call over to the legal department and get somebody's name." He did so, reflecting on the irony of a British official calling on the U.S. State Department to recommend someone to shield him from the importunities of the U.S. State Department.

Alex spoke over the telephone from his house in Georgetown, a part of his late wife's estate. He had been put onto one Eustace Meikkle-john, Esquire, with whom he now exchanged greetings. Alex read him the text of the letter the ambassador had received from Loyalty-Security and agreed to meet with him the following Friday.

"Things are a little different when State is dealing with foreign cit-izens, but most of the security routine is the same thing," Meikkle-john counseled him.

The interval would give Herrendon time to forage for any exchanges, fourteen years ago — or, for that matter, subsequently — with the organized consumer people. He wished he knew where to find Guido Pacelli, who had got him into this mess. Pacelli was a good bit older than Alex, who was in his late forties. Probably Pa-celli was retired. He could hunt him down, if it seemed advisable, or necessary.

What was absolutely required, Herrendon closed his eyes and thought deeply on the matter, was that no investigation by the loyalty/security board should lead to a wider investigation. One that could establish that (Viscount) Alex Herrendon was now and had been for ten years, in London and in Washington, an agent of the Soviet Union performing intelligence work and engaging in espionage. He must get the consumers league business dealt with and satisfy the investigators that there was nothing more to look into.

On impulse he looked over at the framed wedding picture. *For my Alex, with eternal love, Judith.* The picture was taken immediately after the wedding at St. Cecilia's Roman Catholic Church, in Hamden, Connecticut. Judith had appended the date, *December 29, 1927.*

After gazing at the wedding picture he turned to the antique mir-ror behind the desk. He examined his image clinically. His hair was still full, with only traces of gray. His features were regular, his brown eyes wide and expressive. His lower lip was full, his teeth unblem-ished. He did look forty-eight, but not a day older.

He doubted he would ever readjust after Judith's death, though at the hospital, during those awful last weeks, she had pressed him to go on with life "—my beloved Alex." And that last time she had hugged Robin to her. "Make your father live again a whole life, Robin. That's the only way I will truly"—she managed a smile—"rest in peace."

That was two years ago. He hadn't, in the period since then, spent a single evening alone with any woman. He accepted social invitations and, as often as not, enjoyed them; but he never called any of the myriad maidens or widows who were seated, serially, next to him at dinner party after dinner party. He allowed himself to wonder whether he was trying to make up in middle-aged sobriety for a youth that had been anything but regulated. That other life—this one—he had never shared with Judith.

After the session with the lawyer on Friday, Alex came home to his alluringly comfortable living room and began to read a novel, plucked from his complete collection of Anthony Trollope. Robin came in, a special bounce in her stride, to advance on her father and give him a kiss. She would bring him tea. "But after that I'll have to hurry. Can't sit here with you tonight and watch the news." She had a date, and he—her new friend—had tickets to the dress rehearsal of *As You Like It,* which would open at the National Theater the following Monday. Robin was visibly excited. Alex saw in her her mother's radiance.

"Who's the young man?" His voice carried to the kitchen, where Robin was heating the water.

"Oh, Daddy, he's terrific. Tall, handsome, bright—Phi Bete, Columbia—great sense of fun."

"What does he do?"

Robin had steeled herself for the question. She would put off full disclosure as long as possible.

"He works in the Senate."

"For whom?"

"Oh, Daddy, do you want a cookie with tea?"

"Yes. For whom does your beautiful young man work?"

It was no use. "He works for Senator McCarthy."

Her father appeared in the kitchen. "Joe McCarthy?"

"Umm," said Robin, biting on a cookie.

"Oh, my God, Robin." Alex laughed, took his tea, and sat down. "I'm being investigated by the man who is the boss of your boyfriend."

"Daddy, come on. I don't think Senator McCarthy has anything to do with the business you talked about yesterday. And certainly my— he's not exactly my 'boyfriend.' He is somebody I met at a White House party. You'll like him, I'm sure of that, Daddy."

"Well, don't let him come around. He'll become a security risk. Be sure to ask him tonight if Senator McCarthy has located every . . . consumer. No—" Herrendon checked himself immediately. No taunts. Nothing provocative. "Just, well, just have a good time."

The following day, Alex came in from his golf game with Simon Budge, invigorated by the physical exercise, gratified by his score, and indolently relaxed in the clement weather. Robin was upstairs but heard him come in. "Good day, Daddy?"

"Fine day. Shot an eighty-four. I'm thinking maybe of going into tournament golf."

Robin laughed and came down the stairs in a gray cotton suit with starched white collar, lapels, and cuffs. She wore her mother's pearls and gold and ruby earrings.

"And where are you going, all dressed up?"

"I'm going to the races at Laurel."

"Oh? Who with?"

"With my new friend, Harry." She breathed deeply for fear he would ask who else was going.

He didn't.

She kissed him, looked at her watch, and walked down the stairs to P Street. Harry said he would appear at her door in his Chevy at "*exactly* 11:32. I use CIA protocols. Never arrange to meet somebody at 11:30 or 11:35, because that way they'll wobble in one direction or the other on the designated time. When you work for Joe McCarthy, you've *got* to be exact because he *never* is. He told me he'd be ready at eleven. That means he'll be ready at 11:20, which is just right for 11:32 at your door."

"You mean Senator McCarthy will be *in your car?*"

"Yes. And also Jean Kerr. She'll be Mrs. McCarthy soon."

"I'll be there," was all that Robin could manage.

The domestic explosion came the following day.

A picture in the *Washington Post*, two couples, all four figures smiling. The caption: "Coming in with the winner. 'We bet on the winner. Always do!' said Senator Joseph McCarthy. Accompanied here by his fiancée, Jean Kerr, McCarthy aide Harry Bontecou, and date."

A clarification by Herrendon

Harry Bontecou continued to answer questions as Alex Herrendon fired them off. It was on the third day, after breakfast, that Harry came in. He shook off the rain after his brisk walk. They sat down in the study at their customary positions, and Harry said he had done "a lot of thinking" the night before. "Things aren't quite right."

Alex leaned back, apprehensive. He didn't want to run any risk of losing Harry. His concern was sincere. "Is the work too . . . heavy? Too detailed?—"

"No, no. The long hours don't bother me, and I welcome the chance to look back more on that scene, straighten out my own mind on the subject. But what I considered last night is this: I'm as curious about what you know and did as you are about what I knew and did, and of course, what McCarthy knew and did. I'm as interested in what *you* can tell *me* as you are in what *I* can tell *you.*"

"Interested how? You mean interested professionally? Or do you mean—interested personally?"

"Well, both. I spent three years chasing down Communists and pro-Communists. You were a Communist. Worse, you were a spy. I don't want you to tell me again what it was that shook you loose. I read your famous essay in *Encounter* about your reaction to Khrushchev's Twentieth Congress speech in 1956, and that was thirty years ago—"

"Yes, that was what did it." Herrendon reflected. Harry had told him he didn't want to hear about it "again." He could understand. "It obviously pains you that I stayed with the Communists through the show trials, through the Hitler-Stalin pact, through the Iron Curtain—right up until Khrushchev himself, addressing the entire Communist fraternity, dethroned Stalin, to whom I—and a lot of others—well, you know this—swore allegiance." Again he paused. "Well, as you remind me, I gave my reasons in that essay in *Encounter.*"

"I remember them. I read your story with intense curiosity at every level. The Twentieth Congress alienated more American Communists than the Hitler-Stalin pact, it looks like."

"What we were told by Khrushchev on February 24, 1956, was the equivalent of telling us that everything the fascist world had been saying about Stalin for twenty years—was correct. Did you ever run into Howard Fast?"

"No. I know about him, obviously."

"Yes. Well, Howard is of course known as a novelist and historian. But he was an editor of the *Daily Worker* when the Khrushchev speech was leaked. As you know, leaking that speech was a CIA operation. It had been delivered three weeks before. Delivered in the very closed chamber in the Kremlin where the Communist congresses take place.

"Well, the big question, in the offices of the *Worker* when it came in, was: Should we publish Khrushchev's speech? Or bury it? The editor in chief of the *Worker* warned that if they published it, they'd lose ten percent of the members of the Communist Party. Howard Fast said, No, you're wrong: We'll lose *fifty* percent. They finally reckoned there was no way to keep it hidden, so they did publish it. And lost not fifty percent of the members of the party, but ninety percent—or so Howard Fast told someone I know. So I suppose the point I am stressing is the shock value of that speech to some of the Soviet colonials." He paused again and this time got up from his chair and walked toward the window. But after a moment, perhaps afraid he would sound theatrical, he reached for his pipe and sat down: Alex, Lord Herrendon, gone back to work. But he didn't mind describing to Harry—especially to Harry—something of the personal impact.

"What I did not relate in my *Encounter* piece was the agony I felt from then on in coming up in my mind with some means of—atonement. There is much literature on that theme, the great ideological hangovers of such as Koestler and Muggeridge and Utley, Eugene

Lyons—the list is vast. In my own case I thought to make the point I wanted to make by dropping out of sight and living in poverty, doing menial work in a hospital in Liverpool. I swore to myself I'd do it for an entire year. I lasted ten months, and learned then quite by accident—from a hospital cancer specialist who had been called to give treatment in London to a special patient—that my father was terminally ill. I went to him and in his closing hours told him what it was that I had done for over ten years. He communicated his understanding. He couldn't speak, but he nodded his head, in a particular way. He was himself much addicted to lost causes, though not to ignoble causes, as I was."

Harry stopped him. "I understand." And once again attempted to emphasize to Lord Herrendon that "my purposes are not inquisitorial. I don't think we want to go into the question of *why* you had to wait until 1956 to quit the party. People see the light at different times. But I am interested in how you wrestled with the McCarthy problem. I know that your file was pulled out for a going over, because I spotted it on one of those lists we accumulated in McCarthy's office: a list of people the State Department wanted to look into. What I don't remember is what it was that caught the attention of the State Department."

"It was this. Sometime in the thirties, I now forget just when, I signed a petition got up by the National Consumers League protesting utility rates. It turned out that the league was under Communist control. As you can imagine, I was pretty apprehensive. I didn't want a half dozen FBI agents training their microscopes on my past, though I had been pretty careful."

"Okay, okay." Harry was anxious to get with the point he had set out to make. "Listen, Alex: One. You want to do a book on the formation and cultivation of pro-Communist sentiment in the West in the postwar years.

"Two. I'm interested in the anti-Communist sentiment in the West in the postwar years, and of course the two are related. But you've brought on an itch, to look back at the whole Joe McCarthy scene, something I never expected to do."

Alex leaned back in his chair. "Harry, I've no objection to your producing your own scholarly work on the era. I don't see that my own work will suffer in the least—quite the contrary—from your expressing your curiosity and getting from me my own story as a soldier on both fronts of the Cold War."

"Good. It's odd how I can sit and talk fraternally" — Harry, a faint smile on his face, looked up at Alex — "with someone who was doing his best to bring misery to the—" He stopped, then looked away. "Sorry about that. It isn't quite as if you were Marcus Wolf." Harry's reference to the spymaster and master killer of the former East Germany was strong stuff.

"No, at least I wasn't Marcus Wolf. Marcus Wolf, as keeper of the wall in Berlin, tortured and killed. I didn't do that. I'm afraid to ask myself: Would I have done that if the party had asked?"

Harry didn't reply. Neither of the two spoke. Then Alex said, "That was almost forty years ago that I quit the party, but the hangover is still there."

Harry could tell that that was so. Just by looking at the old man. He knew they had that much in common, the difference being critical. He remembered Willmoore's formulation when a fellow faculty member had insisted that both sides in the East-West struggle were moved by ideals. "That's like saying that the man who pushes the old lady out of the way of the bus has a lot in common with the man who pushes the old lady into the way of the bus. They both push old ladies around." Harry thought to pass that one along to Alex, but decided against it. He found himself saying: "Alex, what do you say to some kind of a break tonight? You got any good movie tapes? Maybe *From Russia with Love?*"

Harry threw himself on the floor and played vigorously with Bloor, the big red Labrador.

42

JULY 1953

Harry pursues Robin

"I got to say it, Harry, your romance is taking time away from the struggle for the free world!" McCarthy had suggested Harry join him for a quick supper before returning to work, but Harry said no, he had a date.

"You must be dating that lady five times a week."

"Sorry about that, Joe. I hope you won't denounce me in your speech."

"Oh, the hell with it. Go off to your lady friend. She works for McMahon, I hear."

"Yes, she does. But we don't talk about it."

"Maybe I'll have her bugged." McCarthy laughed.

Harry, momentarily stunned, opened his mouth to return the wisecrack, but quickly changed his mind. He wouldn't involve Joe in his own little problem. He knew somebody in the FBI who would give him advice on how to handle it.

Harry had, in two days, three odd phone calls, the caller hanging up immediately after Harry picked up the phone. It could have been accidental. Or somebody who had read about Harry in the papers, decided to call him, then decided to back out. His name was often printed, as accompanying Senator McCarthy here and there, sitting at his side during hearings, whatever. Harry did think to examine the telephone itself, but found no traces of a bug. But he knew that technology in the bugging business had advanced. He had a friend in the FBI who was taking advanced training as a sweeper.

But then why, other than maybe to listen in on his conversations with Joe, would anyone *want* to bug him? His mind turned, momentarily, to the most conventional uses of wiretaps. They were common in domestic disagreements, or suspicions. What else? He couldn't imagine anyone going to extravagant lengths, in his case, to document his romantic . . . distractions. Though they were getting intense.

The mere thought quickened his pulse, and his ardor was high when he arrived back at his apartment with the chicken, coleslaw, the quart of ice cream, chocolate, and nuts at the ready. And the two wines he would pluck from his ten-bottle cellar.

He had uncorked the white wine when the bell rang.

He had asked her a few weeks before what perfume she wore. She hadn't replied. Now he returned to the subject, asking her the same question.

"It's a secret," she answered.

"Why? Is it a Communist scent?"

"A Communist sent by who?"

"By whom."

"By God, you are inquisitive." She leaned over in the bed and kissed the tip of his nose.

"Kiss me other places."

"You are a dirty old man."

"I am a dirty *young* man. I want to kiss you everywhere."

And he forgot about the name of the perfume. But he was overwhelmed by it. With one hand he held her filled glass. With the other he brought her head to his.

43

Off to the races!

It was Saturday, Wheeling plus. Harry, driving his own car proudly, the second-hand Chevy he had contrived an excuse for pulling out of the garage every day in the week since he bought it, picked up Jean Kerr. Robin would be waiting for them as arranged. They drove to Adler Street and stopped outside Joe McCarthy's apartment building. "Be here sharp at eleven," Joe had instructed him. "That way we can have lunch and catch the first race. We'll take your car, Harry. Okay? Mine ain't fitting for the premier anti-Communist in the Western world." Harry could practically hear him wink over the telephone.

Harry left Jean in the car. Joe — of course — had not been waiting at the door, as he had promised. After a few minutes, Jean stepped outside to avoid the car's heat.

She looked smart and tidy in her coffee-colored silk skirt, her white blouse slightly open, the small ruby and gold earrings visible when she brushed her hair back. At twenty-eight, the five-foot-ten sometime Cherry Blossom Queen of George Washington University was a striking figure. Her blue eyes were wide, her lips ample and determined. She was a two-year veteran of Joe McCarthy's staff, utterly devoted to his cause, affectionately curious about his endless foibles, and engaged by his manners, courage, and determination. When in the company of any staff member she was formal with him. But she was not, on this shining summer day, in an office mood. She had quickly okayed Joe's idea late in the evening in the office after hours and hours of work. His idea was: Let's forget *the whole world,* as he put it. That meant go to the races. Harry was working with them, and Joe said: You come too.

"Did I tell you, Harry, that I usually pick a winner?"

"No," he said. "But if you can guarantee me a winner, I'll bet on the same horse. You know, Jean, you remind me of a horse."

"I what?"

"I mean, the way you like horseplay." This was an office barb. Jean was fastidious and ruled the office as she might a war center. Everything had to be done, no — horseplay. His taunt got from her what he knew it would, that broad smile with the lit eyes, and the slight, shy giggle.

Jean Kerr had worked in advertising before matriculating at George Washington. After three years there, she entered the journalism school at Northwestern, where she studied political science. Back in Washington again, she continued to live with her mother. Mrs. Kerr was a widow and lived in the same house Jean's father had helped to construct as a carpenter and later superintendent in the construction business. Jimmy Kerr (dead in 1946) had railed against the Communists ever since August 23, 1939, when Joseph Stalin signed the non-aggression pact with Adolf Hitler. Jimmy Kerr had for many years, beginning in the Depression, hailed the socialist experiment in the Soviet Union — "They've got to be able to find something better than what we have, Elizabeth." Elizabeth agreed; but then she always agreed with Jimmy, and did so when he denounced the Communists at the Labor Day party. His scorn for Stalin was uninterrupted by Hitler's subsequent attack on Russia in June of the following year, and Jimmy was soon active against the Teamster faction led by Erik Hattersley, an apologist for the Communists. Hattersley, vice president of public affairs in the Teamsters Union, had defended Stalin when he signed up with Hitler and defended Stalin when he fought Hitler. In the forties, after his first heart attack, Jimmy Kerr was reconciled with the Catholic Church. He wrote to Jean at Northwestern that she should be in touch with the Catholic chaplain there to take belated instructions. Jean had been a formal churchgoer to placate her mother. But in Chicago she began to take her faith seriously, and was powerfully influenced by the Catholic chaplain, a follower of Monsignor Fulton Sheen, who, like his

WILLIAM F. BUCKLEY JR.

mentor, spent much time in the pulpit invoking sympathy for the victims of Communism and moral indignation for the perpetrators of life under the Communists. When Henry Wallace made his move on the presidential scene, she did volunteer work for the Republican Party.

Pretty soon Joe came out and, while talking to Harry, who followed him, or tried to, approached at his customary pace, a near jog. He kissed Jeanie on the cheek, ushered her into the rear passenger seat, and inserted himself alongside.

"You may proceed, James." Joe was acting the squire, giving directions to his chauffeur. Harry moved the car forward, first picking up Robin, then heading down to Route One toward Laurel Park, ten miles away in Maryland.

"Kick her up, Harry," instructed Joe. "I've got to bet on the first race. There's a winner there. Name? Tidings!"

"Tidings!" Jeanie burst in. "You must be crazy, Joe. I mean, crazier than we know you are. *I* am going to bet *against* Tidings."

Joe was delighted by the opportunity to tease her.

"How do you go about betting *against* a horse?"

Jeanie was cornered. She turned to Harry, at the wheel, who was enjoying it all, for help. Robin was smilingly silent.

"Well," he ventured, smoothly wending the car past a huge REO truck, "I suppose if you bet on the other eleven horses — how many starters, Joe?"

"Nine—"

"—Bet on the other eight horses, you could say you were betting *against* Tidings. Give up, Joe?"

McCarthy laughed and put his arm around Jeanie.

"Nice try. Now let me tell you about Tidings."

He had been studying the morning sheet and began a practiced recitation of the record and the pedigree of his horse of the day. "Number seven started racing in 1949, two wins. Placed second in Brendon Cup, twenty-five-thousand-dollar stake. Sire, Out of Town — ever see him run, Jeanie? I caught him in California when I was stationed at El Toro in the Marines. Dam, Silky Stuff. Silky stuff like you, Jeanie," he ran his hand over the back of her blouse and love-tapped her behind the neck.

"So what do *I* make out of the name Tidings running in a horse race on the third anniversary of the Tydings Senate hearings? Not that the poor horse should remind us of that little creep—correction, big creep—we spent our working hours with. No, it's a name fortune has stuck in our face so we can avenge ourselves! Make money off Tidings! You like that, Jean?"

When he called her Jean he was in his command mode. ("Jean, get the file on Hanson.")

"All right, all right, Joe. I'll put two dollars on him."

"Which reminds me, Jeanie. You got some cash?"

"Don't *tell* me you are out of cash *again*," Jeanie groaned, opening her pocketbook. "I've got forty-two dollars."

"How much you got, kid?" Joe said. "Mr. Phi Beta Kappa. And don't skimp on me. Give me everything you've got. You can always borrow on that huge salary I am paying you."

"Fifteen or twenty dollars," Harry said at the wheel. "But I happen to know that Robin has a twenty also."

"Of course, it doesn't much matter how much we have now. We'll be rich after the first race. The odds are six to one. That makes—my ten, Jean's forty, Harry's twenty, and Robin's twenty—ninety dollars. Times six, five hundred and forty dollars. We're rich!"

They arrived in time for a hurried lunch. Joe gobbled down his steak, Jean, Harry, and Robin their tunafish sandwiches. Joe asked for a beer but was told no liquor was served at the track. "That's terrible news," he said. "That will throw me off stride." He looked out at the tote board. The odds on Tidings had reduced to five to one. He turned, saying with mock sternness, "Harry, have you been giving out the word that Tidings is going to win?"

He looked out again anxiously at the board. Steady at five to one.

But Tidings had a bad day, and the track ended up with ninety McCarthy, Inc., dollars. Joe was unbothered. This kind of thing had happened to him since he began playing poker with Billy back in Appleton. He looked around for a familiar face. It didn't take long. He knew it wouldn't. Over there, form sheet in hand and walking in his direction, was Henry Inker, paper tycoon from Neenah, Wisconsin. Joe thrust out his hand. One minute later he had borrowed $150—"Jeanie, remind me to send Henry a check on Monday—Henry Inker. Oh. Sorry, Henry. This is Jean Kerr and Harry Bontecou from my staff. And Harry's friend Robin. That Bontecou, Henry, is spelled c-o-u but pronounced k-e-w."

Jean, Harry, and Robin shook hands with Henry and sat down again in the box seats lent to Joe by Urban Van Susteren of Appleton, a hearty McCarthy booster who had the box for the season.

In the third race Joe was triumphant—"How'm I doing?" he beamed at Jeanie—and on the last race he lost it all.

"How'd you do on the day?" Jean asked, back in the car.

"Oh, I don't know, Jeanie. Win some, lose some. That's life." He sighed noisily, intending to draw attention. "Life. What's life without Jeanie? Tell me how much you love me, Jeanie."

"Shut up, Joe. I'm too smart to love you."

"Besides," Harry got into the act, "Jeanie belonged to the Soviet-American Friendship League when she was six."

"You making fun of my work, kid? Communist kid. Remind me to fire him when we get in, Jean."

But now the races were behind him. He fell silent as the car came into Washington. They stopped to let Robin out.

"Tell you what, Harry," Joe said. "Drop me at the office. I got some work to do."

Jean sighed. "Okay, okay. I'll go on up with you."

"Can I help?" Harry said.

"No. You're working on the Philadelphia speech, aren't you?"

"Yes. I'm batting away at home."

"Good. See if you can work into it something about a lousy race-horse called Tidings."

Harry and the intruder, 1951

They were together at Washington National Airport, headed for San Antonio, when Senator McCarthy was paged. Harry, briefcase in hand, waited outside the telephone booth.

Joe came out, a shimmer of sweat on his face. He had not been exercising; he had been eating, and drinking, more. He leaned his increasing bulk against the booth.

"That was Don. There's been a subpoena from Drew Pearson."

Pearson's complaint filled many pages and held that McCarthy had defamed his "professional and personal" life. McCarthy had hired a young, flashy lawyer named Edward Bennett Williams as his counsel. "Surine called Ed Williams, and he says we can't be late on this one, so Don has to pull out of the preparation for the Gillette committee hearings—which means, my boy Harry, that *you* have to do the Gillette-Monroney work. You're the only man on the staff other than Don who can handle that one. We have to furnish an account of every activity undertaken by me or my staff in the Maryland campaign, can you beat it!"

The Gillette-Monroney Committee had been impaneled, after the Tydings Report was filed, to investigate charges against Senator McCarthy that his tactics in the Tydings campaign had been unethical and illegal.

Joe patted Harry on the shoulder. "I'll have to handle the San

Antonio speech on my own. I'm going to let Harry Truman have it tomorrow."

"I know that, Joe. I wrote the speech."

"Yes, of course, sure. But I told you what to say."

"And I tried to say it your way. But I hope you *won't* use the word *impeach.*"

McCarthy put his elbow on the counter. "What other word would you use? Look: Chiang Kai-shek offers to send Nationalist military units to Korea to help solve the mess created by the Truman administration. What does Truman do?

"He stalls.

"I think I'm right; if *he* continues to refuse Nationalist aid, *we* have a duty to ask whether he shouldn't be retired as president. We have to view his performance as a whole. That, coming on top of the firing of General MacArthur—"

"But Joe, dammit, it just isn't that obvious. General MacArthur writes a letter to *Joe Martin,* Republican Minority Leader in the House! MacArthur backs, in that letter, the Martin position on the war—that we should bring in the Nationalist troops. He is in effect urging a different military, in fact a different geopolitical strategy in Korea from that of the commander in chief. I mean, if I gave a speech outlining a mistake I thought *you* were making, you'd have every right to can me, wouldn't you?"

"Yeah, sure. But if the Senate thought *I* was really abusing my authority, they'd have the right to censure *me.* Or even to throw me out."

"But my point is, you *wouldn't* have been abusing your authority if you did something comparable to what Truman did to MacArthur."

"You're a bright kid, Bontekow. But I have to reason it my way. No offense."

"Okay," Harry said. "Now Joe, on the speech you're taking with you. —Don't alter that speech. It's right the way it is."

"Waal, Harry . . . I won't. But I might just give it a little . . . color."

If Joe McCarthy had decided to change it, Harry said to himself, then it would be changed. He let it go. The airplane boarding had begun.

"Good luck. Say hello to San Antonio. And remember the Alamo, Senator."

McCarthy smiled broadly and waved his hand, first at Harry, and then at two or three passers-by who had spotted him and begun to cheer and clap. Harry took a taxi to the office, picked up the bulky file he'd have to go through to answer the queries from the Gillette committee, and set out on foot to his apartment.

The nine-block walk had become a part of his daily regimen, important to him now that he had so little time for the tennis and bicycling he had done while a student at Columbia. Walking down from the Senate building he passed Buster Jensen, aide to Senator Gillette. He was walking with his own heavy briefcase up toward the hill. Jensen stopped.

"Tell you what, Harry. I'll show you mine if you show me yours!"

Harry laughed. "Buster, if you tell me what specific questions you're going to ask my boss on Thursday that would sure lighten my workload."

Jensen was a wag. In a dark whisper: "We're going to find out whether a Communist has *infiltrated* Senator McCarthy's staff. But that's top secret, Harry."

Harry mock-cuffed him on the chin and resumed his walk. "See you Thursday, Buster."

Harry walked up the two flights to his apartment, pulled the key from his pocket, and opened the door on Tracy Allshott. Tracy, dressed in khaki trousers, sport shirt, and sweater, stood there in the interior hallway, papers strewn over the back of the couch.

Neither of them spoke.

Harry closed the door quietly. He contrived to find the door lock behind his back. With his left hand he felt for the door key in his pocket. He wheeled around, inserted it, and locked the door from the inside. The click seemed loud as a bullet shot.

"You will see, Tracy, that I'm extending your visit."

Allshott remained standing. Standing awkwardly, with papers in either hand. He hadn't changed, the near-assertive blondness, the blue-blue eyes. His shirt was open, but then Harry had never seen Allshott with a tie on. He appeared gaunt.

The question flashed through Harry's mind: Was Tracy armed? If he was, Harry would not succeed in putting through an emergency call to the police. If he was not armed, Harry, three inches taller and a graduate of infantry training in hand-to-hand combat, would probably prevail. Whichever, he had best start up an exchange.

With some deliberation, he walked over to the chair behind his desk on the right and sat down.

"So what's up, Tracy? I haven't seen you for a few years."

Tracy let down the papers on the couch and leaned back on the bookshelf. He remained standing. He was breathing heavily.

"What's up is that your boss McCarthy is trying to turn the United States into a fascist dictatorship so we can have another world war."

Harry didn't know whether soft reason would work. He might as well try.

"Why would he be doing that, Tracy? Sit down. Just move those papers behind the couch out of your way."

"Don't try to sweet-talk me, Harry."

"Okay. I can always call the police. But shouldn't we, maybe, try to talk a bit?"

"I don't see how you can *stand yourself*, working for that man."

"Who do you work for, Tracy?"

Tracy looked to the window and said in a solemn tone, "I try to work on the side of history."

"Was it history's idea to break in to my apartment?"

"It's a historically responsible thing to do to expose the crazy mind and doings of your boss McCarthy."

"Well, I've got no answer to that, Tracy. I mean, if you can do—on behalf of history—anything you want to do, how am I supposed to defend, like, the privacy of my apartment? Or my own papers?"

Suddenly it was Tracy Allshott whose voice was that of reason, reason struggling amiably to get out.

"Harry, you just don't understand. Like back at Columbia. You don't *understand*. We're headed toward the great global renunciation of capitalism and war and imperialism."

He pointed to Harry's open file drawer. "What you and—McCarthy—are doing is trying to find everybody who shares my vision of a new history. Let me tell you something, something I never told you at Columbia. My father was a factory owner in Iowa. In 1943—I was seventeen—the union struck. Dad had three hundred workers. Older people, mostly, everybody under thirty-five was off to the war. Dad's factory made bicycle wheels, so there was no wartime antistrike weapon he could wheedle out of Washington. So after the third week we got the goons. The strikers had barricaded the office.

Mum heard them. She told me in French—she's French—that Dad had ordered the strike broken: Two days later they were there. Fifteen of them. There were pictures in the paper. They came with clubs. Great big clubs. Twenty-seven workers were hospitalized, two dead. Dad told the press he knew nothing about the strikebreakers, he thought they had come in from a rival union.

"But the striking union people read the signals. They went back to work. One week later Dad fired twenty-five of them, the union cadre. That's the world some of us—a lot more of us than you think, Harry, never mind how poorly Henry Wallace made out—want to do something about, and a good start on that is to expose your," Tracy's voice now resumed its earlier stridency, "your lying fascist boss."

Allshott moved. His stance was now that of the boxer.

If necessary, Harry calculated, he'd use the brass lamp on his desk as a weapon.

He said calmly, "Well, Tracy, I'm sorry about all that. We'll just have to go our separate ways. I think you'd better go now."

He reached in his pocket for the door key. As he did so, Allshott lunged at him, his head low. With his right hand Harry grabbed the lamp and smashed it as hard as he could—harder than he supposed he could—on the back of Allshott's head.

He called first the ambulance, then the police.

Would he recount the words Tracy had spoken? Or, instead, leave the whole episode as the work of a deranged former roommate. Turned to petty larceny.

Anything, he thought quickly, *anything* to keep Joe McCarthy from emerging as the central figure in an Allshott-Bontecou drama.

He told the police he would not prefer a complaint but he thought himself entitled to knowledge of where Tracy Allshott lived and worked. The sergeant, making notes, agreed to forward him the information.

He saw the two policemen out, Allshott logy, head bowed, following them. Harry dreaded the thought of a long evening devoted to the Gillette hearings. But the research had to be done, and Joe was right that Harry had to do it. No one, except maybe Don and Jean, knew better than Harry what Joe McCarthy did—every day, every week, every month. Harry wished Joe would slow down a bit. He was at it all day long and most of the night, going over the files, speaking on the telephone, preparing final versions of his speeches. He was acting often on a sixth sense. Reviewing a file he'd say to Harry: "I'd bet anything this guy is just plain on the other side. Look at that front record." Then, maybe at one in the morning, he'd say, "Harry, let's have a drink, and maybe just four rounds of draw poker." He would pull out the poker chips he kept in the bottom drawer and open the little office refrigerator Mary had given him for Christmas.

Harry remembered the night in February. Tom Coleman was wintering in Arizona and Joe had been given Coleman's ample house in Madison to stay in. Again it was one in the morning and Harry was working on the speech Joe would deliver the following night at the convention of the Dairy Council. It would be an important speech, with two special tables reserved for his Wisconsin backers.

Finally, Harry said, "I've got to go to sleep, Joe."

"Fine. What time do you want me to wake you?"

Harry yawned. "If you wake me at seven, I can get it done all right."

Harry slept deeply, and when he heard the knock on the door he groaned. Joe was standing outside in his dressing gown with a tray and a hot cup of coffee.

"Thanks, Joe." Harry yawned, grabbing his own robe and heading down the stairs to the study and his typewriter.

"Before you start in, Harry, let me show you something very exciting."

Joe bent down on the floor. He had spread out a large map of China. "Look at this," Joe said on his hands and knees. "That railroad line, Peking to Shanghai. *It is the only railroad line coming into Shanghai.*"

"So?" Harry, sipping his coffee, leaned down to view it.

"If a beachhead were established by the Nationalist Chinese in Shanghai and the railroad was bombed—interdicted—that beachhead could become the capital of the resistance movement. This is a *can-do* proposition, Harry!"

Harry looked over to the wall clock. He rubbed his eyes. The clock said the time was 3:15. He checked his own watch. "God*damnit,* Joe, it's *three-fifteen* in the morning!"

"Yeah, I know, I'm really sorry about that. But I just couldn't keep it to myself, the idea—I'm talking about *the liberation of China!*"

Harry turned to the staircase. "Make that call for eight o'clock, Joe."

It was a tough job, Harry said to himself as he switched on the coffeepot with his left hand, turning the pages on the Gillette-Monroney questionnaire. But *goddamnit,* Bontecou. Stop complaining. I'm riding with a great historical figure. McCarthy's not the kind of person who would have permitted Keelhaul—those were Erik Chadinoff's words to him only last week. Willmoore Sherrill had published a paper backing McCarthy. James Burnham's *The Web of Subversion,* giving a scholar's reading of the systematic infiltration of government by the Communists, was on the presses. The Senate Internal Security Subcommittee had scheduled extensive hearings on the Institute of Pacific Relations, the primary academic support system for the Chinese Communists. Its dominating presence—Owen Lattimore.

Harry had to do what he could. He brought his coffee and a banana to the coffee table and began reading the Gillette-Monroney complaints.

Acheson collects
McCarthyana, 1953

Dean Acheson was cutting up newspapers in his law office at Covington and Burling. However fastidiously he discharged his duties as a
practicing lawyer, his mind was on other things, not least his reputation as secretary of state during the last four years of Harry Truman's
presidency. His daily stimulant — "If you can call it that," he remarked
to his partner and close friend Harold Epison, "the daily ingestion of
poison I inflict on myself" — was what he referred to with some scorn
as "the McCarthy page" in the morning's newspaper. He had been
reluctant to evidence a formal interest in the unspeakable senator.
But in fact he read all references to him and, though only when out
of sight, collected choice items voraciously. He had taken to scissor-
ing out clippings from newspapers (when his secretary wasn't in the
room) and tossing them into his briefcase. But after a few weeks he
decided that it would be better to undertake his project in a more
orderly way. That was when he told his secretary, "Miss Gibson, it is
possible that when I do my memoirs I shall have in them a chapter on
the . . . grotesqueries of Senator McCarthy. For that reason, I shall ask
you to clip out of the papers those articles or editorials I designate
with the initial *M*. These are to be clipped and put in a manila folder,
in the bottom drawer" — he pointed down from where he sat — "over
there."

Day after day, week after week, month after month, the folder grew in size. The methodical Mr. Acheson took to classifying the entries according to his estimate of their ranking. "M-O-3" parsed as "McCarthy-Outrageous-3rd level." "M-P-1" parsed as "McCarthy-Preposterous-1st level." He had other categories, including "T" (for treasonable) and "L" (for laughable). He also reserved a classification for criticisms of McCarthy that he especially savored. His very favorites earned, as one would expect, a "1," whence "M-C-1." Such a discovery in a morning paper would put him in a very good mood, and sometimes he would even drop a quick note of commendation to the author. When Senator Benton said of McCarthy that he was a "hit-and-run propagandist of the Kremlin model," Mr. Acheson had filed the remark as an M-C-2 and dropped a note to Benton, "Bill, nice score today on McMenace. Well done."

This morning's reference to McCarthy by Drew Pearson in his column had caused him to glow. "What he is trying to do is not new. It worked well in Germany and in Russia; all voices except those officially approved were silenced in those lands by intimidation." But he decided against dropping a note to Pearson. He would not wish to run the risk of Pearson's quoting him. He could hardly countenance any public appearance of an ongoing contention between *Dean Gooderham Acheson/ Yale/ Secretary of State* and *Joe McCarthy/ Chicken Farmer/ Marquette*—wherever Marquette was—/ *Junior Senator from*—a state that had lost its senses.

He had dined the week before with defeated Democratic presidential candidate Adlai Stevenson. Dean Acheson enjoyed the company of Stevenson but thought him indecisive. Acheson relished the story Adlai had told him, over drinks at the Metropolitan Club, about the dinner with President Truman. The president was then living across the street at Blair House, while the White House was being rebuilt. Truman had summoned him when Stevenson was still governor of Illinois.

"I walked in the door, and the president said, I mean just after barely saying hello, he said, 'Adlai, I want you to run for president. You should announce the third week in April'—this dinner was in January 1952, Dean—'and say that you will seek a leave of absence as governor of Illinois.'

"I told him I was very flattered by the suggestion, but that I was committed to run for reelection as governor of Illinois—"

WILLIAM F. BUCKLEY JR.

"What did he say?"

"He didn't even *acknowledge* what I had said. He went on and talked about this and that but at dinner repeated *exactly* the same instructions—I was to run for president, announce the third week in April, et cetera. I gave him the same answer. After dinner he walked me to the door and, you guessed it, said the identical thing one more time, and I gave back the identical answer. Then you know what he said, Dean? 'The trouble with you, Adlai, is you're so *indecisive!*'"

They both laughed.

Then Acheson had looked up.

"You know, Adlai, the president was quite correct; you *are* indecisive."

But at least Adlai wasn't equivocal about McCarthy. Acheson had given an M-C-1 to Adlai's designation of McCarthyism before the press club as a "hysterical form of putrid slander" and as "one of the most unwholesome manifestations of our current disorder."

When Harold Epison came into the office of his senior colleague just after five, it was in order to spend an hour on the appeal he was shepherding to the appellate division on behalf of their client, the Kingdom of Iran. But he began by asking Dean whether he had seen the reference to McCarthy—"I caught it in the *New York Daily News*, which I sometimes see. It wasn't in any of the Washington papers"—by Owen Lattimore?

No, Acheson hadn't seen it.

"Somebody apparently asked Lattimore after a speech what he thought of McCarthy. He said—I have this in memory, Dean!—McCarthy is "a base and miserable creature."

"That is a thoughtful summary," Acheson said. He then paused. "Rather a pity it was done by Owen Lattimore. He is not exactly a disinterested party on the McCarthy question. As a matter of fact, Harold—obviously to go no further—it hurts me to say this—I think that miserable creature was substantially right on Lattimore. . . . But that hardly vitiates the soundness of Lattimore's summary on McCarthy." He made a mental note to write down Lattimore's characterization and slip it into his folder.

"You may be interested to know, Harold, that a few Republicans, who are well situated, think McCarthy has gone far enough."

"Surely the question is, What does Ike think?"

Acheson turned his heard slowly, as if to say that the words he would now say were sacredly confidential.

"He is, I am, I think, reliably informed, prepared to move. . . . That is enough on that subject."

"I agree, Dean. How're you getting on with your book?"

"I write every night, five times a week. I try to do five hundred words a day."

"Have you got a title for it yet?"

"Yes. I'm going to call it *A Democrat Looks at His Party*. We've lost a lot of spirit in the Democratic Party in the year since Ike came in. Of course there's a lot of disequilibrium in the country. You will find, Harold, that this is always so after a society completes a major effort— in this case, winning a world war. Churchill's defeat was a symptom of that kind of—letting your breath out. The surprise here was that Mr. Truman defeated Dewey. But that also meant that the opposition never got a chance to exercise its muscles. Not until Ike's victory in 1952."

"So your book is intended to do what?"

"To put the Democratic Party back on its feet, as the civilized party, the intelligent party. A worthwhile project, wouldn't you agree?"

"Of course. But you know, Dean, I hope you will confront head-on the foreign-policy problem. I agree with everything you say about Senator McCarthy. You know that. But it is a fact that we had to fight a war in Korea that President Eisenhower ended—"

"Yes. The war ended officially five months after Eisenhower was elected—and three months after Stalin died."

"Dean, you are being the advocate now. We Democrats did get into that war, we did—I know you hate that word—'lose' China—"

"You are correct that we have to focus very carefully on what is happening in the Soviet Union. We don't know what the triumvirate that's in power now, Khrushchev, Bulganin—I continue to refer to it as a triumvirate, though they executed Beria a week ago, good riddance. What the successors to Stalin are going to do we don't know, but there are no signs they are giving up their commitment to rule the world. But yes, I *am* ready to say this, with great care: I will show you the draft of that chapter. I will say that it is correct that the Communists can't be allowed to go any further. Well, didn't Mr. Truman say that? By engaging them in Korea?

"But the challenge will be to distinguish between the right kind of anti-Communism and McCarthy's anti-Communism. A big difference. Harold, did you see what Henry Reuss said about McCarthy the other day? Reuss was a Democratic contender against McCarthy in 1952, you may remember. I think I may just have a copy of the clipping."

Acheson leaned over and pulled out the bottom left drawer on his desk. "He said, Reuss said, 'Senator McCarthy is a tax-dodging, character-assassinating, racetrack-gambling, complete and contemptible liar."

Acheson's face brightened. He gave the closest he ever gave to a giggle. "I wish I had said that, Harold."

Herrendon decides to act

The morning paper, left as usual on the steps of the house in George-town by the delivery car, was scooped up by Robin before her father's appearance that Sunday morning. ("He likes to 'sleep in' on Sundays," Robin had told Harry. She pronounced the words "sleep in" as her father did, with a trace of discomfort and resignation. Alex had spent many years in America but scrupulously avoided "vernacular argot," as he once described any idiomatic expression that came into use after his graduation from Columbia in 1926.)

"I leafed through the paper, sipping my coffee. *Then I saw it.* I panicked," she told Lucy McAuliffe, her friend and confidante at Senator McMahon's office.

"What did you do?"

"You wouldn't believe it. I actually thought of destroying that whole section of the paper and hoping Dad wouldn't notice. Fat chance I'd get away with it. He might not notice the missing section of the paper. But there must be ten girls my age in the Brit/State/DOD departments he works with, girls I've known and still do. *Somebody* is going to pass the word around that it was me with Senator McCarthy at the racetrack. I don't know how many people would tease my dad about it, but I can guess *somebody* would. What I did do was pull a jacket out of the closet and walk into the street. I decided I needed to give him time. I didn't want to be right there at the kitchen table while he was reading the paper. I walked to the Lauinger library and tried to start in on *War and Peace*."

"*War and Peace*? I'm surprised you're not still there. So then what?"

"Lucy. In July you told me you wanted to get a roomier place to live in but needed a roommate for the second bedroom. Is that offer still open?"

Lucy was agreeably surprised. "Not only open, I've actually seen an apartment *perfect* for two people, two hundred twenty-five dollars, that's one hundred twelve–fifty each—oh. It was *that* bad with your father?"

Robin nodded. A tear came to her eye.

"I couldn't *understand* his vehemence. He went on and on about Senator McCarthy. Then he said that the photograph in the paper would make him the laughingstock of the embassy—I mean, he went on and *on*. He finally said—this was after maybe an hour—I mean in just these exact words, 'Robin. I want you to promise me not to see Harry again.'"

She turned her head away. Lucy waited.

"I went to my room. And this morning I left for work early. We passed each other without talking. It's never been that way with Daddy. So I remembered what you said about looking for an apartment. It's a perfect time anyway, because Daddy has to go to London at the end of the week. When could we move in?"

"I'll find out."

Lucy went out to the public telephone. Senator McMahon did not permit office phones to be used for personal calls. She was back in a few minutes, smiling broadly. But she checked herself.

"I shouldn't be happy over your bad news. But the happy answer is we can move in tomorrow."

Robin thought carefully about how to manage leaving. There would be no point in a dramatic removal of all her clothes and belongings. She would insert into a large suitcase everything she'd need for a few days. Then wait to move her wardrobe until her father had left. She hoped that in the few days remaining before his departure he would soften his opposition to Harry.

It didn't help that the morning's headlines carried updates on two lawsuits against Senator McCarthy, the first by columnist Drew Pearson, the second by former Senator Tydings. The first charged libel and slander and asked for five million one hundred thousand dollars. In the second, Millard Tydings charged that in the campaign for reelection he had lost in 1950, Senator McCarthy and his aide Don Surine had: 1) libeled Tydings, 2) violated Maryland's voting practices laws, and 3) knowingly distributed a photograph of Communist Party head Earl Browder arm in arm with Senator Tydings, an alleged forgery. McCarthy's comment to the press was to the effect that he was surprised *Earl Browder* wasn't suing, to protest his picture alongside "the late Senator Tydings." Alex Herrendon cut the clipping out of the paper and put it in an envelope for Robin, with the note, "Does your boyfriend also give the senator legal advice?"

Three days after settling down with Lucy at Eighteenth and M, Robin steeled herself to call her father. She was astonished by the continuing intensity of his concern.

"Are you still seeing . . . seeing the McCarthy aide?" He sensed what the answer would be.

"Yes, Daddy, I am. I do wish you'd just—just agree to meet him."

"*He is not to come within ten feet of my—of our—house.*"

Robin hung up.

She was crying. She didn't call her father to wish him a safe journey.

Lucy giggled when, two weeks after they had installed themselves in the apartment, she pulled out from her briefcase the "Roommate Protocols," a mimeographed sheet someone, somewhere, had dreamed up. She posted it in the bathroom she shared with Robin. It read,

Whereas ———— and ———— have agreed to take up joint residence at ————, it is hereby agreed between the parties,

THAT checks for the succeeding month's rent will be left in an envelope on the letter tray (if none exists, purchase one) on the 25th of every month, marked "Rent money."

THAT ———— will wash all dishes left in the kitchen from the

day before on even days of the month, and ——— will wash all dishes left in the kitchen from the day before on odd days of the month.

THAT only when specifically requested to do so over the telephone will one party open a letter addressed to the other party.

THAT the living room will be reserved for exclusive use of the two parties on alternate weekends (Saturday, Saturday night, Sunday day).

THAT telephone messages will be taken in behalf of the absent party, and left on the letter tray, without comment.

AND THAT no mention will be initiated by the party in residence when the other party does not occupy his (her) room any night or nights.

What this meant, Robin smiled, for the first time in days, it seemed, and put her signature on the solemn instrument, was that the nights she was spending with Harry would not be a source of conversation the next day.

On Herrendon's return he asked at the embassy whether there had been any movement "on the security business." Simon, friend and golfing companion, detected his distress. He permitted himself to wonder whether Alex had in fact anything to worry about. Was there something other than the silly consumers league petition in his past? Had his relations with Alger Hiss, with whom Alex had traveled on the U.S.S. *Quincy* to Yalta, been other than entirely professional?

Simon put away his concern. But that was on Tuesday. At lunch with him on Friday, at the cafeteria, he thought to comment, "Alex, you're the gloomiest man in Washington these days. Anything I can do?"

Alex shook his head. "Just—family. Robin moved out three weeks ago. Quite right—a twenty-three-year-old shouldn't be stuck in a single house with her father for the rest of her life. But it's lonely at the house without her."

Simon accepted the explanation and they made their golf date.

That night Alex called the private investigating service. He had got the number from his lawyer, Eustace Meikklejohn. The man Eustace had referred him to listened on the phone, paused, and said,

"Do you want to talk to our operative tonight? If so, someone can come to your house at nine."

"Yes, tonight. Nine is fine."

"He will identify himself as 'Cal.' He is to quote to you," there was another pause, "the number 1311. No further identification will be provided. But Mr. Meikklejohn has reassured you about our service."

"Yes. I shall await . . . Cal."

Cal arrived, they talked, and Cal departed.

Robin liked it when Harry slept on, after her own six o'clock rising. The whole McCarthy enterprise straggled into the office in the morning. Everyone was there by ten, and not infrequently Senator McCarthy, who seemed never to need sleep, was there at seven. But everyone worked late, including Harry; though when he spent the evenings with Robin, he was not really working late.

But, he thought late, late at night, with Robin at his side in bed, that in the best sense of it, he didn't believe that when she was with him "work" was outlawed. He would talk happily about problems, questions, dilemmas.

If Joe comes out for a formal invitation to the South Koreans to assert sovereignty over the North, what does it accomplish? Does it make, simply, a historical point, renewing a Geneva accord set aside, everyone seemed to agree, by the war?

He began to talk, on the third night together, about Joe McCarthy. The human being.

He said things he had said to nobody, doubted that he ever would. He began by telling her that she had to put aside the popular legend, canonical among the predominant opinion makers, that Joe simply did not care about factual accuracy.

"Why does he make so many mistakes, then?"

"There are good reasons and bad. He exaggerates. That's bad — but it is also apple-pie American. The priesthood didn't get all that mad at Harry Truman about what he said in 1948 when campaigning. He said that 'powerful forces' were working to 'undermine' American democracy, 'like those that created European fascism.' The whole business, the GOP was run by the real estate lobbies and the National Association of Manufacturers; nobody seemed to mind. But another reason is the fragmentary nature of the stuff that comes in to us. Reports, even rumors—he senses *something* is wrong, but the evidence doesn't congeal. But when it pretty well does, he can't seem to get anywhere with it. Look at Lattimore. The McCarran Committee—and that's not Joe's committee, that's a whole other committee, and its chairman, McCarran, as you know, is a Democrat—did months and *months* of interrogation. And concluded—including six Democratic senators who signed the report—that "Owen Lattimore was a conscious, articulate instrument of the Soviet conspiracy." That was *post* McCarthy. But Lattimore is still a hero out there. Besides, if McCarthy was all that wrong about loyalty/security procedures, how come the Eisenhower administration has kicked out six thousand people on security grounds? Robin?"

"Yes."

"You know what Mark Antony said to Cleopatra?"

"Are you asking me, Have I read Shakespeare? The answer is, Yawp."

"He said—I mean, what comes to my mind right now—is, Antony said to her, 'Do we have to talk about world affairs tonight?' "

They kissed. And they breathed and loved each other. A half hour later she nudged him. "You can't think you have disposed of my problems about your Senator Joe."

"That wouldn't be easy to do. *I* haven't disposed of them. White wine?"

She rose from the bed. "I'll get it. You concentrate."

"On what?"

"On my rear end."

She walked pertly over to the little kitchen. He could hear her voice easily.

"How do you handle the charge that McCarthy has never come up with a *single member of the Communist Party?*"

Harry rose, flipped up his shorts, and walked to his desk. "Okay, I accept the challenge. But only on the understanding that we are dealing with a—synecdoche."

"What's that?"

He took the wine, sat down at his desk, and leafed through a file in his drawer. "It means one part, taken as representative of the whole. 'One thousand oars set out for Sparta.' Means, one thousand men, using one thousand oars, bringing on—how many?—maybe one hundred boats."

"So who's your sinektee?"

"That's syn-ec-do-che. Now you're being serious, right, Robin?"

"Mmm."

"How about Edward G. Posniak, a State Department economist. Here is the *Congressional Record,* July 25, 1950, page 10928. Ready?"

"You may fire when ready, Bontecou."

"'An FBI agent who joined the Communist Party at the request of the Bureau—' the Bureau, that's the FBI—"

"Oh, really? Go on, Harry."

"—the FBI agent who joined the Party '—in 1937 and was expelled from the Communist Party in 1948 and whose record as an informant has been one of complete reliability, stated that [Posniak] was a member of the Communist Party and personally known to him as such.'" Harry looked up.

Robin would not flirt her way out of the problem. "I read you," she said. She sipped her wine and then: "Tell me about growing up with your mom. Mine was divine."

"So is mine."

The intimacy he felt very nearly propelled him to tell her his big secret, about that day searching in his father's trunk. But he stopped.

Even as he did he sensed the totality of Robin for him, his absolute sense that no one else in the entire world could match her company. Yes, he was greedily, hungrily, deliriously happy with her in bed. But before, and after, he sensed a congruity of spirit that made him stop and clench his fists to keep from trembling.

He knew that he would need a more conclusive consummation than the overnight stands. He wouldn't discuss it with her now, though she welcomed discussion on any subject, brightly, inquisitively, playfully, sometimes. Who would ever have thought that she, Robin Herrendon, late at night in his apartment, would hear out the case against Edward G. Posniak!—but he might have been making out the case against Socrates. He'd have to think about the future. And there was the real problem of the hostility of Alex Herrendon. How odd, his total, almost ferocious animosity, just because Harry Bontecou worked for Joe McCarthy. Bloody Brit! Harry decided he'd try to console himself with indignation. Fucking Brit. He has no *business* intruding that way in internal American politics. . . . And after all: If McCarthy was waging the right battle, Great Britain was also a beneficiary. The hell with it. The hell with him.

They went then to sleep, and when his little alarm rang, he rose with her, insisted she lie in bed with the morning paper he retrieved. He brought her coffee and a croissant.

Two days later Alex answered the telephone.

Was he free that night, same time, to see Cal?

Cal arrived promptly in the summer drizzle, removed his raincoat, sat, and brought out a secretarial pad.

"Last night, Subject arrived at 1123 Fifth Street, N.E., at seven-forty-five. She carried a briefcase and a small handbag. Subject did not leave apartment building until this morning at six-fifteen."

Cal asked whether anything further was required.

No, Alex said, rising to take Cal's coat from the rack. "Thank you. I will expect the bill."

Cal left. Alex went to the telephone. He asked for New York information.

"Operator, I want the number, somewhere in the Eighties, West Side, for Mrs. Dorothy Bontecou."

Alex Herrendon
visits Dorothy Bontecou

Dorothy Bontecou had told him she'd rather not meet with him in her house.

Alex understood. "Where, then?"

"I'll make a reservation at Astaire's. I know the people there, and I can get a little table at the far end of the dining room. It's Eighty-first and Columbus. Seven o'clock."

"Thanks, Dorothy. I'll be there."

He lingered outside the door. Astaire's was a utilitarian restaurant. Its front was a thick matted glass on which the restaurant's name showed gold leaf in rococo script. To the right of the window on the inlaid white column a trim green felt frame featured that day's menu. Alex looked through the glass hoping that the table reserved might be visible, however thick the glass through which he had to peer; at least he'd have an idea of Dorothy. He could not dislodge the picture of her in his memory, the striking brunette with the demure and inquisitive expression. He saw her, in memory, lying in bed, her breasts only partly shielded by the bed sheets. He wondered if he would recognize her immediately. She wouldn't have any trouble recognizing him; he knew that from the careful study of his mirror image three weeks ago. He was the same Alex Herrendon she knew.

He entered the restaurant. It was doing brisk Saturday night business. He was dismayed by the noise and bustle but was led not into the main room, but to the left. He passed the cashier, on to what was really a large upholstered booth. Dorothy Bontecou sat at the far corner, opposite. She wore a light blue V-neck dress and pearls. Her hair was gray, but otherwise as before, the simple, feathered curls, the forehead clear. She had been reading a paperback, which now she drew away, extending her hand. He took it and sat down across from her.

The waiter stood by. "Aperitif?"

Alex looked at her. "Still go with sherry on the rocks?"

She nodded.

"And for me, whiskey and soda. Scotch and soda."

They talked about the day's headlines, which spoke of Red China's demand on the UN that it should pull U.S. forces out of Taiwan. "You would think the GIs were an occupying power."

"Yes, it's very strange," Dorothy said. "Who is welcome where. Whose presences are demanded. Did you know that Harry, in the last months of service, was part of the army assigned to guard and repatriate the Russian soldiers and POWs? I haven't talked to Harry, but I know he'd wish there had been a Syngman Rhee in Germany in 1945."

"Yes," Alex said, repressing his own feeling on the matter. President Syngham Rhee of South Korea, ordered by the UN to send back to North Korea the POWs who did not want to return to the Communist north, solved his problem by simply instructing his guards to release the prisoners—just let them go.

"I didn't know that about Harry."

"You know that Harry works for Senator McCarthy?"

"Yes. I do know that. He is mentioned quite often in the press. He travels a lot with the senator."

"I don't like it that Harry is so close to the senator. The whole thing's a mixed-up situation. I am one hundred percent on the senator's side on the broad picture, and that's why Harry went down there, on the anti-Communist enterprise. But it seems to me he's been going wild a lot of the time. You knew Harry was the editor of the *Spectator*?"

Alex nodded. "I competed to join the staff as a sophomore, in 1925, but gave up after two weeks, too much else to do. I didn't make it."

"I remember you competed. You talked to Jesse about pulling out. Yes. Harry's commitment is very strong, on the Communist problem. He fought the Henry Wallace people very hard and studied under Willmoore Sherrill. Do you know about *him*?"

"Again—I've heard about him. The anti-Communist *fons et origo* at Columbia. Remember the term Jesse and I used back then, to describe Nicholas Murray Butler?"

She laughed. " 'Thomas Aquinas, *fons et origo* of scholasticism.' I can't remember, did you teach *me* that, or did I teach *you* that? You were more learned than I, even as a sophomore. On the other hand, *I* had graduated from a Catholic college, was married to an intellectual, and had four years of Latin. I wouldn't have had any trouble on Aquinas being pushed as the 'fountain and origin' of scholasticism."

The drinks came in. They delayed ordering dinner.

"So Harry is communicating Sherrill's Laws to Senator McCarthy. Well, it's hard to know who is instructing McCarthy, except his rampant ego—"

"Alex. Let's not argue McCarthy." They spoke instead of Jesse and his poetry. Alex took courage, draining his glass: Listen: He recited a sonnet.

"That's his most famous, I'd say. It's in a couple of anthologies. By the way, when Jesse spoke those lines he ran the last couplet together: 'Inlaid then with glassed eyes/The movement stilled, the sunlit skies.' No pause."

"I'll remember." He caught the eye of the waiter. He ordered another round of drinks and the menu.

"Alex. Why are you here? It can't be for the pleasure of seeing me after twenty-five years. We made a pretty firm decision back then. I've observed it, zero communications with you—about me, about Jesse, about . . . Harry. And you did the same thing. Though Jesse did hear that you married. I'm glad. Children?"

Alex's throat clutched. "We had a daughter. Judith—my wife— died two years ago."

"I'm sorry, Alex. Jesse died in 1943."

"I knew that. I was at the funeral."

"*You* were at the funeral?"

"Yes. At St. Ignatius. I was in the rear. I saw you, of course. I also saw Harry."

"Divine, wasn't he—isn't he?"

"A very handsome young man." He looked down at the menu. "I knew his age, of course. He must have gone off to war just about that time?"

"One year later, 1944."

They paused. The waiter was hovering over them. They gave him the order for their meal. Dorothy Bontecou ordered the grilled salmon; Alex ordered sweetbreads. Both asked for garlic soup.

"So, Alex, why now?"

"Because our son, Harry, is sleeping with my daughter, Robin."

Dorothy Bontecou turned pale.

Reaching for her purse, she knocked over her cocktail glass. Alex brought out his napkin and caught the liquid before it reached her lap. The waiter appeared. Dorothy mumbled an apology.

"No matter, ma'am, no matter, we have *lots* of tablecloths." He removed the other glasses, the knives, spoons, and forks, the candle, then the tablecloth. Humming a tune, he wiped the table clean, reached in the drawer opposite the cashier for a fresh cloth and napkin, placed the cloth over the table, gave the napkin to Alex, returned the knives, spoons, and forks, the candle, and, finally, Alex's glass. "I will come back with a fresh sherry."

"Thank you, I don't want another drink."

"Okay, ma'am. I'll be along with the soup."

She looked down at the napkin, fiddling with it with both hands.

"I won't say, Are you sure? You wouldn't be here if you weren't sure. Has Robin spoken of any—plans?"

"No. But what you're thinking about can't be ruled out. My opposition, when I learned who she was going out with, was so—explosive—there's the awful possibility they'd—"

"Elope?"

"Yes."

"Oh, God, Alex." Dorothy looked down and spoke with difficulty. "So she has to be told."

"So she has to know about Harry, yes, Dorothy. . . . Does he know—you never told him—his father was . . . somebody else?"

"No."

"He—that would be obvious—never found out about Jesse's problem?"

"How could he? *I* never told him."

"Dorothy, I never showed you this." He reached into the pocket of his coat.

Dorothy put on her glasses. "What is it?"

"A letter from Jesse. Written the day Harry was born. It's not long."

She took the envelope and pulled out a single sheet. She recognized instantly the script. It read,

Dear Alex:

I knew it had happened. I didn't raise my voice. Dorothy wanted a child so desperately, and I couldn't give her one. You have made her very happy. Made us very happy. I am grateful. We will not be in touch again.

Ever, Jesse

Alex spoke to her. "I have to do something about Robin. You have to do something about Harry."

Dorothy got up from her seat. "I really can't have anything to eat. I have to go home. It's not your fault, Alex. I don't blame you . . . for anything."

"I'll walk you home."

"No, Alex. I'll go. I'll . . . take care of Harry. Good night."

The waiter arrived at that moment with the two bowls of soup. He stopped short. Dorothy Bontecou brushed by him on her way out.

"The . . . lady is not feeling too well. Bring me the check, please."

Harry wondered at the telegram from his mother. She was temperamentally averse to melodrama, but here she had wired him, "PLEASE COME IMMEDIATELY. HEALTH ALL RIGHT. DO NOT PHONE. JUST COME. MOM."

He was tempted to disregard her instructions and call her anyway, if only to establish the authenticity of the telegram. But he must guard against being suspicious, he reminded himself: Just because you work for Joe McCarthy, don't start off by doubting that two and two make four. He called Mary Haskell. All he'd need, with Mary, was to say those few words. "Mother needs me."

He was on the train at two and arrived at Pennsylvania Station at seven. He had wired back, "COMING APPROX 7:30. LOVE HARRY."

She opened the door for him, took his coat, and offered him a glass of wine. He took it, closely observing her, apparently unchanged since his last visit a month ago.

She sat down opposite him in the living room.

"Darling Harry, let's start with this. Your father, after we had been married a few years, was disappointed we had no children—"

Harry would put a quick end to the excruciating snail pace.

"Mother. I know about Dad. When I went through his trunk for the insurance information I read the letter from his doctor."

Dorothy stared. "All this time you knew?"

"Yes. What was the point in telling you I knew?"

She paused. "I see. I see. No point. No point. Then you knew, of course, that I had a lover."

"Obviously I had to know that."

"Harry, the first thing I want you to know is that . . . my Jesse and your . . . father were friends."

"That's nice."

The moment he said it he regretted it.

His mother simply went on. "And when your father—when Jesse—found out I was going to have the baby I so terribly wanted— oh, Harry, how I longed for a child—Jesse knew right away who it was."

She turned her head to one side.

"He told me two things. The first was, I must promise never to see him again. The second"—now she broke into sobs—"was that he was very happy, for my sake—and for his."

Harry, got up, went to her, and put his arms around his mother. She wept on, but finally drew breath.

"I can't even imagine," she managed through her tears, "what it would have been like without you, Harry." He soothed her, brushing back her hair, and, in a while, she dabbed her eyes with a handker-chief. She brought it down and gripped the arms of her chair. She turned her head again. And pronounced the words metallically.

"He is Alex Herrendon."

Harry turned slowly. He walked up the stairs to his bedroom. He sat there for a long time, looking every now and then at the tele-phone. Finally his mother knocked.

"You must have something to eat. And you must know that Alex agreed to speak to Robin at the same time I spoke with you. It's nine o'clock. She knows now."

It was when he heard this that Harry collapsed on the bed. His mother stayed outside the closed door. It was an hour before the convulsive sobs died down. She opened the door enough to see Harry, on the bed, fully dressed, face down. She prayed he was asleep. She didn't want to find out.

48

Herrendon talks of
March 1926

It was the tenth day of their collaboration. Alex Herrendon and Harry Bontecou worked every day, Alex working out his passion to put his finger on what he thought the great question raised by the twentieth century: the capacity of totalitarian movements to capture the loyalty not only of multitudes of people, but of intellectuals. And Harry, the historian, wanted to tell the story of the most prominent American figure in the anti-Communist scene in America in the early fifties.

Alex and Harry worked together in the same library, the some-time Red and the sometime Redhunter. They were reaching a level of investigative conviviality that began to affect the nature of their feelings toward one another. It was after a substantial dinner by the fire that Alex brought it up.

"It's becoming a little weary—wouldn't you agree, Harry?—our joint inhibition, our . . . coping with great questions side by side with our refusal to touch on the personal questions?"

He looked over at Harry, whose hand was on the side table, his fingers playing with the coffee cup's handle. Harry said nothing.

"Do you mind, Harry?"

"No. Not really. Go ahead."

Harry's voice was quiet, but Alex found in it a trace of encouragement. He was right—Harry spoke again. "No. I'd like to hear about it. When did you meet my mother?"

Alex poured himself a brandy. "My father brought me to America when I was just seventeen. When you checked in at Columbia as a freshman in those days—I don't know whether that was true in your case, but it was certainly true in 1922—a senior student was assigned to look after you for a couple of weeks. Show you where things are, where you need to go to select your courses. My senior counselor was the tall, blond, blue-eyed, slightly emaciated Jesse Bontecou. He was a World War One veteran and had married the summer before his senior year. He was more than merely formal in the care he took of me. Jesse invited me to his own apartment for dinner. His wife—I find it easier to speak of her so, rather than as your mother—was enchanting, and thought me especially sad and lonely, a young Englishman with absolutely no one to look after him. They took me for weekends at his mother's house on Fire Island—Mrs. Bontecou was a widow, of course.

One night Dorothy had to stay in New York, I forget why. Jesse took me fishing, and at night, sharing his room, Jesse asked if I liked poetry. I replied by quoting to him—in its entirety—I still remember it—one of Shakespeare's soliloquies, the "I come to bury Caesar" one. He was enthralled and asked if I would listen to some of his poetry. I did so, avidly. Jesse was delighted, and from that day until—until four years later, he'd send me a copy of every poem he composed."

"Yes," Harry commented. "He kept them all. They filled three bound volumes. Low Library at Columbia has them."

Alex continued. "His graduation present from his mother, you may or may not have been told—you may have been told and forgotten—was a month in Europe. I saw them off on the *Olympic* early in June. A great party, a dozen of his classmates and a few from my own class who, through me, had got to know him.

"Exactly one day after they set sail I had a desperate telegram from Jesse at sea. He had got word that his mother had died of a heart attack. He knew, because we had chatted about it, that I was at loose ends—Father had planned to take me to England for the summer vacation, but I wasn't especially looking forward to it and hadn't made a reservation, more or less waiting for my father to take the initiative. The long telegram—you didn't have ship-to-shore telephone service in those days—asked me if I could go to their house in Fire Island to look after things. And added that if it suited me, I was welcome to stay there until Jesse and Dorothy got back in August. 'PLEASE CALL MOTHER'S LAWYER AND ADVISE IF YOU CAN DO THIS.' The cable gave the telephone number.

"I called my father, who was in Philadelphia. I think he was rather relieved that he wouldn't have to return to England with me on the same boat—Father never much enjoyed human company. He said I could return to England for a late summer vacation—there were sailings every day back then—or, if I wished, I could remain on Fire Island and 'travel about, get to know something about New England.' He sent me a cashier's check at the Fire Island address.

"So there I was, a—precocious—British student getting ready to enter sophomore year, camped down in a comfortable cottage, in the middle of June, a lovely beach, trees and rosebushes on either side of the house. The family lawyer, old Mr. Ferguson, I think his name was, came in to see me, gave me a list of matters to look after, instructed me to forward utility bills and save all others until Jesse returned, and told me he had signed me up for a guest pass at the Fire Island Club.

"I was deliriously happy. Eighteen years old, with a private dwelling at my disposal, a beach, a village and country club within walking distance, my father's fat check in my pocket. I found it a perfect setting to write my first contribution to the *New Masses*, on the excesses of the capitalist class."

"Did you use your own name?"

"No. Not because I had any notion that twenty years later I'd be engaged in espionage. But because for all that my father was a nonconformist, he would not have liked to see an article in the *New Masses* by Viscount Alex Herrendon."

"Back then the British socialists weren't all that heated up about Soviet Communism, I know."

"Correct, but the Communists were a revolutionary order. And Father didn't want his son associated with socialism of that type. Anyway, I spent a fruitful and pleasant summer at Fire Island and went back to school in the fall."

"Your father and mother and I remained close friends after he graduated. In the fall of my senior year Jesse called. He said he wanted to talk to me. He came in just after I had made myself some soup. He had been drinking. I thought, Oh, my God, there has been a family quarrel! He said he wanted to read me a poem he had just composed. I listened, but not patiently. He hadn't come to my apartment on Ninety-second Street to read me his latest poem. So I said, after clucking my approval of his verse: 'What's the matter, Jesse?' He reached in his pocket and showed me a letter from a doctor. The language was full of technical terms, I remember. But its meaning was very clear. Jesse Bontecou was infertile."

Alex paused. Then he looked up. "Harry, do you want further details? Or can I just say that it was back at the cottage on Fire Island that spring, spending a few days of concentrated reading there. The call for Jesse came in, a former classmate, now at graduate school at Harvard. T. S. Eliot was coming to Cambridge and would give two lectures. Chance of a lifetime! Jesse could meet and talk with the brilliant poet. Dorothy insisted he go. I said I would go back to my apartment in the city. Wouldn't hear of it! I was to stay right there and keep Dorothy . . . company. Jesse would be back in three days."

"That's when it happened?"

"Yes."

"Were you still at the cottage when my father got back?"

"No. I told your mother to tell him I simply had to get back to New York because I hadn't brought enough work with me."

"But you saw him after that?"

"Yes. We both thought I should. But six weeks later she called me. She had been to the doctor. I never saw Jesse again."

BOOK THREE

49

SEPTEMBER 1953

Professor Sherrill
complains about McCarthy

The letter was addressed to "Harry F. Bontecou, Class of 1950." Willmoore Sherrill liked to remind his former students that they were of
junior rank.

Dear Harry,

You are overdue in visiting with me. I remember that you left
Washington to spend your Labor Day vacations with your mother
here in New York even in the hectic years 1950, 1951, and 1952. This
year promises to be more troublesome in the matter of the Communist world-wide offensive, notwithstanding the happy event of
Stalin's death in March, than any one of the preceding years, and it
is concerning recent events and their meaning that I think you
should consult with me. Now, if your plans bring you to New York as
early as September 4, that is the day on which I have agreed to teach
an introductory seminar for my students in the next semester. It
would be instructive to them to hear you talk, and instructive for you
to hear their questions, and perhaps my own. But after they are
gone I'd wish a few hours with you. We can go to the West End Bar
and you can pay the bill since, without knowing the exact figures, I
must assume that an aide to Senator McCarthy is paid more than a
mere tenured associate professor in the department of political science at Columbia. Besides which, you will recall that I was a Trot-

skyite at Cambridge in 1935, which datum will justify your dining with me in order to investigate my subversive past. If my understanding of the ways of Washington is correct (and I teach political science, you will remember), then that would entitle you to reimbursement for our dinner by the United States Treasury. Advise.

Ever, Willmoore Sherrill

Harry enjoyed the archly idiomatic style and the hortatory voice of his former professor. And he held out for "Willmoore," as he had been instructed to call him, sympathy and admiration, and felt also a considerable debt to him. It was he who had given him advice, in 1948, on how to frame the critical debate with the pro-Wallaceite Tom Scott: an important event on campus. Mostly, it was Sherrill who — for Harry — had penetrated the shibboleth so popular with the reigning intelligentsia. It was that the Communists were just another political party, entitled to the same treatment as Republicans or Democrats or, for that matter, socialists.

Dear Willmoore:

Look, these are hard times for the cause, and I wouldn't want to stand two hours before twenty of your trained student assassins to answer questions about Joe McCarthy, which is what they would spend their whole time doing. I ask myself in the morning when I pick up the paper outside my door: Was there *ever* a time when Senator McCarthy didn't dominate the front pages? I mean, it makes *no* difference what he does and says, it is blown up into a story, usually accompanied by denunciations in the editorial pages. And in the *Washington Post*, of course, the almost-daily cartoon by Herblock, whose portraiture is insecure these days: Sometimes, when you see drawings of Joe McCarthy, you can't absolutely tell whether he looks like Hitler or like Genghis Khan. Yesterday he was depicted half-shaven, crawling out of a sewer. So: No, I won't appear at your seminar, but yes, let's dine. September 4 is okay. Unless I hear from you I'll pick you up at your Fellows' suite, 7 P.M.

Harry was on time. Willmoore opened the door dressed with the neat bow tie, wearing an off-yellow shirt, tweed coat, gray flannel pants, cigarette, as ever, between his fingers.

"Come in, Harry. I just got back from a faculty meeting." He removed his jacket. "I could use a drink. Next year I'm going to put in for an increase in salary if I have to attend faculty meetings. You still drinking scotch? One of my students, Henry Gardiner the Seventh, or maybe Eighth, gave me a bottle as a Christmas present, even though his grades don't require my subornation—I'd be giving him a good grade anyway."

Willmoore retrieved ice from the refrigerator in the little kitchen, poured the whiskey and soda, and waved Harry toward the leather couch he had become so familiar with as an undergraduate and friend.

"Now," said Willmoore, sitting himself opposite with his bourbon on the rocks, "let's get down to business. Your McCarthy is hurting us."

Harry decided to stand fast.

"What's Joe—McCarthy—doing that's all that different from what he was doing when you were cheering him on?"

"He's fucking up."

"People said that back in the Wheeling days, though their language was a little better than yours."

"Yes, but Harry, listen to this. In 1950 we had a Democratic administration that was in charge of the future of the country."

Willmoore rose, drink in hand. He liked to stride, forward and back, in the room where he wove his spell on his seminar students.

"Truman accepted Yalta. He went to Potsdam and confirmed the slavery of Poland. His foreign-policy advisers wrote a policy for China that gave the country to the Communists. They invited an aggression in Korea. Soviet agents stole the secrets of the atom bomb. Alger Hiss was convicted of spying even while our president was denouncing his prosecution as a red herring. Henry Wallace captured the left wing of the Democratic Party and, except for a freak, would have cost the election to the Democrats, hardening the Democratic left and putting them in control of their party. But now?—"

"I know what's happened now, Willmoore. Yeah, Eisenhower came in, we sort of stopped the North Koreans, and a lot of security/loyalty risks have been ejected. I guess you can add that Julius and Ethel Rosenberg were executed in June, which made a symbolic point. So what you were saying back then, in June, in your letter to me — that the general will in America was working to 'exclude' the pro-Communists — that's happened. So shouldn't Joe McCarthy get some of the credit?"

Willmoore sat down again. He had brought a folder of newspaper and magazine clippings from a drawer in his desk.

"Now listen here, Harry."

He opened it on the coffee table.

"Your boss McCarthy writes to Senator Thomas Hennings. What *is* Hennings? He is a Democratic senator from Missouri, a lawyer in private life. Your boss McCarthy is struggling to validate his basic case made before the Tydings Committee. Something called the Gillette-Monroney Committee is established, to review your boss McCarthy's conduct during the Tydings campaign. One of the senators who will decide his fate will be Senator Hennings. So what does he ask Hennings to do? To *disqualify* himself from the Gillette committee. Why? Because Hennings's old law firm in St. Louis represents the *St. Louis Post-Dispatch*. So? The *St. Louis Post-Dispatch* editorialized against the Smith Act and the *St. Louis Post-Dispatch* has attacked — your boss McCarthy," Willmoore bent his head over his clipping, "'along the same lines followed by the *Daily Worker*,' to use McCarthy's language.

"Now that's just plain *stupid!* And it argues against the case McCarthy has been trying to make for two years. *Obviously* the *Daily Worker* is going to sound like the Bill of Rights, the Magna Carta, and the Areopagitica when it opposes the Smith Act — which is designed to tattoo and disable American Communist leaders. What did your boss McCarthy —"

"Do you have to say, every *goddamn* time, 'your-boss-McCarthy'?"

Willmoore looked over at his old student, only three years out on his own, so young, quick witted. His head slightly cocked, he smiled, accepting the rebuke.

"I was saying, What does — Joe — *expect* to read in the *Daily Worker*'s denunciation of the Smith Act? '*The Smith Act is wrong because Lenin wouldn't have liked it* and would not have passed any such act against his enemies'? *Obviously* the *Daily Worker* is going to sound like the Bill of Rights whenever it is on the subject of all those freedoms the Communists would of course eliminate if they had power. But the way McCarthy puts it, if you oppose the Smith Act you're being managed by the *Daily Worker*. And so people shake their heads and say to themselves, 'If that's right, then maybe the *Daily Worker* isn't so wrong.' Much more of that kind of thinking and we've had it. He alienates a lot of the right people and *all* the intelligentsia except you and me, Harry."

"—But we do make those points," Harry objected; still, Willmoore strode on.

He felt it had to come up. It was one of the principal reasons he had avoided a meeting with the students.

Roy Cohn.

They met in January. McCarthy needed a chief counsel for the committee he would now head up, the Republicans having taken over the Senate after the November elections. Cohn, the word immediately got out, had himself masterminded a party in his honor, ostensibly given by the FBI's Lewis Nichols. It was Harry's first exposure to the young man who in a matter of days seemed the vortex of Joe McCarthy's world. Senators, congressmen, journalists, made their way to McCarthy's inner counsels often depending on Roy Cohn's opinion of them. He anxiously assumed all the responsibilities for the committee McCarthy hadn't specifically reserved to himself. For all that he was brilliant and quick on his feet, he showed quickly a capacity for critical misjudgment, as in his . . . disastrous "inspection trip" to USIA libraries abroad. Harry was loyal to his boss and stayed out of the way, but there was no way to avoid the probing of Professor Willmoore Sherrill.

"Now tell me, who on earth is this squirt Roy Cohn, and his beautiful Greek companion, David Schine? All of a sudden the entire world learns about their travels. We read, day by day, that they have gone to Paris, Bonn, Berlin, Munich, Vienna, Belgrade, Athens, Rome, Paris again, and London. The impression they mostly leave is that they've never read any books themselves—"

"Roy graduated from Columbia Law School at age nineteen."

"So he can handle college and law school requirements. That doesn't mean anything. *I* ought to know." Willmoore had graduated from college at sixteen. "But the impression they leave—'junketeering gumshoes,' one London critic called them—they swoop down on overseas libraries, demand to see lists of books, refusing to tell anybody at any time what books they're looking for. Says here," he looked down again at his folder, "that they 'spent seven hours in Rome commandeering the presence of the heads of every American agency in Rome,' coming up with? Nothing. They get back to Washington, the laughingstock of the literate world, and your—McCarthy welcomes them like Lewis and Clark. I'm surprised he didn't order a ticker-tape parade up Broadway for them. I repeat, who *is* this guy Cohn?"

"He was hired just before the European trip. Protégé of George Sokolsky." Harry referred to the influential conservative, anti-Communist newspaper columnist. "Roy was on the prosecution team that nailed Julius and Ethel Rosenberg. Joe's very impressed with him. Has him on as counsel to the committee."

"Okay. One week after Cohn and Schine come back, he—your—friend—McCarthy gives a news conference in Savannah. He says in it, according to Associated Press, that 'several U.S. representatives and senators have *known* Communists on their staffs.' So that pisses off a lot of congressmen and senators, right? Then apparently McCarthy realizes this so he simply says to the press he never, *ever* used the word *known.* Anybody believe him? Like nobody. So," again Willmoore looked at his folder, "so they ask what Joe has to say about Bill Benton. Now Joe McCarthy *had* his revenge on Benton, got him defeated in Connecticut, which was super-okay by me. But the press hears from Benton that Joe should be made to give *the names* of these Communists who served on congressional and Senate staffs. And what does Our Joe say?"

He read from his folder. "He says . . . 'I am through paying attention to that odd little mental midget, Benton, whatever he has to say. His complete lack of intelligence makes him too unimportant to waste time on.'"

Willmoore leaned back on the couch, his head almost horizontal, features frozen, as if knocked flat by a bulldozer. "You can't *say* that about a guy like William Benton! You can get away with saying he's screwy-soft on everything from public housing to the World Bank to our policy on the United Nations. But you *can't say* that man—he's a close collaborator of Robert Hutchins, he's vice president of the University of Chicago, chairman of the board of the Encyclopaedia Britannica—you can't say he's a *mental midget.* What are sensible people, and that's who should be on our side on the big issues, going to think? Suppose Our Joe called Einstein a mental midget—which, by the way, I think he is, every time his name shows up on the masthead of one of those peace-with-disarmament committees, even though it is *putrefactive* with pro-Communist history and personnel—are people going to think Einstein is dumb and McCarthy is the only person bright enough to discover this?"

"Benton is no Einstein."

Willmoore stopped. He rose from the sofa. He advanced sternly on Harry. "That was *truly* lame, what you just said. Unbefitting a former student of mine. *Obviously* Benton is not Einstein. They do not have in common that they are both geniuses. They do have in common that they are, neither one of them, mental midgets. Shall we go on?"

Harry was tired, frustrated, and hot. "What do you want me to do, Willmoore? Bat back every pitch you throw out at me? Defend everything Joe—'my-boss-Joe'—has ever done?" He paused for just a moment. Recovered, he said quickly, "Will you give me another drink, or am I being punished for a false analogy?"

Willmoore looked down at Harry and puffed on his cigarette. "What do you want *me* to do, Harry? Cut it out?"

"Why don't you just give me your bottom line."

"It is that McCarthy has now for some months been doing more damage to the anti-Communist cause than help to it."

"Yeah, I know, some people are saying that, Willmoore. But there's another way of looking at it. If Joe McCarthy were crippled, how far back in the wrong direction would the other people go? Do you want to see the disappearance of an effective loyalty/security program, the collapse of organized opposition to accommodationist foreign policy—"

"How far will the other side go with the holes Senator McCarthy has opened up for them?"

"I get your point." Harry drained his drink. "Now, let's talk about other things, okay? Like, Why haven't you been promoted to full professor? I've got a bunch of things on my mind, including how are you doing on your Rousseau book?"

"I'm coming along with it, coming along."

Harry didn't remind him that he had been saying that for six years. They walked out together, sometime student and teacher; companions of the mind, warm friends. Harry did not return to the subject of Joe McCarthy, and he didn't tell Willmoore anything about his own growing reservations.

50

Eisenhower, in the Oval Office,
is irked

President Dwight David Eisenhower looked up from his broad Queen Anne desk in the Oval Office. He had not changed from the picture of him, so widely circulated, taken when he sat down for the first time at the presidential desk, on January 20, 1953. Presidential flag on his right, U.S. flag on his left, oil painting of George Washington behind him, his press secretary seated at his side, clipboard and secretarial pad in hand.

President Eisenhower was a reassuring figure. A little balder than on D-Day, nine years earlier, a few more wrinkles, but nothing more under the chin. D. D. Eisenhower, West Point, 1915, would never gain weight. "He just decided soon after we were married," his wife, Mamie, explained to the interviewer from *Life* magazine one week after Ike's election, "that he wouldn't gain weight. That was the end of it. If he thinks he's putting on weight, he stops eating. Some things are quite simple for Ike."

Handling Joe McCarthy was not a simple problem for Ike. Admirers of the general were abashed by Eisenhower's failure, during the political campaign in the fall, to rebuff Joe McCarthy. The whole world was watching, it seemed, when the two campaigners, one running for president, the other for reelection as senator, appeared jointly in Milwaukee in 1952. How would Ike behave toward the senator who two years before had given a 45,000-word speech the tendency of which was that George Marshall was a partner in a huge conspiracy to undermine the anti-Communist world? James Hagerty, Eisenhower's press chief, had an approach to the problem. Everyone was anticipating the meeting in Milwaukee between Eisenhower and McCarthy. What to do, how to think about, how to act in the context of, McCarthy's famous speech about George Marshall? The answer, Hagerty held out, was: It was simply a "delirious act"—done by young Joe McCarthy without any real thought given to the charges he was making—or, rather, voicing. "Some people, General, don't even think he ever even read it through. McCarthy spoke in the Senate chamber for a couple of hours in a monotone, then dumped the speech into the *Record*. And that was that."

Eisenhower had not been so easily put off. It was only after campaign manager and New Hampshire governor Sherman Adams deployed the language of the military that Ike bent.

"General, it's this simple. We have got to carry the Midwest. Joe McCarthy is God for many voters in the Midwest. They think: Here is somebody who is from our part of the world, who is really raising hell with the people in Washington who lost what in the war you set out to achieve—"

Eisenhower had looked up sharply, his expressive face a mixture of curiosity and indignation.

"—who lost," Governor Adams continued, "I mean, who lost because of much of the *postwar* diplomacy, a war that had been brilliantly won and fought. Now there is no *way* you can afford to simply denounce McCarthy. Renounce your candidacy, if that's what you want to do—you might just as well. Second worst is to appear in Wisconsin with McCarthy—there's no way you can go to Wisconsin at all without *appearing* with him—he owns Wisconsin—and stand way off at one end of the stage from Joe, make it look as if he had yellow fever. Treatment of that kind would be picked up like in two seconds and every pro-McCarthy voter in the country would be furious and looking for a way to avenge Joe—"

"So goddamnit, Adams, get to the point."

"My point is you have to appear side by side with him and smile at least once. And in your speech you've got to say something about Communists in government—"

"I'm *certainly* willing to say something about *that* problem—"

"Obviously not endorsing McCarthy's *specific* charges, just saying it is a continuing responsibility of government to keep the Commies out, and that Truman has done a lousy job, as witness his calling Hiss a red herring."

"I don't want to blast the president. Bad form."

"You don't have to, don't even have to mention him. I'll get up a draft that handles the Truman and the McCarthy problems in the way I think it's got to be done. . . . General, you know everything there is to know about fighting wars. This is a war. In the last war you made common cause with Stalin. You have to make common cause with McCarthy. At least until you get in."

"Jim, I remember what you and Adams told me in Wisconsin," the president said, tapping his pencil on the desk. "I did what you thought was right. Things are different now. That son of a bitch is in my hair, what's left of it, every day. I was never jealous of Arthur" (the reference was to Eisenhower's younger brother) "until last week. Arthur said McCarthy was the 'single most dangerous menace to America.' Have I got that right?"

"Yes, Mr. President. And he said McCarthy reminded him of Adolf Hitler."

"Now that was *wrong* of Arthur. I called, told him so. Shouldn't play around with names like Hitler. Nobody reminds me of Hitler except Hitler. But except for that—I mean, who in the name of *God* does McCarthy think he is? He was exchanging—'declarations!'—with Clement Attlee last month. I don't like Attlee much, Churchill doesn't either, but he *was* prime minister and he heads up the opposition, and it isn't McCarthy's job to issue, what docs the Vatican call them, encyclicals telling people what to do. He's done it to the Brits on their China trade. Sometimes I think he *owns* the Greek merchant fleet, the way he talks about it, tells them what to do—so what do we do about this one? McCarthy says, 'The administration has a lot to learn about the loyalty program.'"

President Eisenhower sat rigid in his chair. He mused, his pencil tapping on the desk. He spoke deliberately, as if postponing a D-Day landing.

"We'll say nothing. *One more time we'll say nothing.* One more time."

51

McCarthy reviews
the hidden memorandum

Late in the afternoon, Joe was shaving. "You've got to do something about that late-afternoon shadow," Jeanie had said on the second day of their honeymoon in Spanish Cay. She had made this complaint before. Perhaps ten times. But now that they were married perhaps it would be different. The other side profiteered from his rapid hair growth. "Herblock has you looking as if you hadn't shaved for three days—"

"Herblock is not going to clean me up if I shave five times a day." For the *Washington Post* cartoonist Herblock, the pursuit of McCarthy was a holy and comprehensive cause.

"Still, Joe. You're going to have to try."

He agreed to try to remember. He had agreed before to try to remember.

Now he was living with Jean at her mother's house, renting from Mrs. Kerr the second-floor apartment on Third Street. McCarthy had a speech to give that night. He would elaborate his charges that the Signal Corps at Fort Monmouth was a mare's nest of loyalty risks.

Roy Cohn had tracked McCarthy down at Spanish Cay in the Bahamas, even though Joe's instructions were that he was not to be disturbed "unless Alger Hiss assassinates the pope." But Cohn was not easily deterred. Reaching McCarthy over shortwave radio in the Bahamas, Roy Cohn told him he had lined up two Signal Corps officers at Fort Monmouth, New Jersey, who were willing to give testimony on loyalty risks in their division. "Very hot stuff, Joe. Serious, heavy stuff. You got to get back here. Apologies to Jeanie."

Jeanie was mad as hell. "Roy can't stand to have you anywhere that doesn't give him access to you every ten minutes." But McCarthy was habituated to criticism of Cohn's habits. He didn't want to fight with Jeanie on this point, but it all added up to one more reason for him to make a big impression about the Signal Corps in his talk to the veterans convention.

The Republicans' sweep in 1952 gave them both houses. That meant, applying the rules of seniority, that Joe McCarthy, beginning his second term, would be handed a committee to head. He became the chairman of the Government Operations Subcommittee. This assignment gave him a broad license. The subcommittee could probe any—operation of government that caught its interest. And arrangements in the Senate were conventional: Whatever caught the interest of the chairman caught the interest of the committee. Senator McCarthy, exercising a power of subpoena, could now bring before his committee very nearly any government official he wished to hear from. There was immediate speculation on whom he would name as chief counsel.

In January, McCarthy gave the name of Roy Cohn, the candidate of George Sokolsky.

Sokolsky was a learned, imperious, dogged newspaper columnist sponsored by the Hearst chain. Early on he had championed McCarthy, adopted his causes, and ventilated, from time to time, opinions on positions and issues that closely corresponded with the views of McCarthy. Sokolsky was highly independent, something of a China scholar, and tended to condescend intellectually to McCarthy. His recommendations were never made obsequiously: George Sokolsky tended to give the impression that anyone he counseled, he was befriending. Moreover, Roy Cohn was about to lose his job. Cohn was a Democrat and as such was named an assistant U.S. attorney in New

York City. But with the Republican sweep, he would have to yield his office to a Republican. He was out of a job.

Roy Cohn was a dazzling twenty-five-year-old. He had graduated from law school at nineteen, as Harry had reminded Professor Sherrill, two years too soon to be permitted to practice. "Fifteen minutes after he became twenty-one," one observer on the scene remarked, "Roy went from clerk-typist to assistant U.S. attorney. He managed to get everybody important to his swearing-in this side of the chief justice." His modus operandi, everyone silently agreed, was this: He knew everybody, he passed along and occasionally husbanded secrets, and he did favors for everyone, in part by blocking further ventilation of rumors he had himself promulgated. ("What I told you about Ruth, Nathan, isn't to go any further. I've told her that you know but that the secret will die with you and me.")

During a busy three years as assistant U.S. attorney, Roy Cohn had helped to prosecute Julius and Ethel Rosenberg, convicted in 1951, electrocuted in 1953, for conspiring to send atomic secrets to the Soviet Union. Joe McCarthy never mentioned the Rosenbergs, even when he was introducing Roy at a banquet or fund-raiser. "How come?" Jeanie was asked by Bazy Tankersley. Jeanie led her to the corner of the room and explained. Six years before, soon after his first election to the Senate in 1946, McCarthy had challenged the nomination of Anna Rosenberg as assistant secretary of defense. Research established that the derogatory information by which McCarthy (and others) had been influenced came from the file of Anna Rosenberg, indeed—but an entirely different Anna Rosenberg. But in the interval, anti-Semites insinuated their conventional insinuations (anyone named Anna Rosenberg was, well, suspicious), whereupon the conventional anti-anti-Semitic press went into its own high gear. A rumor was born, which was that Joe McCarthy was motivated to go after her by anti-Semitism. No friend of Joe McCarthy, as law student, judge, Marine officer, or senatorial candidate, had remarked any trace of anti-Semitism. But McCarthy was keenly anxious to discourage any talk or charges on the subject. Sokolsky was plainspoken on the question: "It won't hurt you to have a Jewish lawyer at your side on the committee."

On getting word from McCarthy that he would be chief counsel,

Roy Cohn planned and consummated a swearing-in ceremony in grand style.

Sam Tilburn spoke of it to Ed Reidy. "Cohn managed to produce J. Edgar Hoover at his swearing-in. Granted, Roy's father is a well-liked judge in New York, but it wasn't the old man who was master of ceremonies at this affair, it was Roy. I was specifically invited. I wondered why. Because I had said an occasional good word about McCarthy? Hell, no, I haven't run into one reporter on the Capitol beat who was *not* invited. But I did go, and so did a couple of others. McCarthy was beaming like a proud father. He told me Roy was 'the most brilliant young person' he ever met—"

"Maybe he is," Ed Reidy commented. "Who's the competition? How many brilliant young people has Joe McCarthy met?"

"I don't know. But you can be sure of this, that the McCarthy committee, with Cohn running it, is off to the races."

The Signal Corps investigation was, for Roy Cohn, a big-stakes race.

Meredith O'Toole stared at the one letter. It had been a crowded week, a terrible week. On Tuesday, the heart seizure. She drove Jimmy to the hospital, they did what they could, but pronounced him dead two hours later. Dead at sixty-one. Then the wake. Then the funeral. Their only son, Bobby, was in Korea. Meredith had for company from the family only her spinster sister. There were others at the funeral, four or five fellow clerks from the FBI and a few friends. The O'Tooles mostly stayed at home. A colleague once twitted Jimmy that anyone who was personal file clerk for J. Edgar Hoover had better look inconspicuous, and act inconspicuous.

But now, on the very afternoon of the funeral, Meredith had undertaken to look at Jimmy's personal papers. He had them in a large safe, a cast-off from old FBI safes replaced by modern equipment after the war. Jimmy had instructed her on what the combination was, and it was written in simple code in the family bible. You always added two to the number shown. So that 4-8-9 would become, in the real world, 6-0-1. 2R meant two revolutions to the right. 1F, one to the left.

She didn't know what was in the safe other than his will, and had little reason to be curious about it, as it was inconceivable that Jimmy had hidden assets. Still, he was a fastidious man, and whatever was there, he'd have wanted Meredith to look at—what else was the point in putting it in a safe and giving her the combination?

But this letter. What was *it* doing in Jimmy's file?

Meredith didn't follow the news carefully, and Jimmy never talked about his work at the FBI. But she was alarmed by what she read. She couldn't quite elaborate for herself what would be the consequences of its disclosure, but—well, it would be serious business, she thought.

She suspended her examination of other material in the safe, what seemed a hundred folders, many of them including newspaper clippings. And of course his last will and testament, which told her nothing she didn't expect. The letter was very much on her mind when she put it back and locked the safe, and went to the kitchen to make some soup and see if she could distract herself with *I Love Lucy* at eight o'clock.

But she couldn't keep her mind even on Lucille Ball. She knew what she was worrying about. That the FBI—that the director— would . . . discover the letter. What would happen then! Certainly she would risk losing her pension, and the thought of this was intolerable. She had to do *something*.

Burn it?

That would have desecrated Jimmy's memory, she concluded. She would say a Rosary and pray for guidance.

The next morning she had resolved what to do. She drew the letter from the safe, inserted it in an envelope, and wrote out the name of the man Jimmy always spoke of as a great American who cared the most for his country. The newspaper accounts of the wedding had said the newlyweds would live with the bride's mother. She looked in the phone book and wrote down the address. She would not trust it to the mail, perhaps to fall into alien hands. She would have it delivered to his house.

She took the bus, the same route as when she took Bobby there, the first semester days, before he could look after himself. She knew the route to Hamilton High School and the parking lot where some of the older boys and girls, those who used the family car, would come in for their late afternoon and evening courses.

She watched the young people coming and going, and decided that the time had come for a leap of faith.

She approached the young redhead about to lock the door of the prewar Ford.

She smiled and spoke directly. "Can you do me a favor?"

The young man, his hair combed, wearing a sport shirt and jeans, answered politely.

"What is it, ma'am?"

"I have a letter here I want delivered to Senator McCarthy at his home—the address is written on the envelope. It is very important to me. If you will do this—Haydock Street is only a few minutes away—I'll give you twenty dollars."

"*Twenty dollars?* . . . You mean when I come back you'll give me twenty dollars?"

"No. If you say you will do it, I will take your word for it and pay you now."

He pulled the car key from his pocket.

Meredith O'Toole smiled, gave him the envelope and a twenty-dollar bill. And said, "Just give it to him, personally, and don't talk about it, that's all."

"Okay, ma'am."

The young man inserted the car key, opened the car door, and drove away.

Meredith O'Toole would never know what happened, she said to herself on the bus going home, but she was certain that Senator McCarthy would do the right thing.

The knock on the bedroom door had to be Mrs. Kerr. McCarthy assumed his landlord was looking for her daughter.

"Jeanie's not home yet, Elizabeth."

"I know. But it's for you, Joe. There's a man here with a package, but he says he can only deliver it to you directly. Do you want to come down, or shall I have him come up?"

"Send him up, dear. I'm in my underwear. I'm shaving, you'll be glad to know."

"Well, I wouldn't want to interrupt *that.*" Elizabeth Kerr—the mirror caught Joe's smile—had joined the anti-McCarthy conspiracy to keep him closely shaved.

In a moment he opened the door to what seemed a boy, not more than eighteen, perhaps twenty. The young man was nervous as he fumbled with one hand in his pocket, pulling out an envelope. He thrust it at McCarthy.

"That's all, Senator."

McCarthy reached for the envelope, eyeing the messenger suspiciously. On impulse he grabbed the parcel from the messenger's left hand and with his right, the messenger's wrist.

"Let me see your credentials, sonny."

The nervous voice replied. "I'm just—freelance, Senator."

"Who's your employer?"

"Nobody. Just somebody." He was not about to betray his benefactor, even though he did not know her name.

McCarthy released his grip and leaned over to pick up the envelope he had dropped. The messenger took that moment to break away and rush through the open door, barreling down the staircase out to the street. McCarthy went to the window and saw him lunge into the car he had parked outside the house, its motor left running, and speed off. McCarthy went to the bathroom and dried off his face. Sitting in his shorts on the bed he opened and read what appeared to be a copy of a letter. It was addressed to "Honorable George E. Allen, Director, Reconstruction Finance Corporation, Washington, D.C." It was typed on the letterhead of the FBI, Office of the Director, marked PERSONAL AND CONFIDENTIAL BY SPECIAL MESSENGER, dated May 29, 1946. The salutation was "Dear George." It was signed "Edgar."

After reading it, Joe continued to sit on the bed. After a moment, he reached into the pocket of his jacket on the chair and pulled out his telephone notebook. He picked up the phone and dialed FAirview 3232. "This is Senator McCarthy," he said to the operator. "I want to talk to the director."

J. Edgar Hoover had not been quite as accessible in recent months, not as much as he had been during the first year, McCarthy thought.

The operator reported back that the director was in conference.

"Then put me through to Lou Nichols."

"Lou? Joe here. Tell the director I want to talk to him like right away, and it's for his own good not to waste any time."

"Nothing I can take care of, Joe? Anything I can do . . ."

"No, Lou. I'm at home. Will be here—Jean's mother's house—LUdgrave 2747—for fifteen minutes. That's fifteen minutes, Lou."

"I understand."

The telephone rang five minutes later.

"Edgar," McCarthy said, wasting no time in greetings, "we need another of your bubble conferences. As I told Lou, what I want to see you about is very much in your own professional interest."

Hoover could be very direct.

"Lou will call your office for a date."

"A date tomorrow?"

Hoover hesitated for a moment. Was he looking at his calendar?

"A date tomorrow," he confirmed.

McCarthy was relieved that Jeanie had not come home during his conversation with the director. Something very weird, and conceivably dangerous, was going on. He'd as soon leave her out of it, at least for the present.

The arrangements were as before. This time McCarthy did not nod off while driving with "Henry" at the wheel. About ten minutes before the car's estimated arrival, after apologizing, Henry requested the senator to put on the proffered eye mask. "The director just plain insists on it. Not that there are that many people who come out here. The director only brings in a very few people here. But it's always this way."

McCarthy donned the mask and, when the car came to a stop, walked, as the autumn light began to fade, from the garage to the front of the house and up the stairs. He climbed to the second floor. The door opened. The director was in his chair, his coat off, his suspenders gripping his loose shirt. They shook hands.

"What you got, Joe?"

McCarthy removed the letter from his pocket.

"First: I haven't the slightest idea how this was slipped to me. None of my usual people. It's four pages, but I'm just going to read you two paragraphs. This," McCarthy said, as he peered intently, examining the document, "is addressed to George Allen. It's signed 'Edgar,' and it's dated May 29, 1946. The first paragraph reads,

"'I thought the President and you would be interested in the following information with respect to certain high government officials operating an alleged espionage network in Washington, D.C., on behalf of the Soviet Government.'"

He looked up at Hoover. The muscles in his face were clenching.

McCarthy returned to the letter. "'Information has been furnished to this Bureau through a source believed to be reliable that there is an enormous Soviet espionage ring in Washington'—this is you talking, Edgar—'operating with the view of obtaining all information possible with reference to atomic energy, its specific use as an instrument of war, and the commercial aspect of the energy in peacetime, and that a number of high government officials whose identities will be set out hereinafter are involved.'

"You then go on—this is your letter, not a forgery, right, Edgar?"

Hoover said nothing.

"You then go on to list department heads in federal divisions that touch on atom energy or the atom bomb. And then you say,

"'The individual who furnished this information has reported that all of the above individuals mentioned are noted for their pro-Soviet leanings, mentioning specifically Alger Hiss of the United Nations Organization.' Then there are two more pages." He looked up at Hoover.

His face was now the famous Hoover red. He ground his back teeth. "What do you want to know, Joe?"

"I want to know if the president of the United States saw your letter. I mean, did you send the same letter to him? You didn't send it just to George Allen, did you?"

Again Hoover was silent.

"Because you know what, Edgar, I doubt that you ever did. I can't imagine Truman, in December 1948, saying the prosecution of Hiss was a red herring if he heard from you in May 1946 that 'a source believed to be reliable' informed the bureau that"—McCarthy looked down—"Hiss was 'noted for . . . pro-Soviet leanings.'"

McCarthy sat back. "You know what I think, Edgar? I think you never told the president about this, and I think you wrote that letter to Allen for the record, and I'm even wondering to myself—Did you actually *send it to him?* And I'm thinking, McCarthy is thinking, that maybe you were *afraid* to deliver it to Truman."

Hoover spoke. "You're not, I mean, you're not—"

"No. *Obviously* I'm not. But I'm thinking there's got to be an explanation for Truman exposing himself the way he did on the Hiss business with you sitting here with incriminating evidence—"

"Whittaker Chambers had plenty of incriminating evidence against Hiss. All of it was available to the president."

"But a lot of people thought Whittaker Chambers was a liar. Nobody thinks you are a liar. What I got to know, Edgar, is something about your source. Because I don't know how many other people have been fingered by this same source who are still in government, and maybe you, like in the Hiss business, aren't about to tell the president who they are and where they're hiding. Edgar, what I have in my hand is—can be—the biggest explosion of your, or my, lifetime."

Hoover got up. He peered at the sketch on the wall behind his desk. *Washington, 1860, Awaiting the Arrival of President-elect Abraham Lincoln.* He paused and then said, "There's one great secret in this town."

McCarthy waited.

"Six people know it."

Again McCarthy sat silent.

"We broke the Soviet code in 1946. The Venona files, we call them. They expose Hiss."

"You didn't tell Truman?"

"I didn't tell him. If *he* was told, others surrounding him would know. And some of them were also named in the Venona files—not, presumably, as agents, like Hiss. The decoding is still going on and will be for years. But the way their names were used—we just had no way of telling. All we could do was watch them." Hoover's normal color had returned. "The one thing I figured we couldn't afford was word getting back to the Kremlin that we had cracked their code."

"You still got it? The Soviet code?"

"Joe, I wouldn't tell you that, and you shouldn't ask me."

"I understand."

"Do you also understand that if you let out what's in that letter, the Soviets are going to know we're onto them? And, incidentally, I'd get fired—overnight. You willing to see me replaced? You know, Joe, you owe me quite a few. I've stood by you. And you know what I've tried to do for—the country."

McCarthy was again silent. He looked up at Hoover. In slow motion he reached into his pocket, brought out the letter, reached his hand over the desk, and dropped it in front of the director.

"I made no copy. I trust you. You got a drink in this here bubble, Edgar?"

"Thanks, Joe."

After Senator McCarthy left, Hoover sat back and pondered the letter left on his desk. McCarthy had guessed correctly. He had never actually delivered it. He had indeed wanted it in his private file, just in case. There was only one human being who had access to it, his file clerk.

He picked up his hot line to his office, to the operator whose only duty it was to attend his line.

"Put me through to my file clerk, what's his name, O'Toole."

"Sir, Jimmy O'Toole died on Tuesday."

Hoover put down the phone slowly.

There was nowhere to go. He'd have to hope and pray that the only copy was the copy that lay on his desk.

52

McCarthy begins
the Monmouth investigation

McCarthy, returned from the Bahamas, convened a meeting of the executive committee of the Government Operations Subcommittee. He told his colleagues—Republican senators Mundt, Dirksen, Potter, and Democratic senators Symington, Jackson, and McClellan— that he intended to go immediately to Fort Monmouth to conduct hearings, with his counsel, Roy Cohn.

He left from his office to the airport and caught a flight to Newark. A lieutenant from the public-relations office of Fort Monmouth was waiting for him. At the base, McCarthy and Cohn entered the room that had been prepared for them together with the stenographer who had been brought in to record the proceedings.

Two hours later Senator McCarthy emerged. Two reporters were there, and a television cameraman. He advised the reporters that Fort Monmouth had a severe loyalty/security problem that required immediate attention. He took reporter Annie Stephenson from the *New York Daily Mirror* to one side. "Annie, keep your eyes on this one. I think we have a real scandal here. Incredible, the army has let this go on. I've scheduled more meetings, tomorrow and maybe the next day."

Two days later he was back in Washington from New Jersey with Roy Cohn, arriving haggard at his office early in the afternoon. He sat down at his desk and asked for Harry.

"Harry's working on your Wilmington speech," Mary Haskell told him on the intercom. "He's working at home."

"Tell Harry—tell Roy to tell Harry—to bring his speech draft to the meeting I'm scheduling. I'm inclined to let the White House have it, Mary. This is too much—"

"Joe, I have some calls for you you'll really want to make. There are the usual hundred press calls, but there's also . . ." Mary looked down at her notes.

"Yes, yes, bring them in, Mary, I'll do what I can. But important, reserve the room at the Hay-Adams—the usual room—order dinner for three. We have to work out the speech and the press release and the executive committee report. Just Roy and Harry. You pacify Don Surine and Frank Carr, I'll pacify Jeanie. Yes, and we'll want one of the girls standing by at the Hay-Adams, maybe from nine o'clock on, to type up the speech. Harry will feed it to her."

"What's going on?" Harry asked when Roy called to summon him to the Hay-Adams meeting.

"Wait till you hear! The two army officers. We get up there. We have a pretty full report on what they were willing to tell us. So we get ready to go, and suddenly they say, 'Sorry, the presidential order says we can't talk.' So then we bring in a fellow called Carl Greenblum, an electrical engineer over at Monmouth. I tell him what I've got on him, and he begins to cry and pleads sick. Then we get Harry Grundfest—ever hear of him? Neurologist at our great alma mater, Columbia. He won't answer questions. I think Joe's got a great opportunity here to blow the lid off the whole mess. What were you doing a speech on?"

"I've written on the United Nations business—"

"Forget it. This is hotter. Nobody cares about the UN."

"Joe cares. I care. A lot of our targets are there under diplomatic immunity—hell, I'm not telling you anything you don't know."

"No, you're not, Harry. Be at the Hay-Adams at six."

Harry drew a deep breath. He was about to say, "Yes, six o'clock," but Roy had hung up.

———

WILLIAM F. BUCKLEY JR.

Harry was reading the *Washington Star* in the cab when the honking began from behind. He looked up. The traffic light had gone green. His cab driver was slumped over the steering wheel. Harry reached over and shook him by the shoulder, but there was no reaction. The honks were increasing in frequency and duration. Harry stepped outside the cab and looked back at the driver in the truck behind him, whose horn was unremitting. He thrust up his right arm, palm raised, and shook his head two or three times vigorously—please would he release the horn. He opened the driver's door and turned up the head of the elderly black man. Harry searched desperately for signs of life.

He found none. The cab was blocking the traffic, now a block long, on the crowded avenue. He managed to think purposefully through the cacophony. He nudged the body of the driver over to the passenger side of the seat, got into the driver's seat, slammed shut the car door, and slipped the car into gear. Driving at a slow speed, he looked for a parking space. Anyplace that wouldn't block the rush-hour file of cars he could see stretching down Constitution Avenue. In desperation he turned up Fifteenth Street and veered sharp left— onto the sidewalk. It was a cop who came running, and a cop was just who Harry wanted to see.

"Looks like a heart attack, officer. You better call an ambulance."

"You wait right here, mister," the young, crew-cut police officer said breathlessly. "Be right back."

Harry waited impatiently while the officer zigzagged across the avenue, dodging the cars, making jerky headway to the police telephone box. It seemed a very long time, though it was not more than five minutes before the officer was back. "The ambulance is on its way!" he reported excitedly. He pulled out a police pad.

What exactly had happened? he asked, his pencil over the pad. Harry told it all, briskly; but it was haltingly taken down, from the "How do you spell Bontecou?" which took much time to write down, to "Who is your employer?" to "How do you spell McCarthy?"

It was 6:45 when he reached room 455 at the Hay-Adams. He was startled to hear Cohn, opening the door, say to him—in Joe's presence, a few feet away—"I thought I told you to be here at six."

Harry looked at him and gave no answer. He hung his coat and walked over to McCarthy, seated in shirtsleeves, tie askew, in an armchair. On the dining table set up to one side of the two armchairs and the sofa opposite were the forks and spoons and knives and napkins, a single rose in a vase, and a bucket of ice and a bottle of Jack Daniels.

"I'm sorry I'm late, Joe. My taxi driver dropped dead in the middle of traffic. Had to stay and answer some questions."

"Don't worry about it, Harry. We've been talking about the Monmouth situation. Roy thinks the time is here to run headlong into Ike on the executive-order issue and maybe—"

"Ike wants to have it both ways," Cohn interrupted. "We've run into a real vipers' nest at Monmouth—took me a lot of hours—"

"Roy's done a great job," McCarthy said, pouring another drink. "Roy's a brilliant fellow, we all know that. But he is really devoted to McCarthy, you know. Harry, bourbon? Or you want something else? Here." He reached for the telephone and rang room service before Harry could speak. "Senator McCarthy here. Send up"—to Harry— "What?"

"A beer would be fine."

"Send up six beers. The dinner? No, ma'am, we're not ready for that. Dinner, say," he looked at his watch, "at eight o'clock." He hung up the phone and looked benignly at Harry. "You were saying, Roy?"

"We ran right into the Truman presidential order forbidding testimony on loyalty/security by federal personnel. I've been saying to Joe: Let's stop fooling around with Ike. He's no good at this kind of stuff, doesn't really care, I expect, too used to dealing diplomatically with everybody in sight, including Joe Stalin's direct representatives in Europe—"

"That's a good point, Roy," McCarthy said. "A very good point. We haven't ever really stressed that point, that Ike got used to dealing with the Communists as allies. Have we?"

"*Never.* When you did the exposé on Marshall, Joe, nobody heard a peep from Ike. He was running for president. He didn't care about Marshall—maybe he even wondered what it was all about, your exposé. Probably figured, Well, the Soviets were on our side, weren't they?"

"Now wait a minute, Roy," Harry said. "Eisenhower has talked about the Communist problem *repeatedly*. He was commander of NATO before he ran for office. What's the purpose of NATO except to stand up against the Russians?"

"Well." Cohn's was a soft tread in retreat. "*Joe* knows what I mean. And right now we've got this Monmouth situation."

"Joe," Harry turned his head, "you want me in on this whole business?"

"I sure as hell do, Harry. I'm counting on you to write the speech I'll give tomorrow. And," he looked over at Cohn, "I want your judgment in the matter."

"Well then I'd better get briefed on the particulars. All I got is what Roy gave me over the phone this afternoon."

"You're dead right. Roy, you bring Harry up to speed. I've got to call Jeanie—" The doorbell rang. "That would be room service. Let 'em in, Roy."

"Harry, you get the door. I'm bringing up my notes."

Harry rose and let the waiter in.

At nine, Alice Mayhue called up from the lobby. "Want her to come up?" Cohn looked at McCarthy.

Harry said: "I can do it. Tell her to go home."

It was after nine o'clock, after dinner. Joe had asked for his steak rare. "Before Jeanie, I used to ask for my steak 'cremated'!" Harry had managed to eat his dinner and take notes. With the coffee he began cautiously on his second beer.

"So what you think, Harry?" McCarthy asked.

"I think you've got clear evidence of loyalty/security neglect at Monmouth. A perfect case for investigation by your committee, Joe. But what's the point in going to war with Eisenhower over this?"

Cohn pounded on the table. "For God's sakes, Harry. Do I have to say it again? It's because of the presidential order forbidding testimony—"

"I know about that, Roy. I wrote a speech for Joe in 1950 questioning that order. I cited Woodrow Wilson. He said—in *Congressional Government*—that the most important function of Congress is its investigative function. We've raised the problem three, four times—"

"You're making my point, Harry. We've jawed about it for years and now we have a very direct example of how that executive gag is preventing any reform, so the time has come to put the blame on the person who is responsible for the perpetuation of the gag order."

"Look, Roy. Look, Joe"—Harry turned to McCarthy. "The constitutional business, separation of powers business—that's an important fight. But because Monmouth is hot isn't a reason to attack Eisenhower directly. If you do, the commotion isn't going to be about Monmouth, it's going to be about McCarthy versus the president. We've got to win the loyalty/security fight *under an Eisenhower administration*. It's crazy to challenge him personally. He isn't clipping fresh congressional wings—he's just staying on with a policy that President Truman came up with—six years ago, in 1948. There isn't any pent-up congressional opposition to that order; it's pretty widely accepted as executive privilege. Why muck up the Monmouth business with a fight against Ike?"

"Why?" Cohn burst in. "Because *that* is the great hindrance to effective congressional investigation!"

"Well, the way to make that point, Roy, is to proceed with the hearings and get the two army officers to say they won't testify. Then let Joe raise the point in the Senate—what do we do about this constitutional logjam? But it should be floated as a where-do-we-go-from-here question, and the way *not* to do it is to go after President Eisenhower in a speech tomorrow."

"Harry." Cohn got up on his feet and turned to the window, looking out on the lighted wing of the hotel, opposite. "Harry, I'm here backing Joe McCarthy. He's gotten where he's gotten by courage and vision. He knows what enemy fire is. You don't. You want to shrink from it. He's not afraid."

McCarthy cleared his throat. "Harry, I think Roy is right. We got to get the word out there, to the whole bureaucracy. When you find the federal government sitting on its ass, doing nothing, you got to come to us. . . . Tell you what. Let's compromise. We won't go after Eisenhower *directly*. But we'll make our point in unmistakable language. We'll invite everybody in government—*everybody*—to tell McCarthy what's going on, right, Roy? Let them know they're welcome and the hell with presidential orders to keep knowledge of subversive activities to themselves."

There was a moment of silence, during which McCarthy poured another drink and nudged a third bottle of beer toward Harry.

"Joe," Harry said, "could I draft that statement for you? I could do it now, in longhand, or bring it to you tomorrow, typed up."

McCarthy looked at his watch. "It's only just after ten. Why not whack away at it here? You got your briefcase, go right ahead. I'm going to look in on the late news on TV. Roy, let's see what's going on in that part of the world that doesn't have the benefit of our advice."

Harry retreated to the end of the room. Joe and Roy watched the end of the football game, waiting for the news that would follow. The network news gave thirty seconds to Senator McCarthy leaving Fort Monmouth, waving his right hand, index and third fingers parted, at the reporters, saying, "I'll be back," with a smile.

53

Ike is angered by McCarthy

"He did *what*?" The curtains were closed in the Oval Office. All the lights had been turned off. It would be so until eleven, at which point the ophthalmologist would reappear, insert two drops of the lotion in each eye, and, after two hours of light-abstinence, his patient would don his glasses and his assistants would let in the sunlight.

"Read it to me. Turn on the picture light, by the Cabinet room. I'll look away."

James Hagerty went off to the front of the room, under the portrait of James Madison, and turned on the picture light. He angled the paper in his hand to make it visible in the dim light.

"What came first, Mr. President, was that Senator McCarthy convened the executive committee of his committee—"

"Which one is that? I forget."

"It's the Senate Government Operations Committee's Permanent Subcommittee on Investigations. They can look into anything, very broad mandate. Anyway, he asked the executive committee to approve a joint declaration criticizing you for keeping in place President Truman's ban on testimony by federal employees to congressional committees on personnel security matters. The majority refused to go along, so McCarthy said he would make his *own* statement. Here's what he said, Mr. President. 'As far as I am concerned'—the senator read this to the press—'As far as I am concerned, I would like to notify the two million federal employees that I feel it is their duty to give us any information which they have about graft, corruption, Communism, treason, and that there is no loyalty to a superior officer which can tower above and beyond their loyalty to their country.'"

Eisenhower broke in. "*No loyalty to a superior officer?* Is that man *crazy?* Loyalty to a superior officer is what democratic structure is all about. It's not just the army. If you don't have loyalty to a superior officer you should quit. Those two million federal government employees *have to have* loyalty to their superiors. Discipline, order, mutual esteem — they don't work under any other arrangement. Was that how McCarthy left it?"

"No, sir. Senator McCarthy wasn't through. His statement to the press says, 'I may say that I hope that the day comes when this administration notifies all federal employees that any information which they have about wrongdoing should be given to any congressional committee which is empowered to take it, period.'"

"Get me Bernie Shanley."

The president, eyes studiously sheltered, waited impatiently. Hagerty, keeping his voice down, told the White House operator to locate the White House counsel and have him come *immediately* to the Oval Office. "Only way I can make it out, Jim, is McCarthy is inviting *two million employees* to defy the presidential interdict against communicating to Congress complaints about security personnel estimates. That would mean anyone with any beef who wants to call any other employee a security risk could write — write to what? What was that one qualifier he used?"

"He said, 'any congressional committee which is empowered to take it.'"

"What in the hell kind of qualification is that? *No* congressional committee is 'empowered' to solicit testimony prohibited by his department head, pursuant to executive order. Never mind Shanley. Get me the attorney general."

At that moment Bernard Shanley walked in. He greeted the president, who recognized his voice and called out to Hagerty, "*Hold the call to Brownell.* Shanley, have you seen what McCarthy did?"

"Can't hardly not see it, Mr. President" — Shanley was an easygoing young lawyer, greatly respected; he had served as editor of the *Harvard Law Review* — "even in this light. It's everywhere. Headlines, radio, television. Drew Pearson took it so hard I fear for his life."

"Better fear for McCarthy's life. Siddown. Now tell me this, Shanley, you're supposed to know everything there is to know about the Constitution and the separation of powers and all that business. What's the best construction a sober supporter of McCarthy could put on that statement of his, inviting mass disobedience?"

"Well, sir, you could take the position that Congress has an ongoing responsibility to monitor the operations of the executive. But Senator McCarthy isn't simply saying that. He is inviting employees to pass individual judgments about whether to obey their superior officer—to obey the chief executive—or interpose a different loyalty and go to a congressional committee. What he's doing is in effect pleading the Nuremberg doctrine. The kind of insubordination he's advocating might be honored by a respectable legal tribunal if your department heads were engaged in sending employees to crematoria. But in this situation the answer to your question is: No supporter of Senator McCarthy could defend him while sober. I mean, while the supporter was sober."

The telephone rang. Hagerty picked it up. He turned to the president. "You want to talk to the attorney general?"

The president fumbled for the telephone in the near dark. Hagerty maneuvered the phone into his hand.

"Yes. Herbert. You're calling about McCarthy, I'd guess. . . ."

The President listened. "You just said McCarthy's is 'an open invitation to violate the law'? Quote unquote. Now I tell you what, Herbert. I want you to go public with that. Use *exactly* that language. Because this is it. The end of Ike's sweet temper. Son of a bitch. Now Herb, you've got a long friendship with Bill Knowland. We need something from the majority leader. Go to work on him to go our way. Maybe we'll hear from some other senators from our distinguished political party, if we can find any with guts."

Jack Hastings, the appointments secretary, walked into the Oval Office from the little room he occupied next door. "The doctor is ready with the drops, sir. Shall I tell him to come in?"

"*God,* yes, and next time I have my eyes examined, tell Walter Reed to send me somebody who doesn't need to make me blind for two hours every time he wants to check my eyesight."

"Well now, Ed," Sam Tilburn said on the line with his daily call to Reidy at the *Indianapolis Star,* "the you-know-what has really hit the fan today. I mean it's coming in every few minutes. You got the wire stories, but you may not yet have got the Flanders quote, or has it come in? . . . No? Well, get this. I'll read it fast, because the wire will have it complete within the hour, if you want the quote in front of you. But listen to this— Oh. You *have* seen the Brownell quote?"

"Yeah, that came in an hour ago. That wasn't so much a surprise. Eisenhower's fed up, and using his attorney general to apply pressure on McCarthy is to be expected. What *really* hurts Joe is Bill Knowland. Here's the right-wing majority leader of the Republican Party, senior senator from California, saying no to his pal McCarthy. Our Joe is treading on highly dangerous and doubtful ground. But go on with Flanders—I like Flanders. He uses colorful language. Amazing what McCarthy does to Flanders, the thoughtful, sort of highbrow, quiet senator. He whiffs McCarthy and he might as well be charging it up in a bull ring."

"What he said isn't so much colorful as apocalyptic. Brace yourself: 'One of the characteristic elements of Communist and fascist theory is at hand, as citizens are set to spy upon each other. Established and responsible government is besmirched. Religion is set against religion, race against race. Churches and parties are split asunder. All is division and confusion. Were the junior senator from Wisconsin in the pay of the Communists he could not have done a better job for them.'"

"Oh, my goodness, Sam." Ed Reidy began to laugh at the display of rhetorical temper, but stopped. He simply repeated himself. "Oh, my goodness."

"Yeah, I feel the same way. Some of the enemies of McCarthy will, if possible, manage to outdo McCarthy. You saw where Robert Hutchins said that under McCarthyism it requires an act of physical courage to give money to Harvard?"

"No. I'll note that. . . . Has Joe come back at Flanders? How can they sit in the same chamber? Granted, Vermont is a fairly long way from Wisconsin, but they are in the same *country.* Did Joe respond?"

"Joe never lets us down. Hang on. . . ." Sam went through his notes. "Here it is: '*I think they should get a man with a net and take him to a good quiet place.*'"

"I'd say Joe won that exchange. But he's not going to win the big one, the one with Ike."

"No—here's another one, just handed to me. Senator Alexander Smith of New Jersey. Not long ago Smith was pleading with Joe to cooperate with the GOP. Lemme see, Smith is . . . 'deeply shocked,' . . . he reads it as 'a defiance of the executive in crisis.' . . . Hold on. It gets better: 'We cannot tolerate one-man government either in the executive or in our legislative body.'"

"You think Joe's going down?"

"I think he was a real asshole on this one, Ed. I mean, he's had the whole liberal world to fight. He's only been a national presence for three years. Why throw the gauntlet at Ike? Among other things, Ike's the most popular man in America, after John Wayne and Arthur Godfrey. Is the old man going to call in his troops and give them marching orders? President/General Eisenhower knows how to do that. . . . How are you going to handle it on the editorial page? Or is *your* old man going to call in and give orders?"

"If Mr. Pulliam gives me orders, I'll follow them. I wouldn't be surprised if the boss—Mr. Pulliam, sir—did call me about this one. I'll wait till the last minute to write the editorial. If you want to get me with anything more you can reach me till seven-thirty. Make that seven-twenty-nine."

Then Ed Reidy and Sam Tilburn went into their daily act, an exaggerated imitation of NBC superstar nightly newsers Chet Huntley and David Brinkley.

"Good night, Ed."

"Good night, Sam."

They both audibly and noisily wept, regularly amusing editorial hands working at close quarters with them, at the terrible prospect of going an entire day until their next telephone conversation.

54

McCarthy questions General Zwicker

The officer who had alerted Roy Cohn to the problem at Fort Monmouth in New Jersey was a brigadier general. He had given Roy Cohn several leads, the most explosive of which, in a matter of weeks, gave way to a bumper-sticker size question intended to intone dark, subversive activity within the heart of the United States Army. The words were: WHO PROMOTED PERESS? Tens of thousands of the stickers were made, distributed, and exhibited. One partisan, carrying a sign with those three words emblazoned on cardboard four feet high, six feet long, walked solemnly for a day up and down Pennsylvania Avenue, opposite the White House.

Peress? Irving Peress was a dentist, an army officer, and—a member of the Communist Party. A hidden member of the party? No, not really. When questioned about it by Fort Monmouth army intelligence he did not hide his membership. The questions that subsequently arose were: How was it that he was a) then promoted (to major, from captain); and b) honorably discharged? (The Communist Party having been declared hostile to the government of the United States, membership in it entailed a discharge from the Army "without honor.")

Dr. Peress did not tranquilize the situation when, asked by a reporter whether he was still a member of the Communist Party, he declined to answer the question, giving rise to the assumption that yes, he was still a Communist.

One month after McCarthy's open invitation to federal employees to give information to congressional committees, Roy Cohn advised the general who had alerted the committee to the security delinquencies at Monmouth that the time had come to give formal testimony, giving him, by telegram, the date on which the hearing would be held. General Zwicker wired back that, after all, he could not testify—because of the presidential ban on testimony to legislative agencies by federal personnel on security matters. General Zwicker had been reminded by John Adams, counsel to the army, of the presidential directive.

Cohn put in a call to the general. He told him he could not possibly get away with any such a defiant act of "disloyalty." He then telephoned McCarthy, who was in New York to visit with Jeanie. The McCarthys had taken a weekend vacation in Mexico with tycoon Clint Murchison and Hollywood actor Ward Bond. Returned to New York, McCarthy was off to Monmouth, and Jean's taxi was hit, her ankle broken. The next day, McCarthy sent her to the hospital. She was now immobilized. McCarthy had a further medical objective, to seek fresh medical advice about his own recurrent problem, inflamed sinuses.

"Zwicker thinks," Cohn said, "he can just back off the whole thing, pleading the executive order. I think you should get in there and let him have it."

McCarthy told Cohn to call a meeting of the committee for the afternoon of the following day to advise General Zwicker to be there unless he wanted to receive a subpoena. McCarthy would arrive in Washington on the ten A.M. Eastern flight. "Tell Harry to meet me," he instructed Mary Haskell. "Roy will be tied up getting ready for the closed session. I got to get Harry going on my speech for tonight." McCarthy would return to New York to speak to the East Side Republican Club. "I want to talk to Harry about that speech and a lot of other things."

Harry was waiting at the Eastern Airlines terminal. He was not surprised by the appearance at the gate of reporters there to wrest something from Joe McCarthy, anything, preferably about the hostile reception given to his Come-All-Ye-Faithful invitation (as the radio wags were calling it) to two million federal employees. But Harry was

WILLIAM F. BUCKLEY JR.

surprised and dismayed by Joe's appearance. Harry had seen him only three days earlier. Now Joe's beard was a day old, his hair seemed thinner and looked as if plastered over his head. His eyes were droopy. At close quarters one could hear him wheeze as he struggled with his sinus. At very close quarters Harry could smell the whiskey.

Joe extruded a smile for the reporters and gave them a wave of the hand. "Sorry, gents. Got a committee meeting waiting for me. Can't keep my fellow senators waiting!" Another wave and he shuffled out, following Harry to the waiting car, his wedding-gift Cadillac.

"Joe," Harry spoke in the car, "you're not keeping any senators waiting, because nobody else is going to be there this afternoon."

Joe had become accustomed to boycotts and threats of boycotts by the Democratic members, Symington, Jackson, and McClellan, even to persistent absences by the overburdened Everett Dirksen, with his legion of fishes to fry; but he was surprised that his fellow Republicans Charles Potter and Karl Mundt would be absent.

"To hell with them. Zwicker's all I care about. I'm going to ask him some hard questions, playing with us this way. Roy's quite right. Zwicker complains to us about the security at Monmouth and now he wants presidential protection to keep him from testifying."

Harry said, "You know, General Zwicker's from Wisconsin."

"Oh?"

"Yes, Stoughton. He did a year at the University of Wisconsin before West Point. . . . Do you know about his war record, Joe?"

McCarthy shook his head—"Turn down the heat, Jeremiah," he called out to the driver. They were traveling slowly in the light snowfall, crossing the Memorial Bridge. "What did you say, Harry?—You know, I think you'd better come up to New York with me after the hearing. I'll have to speak off the cuff to the East Side Republicans. We can discuss what to say on the plane. My sinus is awful." He reached into his briefcase and brought out a flask. "Slug?"

"No, thanks."

Joe McCarthy took a deep swallow, shook his head vigorously, and drew a deep breath through his nose. "There. That's better. You wanted to tell me?—"

"About the war record, Zwicker's. I have it here." He reached in his pocket for a 3x5 card.

"Ralph Zwicker served with the infantry in Normandy, in northern France, in the Ardennes, the Rhineland, and central Europe. His decorations include the Silver Star, the Legion of Merit with Oak Leaf Cluster, the Bronze Star with two Oak Leaf Clusters, Arrowhead, the British Distinguished Service Order, and the French Legion of Honor and Croix de Guerre with Palm. After the war he graduated from the National War College."

"Good man. Should know better than to surrender this late in life."

Harry said nothing. He let Joe talk about the assorted concerns — would Tom Coleman be sore if he and Jeanie canceled the weekend invitation? Did Harry know anything about a planned program by Edward R. Murrow, "He won't be very friendly, I suspect." Harry permitted himself one last sally as they walked up the stairs of the Senate Office Building. "Joe, this is executive session, I know, which provides some protection, but *don't* go overboard—"

"I appreciate the care you take of me, kid. I mean that." He smiled. "Don't worry, Harry."

The examination of General Zwicker began. Harry was seated on McCarthy's left, Cohn on the right. Harry was silent throughout the session.

Roy whispered continuously in Joe's ear after, it seemed, every answer by the witness. Harry couldn't hear the words uttered, but he knew instantly the sense of them because McCarthy was bearing down on the witness, grinding away, just one senator, the others all absent, sitting opposite the general and his two aides, asking the same question, sometimes reworded, more often not, bringing his clenched hand down on the table. Would it ever, ever end, Harry wondered?

Finally it did.

McCarthy seemed to have forgotten that he had asked Harry to go to New York with him — he was engrossed with Roy Cohn. When the committee session ended, Mary Haskell approached McCarthy from her staff seat. Harry heard McCarthy outline his travel plans. Roy would accompany him to New York, he heard him say. There was no mention of Harry. Harry rose quickly and preceded Joe and Roy out of the chamber. Briefcase in hand, he walked the nine blocks to his house. When he got there, he went to the liquor closet, poured out and drank a large jigger of vodka. Impulsively he went to the telephone and dialed Sam Tilburn.

"Sam, is there anything out on the wire about the Zwicker meeting this afternoon?"

"Not a thing. Want to tell me about it, Harry?"

"No. But Sam—" Harry had to talk to someone, someone he knew and trusted; someone who would be familiar with the general scene "—are you free for dinner?"

"Yuh." Sam was a little surprised, but he liked Harry. Besides, Harry kept hot company. "I could arrange that. Would have to be after seven."

"That's good. I want to pick something up to bring along, and it won't be ready till then. Let's say seven-forty-five, at the Monocle."

Harry put down the phone. His head was churning. He poured another vodka, this time carefully measuring the amount. Without giving thought to what he was doing he reached into the cavity in his briefcase reserved for a very private document that reposed there even if months went by without his fondling it. He pulled out the letter he was looking for. He had found it in his mailbox, hand delivered, when he reached the apartment after the terrible meeting in New York with his mother.

It was a single sentence, written in light ink across a page of plain paper.

I will always love you as a brother.

Robin

He stifled a sob.

He had removed her picture from his apartment and destroyed a half-dozen letters, love notes, really, she had written to him during those golden months. When he returned to Washington from the evening with his mother and found her letter, his wretchedness had kept him all but immobile the following day. He managed a single call to Mary Haskell. He thought to write to her but knew he couldn't match the weight of her single line. The best he could think to do was to resolve not to play in his memory his days, and nights, with her. He prayed for powers to forget. But he could not dispose of the letter, which would lie always in that little cavity in his briefcase.

He had fifteen endless minutes to kill before the office would be ready with the transcript he wanted, to read, to check out with the nightmare of that afternoon.

He found himself unaccountably wondering with odd desperation how to make fifteen minutes go by.

The idea came to him suddenly. He reached for his telephone and dialed the number in New York of Willmoore Sherrill.

Time always flew, in conversations with Willmoore.

Sam Tilburn was known to his colleagues as a conscientious and accomplished journeyman. He never sought by-line treatment, though often his name was placed on top of his dispatches by the editor. He was unhesitating in the amplitude of his reporting and resolutely committed to impartiality—opinion was for the editorial pages; a very different thing. Ed could do the editorializing. When off duty, Sam was diffident and unassertive, a patient, undemanding listener. When he lost his leg at age seventeen, he thought himself too disfigured to woo a wife, and by the time he had acquired the physical self-confidence that permitted him to fly with test pilots to write their story, or dive deeply with submariners to document their long ordeals, he had passed the age for romance. He lived sedately, sharing an apartment with a widowed sister.

Sam would never, answering such a call as he had had from Harry Bontecou and meeting him for dinner, precipitate an agenda. Let Harry do whatever he wanted to do in his own way, at his own speed.

Harry held back, sharing a bottle of wine, until after they had both finished their steak, and ordered ice cream and coffee.

"Sam, I want to share something with you, but it's got to be off the record."

"That's always okay, Harry. The usual rules: If I learn about it elsewhere, I'm not under any constraint."

Sam would need no briefing about the background of General Zwicker or about the morning paper's reports on the general's impending collision with the McCarthy committee this afternoon.

"I've got the transcript of what happened today. I've marked the passages I want you to read. The first is Joe—McCarthy—talking. Joe talking after the general said he couldn't testify because of the presidential directive.

"Joe says," Harry looked down at the typescript and read, "'Don't be coy with me, General. . . . Don't you give me double-talk. I am going to keep you here as long as you keep hedging and hawing.' Now read from there—" he handed over the text.

Sam took it and elected to read the passages out loud. He did so in a soft monotone, barren of any expression, as though he were dictating into a recording machine.

General Zwicker: I am not hedging.

The Chairman: Or hawing?

General Zwicker: I am not hawing, and I don't like to have anyone impugn my honesty, which you just about did.

The Chairman: Either your honesty or your intelligence; I can't help impugning one or the other.

The general had not replied.

McCarthy continued.

The Chairman: If there was a general — this is hypothetical — who consented to the promotion of a Communist officer and allowed his honorable discharge, would you think such a general was incompetent and ought to be discharged?

General Zwicker: I don't think I fully understand the question.

The Chairman: You are ordered to answer it, General. You are an employee of the people.

General Zwicker: Yes, sir.

The Chairman: You have a rather important job. I want to know how you feel about getting rid of Communists.

General Zwicker: I'm all for it.

The Chairman: All right. You will answer that question unless you take the Fifth Amendment. I do not care how long we stay here, you are going to answer it.

General Zwicker: Do you mean how I feel toward Communists?

The Chairman: I mean exactly what I asked you, General, nothing else. And anyone with the brains of a five-year-old child can understand that question. The reporter will read it to you as often as you need to hear it so that you can answer it, and then you will answer it.

General Zwicker: Start it over, please.

(The question was reread by the reporter.)

General Zwicker: I do not think he should be removed from the military.

The Chairman: Then, General, you should be removed from any command. Any man who has been given the honor of being promoted to general and who says, 'I will protect another general who protected Communists,' is not fit to wear that uniform. General, I think it is a tremendous disgrace to the army to have this sort of thing given to the public. I intend to give it to them. I have a duty to do that. I intend to repeat to the press exactly what you said. So you know that. You will be back here, General. This time at a public hearing, on Tuesday.

Sam Tilburn finished the droning recitation and resumed his normal voice. The ice cream was untouched, the coffee was getting cold.

"What are you going to do?"

"I—I don't know. But the idea is coming to me."

"You or Cohn?"

"Me or Cohn."

Back in the apartment he felt a great relief. Sam had served as an older brother. Harry had wrenched out of himself the necessary conclusion of the steps that led to it. Willmoore used to quote the philosopher, "Who says A, must say B."

The next morning he called Mary Haskell.

"I got to have a half hour with Joe alone," Harry said. "Can you figure out how that's possible?"

"It ain't easy, Harry." Mary was obviously scanning the senator's appointment book as she spoke.

"It's important, Mary. Bless you, love."

"I know what I can do. He's got a date at six at the suite in the Hay-Adams, same room you had a few weeks ago with Joe and Roy. He's got to be on time because the date is with Eugene Pulliam, and Joe knows that Mr. Pulliam doesn't like to wait around. What I'll do, I'll call Pulliam and tell him the hour for the supper with Joe has been moved up to six-forty-five. You get there at six, you'll have him all alone. I won't tell the senator the Pulliam hour has been moved up. If I did, he'd be late for your date."

"Thanks, Mary."

Harry arrived at the hotel at 5:50. There was no answer when he rang the bell at suite 455. He'd go back to the lobby, fuss around a few minutes at the newsstand, and then come back up. He was there at 6:05. As he lifted his finger to ring, he heard the voice behind him . . . in February 1954, the most recognizable in the country apart from the president's and maybe Edward R. Murrow's.

"Hey there, Harry! How you doing?"

McCarthy took the room key out of his pocket and opened the door. "Come on in. But Harry, you ought to know I'm expecting that newspaper tyrant Gene Pulliam any second, and he doesn't like to share my company with anyone, even my Phi Beta Kappa assistant-speechwriter. What are you doing here?"

Harry didn't want to dissimulate, so he took some shortcuts. "Mary found out Mr. Pulliam couldn't get here till seven, too late to warn you away, but I asked her for the hole so I could talk to you."

"Sure, sure, Harry. Let's order a few . . . beers and wait for the old dragon." He dialed room service and put in his order.

"So what's on your mind, besides the speech tomorrow?"

Harry put it up front. "I think the way things have been going the past few months you are, net, hurting the anti-Communist cause."

Joe looked up, startled.

"I don't understand that, Harry, coming from you. If it was any of those . . . other people. But *you* —"

"It's disordered, Joe. Terribly disordered. You know how I felt about some of the issues, the challenge to Eisenhower and now the treatment of Zwicker, with you scheduled to go back at him in public session tomorrow —"

"That's been put off till Thursday."

"Then with you scheduled to go back at him in public session on Thursday. You've always been frank, and you hit people hard —"

"It's a hard world —"

"I was going to say that. It's a hard world. But the impulse to act has got out of hand. You're losing sight of the strategic picture. You're giving ammunition to the enemy that's going to hurt you and our position on the Soviet Union and for sure on the internal security question."

McCarthy stood up to open the door to room service. The waiter took the glass with the ice and poured it half-full of bourbon.

"Shall I add soda, sir, or water?"

McCarthy shook his head. "Just ice." He slipped a dollar to the waiter. And to Harry, "You don't see that people like Ike and Zwicker are blocking out any possibility of us making real progress?"

"Joe, the White House announced last week that fourteen hundred–odd federal employees had been let go. That's your accomplishment. The loyalty/security system is on its way to making sense—"

"Meanwhile, a known Communist is promoted and given an honorable discharge."

"Joe, Joe. Now hold it. I'm not talking about individual acts of stupidity, like promoting Peress. It's the bigger view of how some people are seeing you. You probably didn't read Walter Lippmann this morning. Well, don't tell me what you think about him, most of which I agree with. But here's what he said, and it matters that *he* said it." Harry pulled the clipping from his pocket.

"'This is the totalitarianism of the man, his cold, calculated, sustained, and ruthless effort to make himself feared. That is why he has been staging a series of demonstrations, each designed to show that he respects nobody, no office, and no institution in the land, and that everyone at whom he growls will run away.' Now Joe, I know there's a lot of horseshit there and I know that Lippmann and that tribe defended Hiss. But what *matters,* Joe, is that some of what Lippmann is thinking and saying he has *reason* to think and say. Who'd read your exchange with Zwicker and not think the same thing?"

McCarthy, twirling his glass in his hand, was silent. He looked truly sad. "Harry, what are you saying? I mean, I'm *glad* to talk these things over with you. That's always true, for how long? How long has it been?"

"Since June 1950. Three and a half years.

"I got to leave you, Joe."

McCarthy was staggered. He stared ahead, then finished his drink. Then struggled for his old composure.

"I can't stop you." He forced a grin. "I suppose I could rescind the Thirteenth Amendment—remember? The guarantee against involuntary servitude? That's what the Lippmann types think I'd want to do. But—just to sort of *explore* the question: What would I have to do to make you change your mind? Other than—take a vow of silence?"

"Dismiss Roy Cohn."

McCarthy looked up. He had heard those words before, just yesterday. He knew that was what Ray Kiermas really wanted. What Mary Haskell wanted. What Jeanie *really* wanted. Yet he seemed astonished at hearing the suggestion put in just that way.

"Roy's a terrific counselor and, er, aide."

"I've watched him carefully. He gives bad, bad advice."

"Harry, I mean, I couldn't just—fire Roy. It would, I mean, it would be, you know, disloyal."

"That's not the right word, Joe. You'd just be saying to him: 'I've got to get different advice from what I've been getting.' That kind of thing happens all the time, the sense that you've got to have a different set of people advising you."

McCarthy was shaking his head. He refilled his glass and drank deeply. He stared down at the glass in his hand. "I just can't *do* that, Harry—"

The doorbell rang. Harry sprang up to open it. It was Pulliam, escorted by an aide. Harry led them into the room.

"I was just leaving, Mr. Pulliam."

"Nice to see you again, Harry." He turned to Joe—Eugene Pulliam would never address a senator by his first name. "Good evening, Senator. I see you have a start on me!" He looked down at the tray and said to his aide, "George, order me a Budweiser beer."

He sat down. McCarthy looked around, slowly. Was Harry still there?

"Harry?"

"Yes, Senator."

"I'll be in touch with you tomorrow."

Harry replied, with some emphasis, "You can reach me at home, Senator, any time you want."

Pulliam dismissed his aide, told him to return at 8:30. Harry, walking out of the room, overheard him starting in. "Now Senator, on this business of inviting all federal employees to . . ."

McCarthy's voice interrupted him. "Gene, sorry, I forgot to tell Harry something, something for the office. Just wait a minute."

He overtook Harry halfway down the hall to the elevator. "Harry, on that speech you're working on." But his voiced edged down, and now his eyes were moist. "Harry, please don't leave me."

Harry couldn't look at him.

McCarthy grabbed him by the shoulders and forced Harry's face toward him. Harry's tears were running down his face. McCarthy bowed his head. He put one hand on Harry's right hand, the other on Harry's upper arm. He squeezed them both tightly. "Harry, I do need you, I really do need you."

But then he shook his head abruptly, loosed his grip on Harry, and went back to the door, to Eugene Pulliam.

55

President Eisenhower
holds a press conference

The next day, everything happened. The *New York Times* had got hold of a transcript of the closed hearing with General Zwicker and printed every word of it. The paragraphs Harry had pointed out to Sam Tilburn were set in boldface type. Willard Edwards, the *Chicago Tribune* correspondent in Washington, was a staunch supporter of McCarthy and a friend of both the senator and Harry. He called Harry on the telephone and asked if they might lunch "at one, one-thirty. I'll pick you up. I've got to be at the White House press conference at ten."

Harry hadn't even finished reading the *Times* stories when the telephone rang again. It was Jean Kerr McCarthy, calling from New York. . . . She *must* see him.

Jean Kerr McCarthy had assigned herself a personal mission. She needed Harry. Needed him for Joe. She had to bring him around.

Harry sensed immediately her purpose.

She went right on, ignoring his stuttered demurral. "I'm in bad shape to press for a meeting with you, Harry, because I won't be able to move from Fort Monmouth, which means nights in New York, for two or three days. That's how long we expect the hearings up here to take. Is there any chance you could get up here?"

Harry said it would be "terribly hard" to make the round trip to New York immediately. This was difficult to bring off. He couldn't plead that he was behind in his work. Jeanie knew the burdens on every member of the staff: It was her job to distribute the work. Harry hadn't yet filed his formal resignation with Ray Kiermas, and he wasn't going to leave Joe in a bind. He'd finish up the talk he had been preparing for Joe to give in Los Angeles, though the way the news was crowding in, Harry couldn't be confident that Joe could get away to go on a thirteen-hour plane trip to California. The hesitation in his voice was picked up by Jeanie: Maybe better, she thought quickly, to put off a meeting with Harry for two or three days.

"I see the problem, Harry. But let's try to schedule a meeting in the next few days." The interval might, just to begin with, permit Harry to get off what Joe had described to her over the telephone as his "moral high horse." She had no intention of disparaging Harry's motives for quitting (she had got the story from Joe, but she moved it about in her mind, and came up with a plausible version she was confident of). But she wanted very badly to succeed in her mission, which was to keep Harry on the staff.

She had told Joe two years ago, "Harry is all decency, tough but *decent,* which figures; that's why he wants to fight the Communists." And she hadn't disguised from Joe in the past months that she thought Roy Cohn was blundering. So now her objective was: Persuade Harry to change his mind. A better prospect of achieving this—her mind raced forward and came to the conclusion: She'd have a better chance if she *didn't* make him come up to New York. Fort Monmouth, in New Jersey, virtually next door, was the pressure cooker of the Zwicker problem.

"I'm going to try to be back in Washington on Wednesday. You know something, Harry," . . . Jean's voice was now the out-of-the-office voice of the statuesque, elegant woman who liked all the normal things, including kings and queens, "I'm kind of anxious to go to the reception for the Queen Mother. I've been a fan of hers a long, long time. Joe promises to make time to go. So maybe after that, or better—how about lunch Thursday? Can we make that a firm date?"

"Sure, Jeanie. Sure."

"Please don't get discouraged, Harry, I couldn't bear it."

What could he say? "We'll fight the good fight, Jeanie."

———

Then, later in the morning came the presidential press conference. Two hundred and fifty-six reporters were panting to hear President Eisenhower denounce Joe McCarthy. Harry, at home, listened eagerly over the radio (presidential press conferences were not shown on live TV). Eisenhower's voice came over, calming, firm, confident. He was speaking from a text, it was easy to deduce. He went right to the subject on everyone's mind. He said that the case of Major Irving Peress had been mishandled and that reforms were under way to prevent such a thing from happening again. He explained that the promotion to major had been routine, automatic: seven thousand doctors and dentists were promoted during the same fortnight. He then said that the administration had never wished any employee to "violate his convictions or principles" when appearing before a congressional committee. But neither did the administration think it right for a federal employee to "submit to any kind of personal humiliation when testifying before congressional committees or elsewhere." That was the sentence that caught the attention of the press.

In the question period, individual reporters all but begged the president to discuss directly Senator McCarthy's call to the federal employees, and the revelations of the *New York Times* that morning about his treatment of General Zwicker. The president declined to say anything more.

The announcer then reported that Senator McCarthy was preparing a "comment" on the presidential press conference that would be broadcast as soon as available—"Stay tuned," the CBS announcer said.

Willard Edwards arrived at Harry's apartment seconds later. He whisked Harry off to La Colie, where, breathless, Willard told the story of what had then happened.

"I knew Joe would rush to answer the White House based on notice that he was going to be criticized. Now get this: As soon as the president had read out his statement, I beat it out of the White House and flagged a cab to go to Joe's office to tell him the president *hadn't mentioned* his name, had obviously deleted it from the early draft prepared for him. By the time I got there, Mary had the full text. She had taken down in shorthand from the radio what Ike actually said. Before she finished doing that, somebody in the office had handed

Joe an Associated Press bulletin on Ike's statement, which *just plain falsely* said that Ike had attacked Joe.

"So what happens? Joe takes his prewritten reply and adds a fiery first sentence. I barrel into Joe's office, read Joe's statement, and holler out "*Hold the presses!*" I tell Joe I was physically there, and Ike had sounded pretty conciliatory. 'You're crazy,' Joe says, and shoves the AP dispatch at me. Mary says, '*Quiet, gentlemen,*' and pulls up her typescript. Joe reads it quickly and acknowledges that the AP was wrong, that they had gone with a different draft, or whatever.

"So—he gives instructions to delete the let's-go-to-war sentence from his opening paragraph. But there are three reporters outside yelling their heads off, and Mary doesn't have time to retype it, so she just pencils out the deleted sentence, and the office gives out the text to the reporters with the bad sentence penciled out. But on the radio, just now—on my way to you!—the newscaster quoted it *whole*—"

"Quoted the sentence Joe deleted?"

"Yeap." He brought out a copy of the McCarthy response to the president from his briefcase and passed it over to Harry.

Harry's eyes traveled to the critical sentence. It read, "Far too much wind has been blowing from high places in defense of this Fifth-Amendment Communist army officer."

Harry was dismayed. His eyes traveled back to the paragraph before the deletion.

> I think that the joy of the critics will be short-lived. When the shout-
> ing and the tumult die, the American people and the president will
> realize that this unprecedented mudslinging against the committee
> by extreme left-wing elements of the press and radio was caused
> because another Fifth Amendment Communist in government was
> finally dug out of the dark recesses and exposed to public view.

Willard Edwards, disconsolate, chattered on.

Harry did not tell him about his resignation.

Harry thought the day intolerable, but it was not over. At four, Sam Tilburn rang him. "I called you at the office. They said you were working at home. Harry, this is for the record. The paper wants a comment from you on the army's release of the Cohn-Schine telephone calls to the army secretary's office."

"The what?"

"You don't know about it?"

Harry hadn't heard. Sam gave him a rundown. A record of dozens of telephone calls to the secretary of the army by Cohn asking for special treatment for David Schine. The news would break the next day. Sam had an early copy.

"Sam, I simply had no wind of this."

"Okay, let's go off the record. Looking at it from here, the sequence is pretty clear to me. One. President Eisenhower meets the press and says nothing really tough about Joe McCarthy. But two, General Eisenhower, who of course has been told by his army secretary about the Cohn phone calls, has meanwhile told the army people to put the evidence all together and—hand it out to the press for publication the next day. That's pretty good generalship, don't you think, Harry? That strikes me as Ike's Hiroshima bomb. And your boy Roy made it all possible."

"A good day to be away from the office, Sam."

"Permanently?"

Harry was not going to say it in as many words, in a telephone call that was on the record. But he knew that Sam knew. All he said was, "Thanks for calling, Sam. I'll be in touch."

Harry longed for some company. He soon had it. Mary Haskell called. "I can't stand another hour in the office, Harry. Take me to dinner, will you?"

56

HANBERRY, 1991

The evaluation of Eisenhower

Alex Herrendon seemed very excited, as he always was when, pausing in his own narrative, he would hear Harry's.

"I always considered Eisenhower a masterly politician. From what you relate I am reinforced in the conclusions I arrived at a long time ago. Would you agree that Ike masterminded the collapse of McCarthy?"

"I know what you're talking about, Alex." Harry rose from his desk to search in the library's Book Index.

"Can I help?"

"I'm looking to see what you have here by Murray Kempton. He's maybe the shrewdest journalist in America on that subject. And others. He did a piece for *Esquire*—"

"Are you talking about 'The Underestimation of Ike'?"

Harry turned, a broad smile on his face. "I say, Alex. You do get around. An important piece. Kempton takes a half dozen political crises, large and small, and shows how Ike handled them without ever giving off the sense that he was manipulating anybody. Did you ever run into him?"

"Kempton?"

"No, Ike."

"Never did. Did you, Harry?"

"Oh, no. Not even close. If I had, it would have been at a large party for the senators and their principal aides. After the army dust-up—we'll take you through that—McCarthy was dropped even from the official White House invitation list. Not even invited to the annual party for senators—*No Joe.*" He paused. "I like that phrase: *No Joe.*"

"No, no, Ho Chin Joe." Alex's face brightened with the frolic. And then snapped back to normal, a trace of wistfulness there. "Ixnay. That doesn't quite work. Does it?"

"No. If you're searching for the matrix, it was *Ho, Ho/Ho Chi Minh*—"

Alex roared in like a trained chorister, "*Is bound to win.*"

"Speaking of Ike, Alex, you are of course aware of the John Birch Society?"

"Yes. The group founded in 1959 by Mr. Robert Welch, a retired candy manufacturer. It lives in the memory that Mr. Welch privately concluded that Eisenhower was an agent of the Communist Party!"

"Yes. The John Birch Society, which he vigorously organized and which swelled to a couple of hundred thousand members in the early sixties, was founded on the thesis that critical public servants were agents of Communism. Although the general literature of the society didn't go so far, a discreetly circulated book by founder Welch arrived at exactly that conclusion, that Ike was a secret Communist. Joe was dead two years before the John Birch Society was founded. But in a way, McCarthy was the first Bircher."

"Defined as what?"

"As someone who believes that subjective intentions can be deduced from objective effects. McCarthy flirted with the notion that George Marshall was a Communist—because he had been ambassador to China and secretary of state when the Nationalists lost China to the Communists, and principal military adviser to Roosevelt and Truman when the Communists got eastern Europe. Joe wouldn't have formulated it that way, but his reflexes were what a few years later people were calling 'Birchite.' "

Alex raised his hand; Harry should stop talking for one minute while Alex wrote down his notes.

————

After dinner that night they put their work aside and played chess. Harry showed his father some moves he had been taught at Camp Plattling by Erik Chadinoff.

"Those must have been czarist chess moves. I don't remember even running into them. Maybe the inventor was off in Gulag."

Alex could do that now, a levity in which Gulag figured. For many years, he couldn't; wouldn't. Harry had been a little that way on the subject of McCarthy. He would never raise his name, but from time to time others did, speaking directly to him or, more often, obliquely when others were present. From almost as far back as Harry could remember, they would, in discussing McCarthy, take the shortcuts about him that finally took over altogether. But Harry would never interpose. He left the subject alone. He was feeling very good about the work he was doing, and the company he was keeping.

WILLIAM F. BUCKLEY JR.

The Army-McCarthy hearings—
an overture

John Adams, counselor to the Department of the Army, reported, of course, to the secretary of the army. But Secretary Stevens was not decisive in thought or deed, and his public personality was so bland and tentative that no threat that came from his lips seemed quite credible. Accordingly, the call from the White House came in not to the secretary, but to John Adams, who knew instantly that he was dealing with the First Team. Sherman Adams of the White House on the phone, backed by Charles Wilson, secretary of defense, backed by Dwight D. Eisenhower, president of the United States.

The call had come in that afternoon from Sherman Adams, their first contact. ("We have no alternative than to call ourselves by our first names. So—John—it's Sherman here.") As ever, Sherman barked out what it was he wished done, which was the way Sherman Adams governed Eisenhower's White House. "I need to speak to you. Not at the White House, not at the Pentagon. I'll meet you at the Madison Hotel dining room at twelve-thirty tomorrow. They have a little out-of-the-way room I use. Tell the maître d' it's—Sherman! who made the reservations." That quick play on first names was as jocular as Governor Sherman Adams ever got.

John Adams was of course prompt, but even so, the rugged Sherman Adams, with his white hair and weather-beaten face, was sitting there waiting for him. The Madison was new and formal, the waiters wearing black ties, the decorations and flowers serving to remind the patrons that they were not eating at the Hilton. He had ordered iced teas for both, without asking John his preferences. They picked out their lunch, and, with the waiter out of the room, Sherman came quickly to the point:

"The president has had it with McCarthy. He told us to come up with two plans. One plan is: Make peace with McCarthy but get the public loyalty hearings out of the way, beginning right away with the army hearings. The second—if that doesn't work—is make war and kill him."

Sherman Adams outlined the plan. He had put it together with Bernard Shanley and Henry Cabot Lodge. Lodge had lost his Senate seat to John F. Kennedy and was now U.S. ambassador to the United Nations, but he served simultaneously as assistant to the president. They had come up with: a proposal. If McCarthy would agree to hold all future hearings in executive, i.e., closed session, the army would agree (they hadn't yet consulted with army secretary Robert Stevens, but that was a formality) to permit designated witnesses to give testimony, on the understanding that executive action would follow, but not publicly, and not subject to legislative review.

"What's the alternative?"

"Here's where you come in. Stevens mentioned over the phone a couple of weeks ago that Roy Cohn was driving the army crazy with his demands for special treatment for his boyfriend, David Schine. I assume that's true, is it?"

"Is it *true?* Lord Almighty, I must have had twenty calls from him myself. He wants, for David Schine, a) weekend passes—so that twenty-six-year-old Schine can 'give critical help with the research' for Senator McCarthy. He wants b) for Schine to be transferred from Fort Dix to Fort McNair, or some other camp within walking distance of Roy Cohn in Washington; and c) he wants Schine to be commissioned, to spare him any further ignominy as a mere private in the army of the United States."

"Who the hell is David Schine, anyway?"

"He is the son of a hotel magnate. His father controls a chain, the Schine Hotels, Inc. Schine graduated from Harvard and was quickly given a sinecure by his dad. He wrote a six-page pamphlet on the meaning of Communism, which his proud dad distributed to every one of his hotel rooms."

"Was it any good?"

"Superficial stuff. But either it attracted Cohn or else the author of it attracted Cohn; they came to be friends, and Cohn foisted David onto McCarthy's staff as an unpaid researcher. The headlines came when they went off on the grand European tour to save European readers from the temptation of reading the wrong books. When he got back, I guess his draft board decided enough was enough. I never got around to finding out how he got the deferrals that kept him out until age twenty-six."

"Why didn't Stevens put his foot down?"

"Well," John Adams let himself say about his boss, "you know Bob. But in a way he did put an end to it. A week or so ago he told me that any call coming in from Roy Cohn had to submit to a routine. The person getting the call, in his office or my office — or any office, though most of the calls come in to Bob and me — would not put him through until after Cohn was politely asked: 'Sir, is this call on the subject of David Schine? If so, my instructions are to say the secretary (or Mr. Adams, or whoever) isn't available.'"

"Did it work?"

"Well, if you don't get through, you don't get through; so Roy hasn't talked to either of us since then. But the most important thing Stevens did was six weeks ago. He instructed his secretary and my secretary to listen in on conversations with Cohn and make notes of what he said and what he asked for."

On hearing this, Sherman Adams took a gleeful gulp from his iced tea. "That dumb little bugger, he thinks he's so bright: He didn't watch his language over the phone? Never suspected somebody might be listening in?"

"Suspected? If he had suspected, would he have said, which he did say — to me — that if Schine is sent overseas, he promised to 'wreck the army'?"

Sherman leaned back in his chair. His lips parted. A grin of satisfaction. "This is good stuff. *Very* good stuff. So." He moved his empty plate away. "We'll try the Peace Plan first. I'll communicate it to Bob Stevens. He can take it to McCarthy. McCarthy'll say no, I believe.

He's not so much interested in security at Monmouth as he is in getting publicity for himself."

"I wouldn't be so sure of that, Sherman. I've heard him talk about pro-Communist infiltration when there wasn't anybody around. And Joe McCarthy is on record as saying that publicity is necessary to fuel genuine reform, and he has a point there." He sipped his tea; he hated tea. "Though I agree with you; I doubt he'll buy the Peace Plan."

The next day, McCarthy made it absolutely clear to Secretary Stevens.

"The answer to your proposal, Bob, is no. This is a government of the people for the people."

The day after that, John Adams began putting together a comprehensive Roy Cohn–Army file, a record of telephone calls, Roy Cohn to officials of the Department of the Army. Subject: Private David Schine. Dates: mid-July 1953 to February 1954.

A week later, on March 11, McCarthy told Jeanie he sensed something was up. Mary Haskell had told him Allan Sims of the *New York Times* had called to ask whether it would be possible to be put through to Senator McCarthy the following morning for comments on an important matter. "He wouldn't tell Mary what the upcoming story is all about."

Roy Cohn too sensed that something was up. Passing him in the Senate corridor, committee member Senator Symington had said, in mysterious tones, "Roy, you'd better prepare for the cross fire."

The cross fire he was talking about was very evident the next day, coast to coast. The headline on the front page of the *New York Times,* stretched over four columns, read, "ARMY CHARGES MCCARTHY AND COHN/THREATENED IT IN TRYING TO OBTAIN/PREFERRED TREATMENT FOR SCHINE." Every daily paper in the country carried the story, with equivalent display.

Roy Cohn was on *Meet the Press* the following Sunday and on the cover of *Time* magazine the following week. There was the sense that D-Day was coming.

———

Joe McCarthy was in New York the day the story broke. In his absence, Dirksen called together the members of the Government Operations Committee. He asked for a secret ballot on the question of whether Roy Cohn should be discharged as chief counsel. The vote was 5–1 in favor of dismissal.

"But I have one qualification," Senator Potter spoke up. "Cohn should be asked to resign. Otherwise it looks like star-chamber procedure. And I think we should go to Joe and just tell him how we feel about it, instead of voting behind his back."

When McCarthy got in from New York, Frank Carr, executive director of the subcommittee, was waiting for him. Carr, age thirty-seven, like Don Surine, had served in the FBI as an agent. He accompanied McCarthy to his desk chair, closed the door to the office, and communicated to him the action of the committee in his absence.

"How'd he take it?" Jean, seated at her desk at the far end of the office, pulled Frank to one side when, ten minutes later, he emerged from Joe's office.

"He didn't just say, No! like right away. He sat there and looked out of the window. Jean, Joe's up against it, and he knows he is."

"What did he *say?*" Jean asked.

"He said he'd go with it"—Jean grabbed Frank Carr's sleeve, a breath of hope on her face—"on one condition. He said he'd go along with it provided Roy agreed. He said he wouldn't pull the rug out from under Roy, not ever. I asked him, 'Do you want me to tell Roy? Get his yes or no?' Joe thought a bit and said, 'Maybe that's a good idea. If he heard it from me, he might think I was putting him under pressure. And Frank—you listening, Frank? We're *not* going to *pressure* Roy.' I said to him—I'm telling you exactly the words I used, Jean, like two minutes ago—I said, 'Joe, I knew Roy was anxious about Schine, but *thirty-seven calls* to the army about him—I mean, we can't blame the majority on the committee for getting . . . for being embarrassed—' He said, 'That's another reason I'm not anxious to see Roy right away. I'd have to chew him out, and I don't want to.'"

Roy Cohn's version of the events was deft, and effective with Joe McCarthy. What is going on, Cohn said, is that the army people are "holding Schine hostage." Unless McCarthy pulled back from his investigation of the army, they'd see to it that Schine was "in effect a prisoner" at Fort Dix.

Quickly, McCarthy's fighting instincts were revived. He countered the army department's blast with the charge, at an impromptu press conference — these could be had almost at any time of day, almost anywhere: McCarthy always had press waiting for him — that Cohn had simply attempted to protect Schine, who had been a "volunteer" assistant to the McCarthy committee before being drafted, from abuse by the army. McCarthy charged further that army counsel John Adams, seeking to take the heat off the army, had allegedly suggested to Cohn that the McCarthy committee investigate, instead, the air force or the navy. "Because," Adams had said, there was "plenty of dirt there." But there were no written transcripts in Senator McCarthy's office, or Roy Cohn's, of any such conversations.

"What we mustn't do," Cohn urged, "is ease up. We've got to give them a real taste of the trouble they get into by simply . . . *ignoring* the loyalty/security question."

McCarthy nodded. "Let's get back to work. And I'll tell Sanctimonious Stu"—Joe had used that before about Senator Symington, and trotted it out again with some relish—"that if they want to fire you they'll have to drumroll you out in a recorded committee vote with me in opposition."

Dirksen and Symington conferred by telephone. "I couldn't go with that, Stu, that would really violate Senate tradition, firing Roy behind the chairman's back."

"Well, if you can't, Ev, then the idea of getting rid of Cohn is out. We'd better batten down the hatches. Meanwhile, Joe's got General Zwicker — he's the Monmouth general who gave us the alert in September — coming down to testify again tomorrow. That's one more committee meeting I'm not going to attend."

"I'll skip it myself," Dirksen said.

58

Viewing Army-McCarthy
on television

Back in Manhattan, for what seemed the first time in years and years, Harry found it possible to notice such a thing as the coming of spring. He walked, coatless and without any sense of irretrievable time lost in doing so, from lunch at Columbia with Willmoore Sherrill, south to his newly rented apartment on Eighty-third Street, a few blocks from his mother. In the two months since leaving Washington, he considered going in the fall to law school, to which he didn't incline but thought prudent. The royalties—from Jesse Bontecou's book—were declining. He checked at the library and took in the publishers' notices of forthcoming books. He winced. Everybody seemed to be coming out with new and competitive poetry anthologies. He was glad to have saved a few dollars while working in Washington. Graduate school was another possibility for the fall. His GI Bill was not entirely consumed. He spoke to Sherrill about the two alternatives. "But you know something, Harry," the associate professor said to him one night after they had attended a Columbia Political Union debate on whether Red China should be seated in the UN, "I'm not sure you've got the right temperament for sedentary scholarship. Your blood runs pretty hot, you know that, kid?—"

"Kid! Cut it out, Willmoore. I'm twenty-seven years old. I fought and was wounded and was promoted and was decorated in a world war. I was editor in chief of the student newspaper, junior Phi Beta

Kappa, and I was three years at the right hand — make that the left hand — of the most conspicuous senator in Washington" (he wondered whether he should add to his accomplishments, "And I almost married my sister") "— so stop this 'kid' stuff. Just because you graduated from college at sixteen doesn't make everybody else a 'kid.'"

Sherrill loved such talk. But then, with the verbal anfractuosities he was so famous for, he circled the subject, Was Harry right for graduate school? "Law school, sure. You get a chance to discharge those passions of yours, though not always in behalf of people, or of causes, you are passionately attracted to. But graduate school? I've spent, I'd say" — Sherrill always exaggerated — "maybe ten years of my life thinking about Rousseau. I don't think you'd want to do that."

"What is there left to discover in Rousseau, after your book on him?"

Willmoore devoured such intimacies. "Are you a writer, Harry? I can't tell yet. The stuff you did for Our Joe had to be a little formulaic; necessarily. By the way, Harry, did you invent the phrase 'I have in my hand a photostatic copy of'? If so, I think you overdid it. You might have altered it a bit, maybe to 'I have in my hand the original of . . .' Have you made a date with Bill Huie?" Sherrill was talking about William Bradford Huie, editor and publisher of the *American Mercury,* a combative and zesty monthly, anti-Communist, a little racy, occasionally philosophical. Harry had thought to apply to work there, if only until the fall term.

"Yes, actually. Next Tuesday. These days I find I'm in no particular hurry. But there is one thing I'm going to do, no matter what."

"Watch the hearings?"

"Yes. I couldn't any more not watch them than turn off the tube at the sixth inning of the World Series."

"As far as I can gather, every living human being with a television set is going to watch Joseph McCarthy versus the U.S. Army, the White House, and almost everybody else. I certainly intend to. Every now and again a seminar may get in the way. But, come to think of it, those hearings will be pretty good grist for a seminar in political theory. I have an idea —"

"I do too. Let's watch them together."

They raised their wine glasses and made a date for April 22, ten A.M.

Editor Huie of the *Mercury* liked what he met and talked to, and when lunch ended offered Harry a job as associate editor and gave the terms. Harry said he'd be glad to try it out but had to say this, that he could not begin until after the Army-McCarthy hearings were concluded. "I have to watch those."

"Fine! That could be your first *Mercury* article!"

"Mr. Huie, you ought to know this. I won't be writing about Joe McCarthy."

Huie's expressive face fell. "In that case I'll pay you fifty percent of the salary I offered earlier."

He grinned, and they shook hands.

"How long do you figure they'll last?"

Harry said the issues had become pretty complicated. "I'd guess they might last as long as two weeks."

Over one hundred reporters crowded into room 500 on the third floor of the Senate building. The four hundred seats in the observers' gallery were covetously occupied.

Grave thought had been given by Chairman Karl Mundt and his counselors to rules and arrangements. On the first day, McCarthy, Cohn, and Surine would occupy the television-oriented twenty-six-foot-long mahogany table. The second table, opposite, put its users' backs to the three stationary cameras. But on odd days they alternated, frontal television exposure being given to the adversaries: Secretary of the Army Robert Stevens and counsel Joseph Welch. The subcommittee's counsel, tall, rangy Tennessean Ray Jenkins, was stationed (immovably) on the right, with his table and the witness stand.

The seating in the comfortable Fellows' suite of Professor Sherrill was less formal. Willmoore sat at one end of a large green felt sofa, occasionally lifting his legs up over its expanse. Harry sat in a deep red leather armchair to one side. The television screen was slightly adjusted to give them equal viewing rights. It had the neat look of a comfortable New England sitting room, but this suite was large enough for the two dozen students who came on Tuesday and Thursday afternoons to take Professor Sherrill's exacting and rewarding seminar, where the emphasis was always on sharp thought, sharply expressed.

Senator John McClellan, senior Democrat on the committee, was permitted to make a statement after Chairman Mundt's introduction. He said, in apocalyptic accents, that the cross-complaints in the case — McCarthy vs. the Army — were "diametrically in conflict" and that he could see no possibility of reconciliation. "It will be an arduous and a difficult task, one that is not pleasant to contemplate, but it is a job that must be done."

There were subsidiary issues, but only two that were critical. Did committee chairman McCarthy and Chief Counsel Cohn abuse their office by improper efforts to influence the army to give preferential treatment to Cohn's friend and sometime committee associate David Schine? The countercharge was that Secretary Stevens had attempted to block the senator's investigation of the army by threatening maltreatment of Schine and an exposure of Cohn's pressures on the army. The second question: Did Senator McCarthy, in his handling of witness General Ralph Zwicker, employ impermissible language and levy unjustified threats?

The rules specified that the committee counsel, Mr. Jenkins, could take as long as he wished to question the witnesses, after which each member of the committee would have ten minutes to ask the witness whatever he wanted. After that, counsel for both sides had ten minutes with the witness. "All examinations in each case shall proceed without interruption except for objections as to materiality and relevancy," the chairman explained.

"There's not *a chance* Joe will abide by that rule," Harry commented.

"I'm not sure he should," Willmoore retorted. "He should have a chance to get into the act."

Harry replied impatiently. "The rules already allow him — or Cohn — to examine the witnesses. The idea is to prevent endless interruptions —"

"*Point of order!*" they heard McCarthy bellow mere minutes after the hearing began. He would use the phrase throughout the day and (they would learn) throughout the hearings.

The telephone rang. It was Professor Peter Salinger of the law school, a personally friendly antagonist of Willmoore. He was calling to activate Willmoore's commitment to appear in Salinger's seminar to discuss classical forensic political argumentation, about which Willmoore had written in a professional journal. "On just that point, Peter, I'm here with a friend, taking in the McCarthy hearings—"

"And I'm here with my wife watching the same thing and trying to squeeze a little work during the breaks. Your hero is an obtrusive bastard."

"He's looking after your rights, Peter. Remind me to tell you about the Soviet Union. Or maybe I'll save it for when I talk to your class."

Salinger laughed. "Just wanted an okay date from you for the class."

"Yes, sure, but answer me this, Peter, since you know a lot about parliamentary rules. If the rules exclude interruption except for 'materiality and relevancy,' who in a congressional situation is there to enforce the rule, only the chairman?"

"Yes, but your man McCarthy has, in this situation, great tactical opportunities, because materiality and relevance are hard to establish. It could theoretically be material to whether Cohn threatened Stevens that Cohn rooted for the navy in the Army-Navy game."

"How would it be different in a courtroom?" he asked the professor of law.

"If a judge thought counsel was abusing his right to call a point of order, he could summon him to the bench to explain his point, rule it immaterial or irrelevant, and send him back to his wigwam. You do that a few times and counsel shuts up, because he's found out he's not getting a chance to make his point to the jury. The jury, this time around, is the television audience. And McCarthy, on asking for a point of order—as we have seen—can rattle on about any point he really wants to make."

"Okay, I'll be there, four P.M., April twenty-ninth."

"Yes, we'd better get back to the Coliseum. Thanks, Willmoore."

He turned to Harry. "Did I miss anything?"

"Just two more points of order by Joe."

The witness before lunch was Major General Miles Reber. He was introduced as a thirty-five-year veteran and a winner of the Distinguished Service Medal. General Reber, the viewers learned, had flown from Germany to testify about the efforts of McCarthy and Cohn to obtain a speedy commission for G. David Schine. Asked by Ray Jenkins whether he thought the recommendation of a promotion for Schine unseemly or wrong, General Reber testified that he hadn't thought the suggestion wrong when made, but that he had thought the ensuing importunities wrong.

Senator McCarthy called for a point of order.

The committee should know, McCarthy said, that the general had a brother, Sam Reber. That Sam Reber was former acting United States high commissioner for Germany and had resigned from the State Department in July 1953, "when charges that he was a bad security risk were being made against him as a result of the investigations of this committee." It was, McCarthy suggested, in retaliation for this exposure of his brother that General Reber now pronounced his hostile conclusions about Roy Cohn.

General Reber responded noisily, pounding his hand in his fist. "I do not know and *have never heard* that my brother retired as a result of *any* action of this committee!" There was much commotion. Senator Jackson expressed himself as appalled by Senator McCarthy's implication. Senator McClellan asked for a ruling on the issue, "because we may be trying members of everybody's family involved before we get through."

Harry focused his eyes on the screen as if to penetrate it. A young woman had appeared from the committee's staff section. She removed carefully an assembly of papers scattered in front of Senator McClellan, who leaned a little bit to the right to give room to the clerk, whose left hand revealed a wedding ring. She replaced the senator's single file with one with six folders. Her light hair fell forward and brushed over her chin. Someone had silently hailed her attention, because she turned quickly in the direction of the camera, her figure sideways. She was heavy with child. "That's . . . that's Robin—"

"So who's Robin?" Willmoore asked, puffing away on his cigarette.

Harry very nearly gave way to temptation. His reply was gagged.

Finally it came out, sounding flat. "She's a girl I used to know. I guess she works now for Senator McClellan."

"Well, pretty soon now you can send her baby a christening gift. She looks okay. Why'd you stop seeing her?"

Harry nearly choked.

He was relieved when Robin slipped out of sight of the camera just as McCarthy's voice boomed in, "Objection, Mr. Chairman. Point of order."

A recess was called. The committee members and witnesses and reporters and gallery and Harry and Willmoore went out for lunch.

They were back on duty at two. The hearings would last until five, with a twenty-minute recess at three-thirty.

"I'm going to have a drink. I figure we've earned it. Harry?"

"Coke, thanks."

Willmoore answered the phone. "Who's calling? . . . Yes. I'll put him on." To Harry, holding out the phone, his hand over the mouthpiece, "It's Jean McCarthy."

Tactfully, Willmoore took his drink into his study, closing the door.

"Hello there, Jeanie. You looked terrific on camera this morning."

Jeanie didn't have time to dally over pleasantries. "Harry, I really want to see you. I'd come to New York this weekend, but Joe needs me. Last night he was up with Roy and Frank until three, got up at six. It'll be that way on through. I do so much want to spend an hour with you. Could you possibly make lunch here on Saturday, day after tomorrow?"

"Of course, Jeanie. Where, when?"

"The Monocle, twelve-thirty. Thank you, dear Harry. You are such a friend."

Willmoore came back into the living room. They watched to the end, and made a date for the following day. At the end of Day One, the television ratings gave the Army-McCarthy hearings an astonishing public endorsement: Gallup reported that 89 percent of the television-viewing public had tuned in.

59

HANBERRY, 1991

The view of the hearings
from abroad

"You were back in England, I know. Was there interest in the Army-McCarthy proceedings?"

"Well, yes there was, Harry. But not at all on the questions ostensibly at stake."

"What do you mean, 'ostensibly'?"

"Reading the material you've assembled for me in the last few days, it seems to me that several very concrete issues were at stake. The first—pure and simple—involved that extraordinary vermiform appendage, Schine. a) Did Schine in any sense govern the movements of the McCarthy machine? The army said yes—all you have to do is look at the record of Cohn's phone calls and the threats he issued. b) Did the army, having Schine safely, so to speak, behind bars in Fort Dix, use this leverage in an attempt to get McCarthy to call off, or mitigate, his investigation?"

"Yes. That's the first part of it, quite right."

"The second: Was McCarthy guilty of indecorum, or even misbehavior? Did his questioning of Zwicker violate implicit codes having to do with the civility of senatorial grilling? And—I gather from the *New York Times* editorial in your batch yesterday—Was McCarthy in general out of control?—as witness not only what he said about General Zwicker, but what he said about various of his colleagues, notably Senators Tydings, Hendrickson, and Gillette."

"Correct."

"Now on *your* question: How were the Army-McCarthy hearings judged in Great Britain? To begin with, they occupied only four or five minutes, at the most—if memory serves—of the nightly news programs. The commentary was entirely partisan. I think it's fair to say that there weren't two dozen Britishers who thought McCarthy had anything whatever of interest to say. But in that connection I have something I'm sure you haven't seen. You may wish to make some use of it. It is an exchange between our Evelyn Waugh and your Willmoore Sherrill. Waugh's letter is included in his published work. After my conversion I saw something of Waugh. Perhaps he took an interest in me because I had inherited my father's title."

"Did Waugh ever take an interest in McCarthy?"

"He reviewed Richard Rovere's blistering book *Senator Joe McCarthy,* which of course you've seen—"

"Actually, Alex, what I told you at the outset is literally true. I have not read any treatment of McCarthy, of whatever length, since he died."

"I can't imagine how you managed that."

"Well, yes, there was always, still is, the odd sentence, the ubiquitous use of the term *McCarthyism.* But no, I didn't read the Rovere book, and I don't know what the pro-McCarthy people said about it."

"Well, my situation is curious, as I said to Evelyn. I *was* a Soviet spy. I *did* have a position in Washington. Granted, not as an employee of the U.S. government, but as a Britisher, someone who was cleared by government security to attend rather important State Department briefings. And one day I was informed that the security mechanism had winced on reading my record. Had someone got wind of it—that more than two years ago I had passed a supersecret document stolen from the secretary of defense to the whole world? No. Because in the thirties I had signed a silly petition got up by a Communist front group. Does one judge McCarthyism by its failure to discover that I had passed a presidential private letter to the entire world? Or by its success in identifying me as a sometime member of one Communist front group?"

"A very interesting question. Which brings up another item you gave me yesterday—again, I hadn't seen the numbers."

"On loyalty/security risks and dismissal?"

"Yes. Here they are." Harry moved the lamp arm down on the folder. "Eisenhower announced in 1954, one month before the Army-McCarthy hearings, the results of seven months' investigations:

"Two thousand four hundred and twenty-nine 'security' risks found in thirty-nine federal agencies. All resigned or were fired."

"The charges:

"Information indicating subversive activities or associations— 422.

"Information indicating sexual perversion—198.

"Information indicating conviction for felonies or misdemeanors—611.

"Information indicating untrustworthiness, drunkenness, mental instability, or possible exposure to blackmail—1,424.

"Of course," Harry said, "depending on the criteria by which these were judged, it was either a reign of terror or a much-overdue personnel reform—"

"*That* takes us straight into the Waugh-Sherrill question. Waugh wrote an approving review of the Rovere book for *The Spectator*. Sherrill spotted in that review an undertone of skepticism. He wrote Waugh—Sherrill's letter was published with Waugh's answer in a Waugh collection—that 'this skepticism thrice surfaced.' He quoted from Waugh's review. 'Mr. Rovere's comments are pungent and, *as far as a foreigner can judge, just*. [But] one of the things which Mr. Rovere might profitably have done and does not do is follow up. There is a curious raggedness (perhaps inevitable) in the accounts of the various inquiries which seem to have ended without findings and of the various men who appear and disappear in the story without acquittal or prosecution. What has happened to everyone? I wish Mr. Rovere would rewrite the book for us ignorant islanders giving us the simple story.'

"Well, Sherrill evidently seized on this skepticism and wrote to Waugh—here, I have it: 'You are quite right; as far as a foreigner can judge, the comments of Richard Rovere on the McCarthy years are "just." The pity is that you are not given the whole story, whence you might judge better.' Sherrill then offered to send other material."

"Did he? Did Waugh read it?"

"Yes. Or he claims he did, and Evelyn was a pretty conscientious scholar. He wrote back to Sherrill, 'McCarthy is certainly regarded by most Englishmen as a regrettable figure. Rovere makes a number of precise charges against his personal honor. Until these are rebutted, those who are sympathetic with his cause must deplore his championship of it.'"

Alex smiled. "Pure Waugh. But it remains for us to explore—in your own book, and in mine—whether this 'bad character' of Joe McCarthy had as an enduring result the discrediting of anti-Communist activity."

"At any rate, Alex, you make it clear what was the British view of things back in those days when all of America was glued to the Army-McCarthy hearings. . . . Yes, I'll have some tea. No. I will not have crumpets. Thanks."

60

Jean McCarthy meets with Harry

Jean Kerr McCarthy walked into the restaurant alone. Though highly recognizable, with her great height, striking face, and figure, she was unrecognized this sleepy Saturday in April at a restaurant that toiled listlessly at noon, saving energy for the heavy, protracted traffic of Saturday nights. Harry was seated in a remote corner of the restaurant, in the back. She approached him and put her arms around his neck. He kissed her, and they sat down.

Would she have a drink? "No, but you go ahead, Harry." He ordered a beer.

"It's not going well," Jean said.

"No, it isn't, Jeanie."

"Joe's difficult. Well, I don't have to tell you. You know," Jean said, picking absentmindedly on a corner of a roll. "What Roy did to Joe on Schine was just plain unforgivable. And Joe *knows* that. Joe told me a month ago, 'Roy thinks that Dave ought to be a general and operate from a penthouse in the Waldorf-Astoria.' It's terrible what Roy has done to Joe, but Joe won't just—get him out."

"I know that, Jeanie."

"Yes, you know that, Harry. Oh my, how we miss you. But how do you read the way it's going?"

"I don't see anything that can clear Roy of what he did. Call after call to the secretary of the army asking for special treatment for his—"

"Boyfriend?" Jean interrupted him. "But we don't want to get into that, do we, Harry? I don't *want* to get into that, but we've got a situation where Roy would call the army, get a weekend pass for Dave — 'to do important committee work' — then they'd both go to the Waldorf-Astoria and live it up, doing whatever, that's their business, but they sure weren't doing important work, or for that matter any work, for Joe McCarthy." She released the roll. ". . . I know, I know, Joe should have put a stop to it when he found out, and even finding out late, he should have called Roy in and said, So long. But he's very stubborn — and very loyal. Now I know that's part of his nature. But that's part also of what's happened to him because of the solid, I mean *solid* wall of criticism, no matter what he does. If he caught a spy with a hydrogen bomb in his briefcase heading for Moscow, they'd say the same things, *fake, dishonest, publicity hound, despot.*"

The waiter was standing by. Jean noticed him. "Harry, will you forgive me? I don't want any lunch. Well, okay. Give me some soup. What kind? Any kind." Harry ordered tuna salad.

"I mean, Harry, if we live in a country that thinks Owen Lattimore is innocent after what Joe came up with, and then what the whole McCarran Committee came up with, then it's hard to see daylight. And Joe now reacts with, you know, something like outrage about what they say about him, just routinely. Did you see Flanders yesterday?"

"It wasn't in the *Times* this morning."

"Well, maybe even they are embarrassed by it." She reached in her pocketbook and brought out the clipping. "Read it. Don't read it out loud, I couldn't bear it."

Harry pocketed it.

"Jeanie, it's gotten all mixed up. People aren't talking about Owen Lattimore. They're talking about Cohn and Schine. And General Zwicker. But remember, it was *Joe* who spoke those words, not Roy."

Jean leaned back in the booth. "Yes, he spoke those words. Would he have said them if Roy hadn't been around egging him on? I don't know."

"They want Roy, and they'll get him. But they also want Joe. And it doesn't look good for him —"

She stopped him. "Let me tell you the kind of thing that happens to Joe. It won't surprise you, after your time with him. But they come in at him from everywhere, no matter what.

"Look. Last month the Queen Mother—the present queen's mother—"

"I know who you're talking about, Jeanie."

"Well, you read she was in town. All the senators were invited to a State Department reception. We got there, oh, twenty minutes late. We got in the door and we could see at the other end of the room— you know, the big reception room?—the receiving line: John Foster Dulles, the Queen Mother, the two ambassadors, a couple of other people. There were still about five or six senators and their wives waiting to go through the line. Somebody spotted Joe coming in, and presto! like that! the line was dispersed, and the Queen Mother was led to the far corner of the room. I mean, it was obvious: *Dismantle the line so the Queen Mother won't have to shake hands with the disreputable McCarthy*. So what happens? Well, there wasn't any line anymore, so Joe and I went to the corner by the entrance, and a waiter brought us drinks and hors d'oeuvres; so we're munching on these, and I look up and—there's the Queen Mother walking *right across the huge hall toward us*." Jean ran her index finger in front of her, right to left, tracing the Queen Mother's path. "She walked to exactly where we were and—introduced herself!

"Well, Joe behaved like a choirboy. And so he says to her nicely that based on what he had read about her travel and social schedule, 'Your majesty is being given a pretty hard time.' And she says, I kid you not, with a broad smile, 'Not as hard a time as they've been giving *you*, Senator!' I mean, can you beat that? Joe smiled like a baby. He'd have killed for her. We chatted maybe five minutes. The next day we got word of the headlines and the captions in the London tabloids. One of them read, 'REDHUNTER SASSES QUEEN MOTHER.' Another, 'DOES JOE THINK QUEEN MOTHER IS LOYALTY RISK?' And the *Mirror*, I think it was: 'QUEEN MOTHER TRAPPED BY HATEMONGER.'"

She brought out her handkerchief.

Harry looked away.

An hour later Jean sipped at her cold coffee. "We're just going to have to do the best we can. It's good to know we've got friends like you,

Harry. And, Harry, I understand about your leaving, I truly do. Now, listen. And this is *completely* my idea. I haven't checked it with Joe. But I wouldn't want even to mention it unless you say okay. I know that back in February you said to Joe, It's Roy or me. If I can get Joe to back off on Roy—would you come back?"

Harry thought quickly. He knew he would never go back. But he couldn't tell her that, not in her distress. He gripped her hand and reflected: There is no way Joe McCarthy will back off Roy Cohn in the middle of this investigation.

So he thought it all right to say, "Let's see, then, Jeanie, see what Joe says. After all, I did quit—"

"I told you, I understand about that. And Joe does too. You'll be a friend of ours as long as—as long as you don't go to work for Senator Flanders!" She smiled her big Irish smile. They walked together to the door.

61

Day thirty-four
of the Army-McCarthy hearings

Harry and Willmoore went out to dinner on the night of May 28 and were silent for a little while. The cocktails mobilized their spirits. They expressed, almost simultaneously, their self-disgust over the time they were giving to the Army-McCarthy hearings.

"They're threatening to last for months." Willmoore sighed, puffing on his cigarette. "And what do we know from watching that we — sort of — didn't know already? And what is it we really care about? Cohn and Schine are two calamities. Joe's jeopardized his career by getting involved with Cohn, though he was making plenty of mistakes before then. And the Cohn-Schine business precipitated some pretty ugly things: All of a sudden, McCarthy releases thirty memoranda done by his office over the months pertaining to calls from Cohn to the army, 'official reasons' for making the calls. What a coincidence. Each of these memos lists, in strangely similar language, the provocation for the *last* Cohn call. Let me practice. Date One. 'Cohn called Stevens/Adams' — take your pick — 'to say that Schine's service would be needed to prepare for the first Monmouth hearing.' Date Two. 'Cohn called Stevens/Adams to say that the absence of Schine is a real encumbrance.' Date Three. 'Cohn called Stevens/Adams to say that the absence of Schine would not deter the committee from going forward.' It looks — wouldn't you agree? — as if McCarthy's office flat *invented* that series of memos. Retroactively put together to account for Cohn's thirty-odd calls to the army asking for special treatment for his pal. The question before the house, Harry, is, Why am I glued to it?"

"And why is practically everyone else in America also watching it?" Harry replied as Willmoore turned the key to his quarters after dinner. "It has a larger audience than the World Series."

"That's simple," Willmoore said. "People watch soap opera, and there's plenty of that here, though lover-boy doesn't run off at night with the girl—wish he did—"

"Quiet a second!" Harry toiled attentively with the sound and with the vertical-hold controls on the television set. He wanted to get the nine P.M. news summary.

"I can understand why *you* are watching, Harry. You're seeing every day the decomposition of someone who was the central figure in your life, engaged in what we both thought—continue to think—was a noble cause. A vital democratic society has two functions, one is inclusive—*bring in the new ideas*, assimilate them. The other is exclusive—*reject unassimilable ideas.* That's what McCarthyism was all about for a while, and what appealed to you. It's a long way from your Paul Appleby, the federal official who said, 'What's the difference between the Democratic Party and the Communist Party? They're both entitled to compete for loyalty.' Bullshit—you're seeing part of that cause go up in smoke. How much of it, I don't know. I'm interested—I know, you are too—in the policy implications of this inferno. Will they rehabilitate Yalta before they're through? And Alger Hiss?"

"I don't know. Yesterday the St. Louis Bar Association sent a unanimous resolution to Mundt, calling for an end to the hearings. 'For the sake of preserving the dignity of governmental processes in the United States.'"

"Fat chance of doing that. The prevalence of the general will was lost under President Andrew Jackson. I taught you, did I not, that Calhoun is a ranking American political theorist?"

"Yes. There was the difficulty that his 'law of the concurrent majority' would have preserved slavery."

"Only as long as the general will in the individual states wanted it."

"All the Negro would have to do was wait, right, Willmoore?"

"When you leapfrog the general will, you get things like civil wars. Right, Harry?"

"When you don't leapfrog the general will, you get things like the prolongation of slavery, right, Willmoore?"

"You're slow on the aspect of statecraft. You very nearly got killed in Belgium because of a failure of statecraft. Fifty million others, less lucky, did get killed. The justification for a military is to avoid military action. The great statesmen in power during the thirties fucked up. McCarthy's doing the same thing. So's Ike, in a way. He might have killed McCarthyism in the bud."

"How?"

"By taking over the movement."

"Oh, Willmoore! Cut it out. Say, are you getting any?"

"That is an insolent question. Yes. You?"

"My romantic energies got aborted a while ago."

"Want to talk about it?"

"No. Maybe sometime." He grinned at his old (forty-two-year-old) teacher. "You'll be the first to know."

But Harry knew he would never speak to anyone, ever, about Robin.

They had another drink and resolved not to mention *one more time* the names of McCarthy or Cohn or Stevens or Welch. Two hours later they agreed to meet at ten the next morning, in time for the next televised hearing.

62

Roy Cohn testifies

Roy Cohn took the stand on April 29, immediately after the luncheon recess. He wore a dark double-breasted suit with the wide shoulders popular during the period. His face seemed one part scowl, one part innocence betrayed. McCarthy, seated at the center of the long table he shared with critical staff members, wore his regular double-breasted blue suit. The camera caught the diminishing hair on the top of his head. On the left was the table for McCarthy committee Democratic members, with newly retained minority counsel Bobby Kennedy seated at the end. The heat in the room was from the packed galleries. No seat was empty.

The initial questioning by Ray Jenkins, the committee counsel with open coat and informal manner, and subsequent grilling by Joseph Welch, counsel for the army, with his bow tie and vest and patron's smile sketched around his eyes, focused on the subject everyone in America would be debating for two days.

Army secretary Stevens, wearing horn-rimmed glasses, white shirt, neat tie, the middle-aged Ivy Leaguer, had testified about the importunate telephone calls from Cohn, in behalf of Schine.

"We kept a very careful count and submit here to the committee a chronology of those telephone calls and the name of the officials who received them; half the time it was me, half the time army counsel John Adams . . ."

In the morning break, Cohn rushed to a pay phone and dialed in to Fort Myer. Schine was on the alert.

"Stevens is making it sound like he never knew you, heard of you, except when I phoned in. But isn't there a photo I saw somewhere that includes Stevens and you?"

Indeed there was such a photo, Schine said. He had had it framed, and it hung in his (civilian) office, in his father's hotel in New York.

"*Go get it,*" Cohn said.

Schine, who had been transferred to Washington's Fort Myer for the duration of the investigation, instructions given to the camp commander to give him freedom of movement for the duration of the hearings, called his father's office and arranged for a clerk to fly to Washington with the framed picture in a package. Schine was there to meet the plane. He took a taxi to the Senate Office Building.

On Cohn's instruction, he gave the packet to freshly recruited McCarthy assistant Jim Juliana, who was told to make copies. In conversation, Roy referred to "the Schine-Stevens" photograph. Juliana turned over the original to Don Surine, who was friendly with a photo technician in the building.

At the afternoon session, Cohn questioned Stevens.

"You make it sound, Mr. Secretary, as if when I telephoned you about Private Schine I was taking great liberties. But isn't it more faithful to the record that I was pursuing a point or two that completely tied in with your own—personal relationship with Schine?"

Secretary Stevens looked up abruptly. "I have no personal relationship with Schine of any sort, sir."

Cohn pounced. He drew from a folder a picture and asked permission to produce it as evidence.

"Permission granted," said Chairman Mundt.

Cohn handed over an enlarged photograph, which a clerk placed on an easel. The television cameras zoomed in. It was a picture of Private Schine, standing, his army hat on, and Secretary of the Army Robert Stevens. The technician, having cropped out committee staff director Frank Carr and Fort Dix commander Colonel Bradley, had given birth to a cuddly photo of Schine—accused, by deploying his instruments Cohn and McCarthy, of threatening the very existence of the army—and Stevens—the secretary of the army, threatened by the private first class and his formidable accomplices.

"It looks like a summit conference between Russia and Luxembourg," Harry commented to Willmoore Sherrill.

Cohn wanted to know how it was, if Secretary Stevens was really as upset as he claimed to be by the behavior of Schine et al., that the secretary should have consented to pose with beatific expression on his face next to the threatening Schine one full week after Stevens's first memorandum detailing his impatience with the Schine question.

Joseph Welch was not pleased to see this unexpected suggestion of a camaraderie between his client and his adversary. He stared at the photograph and began asking questions about it. Roy Cohn answered them, with some sarcasm and sense of satisfaction. A full half hour went by—Where were you when it was taken? How did you get it? How do you know the date of it? Welch was getting nowhere when an aide approached him with a folder. Welch opened it and gave a triumphant howl—someone had passed up a copy of the photograph in its entirety, showing four figures, not just the two, posing.

The photograph had been cropped, Welch proclaimed.

He depicted what Cohn had done—cropping the photograph—as a dire, inexcusable attempt to deceive: "Mr. Cohn has endeavored to suggest to the committee a social familiarity. The kind of thing one might expect between two people photographed together exclusively; whereas the reality was one of those impersonal group shots in which *whoever* happens to be standing around becomes one of several photographed together."

Roy Cohn answered the criticisms with obvious disdain, and the wrangle went on the full three hours. Cohn attempted to explain. The technician to whom the picture had been taken to reproduce was under the impression that Surine cared only to retrieve the Schine-Stevens part of the photograph. Welch all but laughed at what he clearly gave the impression had been a "consummated distortion and an attempted deception."

Committee counsel Ray Jenkins asked Cohn, "You surely understand, Mr. Cohn, the difference between a photograph of two people apart, and a photograph of four people with disparate attachments? The secretary was evidently visiting the camp, met by the camp commander, at the same time that Mr. Carr, on committee business, greeted Private Schine, who had worked for the committee before joining the army—"

Cohn interrupted him. "I can see the difference, Mr. Jenkins. The question is, can Mr. Welch distinguish between fraud and a wholly understandable sequence of events—"

"The witness will permit counsel to finish without interruption."

Cohn wheeled on Mundt. "Mr. Chairman, I am very experienced in correct procedure in courtrooms."

Mundt looked over, in dismay, at McCarthy.

At the end of the session, Cohn and McCarthy walked out of the chamber side by side. McCarthy turned to him. "You were the *worst* witness I ever saw in my entire life."

Cohn appeared, as he did every night except on Saturday, at McCarthy's home at eight. He heard then from the entire inner-court assembly: Joe, Jean, Frank Carr, Jim Juliana, David Schine. Everyone criticized Cohn's performance, not only the fiasco with the photograph but his manner on the stand, insolent, arrogant. Frank Carr said that Roy should retain his own counsel to lead him through the proceedings, especially to stand by during the days, however many they'd be, when he would continue on the witness stand. McCarthy concurred. Cohn was shocked and affronted by the proposal. Here he was, chief counsel to the committee, a brilliant alumnus of courtroom experience—being told he really needed a good lawyer at his side to give him advice.

He asked to be allowed to think about it over the weekend.

Late on Saturday, Cohn drove by McCarthy's house, stepped out of his car, and slipped a letter under McCarthy's door.

A half hour later, McCarthy read it and passed it on to his wife. "Amazing," he said. "Not like Roy, not at all."

Cohn was not only contrite about his performance, he had analyzed it.

I've been studying the transcript, Joe, and thinking back about yesterday and, really, it was even worse than it seems. The words alone may not appear too damaging in cold print, but a certain tone and attitude accompanied them, I know, that made me appear—well, less than self-effacing.

Cohn had gone on to outline three traits in his own behavior, quoting words he had uttered on the stand:

Arrogance: "Roy Cohn is here speaking for Roy Cohn, to give the facts."

Self-Importance: Asked if I could produce the original photograph, I replied I could but indicated the committee had to understand that "I have an awful lot of papers and stuff to attend to and it is not in my possession." I added confidently (and pompously), "I am sure it is under my control."

Condescension: "I will be glad to answer any question that any member of the committee wants to ask." I even advised Ray Jenkins how to conduct his examination of me. ("I wonder if we could do it this way: Could I give you my recollection as to exactly what I did do?")

Having expressed his contrition, Cohn made his own demand. He did not want a lawyer. He wanted to defend himself. He knew the old saw about anyone who defends himself has a fool for a client. "I know, I know. But I have to do it."

He made a concrete proposal. That the next night, when the inner group congregated at Joe's house as usual to prepare for the following day, Roy was to sit as though he were the witness. "Then let everyone fire questions at me, you, Jean, Frank, Jim—treat me the way Ray Jenkins and Joe Welch treat me. Give me a rough time and let me see if I don't satisfy you."

Jean put the letter down. "He certainly does feel bad about yesterday."

"Yes. Bright boy, the way he analyzes that. Well, Jeanie, we can't order him to come in with his own counsel. But let's give him hell when he shows up tomorrow and takes the stand in our living room."

Joe drank to the success of the "new Roy."

As McCarthy met with his inner team every night beginning at eight, John Adams met almost as regularly with army attorney Joseph Welch, but at six, one hour or so after the Senate sessions had concluded. Robert Stevens, army secretary, was brought to the conference when his presence was thought indispensable, which was infrequently. On June 4, Adams and Welch sat down in the conference room they had reserved at the Carroll Arms hotel.

"You'll never guess," Welch began teasingly as they sat down and waited for their coffee.

"What?" Adams enjoyed the manner of the celebrated New England attorney, who above all things enjoyed his own verbal pacing, whether at a conference with clients, performing before a jury, or before a body of senators and twenty million television viewers.

"I made a deal this afternoon—just now—with Big Bad Roy Cohn."

"What's *that* all about?" Adams was curious but unworried. He had had six weeks' experience of Welch before the Senate tribunal. "What do you want me to do, Joseph, to get the details of your deal out of you? Swear you in and depose you?—What did you do for Big Bad Roy and vice versa?"

Welch explained. As they were walking away from the hearing, Cohn had signaled to him and, in a low voice, said, "I'd like to talk to you privately and off the record about something. Something I'd like from you."

"I said to him: 'That's interesting, because there's something I'd like from *you.*'

"We went into an empty Senate room, and I said, 'Who goes first?'

" 'You go ahead, Joe. What's on your mind?'

"I told him. You know about Fred Fisher. Remember Fred Fisher?"

"Your junior partner up in Boston? The guy who joined the National Lawyers Guild when he left law school?"

"The very one." Joe Welch sipped his coffee. "The *New York Times* carried the story back in April. How they got it I don't know. I was going to bring him down to Washington as my assistant, but he came to see me and said he had joined the National Lawyers Guild after law school for a year, and I thought, Well, that's something I certainly do not need in an altercation with Senator Joseph Raymond McCarthy. So I said, 'Fred, you'd better sit this one out.' . . . Not that I think there is a pro-Communist bone in Fred's body. He was just carried away after law school. It was during the Henry Wallace campaign. I wouldn't hesitate to take him anywhere else, and the *New York Times* story certainly hasn't damaged his reputation in Boston. Still, here's what went through my mind, John: If Roy's about to ask me for a favor, which I assumed he was about to do, I might as well ask him for one—to leave Fred Fisher out of it."

"What did he say?" Adams sipped his coffee.

"He said—sure.

"So it was now his turn. Now get this, John, and I don't want you to laugh. I exercised my *renowned* self-control and didn't laugh, not once, I swear to God."

"Come up with it, Joe. I can't wait."

"Well, Cohn didn't want me to poke around about his army record. Or rather, his non–army record. He had got an early warning signal from me." Welch reached for the well-thumbed volumes and went back to the hearing on May 4, last month. "Here's what I said then."

He adjusted his glasses. "I had been fussing about with him on the stand, on the matter of Mr. Cohn's biography, and I reached the matter of his draft status. I said I wanted to hear from him about that. He said he'd be glad to answer any question I put to him. Then I said, 'But I hope I won't have any questions about your draft status.' I said, 'I hope before we go into this matter that you will consult your file or bring it to the stand with you, so you can reel that off to us, what your whole story has been.' He replied, 'Whatever you want.'

"Well," Welch leaned back in his chair, "what young Roy does *not* want is exactly that. After all, he works for the fighting marine, the hero of all patriotic Americans. So I just listened to him, and he explained.

" 'My personal story,' he said, 'is that'—brace yourself, John, 'when I was a sophomore at Columbia, I fell in love with West Point.' "

"In love with West Point? *Roy Cohn?*"

"Quiet. It gets better. So, he said, he got an appointment to West Point. He was *thrilled.* So he goes up there to take the entrance examination. Needless to say, he whizzes through the academic part. But— he just couldn't make it through the physical. He even told me what that physical exam requires applicants to do. I jotted it down. Sixteen push-ups, twenty-eight squat jumps, thirty sit-ups, a sixty-five-foot basketball throw, a one-hundred-forty-foot softball throw, an eight-hundred-yard run in 46.7 seconds. —John, what if it had taken Douglas MacArthur 46.8 seconds? Would we have lost the Second World War? Anyway, he was of course *brokenhearted* not to be entering West Point, presumably in anticipation of a full-fledged army career."

"What then?" John Adams's face was wreathed with a broad-gauge smile.

"He was classified one-A by the draft board. But guess what? The quota was oversubscribed. They stopped drafting young men from the New York area. The draft call in the New York area was resumed two years later. That's *two years* later. When they got around to Roy Cohn, he had enlisted in the national guard as a private. He was transferred to the coast guard and then to headquarters in New York, where," he looked down again at his notes, "he was promoted to sergeant on September 6, 1949. He was pretty soon promoted to warrant officer, and in 1952, first lieutenant in the Judge Advocate General corps. . . . He can't have been very busy doing work for the coast guard or for anybody else, since during those three years he was active full-time as a civilian prosecutor.

"I didn't comment. Cohn went on. He said some people had been imputing to him a draft-dodging background, but of course this simply was not the case and in any event had nothing whatever to do with the questions being debated before the Senate investigating committee—"

"So you said?"

"I said okay. . . . It's true that Cohn's obvious draft dodging isn't going to affect the issues we're discussing—"

"I'm not so sure you're right, Joseph. I mean, what David Schine has been up to is practically the same thing as draft dodging, so that one way of putting it is, really, whether Roy Cohn has been attempting to get for Schine the kind of treatment he got for himself—"

"Just thought of something. Do you suppose Cohn *tried* to fail the West Point physical?"

"Interesting. But what you just peeled off there sounds like pretty tough stuff."

"Yes. But nothing a healthy eighteen-year-old couldn't handle."

"What makes you think Roy is a healthy—was a healthy—eighteen-year-old?"

Welch laughed. "I see your point. He was probably never a healthy anything. Though let's face it, he's pretty agile. His testimony has got a lot better since that first day."

"Okay, so you made the deal. It can't be any special burden to us. So Roy Cohn and Fred Fisher are scot-free, one see-no-evil-hear-no-evil about draft dodging, one indulgence for joining a Communist-run lawyers' organization. But let's get on to the memorandums the McCarthy office allegedly wrote after every one of Roy's phone calls. How are you going to handle them?"

63

Tom Coleman of Wisconsin
suggests a compromise

The Army-McCarthy hearings were suspended on Monday, May 17, for three days, and Harry turned, after breakfast, to his large file on Henry Wallace. He had agreed to plan for the *American Mercury* an article series, "Where Have They Gone?" Huie suggested a descriptive magazine inset that would attract the attention of veterans of the great political wars of 1948—Harry Truman vs. Tom Dewey vs. Henry Wallace vs. Strom Thurmond. He wrote out a lead: "What happened to the Wallace cadre? The truly important players in the Wallace campaign were members of the Communist Party or indistinguishable from members of the Communist Party. Where are they now? Did they see the light? Or are they doing something else? If so, what?"

Harry sat down to reread the articles by Dwight Macdonald in *Politics* and Victor Lasky in *Plain Talk*. Both writers, the renowned, left-oriented, highbrow Macdonald, and the right-wing journalist Lasky, had diligently documented the domination of the Progressive Party by Communists. The phone rang.

While traveling with McCarthy in Wisconsin, Harry had seen a lot of Tom Coleman, and on one trip had spent a night in his house. He was the senior Republican presence in the state, a politically active industrialist who knew, and was respected by, everyone. He had backed Joe McCarthy early in his career. Now he asked Harry to come

to the Waldorf to his suite and "talk about Joe. I've got a specific proposal."

"Tom, did you know I'm no longer . . . connected?"

"Yes, I know. And that's one reason why I think you are just the
right man to do what I have in mind."

Forty-five minutes later, Harry was in suite 33A of the Waldorf
Towers, on the same floor with General and Mrs. Douglas MacArthur,
who had lived at the Waldorf ever since he lost his command in
Korea. Tom Coleman greeted him, always calm, impressive, incor-
ruptible, to the point.

"The hearings are killing the GOP. Ike is in full swing against
Joe, who is losing ground. Ike is careful; he's always careful. But he's
got Nixon in there pretty well deployed. And the polls are showing
McCarthy's attrition, down twelve points just since the hearings
began. Get this as an indicator: Yesterday, Homer Ferguson — our
good conservative senator from Michigan — says he will not ask Joe to
come to Michigan to campaign for him. That is a shot heard 'round
the Republican world."

"I'm not surprised, Tom."

"Well, I've got a plan. Here's the nut of it. One. Persuade Roy to
resign. Two. Persuade John Adams to resign. What does this do?"

The senior statesman got up on his feet, hands in pockets, the shaft
of light from the window illuminating his silver hair. "The army — and
Ike — get what they — and I — and practically everyone — want: Exit
Roy Cohn. What does Joe get? The resignation of Adams, which is the
equivalent of an apology by the army for its stupid treatment of the
Schine case. You got me?"

"I got you, Tom. Are you going to persuade the Communist Party
to resign its commitment to the Soviet Union while you're at it?"

Coleman's was a thin smile. "Youth! The cliché is that youth will
attempt anything. In my experience it's the other way around. Youth
gives up too quickly. In the last two days I've talked to Matthew Ridge-
way. Now, he's one hundred percent on the Stevens side. You must
have caught him on TV the day he strode in, Enter army chief of staff,
sits down during the whole morning right behind Stevens. Can't
make a more conspicuous affirmation than that. Anyway, I laid my
plan out to him. He took his time. He thought about it. And he

didn't then say, 'Let me check it out with Ike, Dulles, the UN, and Hollywood.' He said: 'Count me in. I'll talk to Stevens.' Yesterday morning he called me: Stevens would go with it! They both talked with Adams. He was reluctant, but said pro bono, he'd go with it."

Then Tom Coleman laughed.

"Ever hear about the proud, rich Italian father who was looking for just the right girl to marry his only son? He hires a marriage broker. Broker comes in after three months, he says, 'I got a beautiful match. She's twenty, great girl. Speaks French. Father was ambassador to Great Britain, brother is an up-and-rising young congressman from Massachusetts. Father's very rich.' The old man thinks, then says: Not good enough. So the broker goes off and comes back in another three months. 'This one is terrific. She's twenty-two, very rich family, also speaks perfect French. Wonderful connections. Her older sister is queen of England. She's very beautiful.' The father thinks a bit, then says: 'Okay, I'll go with that one.' Broker puts on coat and hat, heads for the door, says, '*Well now*, that's *half* the battle!'"

Harry laughed. "The other half is Joe-Roy."

"No. The other half is Joe, period. If he goes along, Roy has to go along."

"And my job is to persuade Joe?"

"Yes. I gave it a lot of thought. You've been an intimate friend. You're close to Jean. You haven't uttered a peep since you pulled out. I think you'd be perfect. I mean, as perfect as anybody can be. If Joe wants to commit suicide, we can't stop him."

Harry said, "I'll try."

Back in his apartment, he called Mary Haskell. He could feel, over the phone, her weariness. "Last time you asked me for a private meeting with Joe you ended up quitting. Sure, Harry. I'll set you up. Come on down. Ring me when you get to town."

Harry thought quickly. "Mary, let me put a little edge on it. Make that a meeting with Joe and Jean?"

"Actually, that will be easier than just with Joe. He goes home at night, and for a while, before the troops move in for the agonized reappraisals, Joe and Jean are alone. They'd never mind it if Harry Bontecou showed up."

———

WILLIAM F. BUCKLEY JR.

For almost two hours it was like old times. McCarthy brightened instantly on laying eyes on Harry. Jean's embrace was so prolonged Joe said, "Hey, Harry, that's my wife you're making love to!" Joe opened a bottle of champagne. ("It's left over from the wedding!" Jean told them.) McCarthy sat down and asked after friends in New York, and said after this was all over, he planned to take Jeanie for a vacation—"a month. Maybe even more. On the lake, in Wisconsin. Maybe you could visit us, Harry? That would be great, Harry. Just sitting there in the beautiful woods, a little fishing and maybe swimming, a lot of time to read those books we pile up to read. No television. No telephone."

Joe McCarthy seemed genuinely entranced.

"Well now, Joe, Jeanie, I've got a proposal, something Tom Coleman came up with. It would bring that vacation a lot closer. What Tom says is, everybody is fed up with the hearings. They go on and on and on, don't seem to get anywhere, and he proposes a deal: Your side— you let Roy resign. Their side—they let John Adams go. The public view: Roy is marked down for using too much muscle on behalf of David Schine. John Adams is marked down for using Schine as a bargaining weapon. The big news: The army has agreed!"

Harry looked at Joe apprehensively. There was a quick shutting of the eyelids, the tic that preceded the consolidation of McCarthy's thought. Without looking at Jeanie, he said quietly, "I'll go with it— provided Roy agrees."

Then he turned to Jean. She said, softly, "Thank God you said that, Joe."

McCarthy sighed. "I'll take it up with Roy tonight."

"I don't think I'd be useful sitting at that conference, Joe."

"No, you're right, Harry. Have another beer and go home. I'll call you tomorrow."

When the three regular conferees arrived at eight, Joe told Frank Carr and Don Surine that they should call it a night. "I've got to spend the time tonight alone with Roy."

Roy frowned, but two hours later he agreed to go with the Coleman proposal—on the understanding that he was free to issue his own statement giving the reasons for his resignation.

The following morning, Tom Coleman, speaking to both parties, suggested that both Roy Cohn and John Adams make themselves unavailable throughout the day, to aim at a meeting at six P.M., when the papers would be signed in the presence of Chairman Karl Mundt of the investigating committee. Senator Mundt would then declare the Army-McCarthy hearings suspended sine die, opening the doors to the press.

Roy Cohn took a room in a hotel and began drafting his resignation statement.

John Adams and Secretary Bob Stevens were summoned early in the afternoon to the White House. They sat down with Sherman Adams and Herbert Brownell. The chief of staff didn't give the sense that he was totally in command of himself, and began to talk.

"Bob, John, we, er, here at the White House, have been giving second thought to the Coleman plan. Well, Herb, you tell 'em."

Herbert Brownell was the consummate Park Avenue lawyer, smooth, collected, resolute. "It's this way, gentlemen. Our analysis here is that McCarthy is going down. Whatever he is able to pull, and whatever Roy Cohn comes up with isn't going to excuse the pressures he put on the army for Schine. And McCarthy's strategy of counterattack requires him to be more scattershot even than usual about who he is attacking. So the conclusions here"—Herbert Brownell knew exactly how to convey what he meant by "here"; the Oval Office was five steps down the hall from where they sat—"are that we should go the whole mile, unpleasant though that is."

Brownell turned to John Adams. "You will simply convey to Tom Coleman that, on second thought, you think it wrong to bury questions which are best left to resolution by open democratic discussion."

Nobody talked. There was nothing left to say. They rose, and Sherman Adams said to Stevens, "Mr. Secretary, come with me one minute. The president just wants to say hello."

Roy Cohn had been on the stand nine days. Joseph Welch was in no hurry. His questions were posed languidly. His half smile was almost always there, though occasionally he would exchange it for a furrowed brow and deep frown, as if he had just been notified about Pearl Harbor. It was late in the afternoon session, and Welch kept at it and at it.

"Mr. Cohn, if I told you now that we had a bad situation at Mon-

WILLIAM F. BUCKLEY JR.

mouth, you would want to cure it by sundown if you could, wouldn't you?"

Yes, Cohn replied.

"Mr. Cohn, tell me once more. Every time you learn of a Communist or a spy anywhere, is it your policy to get them out as fast as possible?"

Yes.

"Where in the hell is Welch going with this line of questioning?" Willmoore asked Harry, staring at the television set in the Fellows' suite.

"I don't know. He's fishing, it seems to me."

"May I add my small voice, sir," Welch droned on, "and ask you to tell us what you know about a subversive or a Communist or a spy? Please hurry."

Joe McCarthy snapped.

"Mr. Chairman, in view of that question . . ."

Chairman Mundt: "Have you a point of order?"

"Not exactly, Mr. Chairman. But in view of Mr. Welch's request that the information be given once we know of anyone who might be performing any work for the Communist Party, I think we should tell him that he has in his law firm a young man named Fisher, whom he recommended, incidentally, to do work on this committee, who has been for a number of years a member of an organization which was named, oh, years and years ago, as the legal mouthpiece of the Communist Party—"

Welch looked up and over at Roy Cohn, who shielded his eyes as if to take refuge from McCarthy's violation of the agreement Cohn had negotiated. Cohn began scratching out a note to hand to McCarthy.

McCarthy continued. "I have hesitated bringing that up, but I have been rather bored with your phony requests to Mr. Cohn here that he personally get every Communist out of government before sundown. I am not asking you at this time to explain why you tried to foist Fisher on this committee. Whether you knew Fisher was a member of that Communist organization or not, I don't know. I assume you did not, Mr. Welch, because I get the impression that, while you are quite an actor, you play for a laugh. I don't think you have any conception of the danger of the Communist Party. I don't think you yourself would ever knowingly aid the Communist cause. I think you are unknowingly aiding it when you try to burlesque this hearing in which we are attempting to bring out the facts."

There was absolute silence. All eyes turned to Joseph Welch.

He rose slowly and with a few words ended the public career of Senator Joseph McCarthy.

"Until this moment, Senator, I think I never really gauged your cruelty or your recklessness. Fred Fisher is a young man who went to the Harvard Law School and came into my firm and is starting what looks to be a brilliant career with us."

Joe Welch's voice was heavy with emotion. Tears began to come down his cheek. "Little did I dream you could be so reckless and so cruel as to do an injury to that lad. It is true he is still with Hale and Dorr. It is true that he will continue to be with Hale and Dorr. It is, I regret, equally true that I fear he shall always bear a scar needlessly inflicted by you."

He stopped, and then leaned down to look directly into McCarthy's face.

"Let us not assassinate this lad further, Senator. You have done enough. Have you no sense of decency, sir, at long last? Have you no sense of decency?"

He bowed his head and sat down. The room burst out in sustained, convulsive applause.

McCarthy did not recover.

64

Army counsel Joseph Welch testifies

Lord Herrendon nodded to the technician, as Epson liked to be called when he left his outdoor work maintaining the estate and devoted himself to milord's VCR, computer, and fax problems. "That will do, Epson." The showing of that tape of the Army-McCarthy hearings was arrested. "Surely, Harry, you don't want any more? Stopping the tape now, we leave Mr. Welch in tears. Jolly effective."

"Yes." Harry was seated alongside Alex, facing the television in the library, Epson in command of the remote control. "Very effective. Even after — what? — yes, thirty-seven years."

"Did you sense when you watched it, Harry, that it would have such an impact?"

"No. I knew it was a very bad moment for McCarthy, but maybe my unwillingness to go right there and then to his funeral had something to do with the ridiculousness of Mr. Welch's implications. The business about how what McCarthy had just revealed would be a scar in the young lad's life forever. In the first place, what McCarthy said about junior lawyer Fred Fisher had already been published by the *New York Times,* six weeks earlier, when Welch was thinking of bringing Fisher down as assistant counsel. Anyway, that was 1954, and I had spent three years of my life going over records and interviewing and writing about and corresponding with two thousand people who had joined one Communist front or another, and unless they were real addicts, the difficulties they encountered—most of them encountered zero difficulties—just floated away. I might add—like your difficulty with the National Consumers League, if I remember that that was your . . . front."

"What about the Hollywood Ten?"

"Alex. You are pulling my leg. By the way, recall that the Hollywood Ten had their problem two years before anybody ever heard of McCarthy. The ten Hollywood people who ended up suspended, some of them doing jail sentences for contempt, weren't people who had joined one or two Communist fronts. They were *Communists.* C-o-m-m-u-n-i-s-t-s, not just people who believed in socialized medicine or in unilateral disarmament or in anti-imperialism."

Harry stood up. Alex could not tell if what came from him then was a sigh or just wistfulness. "It was one of Joe McCarthy's ironic legacies that it became almost impossible in future years to say that anyone was a Communist, because you'd be hauled up for committing McCarthyism."

"But the Hollywood Ten—was it established that they were Communists?"

"Alex, you were a deep-cover agent of the Soviet Union. Your involvement with Communism was at a very private, hidden level. You weren't even permitted to *associate* with known Communists—everybody knows that rule. You should remind yourself that there were *actual* Communists, I mean party members and explicit sympathizers; people who voted the Communist ticket. You don't say about somebody like, oh, the singer and actor Paul Robeson, that he was a liberal activist who wanted to see both points of view. He was a *believing* Communist."

"Well, certainly the young lawyer in Mr. Welch's firm was never a Communist?"

"We don't know. I assume he was not, because the single charge made against him was that he joined the National Lawyers Guild, a dumb thing to do, but there were three, four thousand lawyers who did so. Fred Fisher was one: an *ex*-member of the Lawyers Guild; two: He joined it when he was very young; three: He was obviously embarrassed and repentant about it; four: He wasn't working for the Atomic Energy Commission or for the State Department; and five: *Nothing* was more obvious when Welch spoke than that nobody in the *entire world,* let alone in the Boston legal community, was going to hurt Fisher. I never heard his name again, but I'll bet you your castle here that he never had any trouble on account of McCarthy's naming him. More likely he was lionized. Some scar."

"You may be right on that, Harry. But it was if not venal, then a very stupid thing for McCarthy to do."

"*Incredibly* stupid! But the Welch scene was drenched in cynicism. Your videotape won't show it, but Welch wasn't satisfied to weep in the Senate chamber for the benefit of the committee members and the television audience. He walked over, *after the session,* to the press gallery where the press were concentrated, and managed to weep again."

"Let's get some air." Alex Herrendon rose and walked to the window, examining the weather. His profile was sharply etched, and the conformation of his head. Harry stopped breathing for one second. . . . He was looking at himself, twenty years older.

It was warm, a mild British fall. Alex took his walking stick, and father and son walked through the door.

Alex spoke about the troubles Gorbachev was running into in Moscow. The war in Afghanistan was all but abandoned. Every day, everyone, it seemed, wanted more perestroika.

"There's no way they can get more glasnost." Harry chuckled. "There isn't any more to be had. Anybody can say anything now. God, it isn't taking long after the Berlin Wall coming down to change the whole shape of Soviet man."

They completed their half-hour walk. Back in the study, Alex asked, "How much did you see of McCarthy after the Army hearings?"

"I went down to Washington every four or five weeks. I didn't go at dinnertime because Joe, I knew from Jeanie—we talked every week on the phone—was in pretty bad shape, waterlogged, by that time of day. I'd stop in for lunch, or even for just a visit."

"Did he ever talk about his mistakes?"

"No."

"Did he realize that, largely on account of him, the loyalty/security situation got worse than it ever was?"

"No. And there was something else he didn't realize. It was that the old-guard anti-Communists, people like James Burnham, Max Eastman, Eugene Lyons, Christopher Emmett, Sol Levitas, had a tougher time on account of him." Harry looked up. "I remember something very funny. Joe McCarthy was in town, this would have been late fifty-three. He was giving a lunch speech—I wrote it—to the, oh gee, I forget, some organization that met regularly; but I was there. There was standing room only. I was seated way in the back at a table with Gene Lyons. Remember him?"

Alex replied as if to an examiner at St. Paul's School. "Eugene Lyons, U.S. journalist posted in Moscow in the early thirties, turned away from Communism along with Malcolm Muggeridge. Muggeridge wrote his *Winter in Moscow,* Lyons, his *Red Decade.*"

"You have it. Well, time came for the question period. One of the guests asked something or other, and Joe answered with a pretty wild charge. I winced and whispered to Gene, 'God. I wish he hadn't answered that question just that way.' He looked at me—Gene Lyons was a street-smart guy, veteran of the polemical wars. He said, 'Nobody ever said Joe McCarthy was Abraham Lincoln.'

"Hang on a second, let me look at that big collection of yours."

Harry brought back a volume of articles he had inspected a few weeks earlier. He thumbed through it. "Here is something Lyons wrote in—1954. For the *American Legion Monthly.* Ready?"

"Go ahead. My recorder is on."

"He wrote about a meeting at Swarthmore College. It was called 'Six Bold Men.' That's apparently how they designated themselves. Lyons goes on. 'They identified themselves as "the unterrified."' Their theme, I quote Lyons, was 'calculated to prove that Americanism was not yet extinct, but that it was on its last legs.' " Lyons went on, Harry said, to quote Professor Henry Steele Commager: " 'We are now embarked upon a campaign of suppression and oppression more violent, more reckless, more dangerous than any in our history.' Here's Harold Ickes: 'If a man is addicted to vodka he is, ipso facto, a Russian, therefore a Communist.' Lester Markel—editor of the Sunday edition of the *New York Times.* He talked about the advent of a 'black fear in the country brought about by the witch hunters.'

"Gene has a nice collection here. Bertrand Russell is quoted: 'If by some misfortune you were to quote with approval some remark by Jefferson you would probably lose your job and find yourself behind bars.' "

"Does he give a source for that?"

Harry thumbed through the rest of the article. "No. But Eugene Lyons was meticulous. He'd never get something like that wrong, let alone make it up."

"Is there more?"

"Oh, yes." Harry resumed reading. "Bernard DeVoto—Harvard historian—*historian!*—and regular columnist for *Harper's:* 'The hardheaded boys are going to hang the Communist label on everybody who holds ideas offensive to the U.S. Chamber of Commerce, the National Association of Manufacturers, or the steering committee of the Republican Party.' Ever heard of Lawrence Clark Powell?"

"No."

"Well, he was librarian of the University of California. He wrote here for a British publication, 'In this time of inquisitional nationalism, I know that I run a risk in confessing that I possess a French doctor's degree and own an English car. And what dire fate I'd court when I say that I prefer English books?' And—'When Dr. Ralph Turner, a professor of history at Yale, exposed the reign of terror to a convocation of Eastern college students, the latter, after due deliberation, voted McCarthyism a greater threat to America than Communism.' Had enough?"

"It rather hurts my feelings, Harry, that those students didn't appreciate the major efforts I was making as a Soviet agent."

"Which reminds me to ask you—I know you were back in England in the spring of 1954: What foul deeds were you up to?"

"I was put in the deep freeze. My KGB colonel was very concerned over the general sweep being quietly effected after the exposure of Burgess and McLean. All hell broke loose when those two took off for behind the Iron Curtain with a load of British security secrets. It wasn't for twenty years after that, in the seventies, that anybody— including me—had any idea how many people MI5 had overlooked, who were still doing Soviet business inside the British establishment. Including the surveyor of the king's/queen's pictures, Sir Anthony Blount." He paused and smiled—he was enjoying the reminiscence.

"Yes, curious about old Blount. He called on me when I inherited my father's title. He wished to record his special sadness at the death of his fellow socialist, my honorable father." He laughed. "Great heavens, Harry! Do you suppose the first Lord Herrendon, my honorable father, was also a spy?"

"We can laugh about those things now. I take it you did not talk with Blount about old times?"

"No. I didn't know that he was an agent, and he probably didn't know that I had been one. But I will talk about him in my book. And you, Harry?"

"I will too. Dad."

65

SEPTEMBER 1, 1954

The committee votes

SEPTEMBER 1, 1954

A second Senate committee convenes

The Army-McCarthy hearings concluded on June 27, after nine weeks. Thirty-six sessions had been held, 187 hours of, well—jury time. Two million words filled 7,424 pages of transcript. Thirty-two witnesses testified, and a cumulative total of one hundred fifteen thousand spectators viewed live some part of the hearings in the Senate chamber. Radio and television put their loss of revenues from abandoned regularly scheduled broadcasts at ten million dollars plus.

Exactly two months later, the committee filed its report. It was here and there factional—the Republicans saying this, the Democrats that. But there was convergence on some points. Both sides criticized Senator McCarthy's conduct, though the Republicans' language was milder. Both sides criticized Secretary Stevens for his complacent conduct in the face of Roy Cohn's importunities, an interesting division here being that the Democrats were more vigorous than the Republicans in their criticism of Stevens. ("Why should we be surprised?" Sam Tilburn remarked to Ed Reidy in one of their near-nightly conversations on the hearings. "Stevens is a Republican secretary of the army appointed by a Republican president.")

Senator Potter, Republican, filed a separate report. Word had leaked that President Eisenhower, at midpoint in the hearings, had invited Potter to the White House to hear an anti-McCarthy pep talk from Vice President Richard Nixon. Potter, a double amputee in

World War II, was understandably malleable in the presence of the man who had commanded him in that war and was now commander in chief. Senator Potter's report said that "the principal accusation of each side in this controversy was borne out." McCarthy had tolerated the behavior of Cohn, and Stevens/Adams had tolerated the behavior of Cohn: The senators were unanimous in affirming that Stevens and Adams were at fault for trying to appease Cohn rather than objecting immediately and forcefully to his requests for favors for Schine. The senators, again unanimously, criticized McCarthy for inviting all federal employees, against executive orders, to report their complaints to congressional committees.

Senator McCarthy made no comment (this was unprecedented) on the committee's report. Roy Cohn, who had resigned as chief counsel in anticipation of the committee's findings, gave his own statement. "The American people . . . are the jury. They have given me tremendous support in this controversy. Anyone who associates himself with the cause of exposing atheistic Communist infiltration has to contend with partisan politics."

On the same day the findings of the special Senate committee on Army-McCarthy were released, still another special Senate subcommittee convened. This one was headed by Senator Arthur V. Watkins of Utah, and its mandate was to resolve whether Joseph Raymond McCarthy, by (alleged) misbehavior dating back to the Tydings Committee investigations and going forward to his questioning of General Ralph Zwicker should be censured by the Senate. Short of expulsion, the heaviest levy available to the Senate.

WILLIAM F. BUCKLEY JR.

66

Joe McCarthy and Jean, in Wisconsin;
vacationing

The following day, speaking in the Senate chamber, Senator Fulbright said of his colleague, "His abuses have recalled to the minds of
millions the most abhorrent tyrannies which our whole system of
ordered liberty and balanced power was intended to abolish."

Senator McCarthy, intercepted by a reporter at an airport, commented that he no longer paid any attention to anything said by Senator Halfbright. Within the week, Freedom House, founded by the
late Wendell Willkie, a former Republican presidential candidate,
added a comment to the heavy library of evaluations of the senator.
"[McCarthy is] a man who is ever ready to stoop to false innuendo
and commit as dangerous an assault on democracy as any perpetrated in the propaganda of the Communists." The widow of the
president against whom Mr. Willkie had run said that Senator
McCarthy's investigating tactics "look like Mr. Hitler's methods."
And FDR's successor, former president Harry Truman, said simply
that Mr. McCarthy's problems were "pathological" and that he was a
"character assassin."

The day after the report of the Army-McCarthy subcommittee was
filed, Joe and Jean McCarthy left Washington for a vacation at an
undisclosed destination.

On reaching the secluded lakeside house close to Joe's native Appleton, Jean made a careful decision. She wouldn't say anything to Joe about his drinking until the third day. He needed desperately whatever physical repose he could get from two days of sleeping and relaxing at the isolated and ingeniously appointed summer cottage of a friend, Milwaukee manufacturer Bill Brady. Irene Brady had detached an old retainer from the city with instructions that she must cook for the McCarthys, keep the house tidy, stay out of their way in her own room with her own television, and under no circumstances report where she was, or with whom, to friends or family. That was easy. Thelma, an ardent supporter of the senator, welcomed enthusiastically the prospect of "looking after our Joe McCarthy for a few days."

Jean had packed several books, rigorously excluding any book that so much as touched on the problems of the postwar world. She had a novel or two by Jane Austen and by Trollope, plus *Gone with the Wind*, which neither she nor Joe had read, and two murder mysteries by Agatha Christie. On the morning after their arrival she took a book to the terrace and began reading. There was a pier on the lake, and the water was at midsummer warmth. Joe pulled out a long bamboo pole from the garage, some fishing line, and affixed to the hook a piece of raw bacon. He whooped with delight when, a few minutes later, he brought up a sunfish. He caught three more in the succeeding hour and brought them in to Thelma, insisting that she fry them for lunch, never mind that she had prepared a steak. "Steaks last forever, Thelma. Save the steak for dinner."

With lunch, Joe had three Bloody Marys. Pursuant to her resolve, Jean said nothing. She would wait until the next day. Then, she said to herself sternly, *she would be tough!*

After lunch, Joe napped for an hour, read listlessly in one of Jean's novels, and joined her for a half hour's walk up toward the main road and back. At five he turned on the early news hour. Half the figures in Wisconsin shown in the news were men and women he knew from his industrious cultivation of Wisconsin voters. But there was no reference to McCarthy. At six he explored the networks. Once again, no mention. At six-thirty, highball in hand, he looked at the television, dialed around, but had no satisfaction from what he saw and heard. He turned the television off and gave the operator the number in New York for Harry Bontecou, who was quickly on the

　　　　　WILLIAM F. BUCKLEY JR.

line. He chatted contentedly with Harry. He spoke of the Army-McCarthy hearings ("Pretty much predictable, I think. Roy thought so too"). And then about the censure committee.

"Did you see it coming, Harry?" Oh sure, Harry had replied. The Gillette committee, set up to investigate McCarthy's behavior against Tydings in the Maryland campaign, had withered away irresolutely.

"You know, Joe, some senators, like Flanders and Symington, hadn't forgotten that whole business." And then the conduct of McCarthy when questioning General Zwicker revived senatorial sentiment that their colleague deserved a heavy personal rebuke (some senators wished for more than that). Republican members of the Army-McCarthy committee maneuvered desperately not to let the Zwicker business overwhelm the investigation bearing on Army/Adams/Cohn/Schine. The Democrats agreed, but at a price. Republican members had to promise to endorse yet another committee, specifically mandated to look into McCarthy's behavior.

"Joe, you got to have first-class counsel on this one. You've got a lot of the Senate aroused against you, and you can see the heavy hand of the White House in this fight. I know you recommended to Roy that he have counsel and he turned you down, and he was wrong and you were right."

Traditionally, McCarthy would have scorned the idea that he needed counsel at his side in his public life. But Joe McCarthy was tired. The fourth drink of the evening, which he was swallowing as he talked to Harry, did not revive him, not as drinks used to do.

Harry moved quickly after noting the moment's hesitation. "There's a guy, you know him. He's an up-and-coming guy: Edward Bennett Williams."

"Oh, sure. He defended me against Drew Pearson."

"He loves front-page clients. I'm friends with a law professor at Columbia who says he's tremendous, both at trial and as a negotiator."

"Okay, I'll give him a ring." He called out, "Make a note of this, Jeanie. Call Ed Williams in the morning. Good night, Harry, hope things are okay."

After a half hour, Joe was finally reanimated, and had another highball. Jean watched him carefully and made her plans, apprehensive but determined, for the next day. In bed, Joe spoke of the idea of adopting a child. She fondled him and said yes, if she didn't conceive by . . . Christmas, she'd initiate proceedings. "I know exactly where to go."

"Boy or girl?"

"Either one."

"Just so long as it looks like you."

After breakfast, she addressed him.

"Joe. Joe, put down the paper and listen to me."

He looked up. He had a powerful intuitive sense. "You going to talk to me about drinking, aren't you, Jeanie?"

She was startled. "Well, yes. I love you, Joe. The country needs you, Joe. But nobody's going to have you for very long at the rate you're going. The *only* thing to do, Joe, is to kick it. You're a strong man. You can do it. You've got four more years in the Senate —"

"That's all the years I want. I may not even run again in fifty-eight."

"You may not be *able* to run in fifty-eight. Joe, you captured the attention of the American people when they were just *drifting* on the Communist issue. But it's slipping away, and that's not just because there are liberals and Commie sympathizers after you. It's because your judgment is bad, and it's affected by — *booze!*"

She spoke the word emphatically, spoke it as though it were her worst, most vicious enemy, worse even than a nest of Communist vipers waiting to spit their poison into McCarthy's veins.

He walked to the sink, pulled out a bottle of vodka from the cabinet below, and poured himself a drink. "I'll think about what you say, Jeanie. And I love you too, Jeanie. Love you a whole lot. And Jean, it isn't that I could stop if I wanted it. It's that I can't stop. Even for you, Jeanie."

He resumed reading the *Milwaukee Journal.*

67

The censure committee
begins hearings

On September 3, Willmoore Sherrill called Harry, reaching him at the office of the *American Mercury*. "*We did it, we did it!*"

"I thought you'd like that. It's terrific, I think."

The jubilation was over the passage, the day before, of the Communist Control Act, a statute designating the Communist Party of the United States "the agency of a hostile foreign power" and declaring that, as such, it "should be outlawed." That clarification—Was the U.S. Communist Party a domestic, independent political party, or was it an agent of a foreign power?—affirmed the distinction Harry had defended before the Columbia Political Union in 1948, and the theoretical distinction Willmoore had been arguing in his political seminars, "Willmoore's doctrine of clear and present objectionability," graduate student Charles Lichtenstein had dubbed it.

"And would you believe it?" Willmoore said. "It looks as if Congress will override Truman's veto of the Communist Control Act. You heard anything from McCarthy?" he asked.

"Yes, in fact. Jeanie called yesterday, and Joe came on the line, chatted a while. They're on vacation, secluded lake in Wisconsin. He's trying to decompress, but I think he's having a hard time. Joe was never very good—during the time I was with him—at relaxing. The length of a horse race or a poker game was about it."

"I see what you mean. I see him as permanently wound up. Probably affects the booze problem. Leonard Lyons in his column yesterday wrote directly about the booze. I assume you know about it?"

"Yes," Harry said. "It is a problem." He had to stop himself from warning that Willmoore had the same problem.

"Harry, I wish you to know that you are *not* invited to my suite to tune in on the McCarthy censure hearings, whenever *they* come along."

"They're not going to be televised, thank God."

"I hope Joe behaves between now and then. Any chance?"

"I don't know, Willmoore," he said. "I just don't know."

McCarthy professed himself "completely satisfied" with the composition of the select committee deputized to decide whether to recommend a Senate censure. The committee chairman, Senator Arthur Watkins of Utah, was a Republican conservative and also a disciplined jurist.

But two days later the papers quoted a McCarthy speech to the American Legion of Illinois. He told the legion members that the Watkins Committee was engaged in evaluating charges from "nice little boys in the Senate" who had attacked "someone for doing the skunk-hunting job which they didn't have the guts to do."

A reporter from *Time* magazine asked him whether he would call defense witnesses to appear before the Watkins Committee. McCarthy said that this would be a "great waste of time." Besides, he added, some of the statements he was being censured for making he had no inclination whatever to regret. "For instance, it's true I said Senator Flanders was senile. Obviously he is. He can prove he's *not* senile if he can, and wants to."

The next week in Richmond he was asked whether he wished to modify his statements about Senator Hendrickson. About Senator Hendrickson, McCarthy had said that here was "the only human who ever lived so long without brains or guts." Now he seemed to reflect pensively on the reporter's question. Then he said that what he had said about the senator "certainly expressed my feelings then, and expresses my feelings now."

When the committee met, Chairman Watkins was resolved not to permit a spectacle of the kind that had been televised for nine weeks

WILLIAM F. BUCKLEY JR.

in the spring and early summer. Senator McCarthy would be permitted to speak only when testifying as a witness.

Early in the proceedings, McCarthy challenged this ruling, even though his counselor, Edward Bennett Williams, tried to restrain him.

Senator McCarthy: Mr. Chairman . . .

The Chairman: Just a moment, Senator. You have filed no challenge; and, in the first place, I believe it is improper for you to do so, because we have not any jurisdiction.

Senator McCarthy: Mr. Chairman, I should be entitled to know whether or not—

The Chairman: The Senator is out of order.

Senator McCarthy: Can't I get committee counsel to tell me—

The Chairman: The Senator is out of order.

Senator McCarthy: —whether it is true or false?

The Chairman: *The Senator is out of order.* You can go to committee counsel and question him later to find out. That is not for this committee to consider. We are not going to be interrupted by these diversions and sidelines. We are going straight down the line. The committee will be in recess.

The signs multiplied, and they were unfriendly. A national poll showed McCarthy with a heavy loss of support since the close of the Army-McCarthy hearings. Fifty-one percent now disapproved of him, his popularity reduced to thirty-six percent. Columnist James Reston wrote that Joe was now like "an alley fighter in the Supreme Court." And it wasn't only the Watkins verdict that was hurting, Reston analyzed. "He is fenced in for the first time and he is being hurt, for regardless of what the Senate does about his case, each day's hearing is a form of censure of its own."

Defense counsel Williams attempted a technical maneuver. One count in the complaint held up McCarthy's abuse of the Gillette-Monroney Committee as itself censurable. That committee had been set up to investigate McCarthy's activities in the campaign against Millard Tydings in 1950. Williams objected: A Senator cannot be censured, according to the Senate rules, for conduct during a previous session of Congress.

Chairman Watkins researched the point and observed dryly the next day: "We do not agree with you."

Subsequent attempts by Williams to delegitimize the committee, on the grounds that it was violating basic legal principles and lacked legal authority for its procedures, were peremptorily dismissed by Chairman Watkins as "wholly immaterial."

That night Sam Tilburn commented to Ed Reidy, "Poor Ed Williams. He's in alien waters. He's used to arguing before the Supreme Court. All those arguments he's using you can use up there, but not before a legislative committee. Those people make their own rules."

Williams insisted that there was no real difference between his client's having called on federal employees to come up with deleterious information about government personnel and similar appeals from others, including the Internal Security subcommittee on which Watkins sat.

Senator Watkins, grown impatient, snapped that at the rate they were proceeding, "We could go on for months here." He reprimanded Williams.

McCarthy testified that in his famous declaration he had asked only for evidence of wrongdoing, not for classified information. He refused a pointed invitation by Senator Watkins to withdraw, or at least to modify, his call of last February to federal employees.

The subcommittee recessed on September 13 after two weeks of hearings. In just two weeks, on September 27, it issued a sixty-eight-page report.

The country was stunned. The recommendations had been *unanimously* adopted. They were that McCarthy be censured on two counts. On the matter of the Gillette committee, the committee wrote of his treatment of committee member Senator Hendrickson. And on his later conduct, his treatment of General Zwicker.

The closely reasoned report termed McCarthy's statement about Hendrickson (no brains, no guts) "vulgar and insulting" and his conduct toward the committee "contemptuous, contumacious, and denunciatory, without reason or justification, and obstructive to legislative processes."

The six senators called McCarthy's berating of Zwicker "inexcusable and reprehensible." The committee cited a judicial decision that discussed orderly processes of legislative inquiries and then summarized, "The select committee is of the opinion that the very fact that 'the exercise of good taste and good judgment' must be entrusted to those who conduct such investigations places upon them the responsibility of upholding the honor of the Senate. If they do not maintain high standards of fair and respectful treatment, the dishonor is shared by the entire Senate."

68

McCarthy returns to visit
Whittaker Chambers

Jean saw it coming and thought to do the one thing Joe never associated with the turmoil that otherwise moved with him wherever he
went. She called Esther Chambers and asked whether she could bring
Joe around. Esther came quickly back to the phone and told Jean they
would both be welcome.

McCarthy had angered Whittaker Chambers two and one-half
years earlier, at the outset of President Eisenhower's term. In the dispute over the nomination of Charles Bohlen as ambassador to the
Soviet Union, McCarthy had left a large trail when he set out to call
on Chambers. The two men had visited for not more than an hour or
two, but McCarthy had left the pursuing press with the impression
that he had stayed the entire weekend in Westminster, rounding up
adverse information on the nominee—about whom Chambers had
no negative opinion other than that he was a member of the State
Department establishment that had so consistently misread Soviet intentions. Chambers had refused many invitations to disavow
McCarthy, but he had deplored, in correspondence with critically situated friends, McCarthy's misorientation of the anti-Communist
cause.

Chambers greeted him warmly in the cold and bright November
day, the leaves now mostly gone, only traces of gold and red remain-

ing. Jean went to the kitchen to help Esther make the coffee. Esther said, "Whittaker knows what it's like to feel down and out. You know he will be kind, don't worry." Jean had been on edge as the days went quickly by, the vote on censure now scheduled for early the following week.

Jean brought up the question as they waited for the water to boil. "There have been only five votes of censure in the history of the Senate."

"Oh?" Esther responded.

Jean struggled to make light of it. "Only three in this century, Esther, and two of them were for a fistfight on the Senate floor. The other was, well, complicated. It had to do with a vote on a tariff bill and whether somebody with special interests should have been brought in. It was a *very* distinguished senator. Hiram Bingham. Professor, archaeologist. He discovered Machu Picchu—the great Inca city in Peru."

Esther let Jean go on. Then said, "It's certainly not *welcome* news, Jean, but I don't see why it should be, well, the end . . . the end of Joe's career."

Esther carried the coffee and cakes to the living room. Jean prayed to herself that Joe would not ask for a drink. He didn't. And the subject of the impending action never arose. Whittaker was telling stories and laughing. Joe was trying to laugh along with him. He did not succeed, but then Chambers deftly guided the conversation to his farm, the activity surrounding them where they sat, and on to a problem his son, John, was having with the chickens. McCarthy's eyes brightened. He got up. He wanted, he said, to see the chickens. Chambers exchanged a quick glance with Esther, who opened the door to the chilly outside and called out to her son, busy placing winter cover on the windows of the garage.

"John. John, dear. Would you take Senator McCarthy over and show him the chicken shed? Tell him about the problems?" Joe was outside now, and walked briskly with the young man to look in on an earlier preoccupation that had overwhelmed him, back when he was John Chambers's age.

The McCarthys left as the sun went down. The Chamberses waved them good-bye.

"Senator McCarthy is through," Whittaker Chambers told his wife as they made their way back into the house.

That night Chambers wrote to Harry.

> He was a crushed man. I said to the senator just about this: "I want you to know something so that I shall not have to refer to it again. This farm is always a haven for you. When Washington gets too much for you, come here. I want you to know that this will always be so and has nothing to do with political differences."

Chambers took a longer view of the phenomenon of his afternoon visitor.

> Tell your friend Professor Sherrill, who you tell me is outspoken at Columbia on the McCarthy question, that I think it would be a mistake to perpetuate a myth of McCarthy as something he really was not. For the Left will have no trouble in shredding a myth which does not stand on reality. I am urging a decent prudence, unstinting but firm, because I believe that the tighter the Right clings to a myth which will not justify itself, the farther and faster it will be swung away from reality; will be carrying, not a banner, but a burden. Give this man, as a fighter, his due and more than his due. Hamlet has noted the penalties in giving anybody merely his due. But let the Right also know where and when to stop, what is at stake. Of course, time, the obliterator, will take care of much of this.

69

A rally at
Madison Square Garden

The pro-McCarthy forces were by no means to be counted out. William Knowland and Democratic powerhouse Pat McCarran, both prominent in the anti-Communist movement, announced that they would vigorously fight, on the floor, the contemplated censure of Joe McCarthy. Sam Tilburn noted, without surprise, that the Hearst Press was steadfast against censure, as also the *Chicago Tribune* and David Lawrence's *U.S. News & World Report*. The Catholic War Veterans issued a stirring manifesto, and Rear Admiral John G. Crommelin headed up a national committee to collect signatures. He arrived at Senator McCarthy's office on the eve of a rally scheduled at Madison Square Garden with crates of folders, claiming 1.8 million names.

The rally's sponsors were not all crusty Catholic war veterans. They included writers, academics, a former ambassador to the Soviet Union, and a dozen retired generals and admirals.

Thirteen thousand enthusiasts thronged the Garden, with balloons and confetti and a huge brass band that played John Philip Sousa music. What sounded like thirteen thousand voices joined in singing "America the Beautiful." Eight speakers were introduced to robust applause. Former New Jersey governor and sometime secretary of the navy Charles Edison, son of Thomas, spoke of the need to continue to train on the main thing, the Communist threat. Roy Cohn spoke to tumultuous applause. But the audience was hungry for the main event, and when Senator McCarthy appeared, hand in hand with his wife, Jean, the crowd rose to its feet and cheered for ten minutes, as though at a nominating convention applauding a presidential nominee.

McCarthy waved but appeared pale, his jowls accentuated by the floodlights. He had spent twelve days at Bethesda Naval Hospital submitting to painful treatment for an injury to his elbow. Jean, tears in her eyes, her hand waving at the receptive crowd, forced a bright smile. Admiral Crommelin begged for silence, and McCarthy finally began. Within a few seconds the Garden was silent.

He thanked the audience. "From the moment I entered the fight against subversion back in 1950 at Wheeling, West Virginia, the Communists have said that the destruction of me and what I stand for is their number one objective in this country."

Cheers stopped him.

He resumed. "Let me say, incidentally, that it is not easy for a man to assert that he is the symbol of resistance to Communist subversion—that the nation's fate is in some respects tied to his own fate."

There was a smattering of applause. The participants were eager to know what he would say next.

Two days ago, he said, Alger Hiss left jail. "Four years is how long you have to stay in jail for serving as an agent of the Soviet Union." He went on to recount his special targets, with much emphasis on Owen Lattimore. He cited with great pride the White House's own figures, 1,400 dismissed since his crusade began. The Watkins Committee, he declared, was "the victim of a Communist campaign," the "involuntary agent."

"Thank God for 'involuntary,'" Harry whispered to Willmoore, seated with him in the bleachers—

"I would have the American people recognize, and contemplate in dread, the fact that the Communist Party—a relatively small group of deadly conspirators—has now extended its tentacles to that most respected of American bodies, the United States Senate; that it has made a committee of the Senate its unwitting handmaiden."

"Oh, no. *Oh, no!* Edward Bennett Williams, in his office alone the next morning, received the news of the rally the night before. "Get me Senator McCarthy," he told his telephone operator.

WILLIAM F. BUCKLEY JR.

"Joe, you—you—*dumb* bastard! You *promised* me you'd check all public statements with me *the day before yesterday!* I tell you what you've done, Joe. I had a deal made with Lyndon Johnson and Carlson and Case. They were ready to interpret the *least* statement you'd make about Gillette-Hendrickson-Zwicker as clearing you of censurable motivation. You've blown it, Joe. What got *into* you? *Handmaidens of Communism!* I mean, Joe, why, why, *why?*"

"Sorry about that, Ed. But I thought it was a pretty good speech. I mean, that's what it boils down to, isn't it? They *are* handmaidens of Communism, the ones who want to vote censure, aren't they? Look, I copied it down from the dictionary when the fuss exploded this morning. I have it here, listen. . . . 'Handmaiden. Something that serves a useful subordinate purpose; piety as the handmaiden of religious faith.' That's what the censure senators are doing, isn't it?"

Ed Williams hung up on his client.

Sunday, on *Meet the Press,* Senator Sam Ervin, who had remained silent during the first three days of debate, said to TV host Larry Spivak, "If Senator McCarthy *didn't* really believe what he said, that was pretty solid ground for expelling him from the Senate on the grounds of moral incapacity. If McCarthy *did* believe what he said, then he suffers from mental delusions and mental incapacity."

Two days later the Senate voted 67 to 22 to "condemn" Joe McCarthy for the acts cited by the Watkins Committee. The Democrats voted unanimously against him. Senator McCarran had given up pleading for him.

Was there a difference between "condemning" and "censuring"? a reporter asked.

"I guess it wasn't a vote of confidence," Joe said, leaving his office to drive home, where he wept, uncontrollably.

70

APRIL 27, 1957

Harry visits McCarthy

Harry walked up to the door of the little house on Third and North East. Mrs. Kerr had died, so only Joe and Jean and the baby, Tierney, now lived there. Harry didn't get down to Washington very often. He had left the *Mercury* in the fall of 1954 and was embarked now on a dissertation for NYU: subject, The Techniques of Nineteenth-Century Demagogy in England. Jeanie had said on the telephone three weeks before that Harry need never give notice when his plans brought him to Washington. "Just arrive at the door—Joe's always here."

So now Harry rang the bell. He could hear the vacuum cleaner's *whish*. He had to ring again to make it stop. A moment later the door opened. She was in jeans, a long apron, a bandanna tied around her head.

"Come on in, Harry." They embraced. "Joe's in the study. Here, let me take your coat. Quite wrong of you, Harry, putting on a coat, beautiful spring day like this."

"How's he doing?" Harry asked in a low voice.

"Don't worry," Jeanie replied, her voice at natural pitch. "He can't hear us where he is. Not too good, Harry. Doesn't have much interest. Then there's the usual problem. And also his sinus and stuff are bad. I want to take him to Wisconsin in the next month or two, get a real rest."

"From what?" Harry asked, a grain of sharpness in his voice.

"From viewing television serials, I guess."

"It's that bad?"

"It's pretty bad."

"Does he get to the Senate?"

"Once, maybe twice a week. All the stuff that has to be done is done, Ray and Mary attend to that. When it's a matter of a vote in the Senate, Ray comes up with a senator on the other side, and they pair the vote, both senators absent but recorded. The only thing they can't deal with is a constituent—or a professor—or a madman—or a kid—who wants to meet Senator McCarthy. They get told what you'd expect. He's out of town. . . . He's out of the office working on a project. Whatever."

Harry studied the face of his beautiful old confederate. There was an Irish resolution written in it: What is, is. And she would stay there if it meant the rest of her life.

"I went with him to the office last week, just said I wanted to look around, say hello to the staff. You—I know you know—I've been on a leave of absence. Not supposed to clock in there anymore. My salary is next to zero. Anyway, I watched him walking down the Senate hall. Greets everybody like they're his closest friend. You know, Harry, he hasn't said *anything*—not *one word*—against any of the senators who voted censure—did you know that? Not *one*, never. Not even that white-haired old traitor Pat McCarran. There're still one or two reporters who want to interview him. Mostly he says to them, Go talk to Don Surine, or Ray Kiermas, or Mary Haskell. He tells them"—she smiled—"that they know as much about all this stuff as he does at this point."

"Any speaking engagements?"

"He gets a few requests. Almost always says yes. Then about five days before the date, he says no, not feeling up to it. He told Mike Wallace yes on Mike's new coast-to-coast program, and two days later I had to call and say—What did I say? He was sick. Or he had to go to Geneva. I forget. Mike didn't like it. It was his opening show. He got Jim Eastland.

"On the regular lecture business it's Mary Haskell who has to relay the no, and some of the people go *crazy!* They've sold a lot of tickets, they've taken ads in the newspaper, they persuaded the principal to introduce him, they've arranged for buses to bring in students from fifty miles away. Mary just says there's nothing to be done, doctor's orders. Sometimes it's somebody who knows Joe personally, and sometimes they get through to this number here. When that happens I've got to say, 'Joe's asleep,' or 'Joe's at the doctor's office.' Sometimes, if it's somebody I know he was close to, I put Joe on. He's very sweet always, the old Joe. Says things like with his sinus the way it is he's not permitted to fly. They go away, after a while."

"A lot of visitors?"

"Not many. Some of the old gang come in. Dirksen, Goldwater came last week, no, week before last. Forrest Davis was here just last Sunday. He and Joe had a good-old time. He stayed for dinner, and after that they watched the *Ed Sullivan Show* together, laughed quite a lot. You staying for lunch, Harry?"

"You want me to do that, Jeanie?"

"If you want. I'll fix it for three—Tierney's asleep upstairs. Then if you think you ought to go on after visiting with Joe, okay. If you stay for lunch, I'll have something for you."

"Okay."

She led him into the study. Joe was seated in the armchair, the television on. He didn't hear Jeanie until she raised her voice. He turned and saw Harry.

"God-*damnit*, it's good to see you, feller!" He rose from his seat and put his arm around Harry, who took his hand warmly.

Jean nodded to Harry. "I'll get back to work. See you later."

"It's fine to see you, Joe."

McCarthy's eyes glistened with pleasure. Then, furtively, he raised his index finger to his lips. "Shhh!" he whispered. "*Follow me!*"

Harry followed Joe out of the study into the kitchen. They could hear the vacuum cleaner on the second floor. Joe bent over and opened the cabinet drawer under the sink. He ran his hand about the empty space. He stood up. His face was contorted. Surprise, indignation, resolution.

He walked to the bottom of the staircase.

"Jeanie? *Jean-ie!*"

The vacuum stopped.

"Yes, Joe." The voice came down from upstairs.

"Jeanie, it ain't fitting what you did. That's no way to treat Harry, come all this way from New York."

There was a silence. Jean came down the stairs, walked to the corner of the kitchen, reached into her pocket for a key, and used it to open her locker. She pulled out a bottle of vodka and, wordlessly, handed it to him.

"Thank you, Jeanie."

She walked back upstairs. Joe turned to Harry. "Let's go back in the study now, have a little good-old time."

The following Thursday, back in New York, Harry turned on the television to look at the news. The announcer gave the bulletin from the Bethesda Naval Hospital. Senator Joseph McCarthy was dead.

71

HANBERRY, 1991

Harry speaks about
the memorial services

"You went to the funeral, of course. Tell me about it."

"Funny, the flight to Washington was overbooked that morning, and who should I bump into making a scene at the ticket counter— because there wasn't a seat there for some filly he was traveling with? David Schine. I had trouble, that day, exchanging civilities with him. On that plane was me, dear Elena, who I married a month later, Schine, and maybe one hundred priests. I'm exaggerating, of course, but they came from all over the country."

"To concelebrate the mass? Or just to attend it?"

"Both. There wouldn't have been room that day, even at St. Matthew's, for all the clergy at the altar. Let's say there were fifty up there, the rest finding seats wherever they could in an absolutely packed church. The vice president came in, looking solemn. They placed Nixon in the second row. Allen Dulles of the CIA was there; what must have been the whole Congress, maybe excepting Senator Flanders, I guess; and a bunch of generals and admirals—you wouldn't think they had been estranged by the Army-McCarthy episode. Then an incredibly moving eulogy by a monsignor. The music was *something*, like wrestling with death itself. (The organist was obviously a McCarthyite.) Jeanie in black lace, resolute, beautiful, stately. She did a very sweet thing. I was in maybe the tenth row, by the aisle. Walking down the aisle, solo, Vice President Nixon behind her, she spotted me. She put out her hand and brought me to her side, to walk down with her. The music turned tranquil, and we emptied out to the crowd on the street, a million cameras. Just like the old days, only they weren't shouting out questions."

"Did you go on to the funeral in Appleton?"

"No. I didn't much want to go. When he died, four or five newspapermen and radio and TV people hunted me down, wanted to question me, Why had I resigned? et cetera, et cetera—I didn't tell them anything, but I didn't want to be stuck in Wisconsin where I couldn't have said no. They ran the Appleton funeral on TV, extraordinary outpouring. I haven't figured it out even now; Joe went from being almost forgotten to being treated with defiant love and honor. Not quite overnight stuff: There was a quickie tribute in the Senate on the sixth of May—he died on the second—but they had a full-blown tribute in August, and you'd have thought it was George Washington who died."

"Any surprises?"

"Well, yes. There were his old favorites speaking, but a lot who weren't. What was amazing was a kind of unanimity of sentiment about how good he was to his fellow senators. A lot of them talked about Joe's personal traits. It's all published in a government volume. I've got it here. Listen to Lyndon Johnson.

" 'Joe McCarthy had a rare quality which enabled him to touch the hearts and the minds of millions of his fellow men. One thing that can never be disputed is that the name of Joe McCarthy will never be forgotten. There was a quality about the man which compelled respect, and even liking, from his strongest adversaries'—"

"Well, that just plain isn't true. You've shown me what some of those adversaries said about him—and what he said about them."

"Yes, that's absolutely true. But McCarthy's attacks were always public. He never said anything mean about anybody unless there was a camera there. Strangest thing. And that personal manner got through to them, affected their personal judgment. And when Senator Johnson and those others spoke that day—there were thirty-three senators who gave tributes, half of them Democrats—they were speaking for the record, and that is what they said. Quite a few of those who spoke had voted to censure him. For instance, here's Senator Stennis, old-guard South. 'I was attracted to him through his intense interest in humanity and his consistent and unvarying kindness, not only towards his colleagues, but towards everyone.'"

Harry flipped the pages. "Here's Senator Anderson. Clinton Anderson. No friend of McCarthy. 'Generally, I never agreed with his manner of expression nor subscribed to his selection of sentiments. But I never failed to understand where he stood; and that steadfast quality of heart and mind is, I believe, of some value in this Chamber to the American people.'"

"'*Selection of sentiments.*' Oh, dear. Eulogy time."

"But hang on, Alex. Anderson didn't have to volunteer to say *anything*. It's a very long list, the people who paid tribute. Crowned by— Everett Dirksen; king of Orotundity. He really put out. His talk must have lasted twenty minutes. He told an interesting story. I knew about it because Jeanie had confided it to me. But others didn't. He told the assembly that when the debate on censure was raging, Joe's arm acted up, and he was in the hospital, his arm in a cast. Dirksen went to him. Here, let him tell it:

"'The night before I visited him in the hospital, hours were spent drafting the text of three different letters addressed to the president of the Senate, letters which I thought would be helpful. So I sat with Joe McCarthy in the hospital, and he had his arm propped up.

"'I said, "Joe, make it a little easier, because this is a rough go, as you know. I will do the best I can. But look. I have a letter. I am going to read it to you. I want you to sign it. I think it will make the job a little easier." '"

Harry closed the volume. "Well, you guessed it. McCarthy wouldn't consent to sign draft one, which was a pretty straightforward apology on the Zwicker and Hendrickson count; or draft two—which was a milder quasi apology; or even draft three, which was practically a reaffirmation of what he had said. —But listen to old Ev Dirksen." Harry reopened the volume. "This is heady stuff for me, even after thirty years."

Harry's voice registered a profound sadness when he read out, "'What was his reward for this loyalty? Oh, the contumely which was heaped upon him, the imprecations which were hurled against him; the vindictive fury which was unleashed against him; the vilification with all its bitterness which was poured upon him. Mr. President, what is the monument to him? It is not in the feeble words we utter, which will pass on the afternoon breeze. But, rather, it is the living, pulsing shrine of hundreds of thousands of hearts in America as attested to by the letters and other expressions.'"

Alex lifted his hand as if to say: Please, no more.

"Wait. Two more sentences. Ciceronian stuff. 'As I came away' — Dirksen is talking about the funeral at Appleton — 'I thought, He was only forty-eight years old. On the plane returning to Washington there first came into my mind a line one frequently reads in Scriptures. It refers to an individual and the length of his days. Then I thought, What is the worth of a man's days? After all, the length of one's days is not so important. What is important is the worth of one's days, when he is here, measured in terms of achievement and what he has done for the enrichment of mankind. The events in the life of Joe McCarthy tell in large measure the story; as the wind caresses the trees in the great cathedral over the placid waters of the Fox River, I believe it will waken living memories of a man who served his country well, fighting for the perpetuity of the Republic.'"

There was a half second's silence. Then from Alex, "Well. Dirksen said a mouthful, didn't he."

"Yes," Harry said. "In my own book I'll say a mouthful too, not quite the same way, not quite the same thing. Not exactly a funeral eulogy, not like Ev Dirksen. Dirksen was unique. So was Joe."

Alex agreed. "Yes. So was Joe."